THE NEW AGE
OF ENLIGHTENMENT

The origin of women's literary history predates Jane
Austen's birth by well over a hundred years. Yet
until now, there has been precious little attention paid
to those extraordinary women who had the courage
to set their poems, short stories, novels, essays and
plays to paper. Collected here, for the first time, are
nineteen brilliant women of letters and the rich,
delightful, and moving works they have left us
as their legacy.

KATHARINE M. ROGERS teaches literature at Brooklyn
College and at the Graduate Center of the City University of
New York. She has edited *Selected Works of Samuel Johnson*
(Signet Classic), *Eighteenth and Nineteenth Century British
Drama* (Meridian Classic) and is the author of *Feminism in
Eighteenth Century England* (1982).

WILLIAM McCARTHY teaches literature at Iowa State
University, Ames, Iowa. He has also written the literary
biography *Hester Thrale Piozzi* (1985).

The Meridian Anthology of Early Women Writers

British Literary Women from Aphra Behn to Maria Edgeworth, 1660–1800

EDITED BY
Katharine M. Rogers
and
William McCarthy

A MERIDIAN BOOK

MERIDIAN
Published by the Penguin Group
Penguin Books USA Inc., 375 Hudson Street, New York, New York 10014, U.S.A.
Penguin Books Ltd, 27 Wrights Lane, London W8 5TZ, England
Penguin Books Australia Ltd, Ringwood, Victoria, Australia
Penguin Books Canada Ltd, 10 Alcorn Avenue, Toronto, Ontario, Canada M4V 3B2
Penguin Books (N.Z.) Ltd, 182-190 Wairau Road, Auckland 10, New Zealand

Penguin Books Ltd, Registerd Offices: Harmondsworth, Middlesex England

Published by Meridian, an imprint of New American Library, a division of
Penguin Books USA Inc.

BOOKS ARE AVAILABLE AT QUANTITY DISCOUNTS WHEN USED TO
PROMOTE PRODUCTS OR SERVICES. FOR INFORMATION PLEASE
WRITE TO PREMIUM MARKETING DIVISION, PENGUIN BOOKS USA INC.,
375 HUDSON STREET, NEW YORK, NEW YORK 10014.

We wish to thank Oxford University Press for permission to use excerpts for the
following:

Thraliana: The Diary of Mrs. Hester Lynch Thrale 1776–1809, ed. Catherine C. Balderston
(2 vols. 2nd ed., 1951). Reprinted by permission of Oxford University Press. *The Journals
and Letters of Fanny Burney Vol. VIII*, ed. Peter Hughes et al. (1980). Reprinted by
permission of Oxford University Press.
The Complete Letters of Lady Mary Wortley Montagu, ed. Robert Halsband, Vol. 1 (1965),
Vol. 3 (1967). Poem by Lady Mary Wortley Montagu from article by Robert Halsband in
The Augustan Milieu: Essays Presented to Louis A. Landa, ed. Henry K. Miller et al. (170).
Reprinted by permission of Oxford University Press.

REGISTERED TRADEMARK—MARCA REGISTRADA

Library of Congress Cataloging-in-Publication Data

The Meridian anthology of early women writers.

Bibliography
1. English literature—Women authors.   2. English
literature—18th century.   3. English literature—
Early modern, 1500-1700.   4. Women and literature—
Great Britain.   I. Rogers, Katharine M.   II. McCarthy,
William, 1942-
PR1110.W6M4   1987   820'.8'09287   86-33139
ISBN 0-452-00848-4

First Printing, June, 1987

8   9   10   11

PRINTED IN THE UNITED STATES OF AMERICA

Contents

Acknowledgments

Our first thanks go to the people who, often with enthusiasm and always helpfully, sent us their suggestions and even their course syllabi in response to a questionnaire we circulated in the autumn of 1985. We especially thank Professor Sarah English of Meredith College, who collaborated with us in the early stages of text selection, and Maureen Mulvihill, Fellow of the Institute for Research in History, for suggestions and information on Aphra Behn and Ephelia.

Others to whom we are grateful are McCarthy's students in English 571 at Iowa State University in the fall of 1985, especially Craig Klein; Rogers's students in English 702.06 at the Graduate School of the City University of New York; Professors Aubrey Galyon, Kathleen Hickok, and Rosanne G. Potter; the Inter-Library Loan staff at Iowa State University; Cynthia Wall of the Newberry Library; and Wellesley College Library for permission to print two poems from their Anne Finch manuscript.

Editorial Note

For the convenience of the reader we have modernized and Americanized the spelling and punctuation of the texts. In texts such as *Thraliana*, whose published versions retain the characteristics of their authors' manuscripts, we have also expanded abbreviations, changed ampersands to "and's," and supplied quotation marks around speeches.

Introduction

"Towards the end of the eighteenth century," claimed Virginia Woolf, "a change came about which, if I were rewriting history, I should describe more fully and think of greater importance than the Crusades or the Wars of the Roses. The middle-class woman began to write."[1] Janet Todd's new *Dictionary of British and American Women Writers 1660–1800* allows us to estimate the size of the change. It lists 108 British women who published between about 1650 and 1760; and for the half century 1760–1810 it lists 209—almost double the first number in a period less than half as long. In English literary history the first and second halves of the period covered by this anthology have been called the Age of Reason and the Age of Sensibility, or the Age of Pope and the Age of Johnson. But our period may with equal justification be called the Age of the Emerging Woman Writer.

Her freedom to write did not come easily. Aphra Behn, who opens our collection, is considered the first professional woman author in England—the first to earn her living by writing, in direct competition with men. Primarily a playwright, she used all the popular forms of her day. She wrote from financial necessity, but also for fame; her forthright avowal of the second motive shows exceptional boldness for a seventeenth-century woman. But she paid a price for her success—a heavy price, in

---

[1] *A Room of One's Own* (New York: Harcourt Brace Jovanovich, 1929), p. 112.

view of seventeenth-century ideals of womanhood. In the rough-and-tumble literary world of the Restoration, she could not maintain the strict chastity required of women; and sexual liaisons which would have been ignored in a man caused her to be stigmatized as a whore. Moreover, the very acts of publishing and competing with men violated the almost equally essential feminine virtue of modesty.

Behn's most conspicuous successor in the next generation, Delarivière Manley, also took up writing from necessity, made a success of it, and suffered contempt and abuse. Tricked into a fraudulent marriage at fifteen, she lost her chance for a respectable life; needing to support herself, she wrote scandal chronicles and steamy romances. Her contemporaries noticed her lovers and her scurrility rather than her effective political journalism and her feminist insights. Thus the examples of Behn and Manley proved double-edged: they showed that women could support themselves as writers, but that they could do so only at the expense of the modesty and reputation they were taught to value above all else.

Until the mid-eighteenth century, creative women who wanted to preserve their moral and social status avoided open competition and the profit motive. Anne Finch, Countess of Winchilsea, left many of her poems in manuscript, including all the more personal ones. Lady Mary Wortley Montagu prepared her brilliant travel letters for publication, but left them to be printed after her death. Middle-class writers similarly avoided publicity and profit-making: Katherine Philips disclaimed responsibility for the publication of her poems, and Mary Astell seems to have depended on a small income from her family, supplemented by gifts from upper-class friends. Even late in the eighteenth century, Frances Burney went to extraordinary lengths to keep secret the authorship of *Evelina*, her first novel. Her contemporary Hannah More, who did publish in her own name and who achieved unprecedented success (she left an estate of £30,000, all earned by writing), nevertheless took care to discourage her female readers from following her example: "The profession of ladies," she wrote, "is that of daughters, wives, mothers, and mistresses of families."[2]

Every aspiring woman writer, then, had to struggle against

[2]*Strictures on the Modern System of Female Education* (1799; rpt. New York: Garland, 1974), 1:97–98.

inhibitions produced by an ideal of womanliness which required her to be modestly retiring and defined her as a helpmate to man. Women were also handicapped by their lack of experience. They could not go to college, they could not enter government (and were not even supposed to have political ideas), they could not (with any decency or safety) travel alone; they were being pushed out of trades and shopkeeping and had few opportunities of managing money; they could not run away to sea, practice law, perform surgery, enter the Church, initiate relationships with men; even assisting at childbirth was gradually pried out of their hands as midwives were replaced by male accoucheurs. Deprived of access to so much of human experience, they confronted the world as spectators—often, frightened and puzzled spectators. They were, in fact, in much the same position as children.

Like children, women had to depend on men for the conditions of their lives. Excluded from the professions and business, most of them were forced into marriage as their only means of support. Lower-class women could work as farm laborers or servants, but were badly exploited, as we see from Mary Collier's poem "The Woman's Labor." Once married, a wife was morally and legally dominated by her husband. The Church told her it was her duty to obey him; the law gave him control of her property, her earnings, her children, and her person (unless she could prove in court that he actually endangered her life). Generally speaking, her well-being depended upon the goodwill of the men who surrounded her. She could be well educated if her father or brother saw fit to instruct her; she could be an influential hostess and patron, like Elizabeth Montagu, if her husband was willing to pay the bills; she could write and publish if her husband approved of literary activity in women.

Exclusion from higher education not only kept women out of the learned professions; it also weakened confidence in their writing. Until far into the eighteenth century, respected literature was that produced by authors trained in the Greek and Roman classics—Homer, Virgil, Horace, Ovid. Such "manly" literature (as it was called) was considered serious and weighty because it was rooted in knowledge of the approved tradition. This knowledge women in general were denied. (Exceptions like Anna Laetitia Barbauld were lucky: they were blessed with supportive fathers or brothers. That a country working girl like Mary Leapor managed to attain even to literacy—let alone to classical allusion—was correctly regarded as a freak event.) Their lack of classical learning meant that most women were ignorant of modes and styles available to almost any male writer. Manley, for example, could not have written "Imitations of Horace," as Pope did, because she knew no Latin. For her, the place of Homer and Virgil was filled by French romances and Renaissance Italian tales in English translation.

Even if they had learned Latin, women were thought to be incapable of serious writing, as of serious thinking. "What a pox have the women to do with the Muses?" exclaimed one male writer in 1702.[3] Another, reviewing Hester Thrale Piozzi's world history, *Retrospection*, a hundred years later, sneered, "Does a weak woman flattered with folly take up the pen of the historian, and think to add to her reputation and fame?"[4] As the century wore on, however, reviewers (who were almost always male) tended to change their note from savage to patronizing. Hannah More described the kind of reception a woman writer could expect:

> In the judgment passed on her performances, she will have to encounter the mortifying circumstance of having her sex always taken into account, and her highest exertions will probably be received with the qualified approbation, *that it is really extraordinary for a woman.* Men of learning . . . are apt to consider even the happier performances of the other sex as the spontaneous productions of a fruitful but shallow soil.[5]

This presumption of incompetence took its psychological toll even on women as strong as Piozzi and Barbauld. Despite having benefited from an excellent home education, Barbauld doubted the rightness of educating women; Piozzi spoiled her two most ambitious books by anxious disclaimers of any intention to compete with men.

In a society controlled by men, women could gain a right only if men were willing to grant it. Fortunately, some were. Not only did they tolerate female literary efforts, but also, as collaborators, editors, or publishers, they actively promoted them. Some of these men, such as Samuel Johnson, were influential.

[3]*A Comparison between the Two Stages* (1702; rpt. New York: Garland, 1973), p. 26. The anonymous author does, to be sure, assert that he writes "between jest and earnest" (p.vi).
[4]*Anti-Jacobin Review*, 8 (1801): 245.
[5]*Strictures*, 2:12–13.

Johnson has an honorable record of assisting women authors—
Anna Williams the poet, Charlotte Lennox the novelist, Hester
Thrale (before she became Piozzi)—and he understood the importance of what they collectively were doing. "In former times,"
he wrote in 1753, "the pen, like the sword, was considered as
consigned by nature to the hands of men . . . the revolution of
years has now produced a generation of Amazons of the pen,
who with the spirit of their predecessors have set masculine
tyranny at defiance."[6] Another Johnson, the radical publisher
Joseph, printed the works of Barbauld, Mary Hays, and Mary
Wollstonecraft. Biographies of learned women were compiled
by George Ballard (*Memoirs of Several Ladies . . . Who have
been Celebrated for their Writings or Skill in the Learned Languages, Arts and Sciences*, 1752), their achievements were celebrated in verse by John Duncombe (*The Feminiad*, 1754), and
their poems were anthologized by George Colman and Bonnell
Thornton (*Poems by Eminent Ladies*, 1755).

By the end of the century the professional woman writer,
although not altogether secure from sexual denigration, could
compete almost on equal terms with men. The most phenomenal
success was Hannah More's: not only did she make a fortune
with a constant stream of best-sellers (poems, plays, a novel,
conservative political and religious tracts, treatises on education) and organize an extraordinarily influential series of pam-
phlets for the poor (the *Cheap Repository Tracts*, 1795–98), but
she was generally acclaimed as an oracle of wisdom and morality. Not far behind her was Barbauld, who not only dominated
children's literature but also was acknowledged to stand among
the foremost poets—male or female—of the 1780s and 1790s. And
the writer who comes last in our collection, Maria Edgeworth,
was reckoned the leading novelist of her generation. There were
still murmurs and sneers, to be sure: More was derisively called
"the female bishop," and Barbauld got a torrent of abuse for her
criticism of England in her poem *Eighteen Hundred and Eleven*;
female novelists were often dismissed, collectively, as insipid
nonentities. But they were no longer whores. Although Behn
had been a prodigy in her time and had had to flout conventional
notions of female propriety, these women supported themselves
by authorship as a matter of course.

[6]*The Idler and The Adventurer*, ed. W. J. Bate et al. (New Haven: Yale University Press,
1963), pp. 457–58.

This acceptance of women into intellectual life was both manifested and promoted by the Bluestockings, a group of literary minded women—and men—who formed around the wealthy Elizabeth Montagu during the 1750s and 1760s. Their most specific aim was at once quite limited and quite revolutionary: to bring men and women together socially for the purpose of conversation. Thirty years earlier, in Lady Mary Wortley Montagu's day, men and women had rarely mingled except to dance and flirt. To bring them into the same room in order to talk—and to talk about books and ideas and events—amounted to introducing them to each other as equals. One result we have already noticed: increased respect for female intellect by influential men. Another was support for women writers by women. As a member of the group, Elizabeth Carter was encouraged to translate the Greek philosopher Epictetus and made £1000 by her work (1758). Barbauld and Piozzi were also connected with the Montagu circle, and the working-class poet Ann Yearsley was a Bluestocking "discovery."

Family groups provided essential support for some of these achieving women. D'Arblay developed her skills as a social reporter through writing journals for an appreciative family, and Edgeworth wrote primarily to please her family and relied on them for stimulus and criticism. Several of our authors expressed gratitude and devotion to supportive fathers. Mothers, in contrast, are seldom mentioned. The only one with known significant influence, Piozzi's, preached self-abnegation and restriction to her daughter; it was Samuel Johnson who prodded Piozzi into developing interests beyond her home and babies.

The nineteen women included here are a diverse group. Some were blissfully happy wives, some unhappy or separated ones, some mistresses, and some respectable celibates. Most had no children or only one or two, but both Smith and Piozzi bore twelve. About half wrote partly at least for financial support. The majority came from the middle class, but three were aristocrats and three laboring women. In politics, they ranged from ultraconservative (More) to radical (Hays). Some were deeply religious, all gave at least lip service to religion, and a surprising number used Biblical arguments to support their feminist claims; they saw in Christianity not its patriarchal church but its emphasis on an immortal soul unlimited by sexual distinctions. Royalist Finch and radical Hays used Biblical texts to support their claims to spiritual equality, and Astell took great pains, in the

Appendix to her *Reflections on Marriage*, to prove from the Bible that woman was not created inferior. (Only Wollstonecraft was prepared, in Chapter Two of her *Vindication of the Rights of Woman* [1792], to dismiss the Scriptural account of woman's creation as a fabrication by men to justify their domination.)[7]

Women proved their ability to succeed in male-defined literature and, at the same time, they modified it to express their distinctive perceptions and concerns. Sometimes they met men on their own ground with a counterattack. Behn, with characteristic boldness, declared that amusing people with comedies was more valuable than expounding abstruse philosophy and produced Shakespeare as proof that no one needs to be learned in order to write a good play. Polemicists from Astell to Hays and Wollstonecraft countered charges that women were ignorant and frivolous by retorting that they had been made that way by men. The positive form of this retort was, of course, a demand for equal education. This impulse to retaliate cuts right across class lines to unite writers who could hardly have imagined each other's lives. Lady Mary's witty, worldly reply to Swift ("The Reasons that Induced Dr. S[wift] . . .") and the farm worker Mary Collier's earnest doggerel rebuttal of Stephen Duck ("The Woman's Labor") are more significantly alike than they are different: they are defiant rejections of male aspersions.

Sometimes women adapted masculine forms to express their own concerns. Finch transforms the conventional neoclassical love lyric to express her feelings for her husband and satirizes a female fool as an inadequate human being rather than as an annoyance to men ("Ardelia's Answer to Ephelia"). Mary Leapor and Barbauld employ the eighteenth-century idiom of mock heroic to celebrate, respectively, tea-making and gossip ("The Sacrifice") and "Washing-Day." Dismissed by men as trivial, female concerns are embraced by women writers as healthy alternatives to male norms, as Philips sings retired friendship and Behn, in "The Golden Age," magnificently exalts pleasure above honor, virtue, property—all the tyrannies of patriarchal society.

Finally, the demands of "female decorum" and exclusion from public life drove many writers into "underground" forms: the diary, the private letter, the lyric poem addressed to one's self or to one's dearest friend. Because enforced ignorance tended

[7]For a good selection of Wollstonecraft's writings, see *A Mary Wollstonecraft Reader*, ed. Barbara H. Solomon and Paula S. Berggren (New York: New American Library, 1983).

to keep them out of the then traditional literary forms, that new, "modern," eighteenth-century form the novel was the one in which most women writers published. For obvious reasons we are unable to represent the novel here, and can only direct our readers, enthusiastically, to such works as Burney's *Evelina* (1778) or Charlotte Lennox's *The Female Quixote* (1752), realistic and fanciful narratives, respectively, of a young lady's entrance into society, or Elizabeth Inchbald's *A Simple Story* (1791), a penetrating study of the relationship between an incompatible couple.[8]

In novels as well as letters and journals, we find women writers tending to dwell on details of daily life and personal feeling—for in such matters women were allowed authority. Hence we can enjoy Montagu's reportage of what Turkish women thought about her corset, Burney's exposure of the masculine conceit of Dr. King and Dr. Keate, and Piozzi's complaint that a mother cannot keep up intellectual life while raising children. Maria Edgeworth shows similar acute social insight in "The Noble Science of Self-Justification," where she anatomizes the indirect means by which women attain power. The woman spectator is not an agent, may have no power to influence events; but she compensates herself by convincing us that she *sees* them more clearly than any man does.

Posterity, as Virginia Woolf noticed, has not been kind to these writers. Until recently, they hardly appeared in anthologies or academic courses; we lived with a foreshortened history of women's literary achievement, a history in which women appeared to have burst into print all at once with Jane Austen, or perhaps Frances Burney, and in which Aphra Behn was simply a freak. But even Woolf valued them for just one thing— the bare fact that they had written at all and thus had made Austen possible. They are valuable for other reasons also. The eighteenth century was not populated solely by men; women were there too, and from their writings we can learn how the world seemed to them. In them today's women will find foremothers they never knew they had, and a lengthened record of female experience. Finally, in their writings readers and students of literature will find amusement, power, and passion. They were not just forerunners of their betters; they were good themselves.

---

[8]By the end of the century there were actually more female than male novelists. Women were also conspicuous, if not quite so distinguished, as dramatists. Behn in the 1670s, Susannah Centlivre in the early 1700s, Inchbald and Hannah Cowley in the last decades of the century, produced many plays of high quality that were also popular successes.

Aphra Behn
1640–1689

NOTHING is certainly known of Aphra Behn's early life, not even her maiden name; but it does seem that she lived in Surinam for some months, as she claims in *Oroonoko*. After a marriage, apparently brief, to Mr. Behn, she went to Antwerp as a spy during the second Dutch War (1666), returning to London penniless. Possibly influenced by her acquaintance with Thomas Killigrew, manager of one of the two licensed theaters in London, and doubtless encouraged by the voracious demand for new plays after the theaters reopened in 1660, Behn turned to playwriting to support herself. She wrote two conventional tragicomedies that were moderately successful, but found her style with *The Dutch Lover* (1673), a comedy. Nevertheless, it was not well received, partly because of poor acting and costuming, mostly because of prejudice against a woman author. The female playwright had become a serious competitor instead of an entertaining novelty. Provoked, Behn added a vigorously feminist preface to the published play.

She went on to write fifteen (or possibly eighteen) more plays, most of which were successful and many published with her name. They feature ingenious intrigue, amusing characters, and witty courtship scenes. Boldly, and rightly, she claimed that she had written "as many good comedies, as any one man that has writ in our age." The best of them are *Sir Patient Fancy* (1678) and *The Rover* (1677); the latter, together with her farce *The Emperor in the Moon* (1687), held the stage well into the eighteenth century.

Behn also wrote poems (including some lovely songs), translations, and novellas (of which the best is *Oroonoko*, 1688). Her autobiographical claims as narrator of this tale seem to be partially based on fact, as are many of its details. For example, black slaves were generally prisoners of war bought from victorious African kings, and a clear moral distinction was drawn between acquiring slaves by "lawful" purchase and by seizure. The Governor, Lord Willoughby, was indeed expected in Surinam all the while the story is taking place (late 1663–spring 1664; he finally arrived in November); thus awaiting his arrival could have been a plausible pretext (if not a genuine reason) for delaying Oroonoko's emancipation. Behn's use of authentic detail, such as the fauna of Surinam and the Africans' fondness for tobacco, presages Defoe's.

Behn seems to have been an attractive woman, a witty conversationalist, and a warm friend. She knew the witty courtier the Earl of Rochester, the leading actress Elizabeth Barry, and the writers John Dryden and Thomas Otway. She attracted her full share of the ferocious lampoons characteristic of her period, infused with particular venom because of her sex; she was attacked for "the ruin of her face" (at forty-four), for sexual promiscuity, and for getting her lovers to write her plays. Actually, her only proven love affair was a long, unhappy one with a cold bisexual lawyer named John Hoyle. Despite the attacks, Behn, considered the first professional woman author in England, demonstrated that a woman could openly succeed as a writer if she was sufficiently tough.

An Epistle to the Reader, prefixed to The Dutch Lover

Good, Sweet, Honey, Sugar-Candied Reader,

Which I think is more than anyone has called you yet, I must have a word or two with you before you do advance into the treatise; but 'tis not to beg your pardon for diverting you from your affairs by such an idle pamphlet as this is, for I presume you have not much to do and therefore are to be obliged to me for keeping you from worse employment, and if you have a better you may get you gone about your business: but if you will misspend your time, pray lay the fault upon yourself; for I have dealt pretty fairly in the matter, told you in the title page what you are to expect within. Indeed, had I hung a sign of the Immortality of the Soul, of the Mystery of Godliness, or of Ecclesiastical Policy, and then had treated you with Indiscerptibility and Essential Spissitude (words which, though I am no competent judge of, for want of languages,[1] yet I fancy strongly ought to mean just nothing) with a company of apocryphal midnight tales culled out of the choicest insignificant authors; if I had only proved in folio that Apollonius was a naughty knave, or had presented you with two or three of the worst principles transcribed out of the peremptory and ill-natured (though prettily ingenious) Doctor of Malmesbury undigested and ill managed by a silly, saucy, ignorant, impertinent, ill-educated chaplain,[2] I were then indeed sufficiently in fault; but having inscribed Comedy on the beginning of my book, you may guess pretty near what penny-worths you are like to have, and ware your money and your time accordingly. I would not yet be understood to lessen the dignity of plays, for surely they deserve a place among the middle if not the better sort of books; for I have heard the most of that which bears the name of learning, and which has abused such quantities of ink and paper, and continually employs so many ignorant, unhappy souls for ten, twelve, twenty years in the university (who yet poor wretches think they are doing something all the while) as logic, etc. and several other things (that shall be nameless lest I misspell them) are much more absolutely nothing than the arrantest play that e'er was writ. Take notice, reader, I do not assert this purely upon my own knowledge, but I think I have known it very fully proved, both sides being fairly heard, and even some ingenious opposers of it most abominably baffled in the argument: some of which I have got so perfectly by rote, that if this were a proper place for it, I am apt to think myself could almost make it clear; and as I would not undervalue poetry, so neither am I altogether of their judgment who believe no wisdom in the world beyond it. I have often heard indeed (and read) how much the world was anciently obliged to it for most of that which they called science, which my want of letters makes me less assured of than others happily may be: but I have heard some wise men say that no considerable part of useful knowledge was this way communicated, and on the other way, that it hath served to propagate so many idle

---

[1]Greek and Latin, prominent in the education of upper-class men and very rarely taught to women. Behn derisively contrasts the significance of an entertaining comedy with that of more highly esteemed works, tomes on theology or church politics. *Indiscerptibility*, indestructibility because indivisible into parts, and *spissitude*, density, were theoretical attributes of the soul.

[2]Thomas Hobbes, called the Doctor of Malmesbury, was a witty philosopher (1588–1679) whose materialism and anticlericalism verged on atheism. Hence he was constantly attacked by the clergy.

superstitions, as all the benefits it hath or can be guilty of, can never make sufficient amends for; which unaided by the unlucky charms of poetry, could never have possessed a thinking creature such as man. However true this is, I am myself well able to affirm that none of all our English poets, and least the dramatic (so I think you call them) can be justly charged with too great reformation of men's minds or manners, and for that I may appeal to general experiment,[3] if those who are the most assiduous disciples of the stage, do not make the fondest and lewdest crew about this town; for if you should unhappily converse them through the year, you will not find one dram of sense amongst a club of them, unless you will allow for such a little link-boy's ribaldry thick-larded with unseasonable oaths and impudent defiance of God and all things serious; and that at such a senseless damned unthinking rate, as, if 'twere well distributed, would spoil near half the apothecaries' trade and save the sober people of the town the charge of vomits; and it was smartly said (how prudently I cannot tell) by a late learned Doctor, who, though himself no great asserter of a deity (as you'll believe by that which follows), yet was observed to be continually persuading of this sort of men (if I for once may call them so) of the necessity and truth of our religion; and being asked how he came to bestir himself so much this way, made answer that it was because their ignorance and indiscreet debauch make them a scandal to the profession of atheism. And for their wisdom and design I never knew it reach beyond the invention of some notable expedient for the speedier ridding them of their estate (a devilish clog to wit and parts) than other growling mortals know, or battering half-a-dozen fair new windows in a morning after their debauch, whilst the dull unjaunty[4] rascal they belong to is fast asleep. But I'll proceed no farther in their character, because that miracle of wit (in spite of academic frippery) the mighty Eachard hath already done it to my satisfaction;[5] and whoever undertakes a supplement to anything he hath discoursed, had better for their reputation be doing nothing.

Besides this theme is worn too threadbare by the whiffling would-be wits of the town, and of both the stone-blind-eyes of

---

[3]Experience.
[4]Lacking in fashionable ease and sprightliness.
[5]John Eachard, a distinguished clergyman and academic, wrote witty, humorous attacks on freethinkers, including Hobbes (early 1670s).

the kingdom.[6] And therefore to return to that which I before was speaking of, I will have leave to say that in my judgment the increasing number of our latter plays have not done much more towards the amending of men's morals or their wit than hath the frequent preaching, which this last age hath been pestered with (indeed without all controversy they have done less harm), nor can I once imagine what temptation anyone can have to expect it from them; for sure I am no play was ever writ with that design. If you consider tragedy, you'll find their best of characters unlikely patterns for a wise man to pursue: for he that is the Knight of the play, no sublunary feats must serve his Dulcinea; for if he can't bestride the moon, he'll ne'er make good his business to the end, and if he chance to be offended, he must without considering right or wrong confound all things he meets, and put you half-a-score likely tall fellows into each pocket;[7] and truly if he come not something near this pitch I think the tragedy's not worth a farthing; for plays were certainly intended for the exercising of men's passions, not their understandings, and he is infinitely far from wise that will bestow one moment's meditation on such things: And as for comedy, the finest folks you meet with there are still unfitter for your imitation, for though within a leaf or two of the prologue, you are told that they are people of wit, good humor, good manners, and all that: yet if the authors did not kindly add their proper names, you'd never know them by their characters; for whatsoe'er's the matter, it hath happened so spitefully in several plays, which have been pretty well received of late, that even those persons that were meant to be the ingenious censors of the play, have either proved the most debauched or most unwitty people in the company: nor is this error very lamentable, since as I take it comedy was never meant, either for a converting or a conforming ordinance. In short, I think a play the best divertissement that wise men have: but I do also think them nothing so who do discourse as formally about the rules of it, as if 'twere the grand affair of human life. This being my opinion of plays, I studied only to make this as entertaining as I could, which whether I have been successful in, my gentle reader, you may for your shilling judge.[8]

[6]The two universities, Oxford and Cambridge.

[7]The hero of the most prominent type of contemporary tragedy, the heroic play, was like Cervantes' knight Don Quixote in his uncompromising pursuit of glory, devotion to his lady (Dulcinea was Don Quixote's love), and touchy honor.

[8]The printed play would sell for a shilling.

To tell you my thoughts of it, were to little purpose, for were they very ill, you may be sure I would not have exposed it; nor did I so till I had first consulted most of those who have a reputation for judgment of this kind; who were at least so civil (if not kind) to it as did encourage me to venture it upon the stage and in the press: nor did I take their single word for it, but used their reasons as a confirmation of my own.

Indeed that day 'twas acted first, there comes me into the pit, a long, lither, phlegmatic,[9] white, ill-favored, wretched fop, an officer in masquerade newly transported with a scarf and feather out of France, a sorry animal that has nought else to shield it from the uttermost contempt of all mankind, but that respect which we afford to rats and toads, which though we do not well allow to live, yet when considered as a part of God's creation, we make honorable mention of them. A thing, reader—but no more of such a smelt: this thing, I tell ye, opening that which serves it for a mouth, out issued such a noise as this to those that sat about it, that they were to expect a woeful play, God damn him, for it was a woman's. Now how this came about I am not sure, but I suppose he brought it piping hot from some who had with him the reputation of a villainous wit: for creatures of his size of sense talk, without all imagination, such scraps as they pick up from other folks. I would not for a world be taken arguing with such a property[10] as this; but if I thought there were a man of any tolerable parts, who could upon mature delibera-tion distinguish well his right hand from his left, and justly state the difference between the number of sixteen and two, yet had this prejudice upon him; I would take a little pains to make him know how much he errs. For waiving the examination why women having equal education with men were not as capable of knowledge of whatsoever sort as well as they, I'll only say as I have touched before, that plays have no great room for that which is men's great advantage over women, that is learning. We all well know that the immortal Shakespeare's plays (who was not guilty of much more of this than often falls to women's share) have better pleased the world than Jonson's works, though by the way 'tis said that Benjamin was no such rabbi[11] neither, for I am informed that his learning was but grammar

---

[9]Impotent, dull.
[10]Tool, cat's-paw.
[11]Learned man.

high (sufficient indeed to rob poor Sallust of his best orations); and it hath been observed that they are apt to admire him most confoundedly who have just such a scantling of it as he had; and I have seen a man the most severe of Jonson's sect, sit with his hat removed less than a hair's breadth from one sullen posture for almost three hours at *The Alchemist*; who at that excellent play of *Harry the Fourth* (which yet I hope is far enough from farce) hath very hardly kept his doublet whole;[12] but affectation hath always had a greater share both in the actions and discourse of men than truth and judgment have; and for our modern ones, except our most unimitable Laureate,[13] I dare to say I know of none that write at such a formidable rate, but that a woman may well hope to reach their greatest heights. Then for their musty rules of unity,[14] and God knows what besides, if they meant anything, they are enough intelligible and as practicable by a woman; but really methinks they that disturb their heads with any other rule of plays besides the making them pleasant and avoiding of scurrility, might much better be employed in studying how to improve men's too imperfect knowledge of that ancient English game which hight long Laurence:[15] and if comedy should be the picture of ridiculous mankind I wonder anyone should think it such a sturdy task, whilst we are furnished with such precious originals as him I lately told you of; if at least that character do not dwindle into farce, and so become too mean an entertainment for those persons who are used to think. Reader, I have a complaint or two to make to you and I have done. Know then that this play was hugely injured in the acting, for 'twas done so imperfectly as never any was before, which did more harm to this than it could have done to any of another sort; the plot being busy (though I think not intricate) and so requiring a continual attention, which being interrupted by the intolerable negligence of some that acted in it,

[12] Ben Jonson had more classical learning than his contemporary William Shakespeare and commented on Shakespeare's "small Latin and less Greek." However, Behn says, Jonson had only the basic Latin and Greek he would have learned in an Elizabethan grammar school. Jonson's Roman plays, such as *Catiline*, include long passages translated from Latin authors, including the historian Sallust. *The Alchemist* is a comedy by Jonson; Shakespeare's history play *Henry IV* contains many comic scenes.

[13] John Dryden, the leading writer of the age, was Poet Laureate.

[14] Renaissance critics had formalized Aristotle's critical principles into rules, including the unities of time, place, and action: a play must be limited to one plot, which must take place during one day and within one city. Contemporary French playwrights followed these rules, but the English debated their importance.

[15] *To play at Lawrence* meant to do nothing, to laze (Montague Summers).

must needs much spoil the beauty on't. My Dutch Lover spoke but little of what I intended for him, but supplied it with a great deal of idle stuff, which I was wholly unacquainted with until I had heard it first from him; so that jack-pudding[16] ever used to do: which though I knew before, I gave him yet the part, because I knew him so acceptable to most o' th' lighter periwigs[17] about the town, and he indeed did vex me so, I could almost be angry. Yet, but reader, you remember, I suppose a fusty piece of Latin that has passed from hand to hand this thousand years they say (and how much longer I can't tell) in favor of the dead.[18] I intended him a habit[19] much more notably ridiculous, which if ever it be important was so here, for many of the scenes in the three last acts depended upon the mistakes of the Colonel for Haunce,[20] which the ill-favored likeness of their habits is supposed to cause. Lastly my epilogue was promised me by a person who had surely made it good, if any, but he failing of his word, deputed one who has made it as you see, and to make out your penny-worth you have it here. The prologue is by misfortune lost. Now, reader, I have eased my mind of all I had to say, and so *sans* further compliment, Adieu.

The Golden Age

A Paraphrase on a Translation out of French[1]

I.

Blest age! when ev'ry purling stream
    Ran undisturbed and clear,
When no scorned shepherds on your banks were seen,

[16]Buffoon.

[17]All upper-class men wore wigs; light periwigs, being particularly fashionable, would suggest fops.

[18]Edward Angel, who died a few months after the play's première, was a popular comedian. The fusty Latin is "De mortuis nil nisi bonum," "Of the dead [speak] nothing but good."

[19]Costume.

[20]The Colonel (Alonzo) is a romantic lead in *The Dutch Lover*; Haunce van Ezel is the clownish title character, played by Angel.

[1]First published in 1684. Neither the French original nor the translation have been identified. Behn is likely to have treated them very freely.

Tortured by love, by jealousy, or fear;
When an eternal Spring dressed ev'ry bough,
And blossoms fell, by new ones dispossessed;
These their kind shade affording all below,
And those a bed where all below might rest.
The groves appeared all dressed with wreaths of flowers,
And from their leaves dropped aromatic showers,   *10*
Whose fragrant heads in mystic twines above,
Exchanged their sweets, and mixed with thousand kisses,
    As if the willing branches strove
    To beautify and shade the grove
    Where the young wanton Gods of Love
Offer their noblest sacrifice of blisses.

II.

Calm was the air, no winds blew fierce and loud,
The sky was darkened with no sullen cloud;
But all the heav'ns laughed with continued light,
And scattered round their rays serenely bright.   *20*
    No other murmurs filled the ear
    But what the streams and rivers purled,
When silver waves o'er shining pebbles curled;

    Or when young Zephyrs fanned the gentle breeze,
    Gath'ring fresh sweets from balmy flow'rs and trees,
Then bore 'em on their wings to perfume all the air:
    While to their soft and tender play,
    The gray-plumed natives of the shades
    Unwearied sing till Love invades,
Then bill, then sing again, while Love and Music makes   *30*
    the day.

III.

    The stubborn plough had then
Made no rude rapes upon the virgin Earth;
Who yielded of her own accord her plenteous birth,
    Without the aids of men;
    As if within her teeming womb
    All Nature, and all sexes lay,
    Whence new creations ev'ry day

Into the happy world did come:
The roses filled with morning dew,
   Bent down their loaded heads,   *40*
T'adorn the careless shepherds' grassy beds
While still young opening buds each moment grew,
And as those withered, dressed his shaded couch anew;
Beneath whose boughs the snakes securely dwelt,
Not doing harm, nor harm from others felt;
With whom the nymphs did innocently play,
No spiteful venom in the wantons lay;
But to the touch were soft, and to the sight were gay.

IV.

Then no rough sound of war's alarms
Had taught the world the needless use of arms: *50*
   Monarchs were uncreated then,
Those arbitrary rulers over men:
Kings that made laws, first broke 'em, and the gods
By teaching us religion first, first set the world at odds:
   Till then ambition was not known,
That poison to content, bane to repose;
Each swain was lord o'er his own will alone,
His innocence religion was, and laws.
Nor needed any troublesome defense
   Against his neighbor's insolence.   *60*
Flocks, herds, and ev'ry necessary good
Which bounteous Nature had designed for food,
Whose kind increase o'erspread the meads and plains,
Was then a common sacrifice to all th'agreeing swains.

V.

Right and property were words since made,
   When Pow'r taught mankind to invade:
When Pride and Avarice became a trade;
   Carried on by discord, noise and wars,
   For which they bartered wounds and scars;
And to enhance the merchandise, miscalled it Fame,   *70*
   And rapes, invasions, tyrannies
   Was gaining of a glorious name:
Styling their savage slaughters, Victories;

Honor, the error and the cheat
Of the ill-natured busy Great,
Nonsense, invented by the proud,
Fond idol of the slavish crowd,
Thou wert not known in those blest days,
Thy poison was not mixed with our unbounded joys;
Then it was glory to pursue delight,   *80*
And that was lawful all, that Pleasure did invite,
Then 'twas the amorous world enjoyed its reign;
And tyrant Honor strove t' usurp in vain.

VI.

The flow'ry meads, the rivers and the groves,
Were filled with little gay-winged Loves:
   That ever smiled and danced and played,
And now the woods, and now the streams invade,
And where they came all things were gay and glad:
When in the myrtle groves the lovers sat
   Oppressed with a too fervent heat;   *90*
A thousand Cupids fanned their wings aloft,
And through the boughs the yielded air would waft:
Whose parting leaves discovered all below,
And every god his own soft power admired,
And smiled and fanned, and sometimes bent his bow;
Where'er he saw a shepherd uninspired.
The nymphs were free, no nice, no coy disdain
Denied their joys, or gave the lover pain;
The yielding maid but kind resistance makes;
Trembling and blushing are not marks of shame,   *100*
   But the effect of kindling flame:
Which from the sighing burning swain she takes,
While she with tears all soft, and downcast eyes,
Permits the charming conqueror to win the prize.

VII.

The lovers thus, thus uncontrolled did meet,
Thus all their joys and vows of love repeat:
   Joys which were everlasting, ever new
   And every vow inviolably true:
Not kept in fear of Gods, no fond religious cause,

Nor in obedience to the duller laws.   *110*
Those fopperies of the gown were then not known,
Those vain, those politic curbs to keep man in,
Who by a fond mistake created that a sin
Which freeborn we, by right of Nature claim our own.
    Who but the learned and dull moral fool
Could gravely have foreseen, man ought to live by rule?

VIII.

Oh cursed Honor! thou who first didst damn
   A woman to the sin of shame;
      Honor! that robb'st us of our gust,
      Honor! that hindered mankind first,   *120*
At Love's eternal spring to squench² his amorous thirst.
Honor! who first taught lovely eyes the art
   To wound, and not to cure the heart:
With love to invite, but to forbid with awe,
And to themselves prescribe a cruel law;
      To veil 'em from the lookers on,
      When they are sure the slave's undone,
And all the charming'st part of beauty hid;
Soft looks, consenting wishes, all denied.
      It gathers up the flowing hair,   *130*
      That loosely played with wanton air.
The envious net, and stinted order hold
The lovely curls of jet and shining gold;
No more neglected on the shoulders hurled:
Now dressed to tempt, not gratify the world:
Thou, miser Honor, hoard'st the sacred store,
And starv'st thyself to keep thy votaries poor.

IX.

Honor! that put'st our words that should be free
     Into a set formality.
Thou base debaucher of the generous heart,   *140*
That teachest all our looks and actions art;³
    What love designed a sacred gift,

²Quench.
³Skill or craftiness.

What Nature made to be possessed;
Mistaken Honor made a theft,
For glorious love should be confessed:
For when confined, all the poor lover gains
Is broken sighs, pale looks, complaints and pains.
Thou foe to Pleasure, Nature's worst disease,
Thou tyrant over mighty kings,
What mak'st thou here in shepherds' cottages;   150
Why troublest thou the quiet shades and springs?
Be gone, and make thy famed resort
To princes' palaces;
Go deal and chaffer in the trading court,
That busy market for fantastic things;
Be gone and interrupt the short retreat
Of the illustrious and the great;
Go break the politician's sleep,
Disturb the gay ambitious fool,
That longs for scepters, crowns, and rule,   160
Which not his title, nor his wit can keep;
But let the humble honest swain go on
In the blessed paths of the first rate of man,[4]
That nearest were to gods allied
And formed for love alone, disdained all other pride.

X.

Be gone! and let the Golden Age again
Assume its glorious reign;
Let the young wishing maid confess
What all your arts would keep concealed:
The mystery will be revealed,   170
And she in vain denies, whilst we can guess,
She only shows the jilt to teach man how
To turn the false artillery on the cunning foe.
Thou empty vision hence, be gone,
And let the peaceful swain love on;
The swift paced hours of life soon steal away:
Stint not, ye gods, his short lived joy.
The Spring decays, but when the Winter's gone,
The trees and flow'rs anew come on;

[4]That is, man as originally created.

The sun may set, but when the night is fled,   *180*
    And gloomy darkness does retire,
    He rises from his wat'ry bed:
All glorious, gay, all dressed in amorous fire.
    But Sylvia, when your beauties fade,
When the fresh roses on your cheeks shall die,
    Like flow'rs that wither in the shade,
Eternally they will forgotten lie,
And no kind Spring their sweetness will supply.
When snow shall on those lovely tresses lie,
And your fair eyes no more shall give us pain,   *190*
    But shoot their pointless darts in vain,
What will your duller honor signify?
Go boast it then! and see what numerous store
Of lovers will your ruined shrine adore.
    Then let us, Sylvia, yet be wise,
    And the gay hasty minutes prize:
The sun and Spring receive but our short light,
Once set, a sleep brings an eternal night.

Oroonoko:
OR
The History of the Royal Slave

I do not pretend, in giving you the history of this royal slave, to
entertain my reader with adventures of a feigned hero, whose
life and fortunes fancy may manage at the poet's pleasure; nor in
relating the truth, design to adorn it with any accidents, but such
as arrived in earnest to him: And it shall come simply into the
world, recommended by its own proper merits, and natural
intrigues, there being enough of reality to support it and to
render it diverting, without the addition of invention.

I was myself an eyewitness to a great part of what you will
find here set down; and what I could not be witness of, I
received from the mouth of the chief actor in this history, the
hero himself, who gave us the whole transactions of his youth:
And I shall omit, for brevity's sake, a thousand little accidents
of his life, which, however pleasant to us, where history was

scarce and adventures very rare, yet might prove tedious and heavy to my reader, in a world where he finds diversions for every minute, new and strange. But we, who were perfectly charmed with the character of this great man, were curious to gather every circumstance of his life.

The scene of the last part of his adventures lies in a colony in America, called Surinam, in the West Indies.

But before I give you the story of this gallant slave, 'tis fit I tell you the manner of bringing them to these new colonies; those they make use of there, not being natives of the place; for those we live with in perfect amity, without daring to command 'em; but, on the contrary, caress 'em with all the brotherly and friendly affection in the world; trading with them for their fish, venison, buffalo skins, and little rarities; as marmosets, a sort of monkey, as big as a rat or weasel, but of a marvelous and delicate shape, having face and hands like a human creature; and cousheries, a little beast in the form and fashion of a lion, as big as a kitten, but so exactly made, in all parts like that noble beast, that it is it in miniature. Then for little paraketoes, great parrots, macaws, and a thousand other birds and beasts of wonderful and surprising forms, shapes, and colors. For skins of prodigious snakes, of which there are some threescore yards in length; as is the skin of one that may be seen at his Majesty's antiquary's; where are also some rare flies, of amazing forms and colors, presented to 'em by myself; some as big as my fist, some less; and all of various excellencies, such as art cannot imitate. Then we trade for feathers, which they order into all shapes, make themselves little short habits of 'em, and glorious wreaths for their heads, necks, arms and legs, whose tinctures are unconceivable. I had a set of these presented to me, and I gave 'em to the King's Theatre, and it was the dress of the *Indian Queen*,[1] infinitely admired by persons of quality; and was inimitable. Besides these, a thousand little knacks and rarities in nature; and some of art, as their baskets, weapons, aprons, etc. We dealt with 'em with beads of all colors, knives, axes, pins and needles; which they used only as tools to drill holes with in their ears, noses and lips, where they hang a great many little things, as long beads, bits of tin, brass or silver beat thin,

[1] *The Indian Queen*, a heroic play by Sir Robert Howard and John Dryden, was produced at the Theater Royal ("the King's Theater") in 1664 and often revived. Its cast included two Indian queens who might appropriately have worn the narrator's feathered costume.

and any shining trinket. The beads they weave into aprons about a quarter of an ell long, and of the same breadth; working them very prettily in flowers of several colors, which apron they wear just before 'em, as Adam and Eve did the fig-leaves; the men wearing a long strip of linen, which they deal with us for. They thread these beads also on long cotton-threads and make girdles to tie their aprons to, which come twenty times, or more, about the waist, and then cross like a shoulder-belt, both ways, and round their necks, arms, and legs. This adornment, with their long black hair, and the face painted in little specks or flowers here and there, makes 'em a wonderful figure to behold. Some of the beauties, which indeed are finely shaped, as almost all are, and who have pretty features, are charming and novel; for they have all that is called beauty, except the color, which is a reddish yellow; or after a new oiling, which they often use to themselves, they are of the color of a new brick, but smooth, soft and sleek. They are extreme modest and bashful, very shy, and nice of being touched. And though they are all thus naked, if one lives forever among 'em, there is not to be seen an indecent action or glance: and being continually used to see one another so unadorned, so like our first parents before the fall, it seems as if they had no wishes, there being nothing to heighten curiosity, but all you can see, you see at once, and every moment see; and where there is no novelty, there can be no curiosity. Not but I have seen a handsome young Indian dying for love of a very beautiful young Indian maid; but all his courtship was to fold his arms, pursue her with his eyes, and sighs were all his language: While she, as if no such lover were present, or rather as if she desired none such, carefully guarded her eyes from beholding him; and never approached him, but she looked down with all the blushing modesty I have seen in the most severe and cautious of our world. And these people represented to me an absolute idea of the first state of innocence, before man knew how to sin: And 'tis most evident and plain, that simple nature is the most harmless, inoffensive and virtuous mistress. 'Tis she alone, if she were permitted, that better instructs the world, than all the inventions of man: religion would here but destroy that tranquility they possess by ignorance; and laws would but teach 'em to know offense, of which now they have no notion. They once made mourning and fasting for the death of the English governor, who had given his hand to come on such a day to 'em, and neither came nor sent; believing, when a man's word was past, nothing but death could or should prevent his keeping it: And when they saw he was not dead, they asked him what name they had for a man who promised a thing he did not do? The governor told them, Such a man was a *liar*, which was a word of infamy to a gentleman. Then one of 'em replied, *Governor, you are a liar, and guilty of that infamy*. They have a native justice, which knows no fraud; and they understand no vice, or cunning, but when they are taught by the white men. They have plurality of wives; which, when they grow old, serve those that succeed 'em, who are young, but with a servitude easy and respected; and unless they take slaves in war, they have no other attendants.

Those on that continent where I was, had no king; but the oldest war-captain was obeyed with great resignation.

A war-captain is a man who has led them on to battle with conduct and success; of whom I shall have occasion to speak more hereafter, and of some other of their customs and manners, as they fall in my way.

With these people, as I said, we live in perfect tranquility, and good understanding, as it behooves us to do; they knowing all the places where to seek the best food of the country, and the means of getting it; and for very small and unvaluable trifles, supply us with that 'tis impossible for us to get: for they do not only in the woods and over the savannas in hunting supply the parts of hounds, by swiftly scouring through those almost impassable places, and by the mere activity of their feet run down the nimblest deer and other eatable beasts; but in the water, one would think they were gods of the rivers or fellow-citizens of the deep, so rare an art they have in swimming, diving, and almost living in water; by which they command the less swift inhabitants of the floods. And then for shooting, what they cannot take or reach with their hands, they do with arrows; and have so admirable an aim, that they will split almost an hair, and at any distance that an arrow can reach: they will shoot down oranges and other fruit, and only touch the stalk with the dart's point, that they may not hurt the fruit. So that they being on all occasions very useful to us, we find it absolutely necessary to caress 'em as friends, not to treat 'em as slaves, nor dare we do other, their numbers so far surpassing ours in that continent.

Those then whom we make use of to work in our plantations of sugar are negroes, black slaves altogether, who are transported thither in this manner.

Those who want slaves, make a bargain with a master, or a

captain of a ship, and contract to pay him so much apiece, a matter of twenty pound a head, for as many as he agrees for, and to pay for 'em when they shall be delivered on such a plantation: So that when there arrives a ship laden with slaves, they who have so contracted go aboard and receive their number by lot; and perhaps in one lot that may be for ten, there may happen to be three or four men, the rest women and children. Or be there more or less of either sex, you are obliged to be contented with your lot.

Coramantien,[2] a country of blacks so called, was one of those places in which they found the most advantageous trading for these slaves, and thither most of our great traders in that merchandise traffic; for that nation is very warlike and brave: and having a continual campaign, being always in hostility with one neighboring prince or other, they had the fortune to take a great many captives: for all they took in battle were sold as slaves, at least those common men who could not ransom themselves. Of these slaves so taken, the general only has all the profit; and of these generals our captains and masters of ships buy all their freights.

The king of Coramantien was himself a man of an hundred and odd years old, and had no son, though he had many beautiful black wives; for most certainly there are beauties that can charm of that color. In his younger years he had had many gallant men to his sons, thirteen of whom died in battle, conquering when they fell; and he had only left him for his successor one grandchild, son to one of these dead victors, who, as soon as he could bear a bow in his hand and a quiver at his back, was sent into the field to be trained up by one of the oldest generals to war; where, from his natural inclination to arms and the occasions given him, with the good conduct of the old general, he became, at the age of seventeen, one of the most expert captains and bravest soldiers that ever saw the field of Mars: so that he was adored as the wonder of all that world and the darling of the soldiers. Besides, he was adorned with a native beauty so transcending all those of his gloomy race, that he struck an awe and reverence even into those that knew not his quality; as he did into me, who beheld him with surprise and wonder, when afterwards he arrived in our world.

He had scarce arrived at his seventeenth year when, fighting

---

[2]Coramantien was on the Gold Coast, in modern Ghana.

by his side, the general was killed with an arrow in his eye, which the Prince Oroonoko (for so was this gallant Moor called) very narrowly avoided; nor had he, if the general, who saw the arrow shot, and perceiving it aimed at the prince, had not bowed his head between, on purpose to receive it in his own body, rather than it should touch that of the prince, and so saved him.

'Twas then, afflicted as Oroonoko was, that he was proclaimed general in the old man's place: and then it was, at the finishing of that war, which had continued for two years, that the prince came to court, where he had hardly been a month together, from the time of his fifth year to that of seventeen; and 'twas amazing to imagine where it was he learned so much humanity; or, to give his accomplishments a juster name, where 'twas he got that real greatness of soul, those refined notions of true honor, that absolute generosity, and that softness that was capable of the highest passions of love and gallantry, whose objects were almost continually fighting men or those mangled or dead, who heard no sounds but those of war and groans. Some part of it we may attribute to the care of a Frenchman of wit and learning, who, finding it turn to very good account to be a sort of royal tutor to this young black, and perceiving him very ready, apt, and quick of apprehension, took a great pleasure to teach him morals, language and science; and was for it extremely beloved and valued by him. Another reason was, he loved when he came from war, to see all the English gentlemen that traded thither; and did not only learn their language, but that of the Spaniard also, with whom he traded afterwards for slaves.

I have often seen and conversed with this great man, and been a witness to many of his mighty actions; and do assure my reader, the most illustrious courts could not have produced a braver man, both for greatness of courage and mind, a judgment more solid, a wit more quick, and a conversation more sweet and diverting. He knew almost as much as if he had read much: He had heard of and admired the Romans: He had heard of the late civil wars in England, and the deplorable death of our great monarch; and would discourse of it with all the sense and abhorrence of the injustice imaginable.[3] He had an extreme good

---

[3]The English Civil Wars led to the execution of the lawful sovereign, Charles I (1649); the monarchy was restored, in the person of his son Charles II, in 1660. Behn, an ardent royalist, makes royal Oroonoko share her indignation at rebellion against one's king.

and graceful mien, and all the civility of a well-bred great man. He had nothing of barbarity in his nature, but in all points addressed himself as if his education had been in some European court.

This great and just character of Oroonoko gave me an extreme curiosity to see him, especially when I knew he spoke French and English, and that I could talk with him. But though I had heard so much of him, I was as greatly surprised when I saw him as if I had heard nothing of him, so beyond all report I found him. He came into the room, and addressed himself to me and some other women with the best grace in the world. He was pretty tall, but of a shape the most exact that can be fancied: The most famous statuary could not form the figure of a man more admirably turned from head to foot. His face was not of that brown rusty black which most of that nation are, but of perfect ebony or polished jet. His eyes were the most awful[4] that could be seen, and very piercing; the white of 'em being like snow, as were his teeth. His nose was rising and Roman, instead of African and flat. His mouth the finest shaped that could be seen; far from those great turned lips which are so natural to the rest of the negroes. The whole proportion and air of his face was so nobly and exactly formed that, bating his color, there could be nothing in nature more beautiful, agreeable and handsome. There was no one grace wanting that bears the standard of true beauty. His hair came down to his shoulders by the aids of art, which was by pulling it out with a quill and keeping it combed, of which he took particular care. Nor did the perfections of his mind come short of those of his person; for his discourse was admirable upon almost any subject: and whoever had heard him speak would have been convinced of their errors, that all fine wit is confined to the white men, especially to those of Christendom; and would have confessed that Oroonoko was as capable even of reigning well, and of governing as wisely, had as great a soul, as politic maxims, and was as sensible of power, as any prince civilized in the most refined schools of humanity and learning or the most illustrious courts.

This prince, such as I have described him, whose soul and body were so admirably adorned, was (while yet he was in the court of his grandfather, as I said) as capable of love, as 'twas possible for a brave and gallant man to be; and in saying that, I

[4]Awe-inspiring, sublimely impressive. Cf. below, pp. 45, 55, 68.

have named the highest degree of love: for sure great souls are most capable of that passion.

I have already said, the old general was killed by the shot of an arrow by the side of this prince in battle; and that Oroonko was made general. This old dead hero had one only daughter left of his race, a beauty, that to describe her truly, one need say only, she was female to the noble male; the beautiful black Venus to our young Mars; as charming in her person as he, and of delicate virtues. I have seen a hundred white men sighing after her, and making a thousand vows at her feet, all in vain, and unsuccessful. And she was indeed too great for any but a prince of her own nation to adore.

Oroonoko coming from the wars (which were now ended) after he had made his court to his grandfather, he thought in honor he ought to make a visit to Imoinda, the daughter of his foster-father, the dead general; and to make some excuses to her, because his preservation was the occasion of her father's death; and to present her with those slaves that had been taken in this last battle, as the trophies of her father's victories. When he came, attended by all the young soldiers of any merit, he was infinitely surprised at the beauty of this fair Queen of Night, whose face and person was so exceeding all he had ever beheld, that lovely modesty with which she received him, that softness in her look and sighs, upon the melancholy occasion of this honor that was done by so great a man as Oroonoko and a prince of whom she had heard such admirable things; the awfulness[5] wherewith she received him, and the sweetness of her words and behavior while he stayed, gained a perfect conquest over his fierce heart and made him feel, the victor could be subdued. So that having made his first compliments and presented her an hundred and fifty slaves in fetters, he told her with his eyes that he was not insensible of her charms; while Imoinda, who wished for nothing more than so glorious a conquest, was pleased to believe she understood that silent language of new-born love, and, from that moment, put on all her additions to beauty.

The prince returned to court with quite another humor than before; and though he did not speak much of the fair Imoinda, he had the pleasure to hear all his followers speak of nothing but the charms of that maid, insomuch that, even in the presence of

[5]Awe, extreme reverence. Cf. below, p. 25.

the old king, they were extolling her and heightening, if possible, the beauties they had found in her; so that nothing else was talked of, no other sound was heard in every corner where there were whisperers, but Imoinda! Imoinda!

'Twill be imagined Oroonoko stayed not long before he made his second visit; nor, considering his quality, not much longer before he told her, he adored her. I have often heard him say, that he admired[6] by what strange inspiration he came to talk things so soft and so passionate, who never knew love, nor was used to the conversation of women; but (to use his own words) he said, most happily, some new and, till then, unknown power instructed his heart and tongue in the language of love, and at the same time, in favor of him, inspired Imoinda with a sense of his passion. She was touched with what he said, and returned it all in such answers as went to his very heart, with a pleasure unknown before. Nor did he use those obligations ill, that love had done him, but turned all his happy moments to the best advantage; and as he knew no vice, his flame aimed at nothing but honor, if such a distinction may be made in love; and especially in that country, where men take to themselves as many as they can maintain; and where the only crime and sin with woman is to turn her off, to abandon her to want, shame and misery: such ill morals are only practiced in Christian countries, where they prefer the bare name of religion, and, without virtue or morality, think that sufficient. But Oroonoko was none of those professors; but as he had right notions of honor, so he made her such propositions as were not only and barely such; but, contrary to the custom of his country, he made her vows, she should be the only woman he would possess while he lived; that no age or wrinkles should incline him to change; for her soul would be always fine, and always young; and he should have an eternal idea in his mind of the charms she now bore, and should look into his heart for that idea, when he could find it no longer in her face.

After a thousand assurances of his lasting flame and her eternal empire over him, she condescended to receive him for her husband, or rather, received him as the greatest honor the gods could do her.

There is a certain ceremony in these cases to be observed, which I forgot to ask how 'twas performed; but 'twas concluded

[6]Wondered. Cf. below, p. 69.

on both sides, that in obedience to him, the grandfather was to be first made acquainted with the design: For they pay a most absolute resignation to the monarch, especially when he is a parent also.

On the other side, the old king, who had many wives and many concubines, wanted not court-flatterers to insinuate into his heart a thousand tender thoughts for this young beauty; and who represented her to his fancy, as the most charming he had ever possessed in all the long race of his numerous years. At this character, his old heart, like an extinguished brand, most apt to take fire, felt new sparks of love and began to kindle; and now grown to his second childhood, longed with impatience to behold this gay thing, with whom, alas! he could but innocently play. But how he should be confirmed she was this wonder, before he used his power to call her to court (where maidens never came, unless for the king's private use), he was next to consider; and while he was so doing, he had intelligence brought him that Imoinda was most certainly mistress to the Prince Oroonoko. This gave him some chagrin: however, it gave him also an opportunity, one day, when the prince was a hunting, to wait on[7] a man of quality, as his slave and attendant, who should go and make a present to Imoinda, as from the prince; he should then, unknown, see this fair maid and have an opportunity to hear what message she would return the prince for his present, and from thence gather the state of her heart and degree of her inclination. This was put in execution, and the old monarch saw, and burned: He found her all he had heard, and would not delay his happiness, but found he should have some obstacle to overcome her heart; for she expressed her sense of the present the prince had sent her in terms so sweet, so soft and pretty, with an air of love and joy that could not be dissembled, insomuch that 'twas past doubt whether[8] she lov'd Oroonoko entirely. This gave the old king some affliction; but he salved it with this, that the obedience the people pay their king was not at all inferior to what they paid their gods; and what love would not oblige Imoinda to do, duty would compel her to.

He was therefore no sooner got to his apartment, but he sent the royal veil to Imoinda; that is, the ceremony of invitation: He

---

[7]Attend, accompany. (The old king pretends to be an attendant of his agent, who is to bring the present to Imoinda.)
[8]There was no doubt that.

sends the lady he has a mind to honor with his bed a veil, with which she is covered and secured for the king's use; and 'tis death to disobey; besides, held a most impious disobedience.

'Tis not to be imagined the surprise and grief that seized the lovely maid at this news and sight. However, as delays in these cases are dangerous and pleading worse than treason, trembling and almost fainting, she was obliged to suffer herself to be covered and led away.

They brought her thus to court; and the king, who had caused a very rich bath to be prepared, was led into it, where he sat under a canopy, in state, to receive this longed-for virgin; whom he having commanded should be brought to him, they (after disrobing her) led her to the bath, and making fast the doors left her to descend. The king, without more courtship, bade her throw off her mantle and come to his arms. But Imoinda, all in tears, threw herself on the marble on the brink of the bath and besought him to hear her. She told him, as she was a maid, how proud of the divine glory she should have been, of having it in her power to oblige her king; but as by the laws he could not, and from his royal goodness would not take from any man his wedded wife, so she believed she should be the occasion of making him commit a great sin if she did not reveal her state and condition, and tell him, she was another's and could not be so happy to be his.

The king, enraged at this delay, hastily demanded the name of the bold man that had married a woman of her degree without his consent. Imoinda, seeing his eyes fierce, and his hands tremble (whether with age or anger, I know not, but she fancied the last), almost repented she had said so much, for now she feared the storm would fall on the prince; she therefore said a thousand things to appease the raging of his flame and to prepare him to hear who it was with calmness: but before she spoke, he imagined who she meant, but would not seem to do so, but commanded her to lay aside her mantle, and suffer herself to receive his caresses or, by his gods he swore, that happy man whom she was going to name should die, though it were even Oroonoko himself. *Therefore* (said he) *deny this marriage, and swear thyself a maid. That* (replied Imoinda) *by all our powers I do; for I am not yet known to my husband.* 'Tis enough (said the king), *'tis enough both to satisfy my conscience, and my heart.* And rising from his seat, he went and led her into the bath, it being in vain for her to resist.

In this time, the prince, who was returned from hunting, went to visit his Imoinda, but found her gone; and not only so, but heard she had received the royal veil. This raised him to a storm; and in his madness, they had much ado to save him from laying violent hands on himself. Force first prevailed, and then reason: They urged all to him that might oppose his rage; but nothing weighed so greatly with him as the king's old age, uncapable of injuring him with Imoinda. He would give way to that hope, because it pleased him most and flattered best his heart. Yet this served not altogether to make him cease his different passions, which sometimes raged within him, and softened into showers. 'Twas not enough to appease him, to tell him his grandfather was old, and could not that way injure him, while he retained that awful duty which the young men are used there to pay to their grave relations. He could not be convinced he had no cause to sigh and mourn for the loss of a mistress he could not with all his strength and courage retrieve. And he would often cry, *Oh, my friends! were she in walled cities, or confined from me in fortifications of the greatest strength; did enchantments or monsters detain her from me; I would venture through any hazard to free her: But here, in the arms of a feeble old man, my youth, my violent love, my trade in arms, and all my vast desire of glory, avail me nothing. Imoinda is as irrecoverably lost to me as if she were snatched by the cold arms of death: Oh! she is never to be retrieved. If I would wait tedious years, till fate should bow the old king to his grave, even that would not leave me Imoinda free; but still that custom that makes it so vile a crime for a son to marry his father's wives or mistresses would hinder my happiness; unless I would either ignobly set an ill precedent to my successors, or abandon my country and fly with her to some unknown world who never heard our story.*

But it was objected to him, That his case was not the same; for Imoinda being his lawful wife by solemn contract, 'twas he was the injured man, and might, if he so pleased, take Imoinda back, the breach of the law being on his grandfather's side; and that if he could circumvent him, and redeem her from the otan, which is the Palace of the King's Women, a sort of seraglio, it was both just and lawful for him so to do.

This reasoning had some force upon him, and he should have been entirely comforted, but for the thought that she was possessed by his grandfather. However, he loved so well that he was resolved to believe what most favored his hope, and to endeavor to learn from Imoinda's own mouth what only she could satisfy him in, whether she was robbed of that blessing which was only due to his faith and love. But as it was very hard to get a sight of the women (for no men ever entered into the otan, but when the king went to entertain himself with some one of his wives or mistresses; and 'twas death, at any other time, for any other to go in), so he knew not how to contrive to get a sight of her.

While Oroonoko felt all the agonies of love and suffered under a torment the most painful in the world, the old king was not exempted from his share of affliction. He was troubled for having been forced, by an irresistible passion, to rob his son of a treasure, he knew, could not but be extremely dear to him; since she was the most beautiful that ever had been seen, and had besides all the sweetness and innocence of youth and modesty, with a charm of wit surpassing all. He found that, however she was forced to expose her lovely person to his withered arms, she could only sigh and weep there and think of Oroonoko, and oftentimes could not forbear speaking of him, though her life were, by custom, forfeited by owning her passion. But she spoke not of a lover only, but of a prince dear to him to whom she spoke, and of the praises of a man, who, till now, filled the old man's soul with a joy at every recital of his bravery, or even his name. And 'twas this dotage on our young hero that gave Imoinda a thousand privileges to speak of him, without offending, and this condescension in the old king that made her take the satisfaction of speaking of him so very often.

Besides, he many times enquired how the prince bore himself: And those of whom he asked, being entirely slaves to the merits and virtues of the prince, still answered what they thought conduced best to his service; which was, to make the old king fancy that the prince had no more interest in Imoinda and had resigned her willingly to the pleasure of the king; that he diverted himself with his mathematicians, his fortifications, his officers and his hunting.

This pleased the old lover, who failed not to report these things again to Imoinda, that she might, by the example of her young lover, withdraw her heart and rest better contented in his arms. But, however she was forced to receive this unwelcome news, in all appearance with unconcern and content, her heart was bursting within, and she was only happy when she could get alone, to vent her griefs and moans with sighs and tears.

What reports of the prince's conduct were made to the king, he thought good to justify as far as possibly he could by his actions; and when he appeared in the presence of the king, he showed a face not at all betraying his heart; so that in a little time, the old man, being entirely convinced that he was no longer a lover of Imoinda, he carried him with him in his train to the otan, often to banquet with his mistresses. But as soon as he entered one day into the apartment of Imoinda with the king, at the first glance from her eyes, notwithstanding all his determined resolution, he was ready to sink in the place where he stood; and had certainly done so, but for the support of Aboan, a young man who was next to him; which, with his change of countenance, had betrayed him, had the king chanced to look that way. And I have observed, 'tis a very great error in those who laugh when one says, *A negro can change color*: for I have seen 'em as frequently blush and look pale, and that as visibly as ever I saw in the most beautiful white. And 'tis certain that both these changes were evident this day, in both these lovers. And Imoinda, who saw with some joy the change in the prince's face and found it in her own, strove to divert the king from beholding either, by a forced caress, with which she met him; which was a new wound in the heart of the poor dying prince. But as soon as the king was busied in looking on some fine thing of Imoinda's making, she had time to tell the prince, with her angry, but love-darting eyes, that she resented his coldness and bemoaned her own miserable captivity. Nor were his eyes silent, but answered her again, as much as eyes could do, instructed by the most tender and most passionate heart that ever loved: And they spoke so well and so effectually as Imoinda no longer doubted but she was the only delight and darling of that soul she found pleading in 'em its right of love, which none was more willing to resign than she. And 'twas this powerful language alone that in an instant conveyed all the thoughts of their souls to each other; that they both found there wanted but opportunity to make them both entirely happy. But when he saw another door opened by Onahal (a former old wife of the king's, who now had charge of Imoinda) and saw the prospect of a bed of state made ready, with sweets and flowers for the dalliance of the king, who immediately led the trembling victim from his sight into that prepared repose, what rage! what wild frenzies seized his heart! which forcing to keep within bounds, and to suffer without noise, it became the more insupportable, and rent his soul with ten thousand pains. He was forced to retire to vent his groans, where he fell down on a carpet and lay struggling a long time, and only breathing now and then—Oh Imoinda! When Onahal had finished her necessary affair within, shutting the door, she came forth to wait till the king called; and hearing someone sighing in the other room, she passed on and found the prince in that deplorable condition, which she thought needed her aid. She gave him cordials, but all in vain; till finding the nature of his disease, by his sighs, and naming Imoinda, she told him he had not so much cause as he imagined to afflict himself; for if he knew the king so well as she did, he would not lose a moment in jealousy; and that she was confident that Imoinda bore, at this minute, part in his affliction. Aboan was of the same opinion, and both together persuaded him to reassume his courage and all sitting down on the carpet, the prince said so many obliging things to Onahal that he half-persuaded her to be of his party: and she promised him, she would thus far comply with his just desires, that she would let Imoinda know how faithful he was, what he suffered, and what he said.

This discourse lasted till the king called, which gave Oroonoko a certain satisfaction; and with the hope Onahal had made him conceive, he assumed a look as gay as 'twas possible a man in his circumstances could do: and presently after, he was called in with the rest who waited without. The king commanded music to be brought, and several of his young wives and mistresses came all together by his command to dance before him; where Imoinda performed her part with an air and grace so surpassing all the rest, as her beauty was above 'em, and received the present ordained as a prize. The prince was every moment more charmed with the new beauties and graces he beheld in this fair one; and while he gazed, and she danced, Onahal was retired to a window with Aboan.

This Onahal, as I said, was one of the cast mistresses of the old king; and 'twas these (now past their beauty) that were made guardians or gouvernantes to the new and the young ones, and whose business it was to teach them all those wanton arts of love with which they prevailed and charmed heretofore in their turn; and who now treated the triumphing happy ones with all the severity as to liberty and freedom that was possible, in revenge of their honors they rob them of; envying them those satisfactions, those gallantries and presents, that were once made to themselves, while youth and beauty lasted, and which they now saw pass as it were regardless by, and paid only to the bloom-ings. And certainly, nothing is more afflicting to a decayed beauty than to behold in itself declining charms, that were once adored; and to find those caresses paid to new beauties, to which once she laid claim; to hear them whisper, as she passes by, that once was a delicate woman. Those abandoned ladies therefore endeavor to revenge all the despites and decays of time on these flourishing happy ones. And 'twas this severity that gave Oroonoko a thousand fears he should never prevail with Onahal to see Imoinda. But, as I said, she was now retired to a window with Aboan.

This young man was not only one of the best quality but a man extremely well made and beautiful; and coming often to attend the king to the otan, he had subdued the heart of the antiquated Onahal, which had not forgot how pleasant it was to be in love. And though she had some decays in her face, she had none in her sense and wit; she was there agreeable still, even to Aboan's youth: so that he took pleasure in entertaining her with discourses of love. He knew also that to make his court to these she-favorites was the way to be great, these being the persons that do all affairs and business at court. He had also observed that she had given him glances more tender and inviting than she had done to others of his quality. And now, when he saw that her favor could so absolutely oblige the prince, he failed not to sigh in her ear and to look with eyes all soft upon her, and gave her hope that she had made some impressions on his heart. He found her pleased at this, and making a thousand advances to him: but the ceremony ending, and the king departing, broke up the company for that day and his conversation.

Aboan failed not that night to tell the prince of his success, and how advantageous the service of Onahal might be to his amour with Imoinda. The prince was overjoyed with this good news, and besought him if it were possible to caress her so as to engage her entirely, which he could not fail to do, if he complied with her desires: *For then* (said the prince) *her life lying at your mercy, she must grant you the request you make in my behalf.* Aboan understood him and assured him he would make love so effectually that he would defy the most expert mistress of the art to find out whether he dissembled it or had it really. And 'twas with impatience they waited the next opportunity of going to the otan.

The wars came on, the time of taking the field approached;

and 'twas impossible for the prince to delay his going at the head of his army to encounter the enemy; so that every day seemed a tedious year, till he saw his Imoinda: for he believed he could not live if he were forced away without being so happy. 'Twas with impatience therefore that he expected the next visit the king would make; and according to his wish it was not long.

The parley of the eyes of these two lovers had not passed so secretly, but an old jealous lover could spy it; or rather, he wanted not flatterers who told him they observed it: so that the prince was hastened to the camp, and this was the last visit he found he should make to the otan; he therefore urged Aboan to make the best of his last effort and to explain himself so to Onahal that she, deferring her enjoyment of her young lover no longer, might make way for the prince to speak to Imoinda.

The whole affair being agreed on between the prince and Aboan, they attended the king, as the custom was, to the otan; where, while the whole company was taken up in beholding the dancing and antic postures the women-royal made to divert the king, Onahal singled out Aboan, whom she found most pliable to her wish. When she had him where she believed she could not be heard, she sighed to him, and softly cried, *Ah, Aboan! when will you be sensible of my passion? I confess it with my mouth, because I would not give my eyes the lie; and you have but too much already perceived they have confessed my flame; nor would I have you believe that because I am the abandoned mistress of a king, I esteem myself altogether divested of charms: No, Aboan; I have still a rest of beauty enough engaging, and have learned to please too well, not to be desirable. I can have lovers still, but will have none but Aboan.* Madam (replied the half-feigning youth), *you have already, by my eyes, found you can still conquer; and I believe 'tis in pity of me you condescend to this kind confession. But, madam, words are used to be so small a part of our country courtship, that 'tis rare one can get so happy an opportunity as to tell one's heart; and those few minutes we have, are forced to be snatched for more certain proofs of love than speaking and sighing; and such I languish for.*

He spoke this with such a tone, that she hoped it true, and could not forbear believing it; and being wholly transported with joy for having subdued the finest of all the king's subjects to her desires, she took from her ears two large pearls, and commanded him to wear 'em in his. He would have refused 'em, crying, *Madam, these are not the proofs of your love that I expect; 'tis opportunity, 'tis a lone hour only, that can make me happy.* But forcing the pearls into his hand, she whispered softly to him: *Oh! do not fear a woman's invention, when love sets her a thinking.* And pressing his hand, she cried, *This night you shall be happy: Come to the gate of the orange grove, behind the otan, and I will be ready about midnight to receive you.* 'Twas thus agreed, and she left him, that no notice might be taken of their speaking together.

The ladies were still dancing, and the king laid on a carpet with a great deal of pleasure was beholding them, especially Imoinda, who that day appeared more lovely than ever, being enlivened with the good tidings Onahal had brought her, of the constant passion the prince had for her. The prince was laid on another carpet at the other end of the room, with his eyes fixed on the object of his soul; and as she turned or moved, so did they: and she alone gave his eyes and soul their motions. Nor did Imoinda employ her eyes to any other use, than in beholding with infinite pleasure the joy she produced in those of the prince. But while she was more regarding him than the steps she took, she chanced to fall; and so near him as that, leaping with extreme force from the carpet, he caught her in his arms as she fell: and 'twas visible to the whole presence, the joy wherewith he received her. He clasped her close to his bosom, and quite forgot that reverence that was due to the mistress of a king and that punishment that is the reward of a boldness of this nature. And had not the presence of mind of Imoinda (fonder of his safety, than her own) befriended him, in making her spring from his arms and fall into her dance again, he had at that instant met his death; for the old king, jealous to the last degree, rose up in rage, broke all the diversion and led Imoinda to her apartment, and sent out word to the prince to go immediately to the camp; and that if he were found another night in court, he should suffer the death ordained for disobedient offenders.

You may imagine how welcome this news was to Oroonoko, whose unreasonable transport and caress of Imoinda was blamed by all men that loved him: and now he perceived his fault, yet cried, *That for such another moment he would be content to die.*

All the otan was in disorder about this accident; and Onahal was particularly concerned, because on the prince's stay depended her happiness; for she could no longer expect that of Aboan: So that e'er they departed, they contrived it so, that the prince and he should both come that night to the grove of the otan, which was all of oranges and citrons, and that there they would wait her orders.

They parted thus with grief enough till night, leaving the king in possession of the lovely maid. But nothing could appease the jealousy of the old lover; he would not be imposed on, but would have it that Imoinda made a false step on purpose to fall into Oroonoko's bosom, and that all things looked like a design on both sides; and 'twas in vain she protested her innocence. He was old and obstinate, and left her more than half assured that his fear was true.

The king going to his apartment, sent to know where the prince was, and if he intended to obey his command. The messenger returned and told him, he found the prince pensive and altogether unprepared for the campaign; that he lay negligently on the ground and answered very little. This confirmed the jealousy of the king, and he commanded that they should very narrowly and privately watch his motions; and that he should not stir from his apartment, but one spy or other should be employed to watch him: So that the hour approaching, wherein he was to go to the citron grove, and taking only Aboan along with him, he leaves his apartment, and was watched to the very gate of the otan, where he was seen to enter, and where they left him, to carry back the tidings to the king.

Oroonoko and Aboan were no sooner entered, but Onahal led the prince to the apartment of Imoinda; who, not knowing anything of her happiness, was laid in bed. But Onahal only left him in her chamber, to make the best of his opportunity, and took her dear Aboan to her own; where he showed the height of complaisance for his prince, when, to give him an opportunity, he suffered himself to be caressed in bed by Onahal.

The prince softly wakened Imoinda, who was not a little surprised with joy to find him there; and yet she trembled with a thousand fears. I believe he omitted saying nothing to this young maid that might persuade her to suffer him to seize his own and take the rights of love. And I believe she was not long resisting those arms where she so longed to be, and having opportunity, night, and silence, youth, love and desire, he soon prevailed, and ravished in a moment what his old grandfather had been endeavoring for so many months.

'Tis not to be imagined the satisfaction of these two young lovers; nor the vows she made him, that she remained a spotless maid till that night, and that what she did with his grandfather had robbed him of no part of her virgin-honor; the gods, in mercy and justice, having reserved that for her plighted lord, to whom of right it belonged. And 'tis impossible to express the transports he suffered, while he listened to a discourse so charming from her loved lips and clasped that body in his arms, for whom he had so long languished; and nothing now afflicted him, but his sudden departure from her; for he told her the necessity and his commands, but should depart satisfied in this, That since the old king had hitherto not been able to deprive him of those enjoyments which only belonged to him, he believed for the future he would be less able to injure him: so that, abating the scandal of the veil, which was no otherwise so, than that she was wife to another, he believed her safe, even in the arms of the king, and innocent; yet would he have ventured at the conquest of the world, and have given it all to have had her avoid that honor of receiving the royal veil. 'Twas thus, between a thousand caresses, that both bemoaned the hard fate of youth and beauty, so liable to that cruel promotion: 'twas a glory that could well have been spared here, though desired and aimed at by all the young females of that kingdom.

But while they were thus fondly employed, forgetting how time ran on, and that the dawn must conduct him far away from his only happiness, they heard a great noise in the otan and unusual voices of men; at which the prince, starting from the arms of the frightened Imoinda, ran to a little battle-ax he used to wear by his side; and having not so much leisure as to put on his habit, he opposed himself against some who were already opening the door: which they did with so much violence that Oroonoko was not able to defend it; but was forced to cry out with a commanding voice, *Whoever ye are that have the boldness to attempt to approach this apartment thus rudely; know, that I, the Prince Oroonoko; will revenge it with the certain death of him that first enters: Therefore, stand back, and know, this place is sacred to love and me this night; tomorrow 'tis the king's.*

This he spoke with a voice so resolved and assured that they soon retired from the door; but cried, *'Tis by the king's command we are come; and being satisfied by thy voice, O prince, as much as if we had entered, we can report to the king the truth of all his fears, and leave thee to provide for thy own safety, as thou art advised by thy friends.*

At these words they departed, and left the prince to take a short and sad leave of his Imoinda; who, trusting in the strength of her charms, believed she should appease the fury of a jealous king, by saying she was surprised, and that it was by force of arms he got into her apartment. All her concern now was for his life, and therefore she hastened him to the camp, and with much ado prevailed on him to go. Nor was it she alone that prevailed; Aboan and Onahal both pleaded, and both assured him of a lie that should be well enough contrived to secure Imoinda. So that at last, with a heart sad as death, dying eyes, and sighing soul, Oroonoko departed and took his way to the camp.

It was not long after, the king in person came to the otan; where beholding Imoinda with rage in his eyes, he upbraided her wickedness and perfidy; and threatening her royal lover, she fell on her face at his feet, bedewing the floor with her tears and imploring his pardon for a fault which she had not with her will committed; as Onahal, who was also prostrate with her, could testify: That, unknown to her, he had broke into her apartment and ravished her. She spoke this much against her conscience; but to save her own life, 'twas absolutely necessary she should feign this falsity. She knew it could not injure the prince, he being fled to an army that would stand by him against any injuries that should assault him. However this last thought of Imoinda's being ravished changed the measures of his revenge; and whereas before he designed to be himself her executioner, he now resolved she should not die. But as it is the greatest crime in nature amongst 'em to touch a woman after having been possessed by a son, a father, or a brother, so now he looked on Imoinda as a polluted thing, wholly unfit for his embrace; nor would he resign her to his grandson, because she had received the royal veil: He therefore removed her from the otan, with Onahal; whom he put into safe hands, with orders they should be both sold off as slaves to another country, either Christian or heathen, 'twas no matter where.

This cruel sentence, worse than death, they implored might be reversed; but their prayers were vain, and it was put in execution accordingly, and that with so much secrecy, that none, either without or within the otan, knew anything of their absence, or their destiny.

The old king nevertheless executed this with a great deal of reluctancy; but he believed he had made a very great conquest over himself when he had once resolved, and had performed what he resolved. He believed now that his love had been unjust; and that he could not expect the gods, or Captain of the Clouds (as they call the unknown power) would suffer a better consequence from so ill a cause. He now begins to hold Oroonoko excused and to say, he had reason for what he did: And now everybody could assure the king how passionately Imoinda was beloved by the prince; even those confessed it now, who said the contrary before, his flame was not abated. So that the king being old and not able to defend himself in war, and having no sons of all his race remaining alive, but only this, to maintain him on his throne; and looking on this as a man disobliged, first by the rape of his mistress, or rather wife, and now by depriving him wholly of her, he feared, might make him desperate and do some cruel thing, either to himself or his old grandfather the offender, he began to repent him extremely of the contempt he had, in his rage, put on Imoinda. Besides he considered he ought in honor to have killed her for this offense, if it had been one. He ought to have had so much value and consideration for a maid of her quality, as to have nobly put her to death, and not to have sold her like a common slave; the greatest revenge and the most disgraceful of any, and to which they a thousand times prefer death and implore it; as Imoinda did, but could not obtain that honor. Seeing therefore it was certain that Oroonoko would highly resent this affront, he thought good to make some excuse for his rashness to him; and to that end, he sent a messenger to the camp, with orders to treat with him about the matter, to gain his pardon, and to endeavor to mitigate his grief; but that by no means he should tell him she was sold, but secretly put to death: for he knew he should never obtain his pardon for the other.

When the messenger came, he found the prince upon the point of engaging with the enemy; but as soon as he heard of the arrival of the messenger, he commanded him to his tent, where he embraced him, and received him with joy: which was soon abated by the downcast looks of the messenger, who was instantly demanded the cause by Oroonoko; who, impatient of delay, asked a thousand questions in a breath, and all concerning Imoinda. But there needed little return; for he could almost answer himself of all he demanded from his sighs and eyes. At last the messenger casting himself at the prince's feet, and kissing them with all the submission of a man that had something to implore which he dreaded to utter, he besought him to hear with calmness what he had to deliver to him and to call up all his noble and heroic courage, to encounter with his words and defend himself against the ungrateful things he must relate. Oroonoko replied, with a deep sigh and a languishing voice,—*I am armed against their worst efforts—For I know they will tell me, Imoinda is no more—and after that, you may spare the rest.* Then, commanding him to rise, he laid himself on a carpet, under a rich pavilion, and remained a good while silent and was hardly heard to sigh. When he was come a little to himself, the messenger asked him leave to deliver that part of his embassy which the prince had not yet divined: And the prince cried, *I permit thee*——Then he told him the affliction the old king was in for the rashness he had committed in his cruelty to Imoinda; and how he deigned to ask pardon for his offense and to implore the prince would not suffer that loss to touch his heart too sensibly, which now all the gods could not restore him, but might recompense him to glory, which he begged he would pursue; and that death, that common revenger of all injuries, would soon even the account between him and a feeble old man.

Oroonoko bade him return his duty to his lord and master and to assure him, there was no account of revenge to be adjusted between them: if there were, 'twas he was the aggressor, and that death would be just, and, maugre his age, would see him righted; and he was contented to leave his share of glory to youths more fortunate and worthy of that favor from the gods: That henceforth he would never lift a weapon or draw a bow, but abandon the small remains of his life to sighs and tears and the continual thoughts of what his lord and grandfather had thought good to send out of the world, with all that youth, that innocence and beauty.

After having spoken this, whatever his greatest officers and men of the best rank could do, they could not raise him from the carpet, or persuade him to action and resolutions of life; but commanding all to retire, he shut himself into his pavilion all that day, while the enemy was ready to engage: and wondering at the delay, the whole body of the chief of the army then addressed themselves to him, and to whom they had much ado to get admittance. They fell on their faces at the foot of his carpet, where they lay and besought him with earnest prayers and tears to lead them forth to battle, and not let the enemy take advantages of them; and implored him to have regard to his glory and to the world, that depended on his courage and conduct.

But he made no other reply to all their supplications, but this, That he had now no more business for glory; and for the world, it was a trifle not worth his care: *Go* (continued he, sighing) *and divide it amongst you, and reap with joy what you so vainly prize, and leave me to my more welcome destiny.*

They then demanded what they should do, and whom he would constitute in his room, that the confusion of ambitious youth and power might not ruin their order and make them a prey to the enemy. He replied, he would not give himself the trouble—but wished 'em to choose the bravest man amongst 'em, let his quality or birth be what it would: *For, oh my friends! (said he) it is not titles make men brave or good; or birth that bestows courage and generosity, or makes the owner happy. Believe this, when you behold Oroonoko the most wretched, and abandoned by fortune, of all the creation of the gods.* So turning himself about, he would make no more reply to all they could urge or implore.

The army beholding their officers return unsuccessful, with sad faces and ominous looks that presaged no good luck, suffered a thousand fears to take possession of their hearts and the enemy to come even upon them, before they would provide for their safety by any defense: and though they were assured by some, who had a mind to animate them, that they should be immediately headed by the prince, and that in the meantime Aboan had orders to command as general; yet they were so dismayed for want of that great example of bravery that they could make but a very feeble resistance; and at last, downright fled before the enemy, who pursued 'em to the very tents, killing 'em. Nor could all Aboan's courage, which that day gained him immortal glory, shame 'em into a manly defense of themselves. The guards that were left behind about the prince's tent, seeing the soldiers flee before the enemy and scatter themselves all over the plain in great disorder, made such outcries as roused the prince from his amorous slumber, in which he had remained buried for two days, without permitting any sustenance to approach him. But, in spite of all his resolutions, he had not the constancy of grief to that degree as to make him insensible of the danger of his army; and in that instant he leaped from his couch, and cried—*Come, if we must die, let us meet death the noblest way; and 'twill be more like Oroonoko to encounter him at an army's head, opposing the torrent of a conquering foe, than lazily on a couch, to wait his lingering*

*pleasure, and die every moment by a thousand racking thoughts;
or be tamely taken by an enemy, and led a whining lovesick
slave to adorn the triumphs of Jamoan, that young victor, who
already is entered beyond the limits I have prescribed him.*

While he was speaking, he suffered his people to dress him for
the field; and sallying out of his pavilion, with more life and
vigor in his countenance than ever he showed, he appeared like
some divine power descended to save his country from destruction: and his people had purposely put him on all things that
might make him shine with most splendor, to strike a reverent
awe into the beholders. He flew into the thickest of those that
were pursuing his men; and being animated with despair, he
fought as if he came on purpose to die, and did such things as
will not be believed that human strength could perform; and
such as soon inspired all the rest with new courage and new
order. And now it was that they began to fight indeed; and so, as
if they would not be outdone even by their adored hero; who,
turning the tide of the victory, changing absolutely the fate of
the day, gained an entire conquest: and Oroonoko having the
good fortune to single out Jamoan, he took him prisoner with his
own hand, having wounded him almost to death.

This Jamoan afterwards became very dear to him, being a
man very gallant and of excellent graces and fine parts; so that
he never put him amongst the rank of captives, as they used to
do, without distinction, for the common sale or market, but kept
him in his own court, where he retained nothing of the prisoner
but the name, and returned no more into his own country; so
great an affection he took for Oroonoko, and by a thousand tales
and adventures of love and gallantry flattered[9] his disease of
melancholy and languishment: which I have often heard him
say, had certainly killed him, but for the conversation of this
prince and Aboan, and the French governor[10] he had from his
childhood, of whom I have spoken before, and who was a man
of admirable wit, great ingenuity and learning; all which he had
infused into his young pupil. This Frenchman was banished out
of his own country for some heretical notions he held: and though
he was a man of very little religion, he had admirable morals and
a brave soul.

After the total defeat of Jamoan's army, which all fled or were

[9]Charmed away.
[10]Tutor.

left dead upon the place, they spent some time in the camp; Oroonoko choosing rather to remain awhile there in his tents than to enter into a palace or live in a court where he had so lately suffered so great a loss. The officers therefore, who saw and knew his cause of discontent, invented all sorts of diversions and sports to entertain their prince: so that what with those amusements abroad, and others at home, that is, within their tents, with the persuasions, arguments, and care of his friends and servants that he more peculiarly prized, he wore off in time a great part of that chagrin and torture of despair, which the first effects of Imoinda's death had given him; insomuch as having received a thousand kind embassies from the king and invitation to return to court, he obeyed, though with no little reluctancy: and when he did so, there was a visible change in him, and for a long time he was much more melancholy than before. But time lessens all extremes and reduces 'em to mediums and unconcern: but no motives[11] of beauties, though all endeavored it, could engage him in any sort of amour, though he had all the invitations to it, both from his own youth and others' ambitions and designs.

Oroonoko was no sooner returned from this last conquest and received at court with all the joy and magnificence that could be expressed to a young victor, who was not only returned triumphant but beloved like a deity, than there arrived in the port an English ship.

The master of it had often before been in these countries and was very well known to Oroonoko, with whom he had trafficked for slaves and had used to do the same with his predecessors.

This commander was a man of a finer sort of address and conversation, better bred and more engaging, than most of that sort of men are; so that he seemed rather never to have been bred out of a court than almost all his life at sea. This captain therefore was always better received at court than most of the traders of those countries were; and especially by Oroonoko, who was more civilized, according to the European mode, than any other had been, and took more delight in the white nations and, above all, men of parts and wit. To this captain he sold abundance of his slaves; and for the favor and esteem he had for him, made him many presents and obliged him to stay at court as long as possibly he could. Which the captain seemed to take

[11]Inducements.

as a very great honor done him, entertaining the prince every day with globes and maps, and mathematical discourses and instruments; eating, drinking, hunting, and living with him with so much familiarity that it was not to be doubted but he had gained very greatly upon the heart of this gallant young man. And the captain, in return of all these mighty favors, besought the prince to honor his vessel with his presence, some day or other at dinner, before he should set sail: which he condescended to accept and appointed his day. The captain, on his part, failed not to have all things in a readiness, in the most magnificent order he could possibly: And the day being come, the captain in his boat, richly adorned with carpets and velvet cushions, rowed to the shore to receive the prince; with another long-boat, where was placed all his music and trumpets, with which Oroonoko was extremely delighted; who met him on the shore, attended by his French governor, Jamoan, Aboan, and about a hundred of the noblest of the youths of the court: And after they had first carried the prince on board, the boats fetched the rest off; where they found a very splendid treat, with all sorts of fine wines; and were as well entertained as 'twas possible in such a place to be.

The prince having drunk hard of punch and several sorts of wine, as did all the rest (for great care was taken they should want nothing of that part of the entertainment), was very merry, and in great admiration of the ship, for he had never been in one before; so that he was curious of beholding every place where he decently might descend. The rest, no less curious, who were not quite overcome with drinking, rambled at their pleasure fore and aft, as their fancies guided 'em: So that the captain, who had well laid his design before, gave the word and seized on all his guests; they clapping great irons suddenly on the prince, when he was leaped down into the hold to view that part of the vessel, and locking him fast down, secured him. The same treachery was used to all the rest; and all in one instant, in several places of the ship, were lashed fast in irons and betrayed to slavery. That great design over, they set all hands to work to hoist sail; and with as treacherous as fair a wind they made from the shore with this innocent and glorious prize, who thought of nothing less than such an entertainment.

Some have commended this act as brave in the captain; but I will spare my sense of it, and leave it to my reader to judge as he pleases. It may be easily guessed in what manner the prince resented his indignity, who may be best resembled to a lion taken in a toil, so he raged, so he struggled for liberty, but all in vain; and they had so wisely managed his fetters that he could not use a hand in his defense to quit himself of a life that would by no means endure slavery; nor could he move from the place where he was tied to any solid part of the ship against which he might have beat his head and have finished his disgrace that way. So that being deprived of all other means, he resolved to perish for want of food; and pleased at last with that thought, and toiled and tired by rage and indignation, he laid himself down, and sullenly resolved upon dying, and refused all things that were brought him.

This did not a little vex the captain, and the more so, because he found almost all of 'em of the same humor; so that the loss of so many brave slaves, so tall and goodly to behold, would have been very considerable: He therefore ordered one to go from him (for he would not be seen himself) to Oroonoko, and to assure him, he was afflicted for having rashly done so unhospitable a deed, and which could not be now remedied, since they were far from shore; but since he resented it in so high a nature, he assured him he would revoke his resolution, and set both him and his friends ashore on the next land they should touch at; and of this the messenger gave him his oath, provided he would resolve to live. And Oroonoko, whose honor was such as he never had violated a word in his life himself, much less a solemn asseveration, believed in an instant what this man said; but replied, he expected for a confirmation of this, to have his shameful fetters dismissed.[12] This demand was carried to the captain, who returned him answer, That the offense had been so great which he had put upon the prince, that he durst not trust him with liberty while he remained in the ship, for fear lest by a valor natural to him and a revenge that would animate that valor, he might commit some outrage fatal to himself and the king his master, to whom this vessel did belong. To this Oroonoko replied, He would engage his honor to behave himself in all friendly order and manner, and obey the command of the captain, as he was lord of the king's vessel and general of those men under his command.

This was delivered to the still doubting captain, who could not resolve to trust a heathen, he said, upon his parole, a man that

[12]Put off.

had no sense or notion of the God that he worshiped. Oroonoko then replied, He was very sorry to hear that the captain pretended to the knowledge and worship of any gods, who had taught him no better principles than not to credit as he would be credited. But they told him, the difference of their faith occasioned that distrust: for the captain had protested to him upon the word of a Christian, and sworn in the name of a great God; which if he should violate, he would expect eternal torment in the world to come. *Is that all the obligation he has to be just to his oath?* (replied Oroonoko) *Let him know, I swear by my honor; which to violate, would not only render me contemptible and despised by all brave and honest men, and so give myself perpetual pain, but it would be eternally offending and displeasing all mankind; harming, betraying, circumventing, and outraging all men. But punishments hereafter are suffered by one's self; and the world takes no cognizance whether this GOD have revenged 'em or not, 'tis done so secretly, and deferred so long: while the man of no honor suffers every moment the scorn and contempt of the honester world, and dies every day ignominiously in his fame, which is more valuable than life. I speak not this to move belief, but to show you how you mistake when you imagine, That he who will violate his honor, will keep his word with his gods.* So, turning from him with a disdainful smile, he refused to answer him, when he urged him to know what answer he should carry back to his captain; so that he departed without saying any more.

The captain pondering and consulting what to do, it was concluded that nothing but Oroonoko's liberty would encourage any of the rest to eat, except the Frenchman, whom the captain could not pretend to keep prisoner, but only told him, he was secured because he might act[13] something in favor of the prince, but that he should be freed as soon as they came to land. So that they concluded it wholly necessary to free the prince from his irons, that he might show himself to the rest; that they might have an eye upon him, and that they could not fear a single man.

This being resolved, to make the obligation the greater, the captain himself went to Oroonoko; where, after many compliments and assurances of what he had already promised, he receiving from the prince his parole and his hand for his good behavior, dismissed his irons and brought him to his own cabin;

[13]Do.

where, after having treated and reposed him a while (for he had neither eat nor slept in four days before), he besought him to visit those obstinate people in chains, who refused all manner of sustenance; and entreated him to oblige 'em to eat and assure 'em of their liberty on the first opportunity.

Oroonoko, who was too generous not to give credit to his words, showed himself to his people, who were transported with excess of joy at the sight of their darling prince; falling at his feet and kissing and embracing him; believing, as some divine oracle, all he assured 'em. But he besought 'em to bear their chains with that bravery that became those whom he had seen act so nobly in arms; and that they could not give him greater proofs of their love and friendship, since 'twas all the security the captain (his friend) could have against the revenge, he said, they might possibly justly take, for the injuries sustained by him. And they all, with one accord, assured him, they could not suffer enough, when it was for his repose and safety.

After this, they no longer refused to eat, but took what was brought 'em and were pleased with their captivity, since by it they hoped to redeem the prince, who, all the rest of the voyage, was treated with all the respect due to his birth, though nothing could divert his melancholy; and he would often sigh for Imoinda, and think this a punishment due to his misfortune in having left that noble maid behind him that fatal night in the otan, when he fled to the camp.

Possessed with a thousand thoughts of past joys with this fair young person, and a thousand griefs for her eternal loss, he endured a tedious voyage, and at last arrived at the mouth of the river of Surinam, a colony belonging to the king of England, and where they were to deliver some part of their slaves. There the merchants and gentlemen of the country, going on board to demand those lots of slaves they had already agreed on, and amongst those, the overseers of those plantations where I then chanced to be, the captain, who had given the word, ordered his men to bring up those noble slaves in fetters, whom I have spoken of; and having put 'em, some in one and some in other lots, with women and children (which they call pickaninnies), they sold 'em off, as slaves, to several merchants and gentlemen; not putting any two in one lot, because they would separate 'em far from each other; nor daring to trust 'em together, lest rage and courage should put 'em upon contriving some greater action, to the ruin of the colony.

Oroonoko was first seized on and sold to our overseer, who had the first lot, with seventeen more of all sorts and sizes, but not one of quality with him. When he saw this, he found what they meant; for, as I said, he understood English pretty well; and being wholly unarmed and defenseless, so as it was in vain to make any resistance, he only beheld the captain with a look all fierce and disdainful, upbraiding him with eyes that forced blushes on his guilty cheeks; he only cried in passing over the side of the ship: *Farewell, sir, 'tis worth my sufferings, to gain so true a knowledge both of you, and of your gods by whom you swear.* And desiring those that held him to forbear their pains, and telling 'em he would make no resistance, he cried, *Come, my fellow slaves, let us descend, and see if we can meet with more honor and honesty in the next world we shall touch upon.* So he nimbly leapt into the boat, and showing no more concern, suffered himself to be rowed up the river with his seventeen companions.

The gentleman that bought him was a young Cornish gentleman, whose name was Trefry; a man of great wit and fine learning, and was carried into those parts by the Lord Governor, to manage all his affairs. He reflecting on the last words of Oroonoko to the captain, and beholding the richness of his vest, no sooner came into the boat, but he fixed his eyes on him; and finding something so extraordinary in his face, his shape and mien, a greatness of look and haughtiness in his air, and finding he spoke English, had a great mind to be enquiring into his quality and fortune: which, though Oroonoko endeavored to hide, by only confessing he was above the rank of common slaves, Trefry soon found he was yet something greater than he confessed; and from that moment began to conceive so vast an esteem for him that he ever after loved him as his dearest brother and showed him all the civilities due to so great a man.

Trefry was a very good mathematician and a linguist, could speak French and Spanish; and in the three days they remained in the boat (for so long were they going from the ship to the plantation) he entertained Oroonoko so agreeably with his art and discourse that he was no less pleased with Trefry, than he was with the prince; and he thought himself, at least, fortunate in this, that since he was a slave, as long as he would suffer himself to remain so, he had a man of so excellent wit and parts for a master. So that before they had finished their voyage up the river, he made no scruple of declaring to Trefry all his fortunes, and most part of what I have here related, and put himself wholly into the hands of his new friend, whom he found resenting all the injuries were done him, and was charmed with all the greatnesses of his actions; which were recited with that modesty and delicate sense as wholly vanquished him and subdued him to his interest. And he promised him on his word and honor he would find the means to re-conduct him to his own country again; assuring him, he had a perfect abhorrence of so dishonorable an action; and that he would sooner have died than have been the author of such a perfidy. He found the prince was very much concerned to know what became of his friends and how they took their slavery; and Trefry promised to take care about the enquiring after their condition, and that he should have an account of 'em.

Though, as Oroonoko afterwards said, he had little reason to credit the words of a backearary;[14] yet he knew not why, but he saw a kind of sincerity and awful truth in the face of Trefry; he saw an honesty in his eyes, and he found him wise and witty enough to understand honor: for it was one of his maxims, *A man of wit could not be a knave or villain.*

In their passage up the river, they put in at several houses for refreshment; and ever when they landed, numbers of people would flock to behold this man: not but their eyes were daily entertained with the sight of slaves, but the fame of Oroonoko was gone before him, and all people were in admiration of his beauty. Besides, he had a rich habit on, in which he was taken, so different from the rest, and which the captain could not strip him of, because he was forced to surprise his person in the minute he sold him. When he found his habit made him liable, as he thought, to be gazed at the more, he begged Trefry to give him something more befitting a slave, which he did, and took off his robes: Nevertheless he shone through all, and his osenbrigs (a sort of brown holland suit he had on) could not conceal the graces of his looks and mien; and he had no less admirers than when he had his dazzling habit on: The royal youth appeared in spite of the slave, and people could not help treating him after a different manner, without designing it. As soon as they approached him, they venerated and esteemed him; his eyes insensibly commanded respect, and his behavior insinuated it into every soul. So that there was nothing talked of but this young

---

[14]Contemptuous word for a colonial planter, probably derived from *tobacco.*

and gallant slave, even by those who yet knew not that he was a prince.

I ought to tell you that the Christians never buy any slaves but they give 'em some name of their own, their native ones being likely very barbarous and hard to pronounce; so that Mr. Trefry gave Oroonoko that of Cæsar; which name will live in that country as long as that (scarce more) glorious one of the great Roman: for 'tis most evident he wanted no part of the personal courage of that Cæsar, and acted things as memorable, had they been done in some part of the world replenished with people and historians, that might have given him his due. But his misfortune was, to fall in an obscure world, that afforded only a female pen to celebrate his fame; though I doubt not but it had lived from others' endeavors, if the Dutch, who immediately after his time took that country, had not killed, banished and dispersed all those that were capable of giving the world this great man's life, much better than I have done. And Mr. Trefry, who designed it, died before he began it, and bemoaned himself for not having undertook it in time.

For the future therefore I must call Oroonoko Cæsar, since by that name only he was known in our western world, and by that name he was received on shore at Parham House, where he was destined a slave. But if the king himself (God bless him) had come ashore, there could not have been greater expectation by all the whole plantation, and those neighboring ones, then was on ours at that time; and he was received more like a governor than a slave: notwithstanding, as the custom was, they assigned him his portion of land, his house and his business up in the plantation. But as it was more for form than any design to put him to his task, he endured no more of the slave but the name and remained some days in the house, receiving all visits that were made him, without stirring towards that part of the plantation where the negroes were.

At last, he would needs go view his land, his house, and the business assigned him. But he no sooner came to the houses of the slaves, which are like a little town by itself, the negroes all having left work, but they all came forth to behold him and found he was that prince who had, at several times, sold most of 'em to these parts; and from a veneration they pay to great men, especially if they know 'em, and from the surprise and awe they had at the sight of him, they all cast themselves at his feet, crying out, in their language, *Live, O King! Long live, O King!* and kissing his feet, paid him even divine homage.

Several English gentlemen were with him, and what Mr. Trefry had told 'em was here confirmed, of which he himself before had no other witness than Cæsar himself: But he was infinitely glad to find his grandeur confirmed by the adoration of all the slaves.

Cæsar, troubled with their over-joy, and over-ceremony, besought 'em to rise, and to receive him as their fellow-slave; assuring them he was no better. At which they set up with one accord a most terrible and hideous mourning and condoling, which he and the English had much ado to appease: but at last they prevailed with 'em, and they prepared all their barbarous music, and everyone killed and dressed something of his own stock (for every family has their land apart, on which, at their leisure-times, they breed all eatable things) and clubbing it together, made a most magnificent supper, inviting their grandee captain, their prince, to honor it with his presence; which he did, and several English with him, where they all waited on him, some playing, others dancing before him all the time, according to the manners of their several nations, and with unwearied industry endeavoring to please and delight him.

While they sat at meat, Mr. Trefry told Cæsar that most of these young slaves were undone in love with a fine she-slave, whom they had had about six months on their land; the prince, who never heard the name of love without a sigh, nor any mention of it without the curiosity of examining further into that tale, which of all discourses was most agreeable to him, asked how they came to be so unhappy, as to be all undone for one fair slave? Trefry, who was naturally amorous and loved to talk of love as well as anybody, proceeded to tell him, they had the most charming black that ever was beheld on their plantation, about fifteen or sixteen years old, as he guessed; that for his part he had done nothing but sigh for her ever since she came; and that all the white beauties he had seen never charmed him so absolutely as this fine creature had done; and that no man, of any nation, ever beheld her that did not fall in love with her; and that she had all the slaves perpetually at her feet; and the whole country resounded with the fame of Clemene, for so (said he) we have christened her: but she denies us all with such a noble disdain, that 'tis a miracle to see, that she who can give such eternal desires, should herself be all ice and all unconcern. She is adorned with the most graceful modesty that ever beautified youth; the softest sigher—that, if she were capable of love one would swear she languished for some absent happy man; and so retired, as if she feared a rape even from the god of day, or that the breezes would steal kisses from her delicate mouth. Her task of work, some sighing lover every day makes it his petition to perform for her; which she accepts blushing, and with reluctancy, for fear he will ask her a look for a recompence, which he dares not presume to hope; so great an awe she strikes into the hearts of her admirers, *I do not wonder* (replied the prince) *that Clemene should refuse slaves, being, as you say, so beautiful; but wonder how she escapes those that can entertain her as you can do: or why, being your slave, you do not oblige her to yield? I confess* (said Trefry), *when I have, against her will, entertained her with love so long as to be transported with my passion even above decency, I have been ready to make use of those advantages of strength and force nature has given me: But, oh! she disarms me with that modesty and weeping, so tender and so moving, that I retire, and thank my stars she overcame me.* The company laughed at his civility to a slave, and Cæsar only applauded the nobleness of his passion and nature, since that slave might be noble or, what was better, have true notions of honor and virtue in her. Thus passed they this night, after having received from the slaves all imaginable respect and obedience.

The next day, Trefry asked Cæsar to walk when the heat was allayed, and designedly carried him by the cottage of the fair slave, and told him she whom he spoke of last night lived there retired: *But* (says he) *I would not wish you to approach; for I am sure you will be in love as soon as you behold her.* Cæsar assured him, he was proof against all the charms of that sex; and that if he imagined his heart could be so perfidious to love again, after Imoinda, he believed he should tear it from his bosom. They had no sooner spoke, but a little shock-dog that Clemene had presented her, which she took great delight in, ran out; and she, not knowing anybody was there, ran to get it in again, and bolted out on those who were just speaking of her: when seeing them, she would have run in again, but Trefry caught her by the hand, and cried, *Clemene however you fly a lover, you ought to pay some respect to this stranger* (pointing to Cæsar). But she, as if she had resolved never to raise her eyes to the face of a man again, bent 'em the more to the earth when he spoke, and gave the prince the leisure to look the more at her. There needed no long gazing or consideration to examine who this fair creature was; he soon saw Imoinda all over her; in a minute he saw her face, her shape, her air, her modesty, and all that called forth his soul with joy at his eyes and left his body destitute of almost life: it stood without motion, and for a minute knew not that it had a being; and, I believe, he had never come to himself so oppressed he was with over-joy, if he had not met with this allay, that he perceived Imoinda fall dead in the hands of Trefry. This awakened him, and he ran to her aid and caught her in his arms, where by degrees she came to herself; and 'tis needless to tell with what transports, what ecstasies of joy, they both awhile beheld each other, without speaking; then snatched each other to their arms, then gaze again, as if they still doubted whether they possessed the blessing they grasped: but when they recovered their speech, 'tis not to be imagined what tender things they expressed to each other; wondering what strange fate had brought them again together. They soon informed each other of their fortunes and equally bewailed their fate; but at the same time they mutually protested that even fetters and slavery were soft and easy and would be supported with joy and pleasure, while they could be so happy to possess each other and to be able to make good their vows. Cæsar swore he disdained the empire of the world while he could behold his Imoinda; and she despised grandeur and pomp, those vanities of her sex, when she could gaze on Oroonoko. He adored the very cottage where she resided, and said, That little inch of the world would give him more happiness than all the universe could do; and she vowed, it was a palace, while adorned with the presence of Oroonoko.

Trefry was infinitely pleased with this novel,[15] and found this Clemene was the fair mistress of whom Cæsar had before spoke; and was not a little satisfied that heaven was so kind to the prince as to sweeten his misfortunes by so lucky an accident; and leaving the lovers to themselves, was impatient to come down to Parham House (which was on the same plantation) to give me an account of what had happened. I was as impatient to make these lovers a visit, having already made a friendship with Cæsar, and from his own mouth learned what I have related; which was confirmed by his Frenchman, who was set on shore to seek his fortune, and of whom they could not make a slave because a Christian; and he came daily to Parham

[15]Piece of news.

Hill to see and pay his respects to his pupil prince. So that concerning and interesting myself in all that related to Cæsar, whom I had assured of liberty as soon as the governor arrived, I hasted presently to the place where these lovers were, and was infinitely glad to find this beautiful young slave (who had already gained all our esteems, for her modesty and her extraordinary prettiness) to be the same I had heard Cæsar speak so much of. One may imagine then we paid her a treble respect; and though from her being carved in fine flowers and birds all over her body, we took her to be of quality before, yet when we knew Clemene was Imoinda, we could not enough admire her.

I had forgot to tell you that those who are nobly born of that country are so delicately cut and raised all over the fore-part of the trunk of their bodies that it looks as if it were japanned, the works being raised like high point round the edges of the flowers. Some are only carved with a little flower or bird at the sides of the temples, as was Cæsar; and those who are so carved over the body, resemble our ancient Picts that are figured in the chronicles, but these carvings are more delicate.

From that happy day Cæsar took Clemene for his wife, to the general joy of all people; and there was as much magnificence as the country would afford at the celebration of this wedding: and in a very short time after she conceived with child, which made Cæsar even adore her, knowing he was the last of his great race. This new accident made him more impatient of liberty, and he was every day treating with Trefry for his and Clemene's liberty, and offered either gold or a vast quantity of slaves, which should be paid before they let him go, provided he could have any security that he should go when his ransom was paid. They fed him from day to day with promises, and delayed him till the Lord Governor should come; so that he began to suspect them of falsehood, and that they would delay him till the time of his wife's delivery and make a slave of that too: for all the breed is theirs to whom the parents belong. This thought made him very uneasy, and his sullenness gave them some jealousies[16] of him; so that I was obliged, by some persons who feared a mutiny (which is very fatal sometimes in those colonies that abound so with slaves, that they exceed the whites in vast numbers) to discourse with Cæsar and to give him all the satisfaction I possibly could: They knew he and Clemene were scarce an hour

[16]Suspicions, mistrust.

in a day from my lodgings; that they eat with me, and that I obliged 'em in all things I was capable of. I entertained them with the loves of the Romans and great men, which charmed him to my company; and her, with teaching her all the pretty works that I was mistress of, and telling her stories of nuns, and endeavoring to bring her to the knowledge of the true God: But of all discourse, Cæsar liked that the worst, and would never be reconciled to our notions of the Trinity, of which he ever made a jest; it was a riddle he said would turn his brain to conceive, and one could not make him understand what faith was. However, these conversations failed not altogether so well to divert him, that he liked the company of us women much above the men, for he could not drink, and he is but an ill companion in that country that cannot. So that obliging him to love us very well, we had all the liberty of speech with him, especially myself, whom he called his Great Mistress; and indeed my word would go a great way with him. For these reasons I had opportunity to take notice to him, that he was not well pleased of late, as he used to be; was more retired and thoughtful; and told him, I took it ill he should suspect we would break our words with him and not permit both him and Clemene to return to his own kingdom, which was not so long a way, but when he was once on his voyage he would quickly arrive there. He made me some answers that showed a doubt in him, which made me ask, what advantage it would be to doubt? It would but give us a fear of him, and possibly compel us to treat him so as I should be very loath to behold: that is, it might occasion his confinement. Perhaps this was not so luckily spoke of me, for I perceived he resented that word, which I strove to soften again in vain: However, he assured me that whatsoever resolutions he should take, he would act nothing upon the white people; and as for myself, and those upon that plantation where he was, he would sooner forfeit his eternal liberty, and life itself, than lift his hand against his greatest enemy on that place. He besought me to suffer no fears upon his account, for he could do nothing that honor should not dictate; but he accused himself for having suffered slavery so long: yet he charged that weakness on love alone, who was capable of making him neglect even glory itself; and for which now he reproached himself every moment of the day. Much more to this effect he spoke, with an air impatient enough to make me know he would not be long in bondage; and though he suffered only the name of a slave, and had nothing of the toil and labor of one, yet that was sufficient to render him uneasy; and he had been too long idle, who used to be always in action and in arms. He had a spirit all rough and fierce and that could not be tamed to lazy rest; and though all endeavors were used to exercise himself in such actions and sports as this world afforded, as running, wrestling, pitching the bar, hunting and fishing, chasing and killing tigers[17] of a monstrous size, which this continent affords in abundance; and wonderful snakes, such as Alexander is reported to have encountered at the river of Amazons, and which Cæsar took great delight to overcome; yet these were not actions great enough for his large soul, which was still panting after more renowned actions.

Before I parted that day with him, I got, with much ado, a promise from him to rest yet a little longer with patience and wait the coming of the Lord Governor, who was every day expected on our shore: he assured me he would, and this promise he desired me to know was given perfectly in complaisance to me, in whom he had an entire confidence.

After this, I neither thought it convenient to trust him much out of our view, nor did the country, who feared him; but with one accord it was advised to treat him fairly and oblige him to remain within such a compass, and that he should be permitted as seldom as could be to go up to the plantations of the negroes; or, if he did, to be accompanied by some that should be rather in appearance attendants than spies. This care was for some time taken, and Cæsar looked upon it as a mark of extraordinary respect, and was glad his discontent had obliged 'em to be more observant to him; he received new assurance from the overseer, which was confirmed to him by the opinion of all the gentlemen of the country, who made their court to him. During this time that we had his company more frequently than hitherto we had had, it may not be unpleasant to relate to you the diversions we entertained him with, or rather he us.

My stay was to be short in that country, because my father died at sea and never arrived to possess the honor designed him (which was Lieutenant-General of six and thirty islands besides the continent of Surinam), nor the advantages he hoped to reap by them: so that though we were obliged to continue on our voyage, we did not intend to stay upon the place. Though, in a word, I must say thus much of it; that certainly had his late

[17]Jaguars.

Majesty, of sacred memory, but seen and known what a vast and charming world he had been master of in that continent, he would never have parted so easily with it to the Dutch.[18] 'Tis a continent whose vast extent was never yet known and may contain more noble earth than all the universe beside; for, they say, it reaches from east to west one way as far as China and another to Peru[19]. It affords all things both for beauty and use; 'tis there eternal spring, always the very months of April, May and June, the shades are perpetual, the trees bearing at once all degrees of leaves and fruit, from blooming buds to ripe autumn: groves of oranges, lemons, citrons, figs, nutmegs, and noble aromatics, continually bearing their fragrance. The trees appearing all like nosegays adorned with flowers of different kinds, some are all white, some purple, some scarlet, some blue, some yellow; bearing at the same time ripe fruit and blooming young, or producing every day new. The very wood of all these trees has an intrinsic value above common timber; for they are, when cut, of different colors, glorious to behold, and bear a price considerable, to inlay withal. Besides this, they yield rich balm and gums; so that we make our candles of such an aromatic substance as does not only give a sufficient light, but, as they burn, they cast their perfumes all about. Cedar is the common firing, and all the houses are built with it. The very meat we eat, when set on the table, if it be native, I mean of the country, perfumes the whole room; especially a little beast called an armadillo, a thing which I can liken to nothing so well as a rhinoceros; 'tis all in white armor, so jointed, that it moves as well in it, as if it had nothing on: this beast is about the bigness of a pig of six weeks old. But it were endless to give an account of all the divers wonderful and strange things that country affords, and which we took a very great delight to go in search of, though those adventures are oftentimes fatal, and at least dangerous: But while we had Cæsar in our company on these designs, we feared no harm, nor suffered any.

As soon as I came into the country, the best house in it was presented me, called St. John's Hill. It stood on a vast rock of white marble, at the foot of which the river ran a vast depth

[18]By the treaty of Breda (1667), which ended the Second Anglo-Dutch War, England ceded Surinam to the Dutch.

[19]The boundaries of Surinam were not clearly defined: it extended indefinitely into the South American continent. Its actual climate is unpleasantly hot and humid; Behn was influenced by the contemporary tendency to visualize the New World as an earthly paradise.

down, and not to be descended on that side; the little waves still dashing and washing the foot of this rock, made the softest murmurs and purlings in the world; and the opposite bank was adorned with such vast quantities of different flowers eternally blowing, and every day and hour new, fenced behind 'em with lofty trees of a thousand rare forms and colors, that the prospect was the most ravishing that sands[20] can create. On the edge of this white rock, towards the river, was a walk or grove of orange and lemon trees, about half the length of the Mall here,[21] whose flowery and fruit-bearing branches met at the top and hindered the sun, whose rays are very fierce there, from entering a beam into the grove; and the cool air that came from the river made it not only fit to entertain people in, at all the hottest hours of the day, but refreshed the sweet blossoms and made it always sweet and charming; and sure, the whole globe of the world cannot show so delightful a place as this grove was: Not all the gardens of boasted Italy can produce a shade to outvie this, which nature had joined with art to render so exceeding fine; and 'tis a marvel to see how such vast trees, as big as English oaks, could take footing on so solid a rock, and in so little earth as covered that rock: But all things by nature there are rare, delightful and wonderful. But to our sports.

Sometimes we would go surprising and in search of young tigers in their dens, watching when the old ones went forth to forage for prey; and oftentimes we have been in great danger and have fled apace for our lives, when surprised by the dams. But once, above all other times, we went on this design, and Caesar was with us; who had no sooner stolen a young tiger from her nest, but going off, we encountered the dam, bearing a buttock of a cow, which she had torn off with her mighty paw, and going with it towards her den: we had only four women, Caesar, and an English gentleman, brother to Harry Marten the great Oliverian;[22] we found there was no escaping this enraged and ravenous beast. However, we women fled as fast as we could from it; but our heels had not saved our lives, if Cæsar had not laid down his cub, when he found the tiger quit her prey to make the more speed towards him; and taking Mr. Marten's

[20]Tracts of sand along the shore of a river.

[21]A fashionable promenade along St. James's Park, London.

[22]Harry Marten was a conspicuous opponent of the King during the Civil Wars; he sometimes, though not consistently, supported Oliver Cromwell, a major leader on the Parliamentary side.

sword, desired him to stand aside, or follow the ladies. He obeyed him; and Cæsar met this monstrous beast of mighty size and vast limbs, who came with open jaws upon him; and fixing his awful stern eyes full upon those of the beast, and putting himself into a very steady and good aiming posture of defense, ran his sword quite through her breast down to her very heart, home to the hilt of the sword: the dying beast stretched forth her paw, and going to grasp his thigh, surprised with death in that very moment, did him no other harm than fixing her long nails in his flesh very deep, feebly wounded him, but could not grasp the flesh to tear off any. When he had done this, he holloed to us to return: which, after some assurance of his victory, we did, and found him lugging out the sword from the bosom of the tiger, who was laid in her blood on the ground; he took up the cub, and with an unconcern that had nothing of the joy or gladness of a victory, he came and laid the whelp at my feet. We all extremely wondered at his daring and at the bigness of the beast, which was about the height of an heifer, but of mighty great and strong limbs.

Another time being in the woods, he killed a tiger which had long infested that part, and borne away abundance of sheep and oxen and other things that were for the support of those to whom they belonged: abundance of people assailed this beast, some affirming they had shot her with several bullets quite through the body, at several times: and some swearing they shot her through the very heart, and they believed she was a devil, rather than a mortal thing. Cæsar had often said, he had a mind to encounter this monster, and spoke with several gentlemen who had attempted her; one crying, I shot her with so many poisoned arrows, another with his gun in this part of her, and another in that: so that he remarking all these places where she was shot, fancied still he should overcome her, by giving her another sort of a wound than any had yet done, and one day said (at the table) *What trophies and garlands, ladies, will you make me, if I bring you home the heart of this ravenous beast, that eats up all your lambs and pigs?* We all promised he should be rewarded at all our hands. So taking a bow, which he chose out of a great many, he went up into the wood with two gentlemen, where he imagined this devourer to be; they had not passed very far in it, but they heard her voice, growling and grumbling, as if she were pleased with something she was doing. When they came in view, they found her muzzling in the belly of a new ravished sheep, which she had torn open; and seeing her self approached, she took fast hold of her prey with her fore paws and set a very fierce raging look on Cæsar, without offering to approach him, for fear at the same time of losing what she had in possession. So that Cæsar remained a good while, only taking aim and getting an opportunity to shoot her where he designed: 'twas some time before he could accomplish it; and to wound her, and not kill her, would but have enraged her the more, and endangered him. He had a quiver of arrows at his side, so that if one failed, he could be supplied; at last, retiring a little, he gave her opportunity to eat, for he found she was ravenous, and fell to as soon as she saw him retire, being more eager of her prey than of doing new mischiefs: when he going softly to one side of her, and hiding his person behind certain herbage that grew high and thick, he took so good aim that, as he intended, he shot her just into the eye, and the arrow was sent with so good a will and so sure a hand that it stuck in her brain and made her caper and become mad for a moment or two; but being seconded by another arrow, she fell dead upon the prey. Cæsar cut her open with a knife, to see where those wounds were that had been reported to him and why she did not die of 'em. But I shall now relate a thing that, possibly, will find no credit among men, because 'tis a notion commonly received with us that nothing can receive a wound in the heart and live: But when the heart of this courageous animal was taken out, there were seven bullets of lead in it, the wound seamed up with great scars, and she lived with the bullets a great while, for it was long since they were shot: This heart the conqueror brought up to us, and 'twas a very great curiosity, which all the country came to see; and which gave Cæsar occasion of many fine discourses of accidents in war and strange escapes.

At other times he would go a fishing; and discoursing on that diversion, he found we had in that country a very strange fish, called a numb-eel[23] (an eel of which I have eaten) that while it is alive, it has a quality so cold, that those who are angling, though with a line of ever so great a length, with a rod at the end of it, it shall, in the same minute the bait is touched by this eel, seize him or her that holds the rod with a numbness that shall deprive 'em of sense for a while and some have fallen into the water, and others dropped as dead, on the banks of the rivers where they

[23]Electric eel.

stood, as soon as this fish touches the bait. Cæsar used to laugh at this and believed it impossible a man could lose his force at the touch of a fish; and could not understand that philosophy, that a cold quality should be of that nature; however, he had a great curiosity to try whether it would have the same effect on him it had on others, and often tried, but in vain. At last, the sought-for fish came to the bait, as he stood angling on the bank; and instead of throwing away the rod or giving it a sudden twitch out of the water, whereby he might have caught both the eel and have dismissed[24] the rod before it could have too much power over him; for experiment-sake, he grasped it but the harder, and fainting fell into the river; and being still possessed of the rod, the tide carried him, senseless as he was, a great way till an Indian boat took him up; and perceived, when they touched him, a numbness seize them, and by that knew the rod was in his hand; which with a paddle (that is, a short oar) they struck away, and snatched it into the boat, eel and all. If Cæsar was almost dead with the effect of this fish, he was more so with that of the water, where he had remained the space of going a league, and they found they had much ado to bring him back to life; but at last they did, and brought him home, where he was in a few hours well recovered and refreshed, and not a little ashamed to find he should be overcome by an eel, and that all the people who heard his defiance, would laugh at him. But we cheered him up; and he being convinced, we had the eel at supper, which was a quarter of an ell about, and most delicate meat and was of the more value, since it cost so dear as almost the life of so gallant a man.

About this time we were in many mortal fears about some disputes the English had with the Indians; so that we could scarce trust ourselves, without great numbers, to go to any Indian towns or place where they abode, for fear they should fall upon us, as they did immediately after my coming away; and the place being in the possession of the Dutch, they used them not so civilly as the English; so that they cut in pieces all they could take, getting into houses, and hanging up the mother and all her children about her; and cut a footman, I left behind me, all in joints, and nailed him to trees.

This feud began while I was there; so that I lost half the satisfaction I proposed, in not seeing and visiting the Indian

[24]Got rid of.

towns. But one day, bemoaning of our misfortunes upon this account, Cæsar told us, we need not fear, for if we had a mind to go, he would undertake to be our guard. Some would, but most would not venture: About eighteen of us resolved and took barge; and after eight days, arrived near an Indian town: But approaching it, the hearts of some of our company failed, and they would not venture on shore; so we polled, who would, and who would not. For my part, I said, if Cæsar would, I would go. He resolved; so did my brother and my woman, a maid of good courage. Now, none of us speaking the language of the people, and imagining we should have a half diversion in gazing only, and not knowing what they said, we took a fisherman that lived at the mouth of the river, who had been a long inhabitant there, and obliged him to go with us: But because he was known to the Indians, as trading among 'em, and being, by long living there, become a perfect Indian in color, we, who had a mind to surprise 'em by making them see something they never had seen (that is, white people), resolved only myself, my brother and woman should go: so Cæsar, the fisherman, and the rest, hiding behind some thick reeds and flowers that grew in the banks, let us pass on towards the town, which was on the bank of the river all along. A little distant from the houses, or huts, we saw some dancing, others busied in fetching and carrying of water from the river. They had no sooner spied us, but they set up a loud cry, that frighted us at first; we thought it had been for those that should kill us, but it seems it was of wonder and amazement. They were all naked, and we were dressed so as is most commode[25] for the hot countries, very glittering and rich; so that we appeared extremely fine: my own hair was cut short, and I had a taffeta cap, with black feathers on my head; my brother was in a stuff suit, with silver loops and buttons, and abundance of green ribbon. This was all infinitely surprising to them; and because we saw them stand still till we approached 'em, we took heart and advanced, came up to 'em, and offered 'em our hands; which they took, and looked on us round about, calling still for more company; who came swarming out, all wondering, and crying out *tepeeme*: taking their hair up in their hands, and spreading it wide to those they called out to; as if they would say (as indeed it signified) *numberless wonders,* or not to be recounted, no more than to number the hair of their heads. By

---

[25]Suitable.

degrees they grew more bold, and from gazing upon us round, they touched us, laying their hands upon all the features of our faces, feeling our breasts and arms, taking up one petticoat, then wondering to see another; admiring our shoes and stockings, but more our garters, which we gave 'em, and they tied about their legs, being laced with silver lace at the ends; for they much esteem any shining things. In fine, we suffered 'em to survey us as they pleased and we thought they would never have done admiring us. When Cæsar and the rest saw we were received with such wonder, they came up to us; and finding the Indian trader whom they knew (for 'tis by these fishermen, called Indian traders, we hold a commerce with 'em; for they love not to go far from home, and we never go to them), when they saw him therefore, they set up a new joy, and cried in their language, *Oh! here's our* tiguamy, *and we shall now know whether those things can speak.* So advancing to him, some of 'em gave him their hands, and cried, *Amora tiguamy;* which is as much as, *How do you do*; or, *welcome, friend:* and all, with one din, began to gabble to him, and asked, if we had sense and wit? If we could talk of affairs of life and war, as they could do? If we could hunt, swim, and do a thousand things they use? He answered 'em. We could. Then they invited us into their houses and dressed venison and buffalo for us, and going out, gathered a leaf of a tree, called a *sarumbo* leaf, of six yards long, and spread it on the ground for a tablecloth; and cutting another in pieces, instead of plates, set us on little low Indian stools, which they cut out of one entire piece of wood, and paint in a sort of Japan-work. They serve everyone their mess on these pieces of leaves; and it was very good, but too high-seasoned with pepper. When we had eat, my brother and I took out our flutes and played to 'em, which gave 'em new wonder; and I soon perceived, by an admiration that is natural to these people, and by the extreme ignorance and simplicity of 'em, it were not difficult to establish any unknown or extravagant religion among them, and to impose any notions or fictions upon 'em. For seeing a kinsman of mine set some paper on fire with a burning-glass, a trick they had never before seen, they were like to have adored him for a god and begged he would give 'em the characters or figures of his name, that they might oppose it against winds and storms; which he did, and they held it up in those seasons, and fancied it had a charm to conquer them and kept it like a holy relic. They are very superstitious and called him the great *peeie*, that is, *prophet*. They showed us their Indian *peeie*, a youth of about sixteen years old, as handsome as Nature could make a man. They consecrate a beautiful youth from his infancy, and all arts are used to complete him in the finest manner, both in beauty and shape: He is bred to all the little arts and cunning they are capable of; to all the legerdemain tricks and sleight of hand, whereby he imposes upon the rabble; and is both a doctor in physic and divinity: And by these tricks makes the sick believe he sometimes eases their pains, by drawing from the afflicted part little serpents or odd flies or worms or any strange thing; and though they have besides undoubted good remedies for almost all their diseases, they cure the patient more by fancy than by medicines, and make themselves feared, loved and reverenced. This young *peeie* had a very young wife, who seeing my brother kiss her, came running and kissed me. After this they kissed one another, and made it a very great jest, it being so novel; and new admiration and laughing went round the multitude, that they never will forget that ceremony, never before used or known. Cæsar had a mind to see and talk with their war-captains, and we were conducted to one of their houses, where we beheld several of the great captains who had been at council: But so frightful a vision it was to see 'em, no fancy can create; no sad dreams can represent so dreadful a spectacle. For my part, I took 'em for hobgoblins or fiends rather than men: but however their shapes appeared, their souls were very humane and noble; but some wanted their noses, some their lips, some both noses and lips, some their ears, and others cut through each cheek, with long slashes, through which their teeth appeared: they had several other formidable wounds and scars, or rather dismemberings. They had *comitias*, or little aprons before 'em; and girdles of cotton with their knives naked stuck in it; a bow at their back and a quiver of arrows on their thighs; and most had feathers on their heads of divers colors. They cried *Amora tiguamy* to us at our entrance, and were pleased we said as much to them: They seated us, and gave us drink of the best sort, and wondered as much as the others had done before, to see us. Cæsar was marveling as much at their faces, wondering how they should all be so wounded in war; he was impatient to know how they all came by those frightful marks of rage or malice, rather than wounds got in noble battle: They told us by our interpreter, That when any war was waging, two men, chosen out by some old captain whose fighting was past, and who could only teach the theory of war, were to stand in competition for the generalship, or great war-captain; and being brought before the old judges, now past labor, they are asked, What they dare do, to show they are worthy to lead an army? When he who is first asked, making no reply, cuts off his nose, and throws it contemptibly[26] on the ground; and the other does something to himself that he thinks surpasses him, and perhaps deprives himself of lips and an eye: so they slash on till one gives out, and many have died in this debate. And it's by a passive valor they show and prove their activity; a sort of courage too brutal to be applauded by our black hero; nevertheless, he expressed his esteem of 'em.

In this voyage Cæsar begat so good an understanding between the Indians and the English that there were no more fears or heart-burnings during our stay, but we had a perfect, open, and free trade with 'em. Many things remarkable and worthy reciting we met with in this short voyage, because Cæsar made it his business to search out and provide for our entertainment, especially to please his dearly adored Imoinda, who was a sharer in all our adventures; we being resolved to make her chains as easy as we could, and to compliment the prince in that manner that most obliged him.

As we were coming up again, we met with some Indians of strange aspects; that is, of a larger size and other sort of features than those of our country. Our Indian slaves, that rowed us, asked 'em some questions; but they could not understand us, but showed us a long cotton string with several knots on it and told us, they had been coming from the mountains so many moons as there were knots: they were habited in skins of a strange beast, and brought along with 'em bags of gold-dust; which, as well as they could give us to understand, came streaming in little small channels down the high mountains when the rains fell; and offered to be the convoy to anybody, or persons, that would go to the mountains.[27] We carried these men up to Parham, where they were kept till the Lord Governor came: And because all the country was made to be going on this golden adventure, the Governor, by his letters commanded (for they sent some of the gold to him) that a guard should be set at the

[26]Contemptuously.
[27]Possibly these Indians were Incas, who were of a different physical type from those of Surinam, had more gold, and kept records by means of knotted strings called *quipus*.

mouth of the river of Amazons (a river so called, almost as broad as the river of Thames) and prohibited all people from going up that river, it conducting to those mountains of gold. But we going off for England before the project was further prosecuted, and the Governor being drowned in a hurricane, either the design died, or the Dutch have the advantage of it: And 'tis to be bemoaned what his Majesty lost by losing that part of America.

Though this digression is a little from my story, however, since it contains some proofs of the curiosity and daring of this great man, I was content to omit nothing of his character.

It was thus for some time we diverted him; but now Imoinda began to show she was with child, and did nothing but sigh and weep for the captivity of her lord, herself, and the infant yet unborn; and believed if it were so hard to gain the liberty of two, 'twould be more difficult to get that for three. Her griefs were so many darts in the great heart of Cæsar, and taking his opportunity one Sunday, when all the whites were overtaken in drink, as there were abundance of several trades and slaves for four years, that inhabited among the negro houses,[28] and Sunday being their day of debauch (otherwise they were a sort of spies upon Cæsar), he went, pretending out of goodness to 'em, to feast among 'em, and sent all his music and ordered a great treat for the whole gang, about three hundred negroes, and about an hundred and fifty were able to bear arms, such as they had, which were sufficient to do execution with spirits accordingly: For the English had none but rusty swords that no strength could draw from a scabbard; except the people of particular quality, who took care to oil 'em, and keep 'em in good order: The guns also, unless here and there one, or those newly carried from England, would do no good or harm; for 'tis the nature of that country to rust and eat up iron or any metals but gold and silver. And they are very unexpert at the bow, which the negroes and Indians are perfect masters of.

Cæsar, having singled out these men from the women and children, made an harangue to 'em of the miseries and ignominies of slavery; counting up all their toils and sufferings, under such loads, burdens and drudgeries as were fitter for beasts than men; senseless brutes, than human souls. He told 'em, it was not

---

[28]Whites—transported convicts and indentured servants—were enslaved for a limited period of years; they worked and lived alongside the black slaves.

for days, months or years, but for eternity; there was no end to
be of their misfortunes: They suffered not like men, who might
find a glory and fortitude in oppression; but like dogs, that loved
the whip and bell and fawned the more they were beaten: That
they had lost the divine quality of men and were become insensible asses, fit only to bear: nay, worse; an ass, or dog, or horse,
having done his duty, could lie down in retreat and rise to work
again, and while he did his duty, endured no stripes; but men,
villainous, senseless men, such as they toiled on all the tedious
week till *Black Friday*: and then, whether they worked or not,
whether they were faulty or meriting, they, promiscuously, the
innocent with the guilty, suffered the infamous whip, the sordid
stripes, from their fellow-slaves, till their blood trickled from all
parts of their body; blood whose every drop ought to be revenged with a life of some of those tyrants that impose it. *And
why* (said he) *my dear friends and fellow-sufferers, should we be
slaves to an unknown people? Have they vanquished us nobly in
fight? Have they won us in honorable battle? And are we by the
chance of war become their slaves? This would not anger a
noble heart; this would not animate a soldier's soul: no, but we
are bought and sold like apes or monkeys, to be the sport of
women, fools and cowards; and the support of rogues and
renegades, that have abandoned their own countries for rapine,
murders, theft and villainies. Do you not hear every day how
they upbraid each other with infamy of life, below the wildest
savages? And shall we render obedience to such a degenerate
race, who have no one human virtue left, to distinguish them
from the vilest creatures? Will you, I say, suffer the lash from
such hands?* They all replied with one accord, *No, no, no;*
(Cæsar) *has spoke like a great captain, like a great king.*

After this he would have proceeded, but was interrupted by a
tall negro of some more quality than the rest; his name was
Tuscan, who bowing at the feet of Cæsar, cried, *My lord, we
have listened with joy and attention to what you have said; and
were we only men, would follow so great a leader through the
world: But Oh! consider we are husbands, and parents too, and
have things more dear to us than life; our wives and children,
unfit for travel in those unpassable woods, mountains and bogs.
We have not only difficult lands to overcome, but rivers to wade,
and mountains to encounter; ravenous beasts of prey.*——To
this Cæsar replied, *That honor was the first principle in nature,
that was to be obeyed; but as no man would pretend to that,*

without all the acts of virtue, compassion, charity, love, justice, and reason; he found it not inconsistent with that, to take equal care of their wives and children, as they would of themselves; and that he did not design, when he led them to freedom and glorious liberty, that they should leave that better part of themselves to perish by the hand of the tyrant's whip; but if there were a woman among them so degenerate from love and virtue, to choose slavery before the pursuit of her husband, and with the hazard of her life to share with him in his fortunes; that such a one ought to be abandoned, and left as a prey to the common enemy.

To which they all agreed—and bowed. After this, he spoke of the impassable woods and rivers, and convinced them, the more danger the more glory. He told them that he had heard of one Hannibal, a great captain, had cut his way through mountains of solid rocks,[29] and should a few shrubs oppose them, which they could fire before 'em? No, 'twas a trifling excuse to men resolved to die or overcome. As for bogs, they are with a little labor filled and hardened; and the rivers could be no obstacle, since they swam by nature, at least by custom, from the first hour of their birth: That when the children were weary, they must carry them by turns, and the woods and their own industry would afford them food. To this they all assented with joy.

Tuscan then demanded what he would do: He said they would travel towards the sea, plant a new colony, and defend it by their valor; and when they could find a ship, either driven by stress of weather or guided by providence that way, they would seize it and make it a prize, till it had transported them to their own countries: at least they should be made free in his kingdom, and be esteemed as his fellow-sufferers, and men that had the courage and the bravery to attempt, at least, for liberty, and if they died in the attempt, it would be more brave than to live in perpetual slavery.

They bowed and kissed his feet at this resolution, and with one accord vowed to follow him to death, and that night was appointed to begin their march. They made it known to their wives, and directed them to tie their hamaca[30] about their shoulders and under their arm, like a scarf, and to lead their children

[29]Hannibal of Carthage, a great African general, would naturally have inspired Oroonoko. Hannibal brought his army down through the Alps to attack Rome.
[30]Hammock. *Hamaca* is the Spanish original, derived from the word used by the Arawak Indians.

that could go and carry those that could not. The wives, who pay an entire obedience to their husbands, obeyed, and stayed for 'em where they were appointed: The men stayed but to furnish themselves with what defensive arms they could get; and all met at the rendezvous, where Cæsar made a new encouraging speech to 'em and led 'em out.

But as they could not march far that night, on Monday early, when the overseers went to call 'em all together to go to work, they were extremely surprised to find not one upon the place, but all fled with what baggage they had. You may imagine this news was not only suddenly spread all over the plantation, but soon reached the neighboring ones; and we had by noon about 600 men, they call the militia of the country, that came to assist us in the pursuit of the fugitives; but never did one see so comical an army march forth to war. The men of any fashion would not concern themselves, though it were almost the common cause; for such revoltings are very ill examples and have very fatal consequences oftentimes in many colonies: But they had a respect for Cæsar, and all hands were against the Parhamites (as they called those of Parham Plantation), because they did not in the first place love the Lord Governor; and secondly, they would have it, that Cæsar was ill used, and baffled with; and 'tis not impossible but some of the best in the country was of his council in this flight, and depriving us of all the slaves; so that they of the better sort would not meddle in the matter. The deputy-governor, of whom I have had no great occasion to speak, and who was the most fawning fair-tongued fellow in the world, and one that pretended the most friendship to Cæsar, was now the only violent man against him; and though he had nothing, and so need fear nothing, yet talked and looked bigger than any man. He was a fellow whose character is not fit to be mentioned with the worst of the slaves. This fellow would lead his army forth to meet Cæsar, or rather to pursue him. Most of their arms were of those sort of cruel whips they call *cat with nine tails*; some had rusty useless guns for show; others old basket hilts, whose blades had never seen the light in this age; and others had long staffs and clubs. Mr. Trefry went along, rather to be a mediator than a conqueror in such a battle; for he foresaw and knew, if by fighting they put the negroes into despair, they were a sort of sullen fellows that would drown or kill themselves before they would yield; and he advised that fair means was best: But Byam was one that abounded in his own wit and would take his own measures.

It was not hard to find these fugitives; for as they fled, they were forced to fire and cut the woods before 'em; so that night or day they pursued 'em by the light they made, and by the path they had cleared. But as soon as Cæsar found he was pursued, he put himself in a posture of defense, placing all the women and children in the rear; and himself, with Tuscan by his side, or next to him, all promising to die or conquer. Encouraged thus, they never stood to parley, but fell on pell-mell upon the English, and killed some and wounded a great many; they having recourse to their whips, as the best of their weapons. And as they observed no order, they perplexed the enemy so sorely, with lashing 'em in the eyes; and the women and children seeing their husbands so treated, being of fearful cowardly dispositions, and hearing the English cry out, *Yield, and live! Yield, and be pardoned!* they all run in amongst their husbands and fathers, and hung about them, crying out, *Yield! Yield! and leave Cæsar to their revenge*: that by degrees the slaves abandoned Cæsar and left him only Tuscan and his heroic Imoinda, who grown big as she was, did nevertheless press near her lord, having a bow and a quiver full of poisoned arrows, which she managed with such dexterity that she wounded several and shot the governor into the shoulder; of which wound he had like to have died, but that an Indian woman, his mistress, sucked the wound and cleansed it from the venom: But however, he stirred not from the place till he had parleyed with Cæsar, who he found was resolved to die fighting and would not be taken; no more would Tuscan or Imoinda. But he, more thirsting after revenge of another sort than that of depriving him of life, now made use of all his art of talking and dissembling, and besought Cæsar to yield himself upon terms which he himself should propose, and should be sacredly assented to and kept by him. He told him, It was not that he any longer feared him, or could believe the force of two men and a young heroine could overthrow all them, and with all the slaves now on their side also; but it was the vast esteem he had for his person, the desire he had to serve so gallant a man and to hinder himself from the reproach hereafter of having been the occasion of the death of a prince whose valor and magnanimity deserved the empire of the world. He protested to him, he looked upon this action as gallant and brave, however tending to the prejudice of his lord and master, who would by it have lost so considerable a number of slaves; that this flight of his should be looked on as a heat of youth and a rashness of a too forward courage and an unconsidered impatience of liberty, and no more; and that he labored in vain to accomplish that which they would effectually perform as soon as any ship arrived that would touch on his coast: *So that if you will be pleased* (continued he) *to surrender yourself, all imaginable respect shall be paid you; and yourself, your wife and child, if it be born here, shall depart free out of our land.* But Cæsar would hear of no composition; though Byam urged, if he pursued and went on in his design, he would inevitably perish, either by great snakes, wild beasts, or hunger; and he ought to have regard to his wife, whose condition required ease, and not the fatigues of tedious travel, where she could not be secured from being devoured. But Cæsar told him, there was no faith in the white men or the gods they adored; who instructed them in principles so false that honest men could not live amongst them; though no people professed so much, none performed so little: That he knew what he had to do when he dealt with men of honor; but with them a man ought to be eternally on his guard, and never to eat and drink with Christians, without his weapon of defense in his hand; and, for his own security, never to credit one word they spoke. As for the rashness and inconsiderateness of his action, he would confess the governor is in the right; and that he was ashamed of what he had done, in endeavoring to make those free who were by nature slaves, poor wretched rogues, fit to be used as Christians' tools; dogs, treacherous and cowardly, fit for such masters; and they wanted only but to be whipped into the knowledge of the Christian gods, to be the vilest of all creeping things; to learn to worship such deities as had not power to make them just, brave, or honest: In fine, after a thousand things of this nature, not fit here to be recited, he told Byam, he had rather die than live upon the same earth with such dogs. But Trefry and Byam pleaded and protested together so much, that Trefry, believing the governor to mean what he said and speaking very cordially himself, generously put himself into Cæsar's hands and took him aside and persuaded him, even with tears, to live, by surrendering himself, and to name his conditions. Cæsar was overcome by his wit and reasons, and in consideration of Imoinda and demanding what he desired, and that it should be ratified by their hands in writing, because he had perceived that was the common way of contract between man and man amongst the whites; all this was performed, and Tuscan's pardon was put in, and they surrendered to the governor, who walked peaceably down into the plantation with them, after giving orders to bury their dead. Cæsar was very much toiled with the bustle of the day, for he had fought like a fury; and what mischief was done, he and Tuscan performed alone; and gave their enemies a fatal proof that they durst do anything and feared no mortal force.

But they were no sooner arrived at the place where all the slaves receive their punishments of whipping, but they laid hands on Cæsar and Tuscan, faint with heat and toil; and surprising them, bound them to two several stakes and whipped them in a most deplorable and inhuman manner, rending the very flesh from their bones, especially Cæsar, who was not perceived to make any moan or to alter his face, only to roll his eyes on the faithless governor and those he believed guilty, with fierceness and indignation; and to complete his rage, he saw every one of those slaves, who but a few days before adored him as something more than mortal, now had a whip to give him some lashes, while he strove not to break his fetters; though if he had, it were impossible: but he pronounced a woe and revenge from his eyes, that darted fire, which was at once both awful and terrible to behold.

When they thought they were sufficiently revenged on him, they untied him, almost fainting with loss of blood from a thousand wounds all over his body; from which they had rent his clothes, and led him bleeding and naked as he was, and loaded him all over with irons, and then rubbed his wounds, to complete their cruelty, with Indian pepper, which had like to have made him raving mad; and in this condition made him so fast to the ground that he could not stir, if his pains and wounds would have given him leave. They spared Imoinda, and did not let her see this barbarity committed toward her lord, but carried her down to Parham and shut her up; which was not in kindness to her, but for fear she should die with the sight or miscarry, and then they should lose a young slave and perhaps the mother.

You must know, that when the news was brought on Monday morning that Cæsar had betaken himself to the woods, and carried with him all the negroes, we were possessed with extreme fear, which no persuasions could dissipate, that he would secure himself till night and then, that he would come down and cut all our throats. This apprehension made all the females of us fly down the river to be secured; and while we were away, they acted this cruelty; for I suppose I had authority and interest enough there, had I suspected any such thing, to have prevented it: but we had not gone many leagues, but the news overtook us that Cæsar was taken and whipped like a common slave. We met on the river with Colonel Marten, a man of great gallantry, wit, and goodness, and whom I have celebrated in a character of my new comedy, by his own name, in memory of so brave a man:[31] He was wise and eloquent, and, from the fineness of his parts, bore a great sway over the hearts of all the colony: He was a friend to Cæsar and resented this false dealing with him very much. We carried him back to Parham, thinking to have made an accommodation; when he came, the first news we heard was that the governor was dead of a wound Imoinda had given him; but it was not so well. But it seems, he would have the pleasure of beholding the revenge he took on Cæsar; and before the cruel ceremony was finished, he dropped down; and then they perceived the wound he had on his shoulder was by a venomed arrow, which, as I said, his Indian mistress healed by sucking the wound.

We were no sooner arrived, but we went up to the plantation to see Cæsar; whom we found in a very miserable and inexpressible condition; and I have a thousand times admired how he lived in so much tormenting pain. We said all things to him that trouble, pity and good nature could suggest, protesting our innocency of the fact and our abhorrence of such cruelties; making a thousand professions and services to him and begging as many pardons for the offenders, till we said so much that he believed we had no hand in his ill treatment: but told us, He could never pardon Byam; as for Trefry, he confessed he saw his grief and sorrow for his suffering, which he could not hinder, but was like to have been beaten down by the very slaves for speaking in his defense: But for Byam, who was their leader, their head—and should, by his justice and honor, have been an example to 'em—for him he wished to live to take a dire revenge of him; and said, *It had been well for him, if he had sacrificed me instead of giving me the contemptible whip.* He refused to talk much; but begging us to give him our hands, he took them, and protested never to lift up his to do us any harm. He had a great respect for Colonel Marten and always took his counsel like that of a parent; and assured him, he would obey him in anything

---

[31]George Marteen is the brave and dashing hero of *The Younger Brother*, a play that Behn worked on during the 1680s, although it was not produced until after her death (1696).

but his revenge on Byam: *Therefore* (said he) *for his own safety, let him speedily dispatch me; for if I could dispatch myself, I would not, till that justice were done to my injured person and the contempt of a soldier: No, I would not kill myself, even after a whipping, but will be content to live with that infamy and be pointed at by every grinning slave, till I have completed my revenge; and then you shall see, that Oroonoko scorns to live with the indignity that was put on Cæsar.* All we could do could get no more words from him; and we took care to have him put immediately into a healing bath to rid him of his pepper, and ordered a chirurgeon to anoint him with healing balm, which he suffered, and in some time he began to be able to walk and eat. We failed not to visit him every day, and to that end had him brought to an apartment at Parham.

The governor had no sooner recovered and had heard of the menaces of Cæsar, but he called his council, who (not to disgrace them, or burlesque the Government there) consisted of such notorious villains as Newgate never transported,[32] and, possibly, originally were such, who understood neither the laws of God or man, and had no sort of principles to make them worthy the name of men; but at the very council table would contradict and fight with one another and swear so bloodily, that 'twas terrible to hear and see 'em. (Some of 'em were afterwards hanged when the Dutch took possession of the place, others sent off in chains.) But calling these special rulers of the nation together and requiring their counsel in this weighty affair, they all concluded that (damn 'em) it might be their own cases; and that Cæsar ought to be made an example to all the negroes, to fright 'em from daring to threaten their betters, their lords and masters: and at this rate no man was safe from his own slaves; and concluded, *nemine contradicente*,[33] that Cæsar should be hanged.

Trefry then thought it time to use his authority and told Byam, his command did not extend to his lord's plantation; and that Parham was as much exempt from the law as Whitehall;[34] and that they ought no more to touch the servants of the lord——(who there represented the king's person) than they could those about the king himself; and that Parham was a sanctuary; and though

---

[32]Convicted felons who were not hanged were transported to the American colonies often after confinement in Newgate, a prison in London.

[33]Unanimously.

[34]Behn parallels Parham, the royal governor's residence, with Whitehall, the king's palace in London.

his lord were absent in person, his power was still in being there, which he had entrusted with him, as far as the dominions of his particular plantations reached, and all that belonged to it: the rest of the country, as Byam was lieutenant to his lord, he might exercise his tyranny upon. Trefry had others as powerful, or more, that interested themselves in Cæsar's life and absolutely said he should be defended. So turning the governor and his wise council out of doors (for they sat at Parham House), we set a guard upon our lodging-place and would admit none but those we called friends to us and Cæsar.

The governor having remained wounded at Parham till his recovery was completed, Cæsar did not know but he was still there, and indeed, for the most part, his time was spent there: for he was one that loved to live at other people's expense, and if he were a day absent, he was ten present there; and used to play and walk and hunt and fish with Cæsar. So that Cæsar did not at all doubt, if he once recovered strength, but he should find an opportunity of being revenged on him; though, after such a revenge, he could not hope to live; for if he escaped the fury of the English mobile,[35] who perhaps would have been glad of the occasion to have killed him, he was resolved not to survive his whipping; yet he had some tender hours, a repenting softness, which he called his fits of cowardice, wherein he struggled with love for the victory of his heart, which took part with his charming Imoinda there: but, for the most part, his time was passed in melancholy thoughts and black designs. He considered, if he should do this deed, and die either in the attempt or after it, he left his lovely Imoinda a prey or at best a slave to the enraged multitude; his great heart could not endure that thought: *Perhaps* (said he) *she may be first ravished by every brute; exposed first to their nasty lusts and then a shameful death:* No, he could not live a moment under that apprehension, too insupportable to be borne. These were his thoughts, and his silent arguments with his heart, as he told us afterwards: so that now resolving not only to kill Byam, but all those he thought had enraged him; pleasing his great heart with the fancied slaughter he should make over the whole face of the plantation, he first resolved on a deed that (however horrid it first appeared to us all) when we had heard his reasons, we thought it brave and just. Being able to walk and, as he believed, fit for the execution of his great

[35]Mob, rabble.

design, he begged Trefry to trust him into the air, believing a
walk would do him good, which was granted him: and taking
Imoinda with him as he used to do in his more happy and calmer
days, he led her up into a wood, where (after a thousand sighs,
and long gazing silently on her face, while tears gushed, in spite
of him, from his eyes) he told her his design, first, of killing her,
and then his enemies, and next himself, and the impossibility of
escaping, and therefore he told her the necessity of dying. He
found the heroic wife faster pleading for death than he was to
propose it, when she found his fixed resolution; and, on her
knees, besought him not to leave her a prey to his enemies. He
(grieved to death) yet pleased at her noble resolution, took her
up, and embracing of her with all the passion and languishment
of a dying lover, drew his knife to kill this treasure of his soul,
this pleasure of his eyes; while tears trickled down his cheeks,
hers were smiling with joy she should die by so noble a hand and
be sent into her own country (for that's their notion of the next
world) by him she so tenderly loved and so truly adored in this:
For wives have a respect for their husbands equal to what any
other people pay a deity, and when a man finds any occasion to
quit his wife, if he love her, she dies by his hand; if not, he sells
her or suffers some other to kill her. It being thus, you may
believe the deed was soon resolved on; and 'tis not to be
doubted, but the parting, the eternal leave-taking of two such
lovers, so greatly born, so sensible, so beautiful, so young, and
so fond, must be very moving, as the relation of it was to me
afterwards.

All that love could say in such cases being ended, and all the
intermitting irresolutions being adjusted, the lovely, young and
adored victim lays herself down before the sacrificer; while he,
with a hand resolved and a heart-breaking within, gave the fatal
stroke, first cutting her throat and then severing her yet smiling
face from that delicate body, pregnant as it was with the fruits of
tenderest love. As soon as he had done, he laid the body decently on leaves and flowers, of which he made a bed, and
concealed it under the same coverlet of Nature; only her face
he left yet bare to look on: But when he found she was dead and
past all retrieve, never more to bless him with her eyes and soft
language, his grief swelled up to rage; he tore, he raved, he
roared like some monster of the wood, calling on the loved name
of Imoinda. A thousand times he turned the fatal knife that did
the deed toward his own heart, with a resolution to go immedi-

ately after her; but dire revenge, which was now a thousand times more fierce in his soul than before, prevents him: and he would cry out, *No, since I have sacrificed Imoinda to my revenge, shall I lose that glory which I have purchased so dear, as at the price of the fairest, dearest, softest creature that ever Nature made? No, no!* Then at her name grief would get the ascendant of rage, and he would lie down by her side and water her face with showers of tears, which never were wont to fall from those eyes; and however bent he was on his intended slaughter, he had not power to stir from the sight of this dear object, now more beloved and more adored than ever.

He remained in this deplorable condition for two days and never rose from the ground where he had made her sad sacrifice; at last rousing from her side and accusing himself with living too long, now Imoinda was dead, and that the deaths of those barbarous enemies were deferred too long, he resolved now to finish the great work: but offering to rise, he found his strength so decayed that he reeled to and fro, like boughs assailed by contrary winds; so that he was forced to lie down again and try to summon all his courage to his aid. He found his brains turned round, and his eyes were dizzy, and objects appeared not the same to him they were wont to do; his breath was short, and all his limbs surprised with a faintness he had never felt before. He had not eaten in two days, which was one occasion of his feebleness, but excess of grief was the greatest, yet still he hoped he should recover vigor to act his design, and lay expecting it yet six days longer; still mourning over the dead idol of his heart and striving every day to rise, but could not.

In all this time you may believe we were in no little affliction for Cæsar and his wife: Some were of opinion he was escaped, never to return; others thought some accident had happened to him: but however, we failed not to send out a hundred people several ways to search for him. A party of about forty went that way he took, among whom was Tuscan, who was perfectly reconciled to Byam: They had not gone very far into the wood, but they smelled an unusual smell, as of a dead body; for stinks must be very noisome that can be distinguished among such a quantity of natural sweets as every inch of that land produces: so that they concluded they should find him dead, or somebody that was so; they passed on towards it, as loathsome as it was, and made such rustling among the leaves that lie thick on the ground, by continual falling, that Cæsar heard he was approached: and though he had, during the space of these eight days, endeavored to rise, but found he wanted strength, yet looking up, and seeing his pursuers, he rose and reeled to a neighboring tree, against which he fixed his back; and being within a dozen yards of those that advanced and saw him, he called out to them and bid them approach no nearer, if they would be safe. So that they stood still and, hardly believing their eyes, that would persuade them that it was Cæsar that spoke to 'em, so much was he altered, they asked him what he had done with his wife, for they smelled a stink that almost struck them dead. He pointing to the dead body, sighing, cried, *Behold her there.* They put off the flowers that covered her with their sticks, and found she was killed, and cried out, *Oh, monster! that hast murdered thy wife.* Then asking him, why he did so cruel a deed. He replied, He had no leisure to answer impertinent questions: *You may go back* (continued he) *and tell the faithless governor, he may thank fortune that I am breathing my last; and that my arm is too feeble to obey my heart, in what it had designed him:* But his tongue faltering and trembling, he could scarce end what he was saying. The English taking advantage by his weakness, cried, *Let us take him alive by all means.* He heard 'em; and, as if he had revived from a fainting or a dream, he cried out, *No, gentlemen, you are deceived; you will find no more Cæsars to be whipped; no more find a faith in me: feeble as you think me, I have strength yet left to secure me from a second indignity.* They swore all anew; and he only shook his head and beheld them with scorn. Then they cried out, *Who will venture on this single man? Will nobody?* They stood all silent while Cæsar replied, *Fatal will be the attempt to the first adventurer, let him assure himself* (and, at that word, held up his knife in a menacing posture): *Look ye, ye faithless crew,* said he, *'tis not life I seek, nor am I afraid of dying* (and at that word, cut a piece of flesh from his own throat, and threw it at 'em), *yet still I would live if I could, till I had perfected my revenge: But, oh! it cannot be; I feel life gliding from my eyes and heart; and if I make not haste, I shall fall a victim to the shameful whip.* At that, he ripped up his own belly and took his bowels and pulled 'em out with what strength he could; while some, on their knees imploring, besought him to hold his hand. But when they saw him tottering, they cried out, *Will none venture on him?* A bold Englishman cried, *Yes, if he were the devil* (taking courage when he saw him almost dead), and swearing a horrid oath for his farewell to the world, he rushed on him. Cæsar with his armed hand, met him so fairly as stuck him to the heart, and he fell dead at his feet. Tuscan seeing that, cried out, *I love thee, O Cæsar! and therefore will not let thee die, if possible*; and running to him, took him in his arms: but, at the same time, warding a blow that Cæsar made at his bosom, he received it quite through his arm; and Cæsar having not the strength to pluck the knife forth, though he attempted it, Tuscan neither pulled it out himself, nor suffered it to be pulled out, but came down with it sticking in his arm; and the reason he gave for it was, because the air should not get into the wound. They put their hands across and carried Cæsar between six of 'em, fainting as he was, and they thought dead, or just dying; and they brought him to Parham and laid him on a couch, and had the chirurgeon immediately to him, who dressed his wounds, and sewed up his belly, and used means to bring him to life, which they effected. We ran all to see him; and, if before we thought him so beautiful a sight, he was now so altered that his face was like a death's-head blacked over, nothing but teeth and eyeholes: For some days we suffered nobody to speak to him, but caused cordials to be poured down his throat, which sustained his life, and in six or seven days he recovered his senses: For, you must know, that wounds are almost to a miracle cured in the Indies; unless wounds in the legs, which they rarely ever cure.

When he was well enough to speak, we talked to him and asked him some questions about his wife and the reasons why he killed her; and he then told us what I have related of that resolution and of his parting, and he besought us he would let him die, and was extremely afflicted to think it was possible he might live: he assured us, if we did not dispatch him, we would prove very fatal to a great many. We said all we could to make him live and gave him new assurances; but he begged we would not think so poorly of him or of his love to Imoinda to imagine we could flatter him to life again: but the chirurgeon assured him he could not live, and therefore he need not fear. We were all (but Cæsar) afflicted at this news, and the sight was ghastly: His discourse was sad; and the earthy smell about him so strong, that I was persuaded to leave the place for some time (being myself but sickly, and very apt to fall into fits of dangerous illness upon any extraordinary melancholy). The servants, and Trefry, and the chirurgeons, promised all to take what possible care they could of the life of Cæsar; and I, taking boat, went with other company to Colonel Marten's, about three days journey down the river. But I was no sooner gone, than the governor, taking Trefry about some pretended earnest business, a day's journey up the river, having communicated his design to one Banister, a wild Irish man, and one of the council, a fellow of absolute barbarity, and fit to execute any villainy, but rich; he came up to Parham, and forcibly took Cæsar, and had him carried to the same post where he was whipped; and causing him to be tied to it, and a great fire made before him, he told him, he should die like a dog, as he was. Cæsar replied, This was the first piece of bravery that ever Banister did, and he never spoke sense till he pronounced that word; and, if he would keep it, he would declare in the other world that he was the only man, of all the whites, that ever he heard speak truth. And turning to the men that had bound him, he said, *My friends, am I to die, or to be whipped?* And they cried, *Whipped! no, you shall not escape so well.* And then he replied, smiling, *A blessing on thee*; and assured them, they need not tie him, for he would stand fixed like a rock and endure death so as should encourage them to die: *But if you whip me* (said he) *be sure you tie me fast*.

He had learned to take tobacco; and when he was assured he should die, he desired they would give him a pipe in his mouth, ready lighted; which they did: And the executioner came, and first cut off his members, and threw them into the fire; after that, with all ill-favored knife, they cut off his ears and his nose and burned them; he still smoked on, as if nothing had touched him; then they hacked off one of his arms, and still he bore up, and held his pipe; but at the cutting off the other arm, his head sunk, and his pipe dropped; and he gave up the ghost, without a groan or a reproach. My mother and sister were by him all the while, but not suffered to save him; so rude and wild were the rabble, and so inhuman were the justices who stood by to see the execution, who after paid dearly enough for their insolence. They cut Cæsar in quarters and sent them to several of the chief plantations: One quarter was sent to Colonel Marten, who refused it and swore, he had rather see the quarters of Banister and the governor himself than those of Cæsar on his plantations; and that he could govern his negroes, without terrifying and grieving them with frightful spectacles of a mangled king.

Thus died this great man, worthy of a better fate and a more sublime wit than mine to write his praise: Yet, I hope, the reputation of my pen is considerable enough to make his glorious name to survive to all ages, with that of the brave, the beautiful, and the constant Imoinda.

Anne Finch,
Countess of Winchilsea

1661–1720

A NNE FINCH was fortunate in her social position, her loving and appreciative husband, and the political chance that removed them from public life. She was born into the county aristocracy, lost her father when she was five months old, her mother when she was three, and her stepfather when she was ten. In 1683 she became a maid of honor to Mary of Modena, wife of James, Duke of York, and met the wits of the brilliant but cynical Restoration court. Heneage Finch, a gentleman of the bedchamber to the Duke, fell in love with her; and they married in 1684. The marriage was childless, but blissfully happy and congenial; far from disparaging his wife's intellectual interests, as would the average Restoration husband, Heneage actively encouraged her to write poetry.

Heneage Finch held several political positions after James succeeded to the throne as James II, but lost everything when he was deposed and exiled in 1688. For several years the Finches had no income or settled home. Anne, moreover, was personally grief-stricken because of her devotion to Mary of Modena. This triggered her most serious bout with depression (then called "the spleen"), a malady that afflicted her periodically throughout her life. Things improved for the Finches when Heneage's nephew became Earl of Winchilsea in 1690 and invited them to reside at Eastwell, the family seat in Kent. There they lived in happy retirement, enjoying nature and a congenial circle of friends, Anne writing poetry and Heneage pursuing antiquarian research. On visits to London they associated with Swift, Prior, Pope, and Gay.

In 1712 the Earl died, and Heneage succeeded to the title. The following year, Anne published a volume of her poems, originally without and then with her name; it included about half the poems in this selection, excluding the more personal and feminist ones. Finch wrote

77

in the popular forms of her day—love lyric, satire, fable, Pindaric ode, meditation on nature, comic narrative, and devotional poem (as well as drama, Miltonic burlesque, and scriptural paraphrase). Yet as a woman she expressed Augustan attitudes with a difference: her love lyrics tend to be more personally felt than the men's, and she shows a distinctive concern about freedom.

The Introduction

Did I my lines intend for public view,
How many censures, would their faults pursue.
Some would, because such words they do affect,
Cry they're insipid, empty, uncorrect.
And many have attained, dull and untaught,
The name of wit, only by finding fault.
True judges might condemn their want of wit,
And all might say, they're by a woman writ.
Alas! a woman that attempts the pen,
Such an intruder on the rights of men,   10
Such a presumptuous creature is esteemed,
The fault can by no virtue be redeemed.
They tell us, we mistake our sex and way;
Good breeding, fashion, dancing, dressing, play
Are the accomplishments we should desire;
To write, or read, or think, or to enquire
Would cloud our beauty, and exhaust our time,
And interrupt the conquests of our prime;
Whilst the dull manage of a servile house
Is held by some, our utmost art, and use.   20
      Sure 'twas not ever thus, nor are we told
Fables, of women that excelled of old;
To whom, by the diffusive hand of Heaven
Some share of wit and poetry was given.
On that glad day, on which the Ark returned,
The holy pledge, for which the land had mourned,
The joyful tribes attend it on the way,
The Levites do the sacred charge convey,
Whilst various instruments before it play;
Here, holy virgins in the concert join,   30

The louder notes to soften and refine,
And with alternate verse, complete the hymn divine.
Lo! the young poet, after God's own heart,
By Him inspired and taught the Muses' art,
Returned from conquest, a bright chorus meets,
That sing his slain ten thousand in the streets.
In such loud numbers they his acts declare,
Proclaim the wonders of his early war,
That Saul upon the vast applause does frown,
And feels its mighty thunder shake the crown.   *40*
What, can the threatened judgment now prolong?
Half of the kingdom is already gone;
The fairest half, whose influence guides the rest,
Have David's empire o'er their hearts confessed.
　　A woman here leads fainting Israel on,
She fights, she wins, she triumphs with a song,
Devout, majestic, for the subject fit,
And far above her arms exalts her wit,
Then, to the peaceful, shady palm withdraws,
And rules the rescued nation with her laws.[1]   *50*
How are we fallen, fallen by mistaken rules?
And Education's more than Nature's fools,
Debarred from all improvements of the mind
And to be dull, expected and designed;
And if someone would soar above the rest,
With warmer fancy and ambition pressed,
So strong, th' opposing faction still appears,
The hopes to thrive can ne'er outweigh the fears;
Be cautioned then, my Muse, and still retired;
Nor be despised, aiming to be admired;   *60*
Conscious of wants, still with contracted wing,
To some few friends, and to thy sorrows sing;
For groves of laurel thou wert never meant;
Be dark enough thy shades, and be thou there content.

---

[1]Lines 25–50 refer to three episodes in the Old Testament: (1) the Israelites sang and played instruments to celebrate bringing the Ark of the Covenant into Jerusalem (I Chronicles 15. The "holy virgins," however, seem to be Finch's addition.); (2) the women of Israel, greeting the victorious David ("the young poet, after God's own heart") with songs, praised his achievement over King Saul's (I Samuel 18); (3) the judge Deborah led the Israelites to victory and then composed a triumphal song (Judges 4, 5).

Fragment

So here confined, and but to female clay,
Ardelia's[1] soul mistook the rightful way:
Whilst the soft breeze of pleasure's tempting air
Made her believe, felicity was there;
And basking in the warmth of early time,
To vain amusements dedicate her prime.
Ambition next allured her tow'ring eye;
For Paradise she heard was placed on high,
Then thought, the Court with all its glorious show
Was sure above the rest, and Paradise below.   *10*
There placed too soon the flaming sword appeared
Removed those powers, whom justly she revered,
Adhered too in their wreck, and in their ruin shared.[2]
Now by the wheel's inevitable round,
With them thrown prostrate to the humble ground,
No more she takes (instructed by that Fall)
For fixed, or worth her thought, this rolling ball:
Towards a more certain station she aspires,
Unshaken by revolts, and owns no less desires.
But all in vain are prayers, ecstatic thoughts,   *20*
Recovered moments, and retracted faults,
Retirement, which the world *moroseness* calls,
Abandoned pleasures in monastic walls;[3]
These, but at distance, towards that purpose tend,
The lowly means to an exalted end;
Which He must perfect, who allots her stay,
And that, accomplished, will direct the way.
Pity her restless cares and weary strife,
And point some issue to escaping life;
Which so dismissed, no pen or human speech   *30*

[1]Finch's poetic name for herself. (Such idealized names were common in the poetry of the period.)

[2]The "powers" were King James II and his Queen, Mary of Modena. When the sovereigns were deposed, the Finches remained loyal to them and lost their position at Court as ruinously as did Adam and Eve when they were expelled from Paradise by an angel with a flaming sword (line 11) after the Fall (line 16).

[3]The "monastic walls" were those of Wye College, a former priory (Finch). This was a family property where the Finches lived for some time. See "An Apology for My Fearful Temper."

Th' ineffable Recess can ever teach:
Th' Expanse, the Light, the Harmony, the Throng,
The Bride's Attendance, and the Bridal Song,
The numerous Mansions, and th' immortal Tree,
No eye, unpurged by death, must ever see,
Or waves which through that wond'rous city[4] roll.
Rest then content, my too impatient soul;
Observe but here the easy precepts given,
Then wait with cheerful hope, till Heaven be known in Heaven.

On Myself

Good Heaven, I thank thee, since it was designed
I should be framed, but of the weaker kind,
That yet, my soul is rescued from the love
Of all those trifles which their passions move.
Pleasures, and praise, and plenty have with me
But their just value. If allowed they be,
Freely and thankfully as much I taste
As will not reason or religion waste.
If they're denied, I on myself can live,
And slight those aids unequal chance does give.
When in the sun, my wings can be displayed,
And in retirement, I can bless the shade.

A Letter to Daphnis,[1] April 2, 1685

This to the crown and blessing of my life,
The much loved husband of a happy wife.
To him whose constant passion found the art
To win a stubborn and ungrateful heart;

---

[4]The Heavenly Jerusalem of the Biblical Book of Revelation.
[1]Finch's poetic name for her husband, derived from Greek pastoral. In the next poem, she calls him Flavio.

And to the world by tenderest proof discovers[2]
They err, who say that husbands can't be lovers.
With such return of passion as is due,
Daphnis I love, Daphnis my thoughts pursue,
Daphnis, my hopes, my joys, are bounded all in you:
Even I, for Daphnis', and my promise', sake,
What I in women censure, undertake.
But this from love, not vanity, proceeds;
You know who writes, and I who 'tis that reads.
Judge not my passion by my want of skill,
Many love well, though they express it ill;
And I your censure could with pleasure bear,
Would you but soon return, and speak it here.

To Mr. F[inch] Now Earl of W[inchilsea]

*Who going abroad, had desired Ardelia to write some verses
upon whatever subject she thought fit, against his return in the
evening*

Written in the year 1689

No sooner, FLAVIO, was you gone,
But, your injunction thought upon,
   ARDELIA took the pen;
Designing to perform the task,
Her FLAVIO did so kindly ask,
   Ere he returned again.

Unto Parnassus straight she sent,
And bid the messenger that went
   Unto the Muses' Court,
Assure them, she their aid did need,
And begged they'd use their utmost speed,
   Because the time was short.

The hasty summons was allowed;
And being well-bred, they rose and bowed,

10

   [2]Reveals.

And said, they'd post away;
That well they did ARDELIA know,
And that no female's voice below
　　They sooner would obey:

That many of that rhyming train,
On like occasions, sought in vain　　　　　　　　*20*
　　Their industry t'excite;
But for ARDELIA all they'd leave:
Thus flattering can the Muse deceive,
　　And wheedle us to write.

Yet, since there was such haste required;
To know the subject 'twas desired,
　　On which they must infuse;
That they might temper words and rules,
And with their counsel carry tools,
　　As country-doctors use.　　　　　　　　　　　*30*

Wherefore to cut off all delays,
'Twas soon replied, a *husband's* praise
　　(Though in these looser times)
ARDELIA gladly would rehearse
A *husband's*, who indulged her verse,
　　And now required her rhymes.

A *husband!* echoed all around:
And to Parnassus sure that sound
　　Had never yet been sent;
Amazement in each face was read,　　　　　　　　*40*
In haste th' affrighted sisters fled,
　　And unto Council went.

Erato cried, since Grisel's days,
Since Troy-Town pleased, and *Chevy Chase*,
　　No such design was known;[1]
And 'twas their business to take care,
It reached not to the public ear,
　　Or got about the Town:

Nor came where evening *beaux* were met

---

[1]Erato is the Muse of love poetry. Grisel or Griselda was the model of a patient, devoted wife, celebrated in medieval literature. "Troy-Town," referring to Homer's *Iliad* or possibly John Lydgate's *Troy-book* (1412–1420), and the old ballad "Chevy Chase" (fifteenth century) are examples of literature hopelessly out of fashion.

O'er *billet-doux* and chocolate,   *50*
   Lest it destroyed the house;[2]
For in that place, who could dispense
(That wore his clothes with common sense)
   With mention of a *spouse?*[3]

'Twas put unto the vote at last,
And in the negative it passed,
   None to her aid should move;
Yet since ARDELIA was a friend,
Excuses 'twas agreed to send,
   Which plausible might prove: *60*

That Pegasus of late had been
So often rid through thick and thin,
   With neither fear nor wit;
In *panegyric* been so spurred,
He could not from the stall be stirred,
   Nor would endure the bit.[4]

Melpomene had given a bond,
By the new House alone to stand,
   And write of war and strife;
Thalia, she had taken fees,   *70*
And stipends from the patentees,
   And durst not for her life.[5]

Urania[6] only liked the choice;
Yet not to thwart the public voice,
   She whispering did impart:
They need no foreign aid invoke,
No help to draw a moving stroke,
   Who dictate from the heart.

Enough! the pleased ARDELIA cried;
And slighting every Muse beside,   *80*
   Consulting now her breast,

[2]Probably a coffee- or chocolate-house, where fashionable men would gather.
[3]"Dispense with" means endure, put up with.
[4]Pegasus has been overworked in the composition of poetical tributes to William, the new King (Myra Reynolds).
[5]Melpomene and Thalia, the Muses of tragedy and comedy, are committed to inspiring only work for the licensed theater ("House") in London, whose managers held a patent from the government.
[6]Urania is the Muse of heavenly love.

Perceived that every tender thought,
Which from abroad she'd vainly sought,
  Did there in silence rest:

And should unmoved that post maintain,
Till in his quick return again,
  Met in some neighboring grove,
(Where vice nor vanity appear)
Her Flavio them alone might hear,
  In all the sounds of love.   *90*

For since the world does so despise
Hymen's endearments and its ties,
  They should mysterious be;
Till we that pleasure too possess
(Which makes their fancied Happiness)
  Of stolen secrecy.

Ardelia's Answer to Ephelia,

*who had invited her to come to her in town—reflecting on the
coquetry and detracting humor of the age*

Me, dear Ephelia, me, in vain you court
With all your powerful influence, to resort
To that great Town, where friendship can but have
The few spare hours which meaner pleasures leave.
No! Let some shade, or your large palace be
Our place of meeting, love, and liberty;
To thoughts, and words, and all endearments free.
But to those walls excuse my slow repair;
Who have no business or diversion there;
No dazzling beauty to attract the gaze   *10*
Of wondering crowds to my applauded face;
Nor to my little wit, th' ill nature joined,
To pass a general censure on mankind:
To call the young and unaffected, fools;
Dull all the grave, that live by moral rules;
To say the soldier brags who, asked, declares
The nice escapes and dangers of his wars,
The poet's vain, that knows his unmatched worth,

And dares maintain what the best Muse brings forth:
Yet this the humor of the age is grown,   20
And only conversation of the Town.
In satire versed and sharp detraction, be,
And you're accomplished for all company.

II

When my last visit, I to London made,
Me, to Almeria, wretched chance, betrayed;
The fair Almeria, in this art so known,
That she discerns all failings, but her own.
With a loud welcome and a strict embrace,
Kisses on kisses, in a public place,
Sh' extorts a promise, that next day I dine   30
With her, who for my sight did hourly pine;
And wonders how so far I can remove,
From the *beau monde*, and the dull country love;
Yet vows, if but an afternoon 'twould cost
To see me there, she could resolve almost
To quit the Town and for that time, be lost.
My word I keep, we dine, then rising late,
Take coach, which long had waited at the gate.
About the streets a tedious ramble go,
To see this monster, or that wax work show,   40
Or anything, that may the time bestow.
When by a church we pass, I ask to stay,
Go in, and my devotions humbly pay
To that great Power, whom all the wise obey.
Whilst the gay thing, light as her feathered dress,
Flies round the coach, and does each cushion press,
Through every glass[1] her several graces shows,
This, does her face, and that, her shape expose,
To envying beauties and admiring *beaux*.
One stops, and as expected, all extolls,   50
Clings to the door, and on his elbow lolls,
Thrusts in his head, at once to view the fair,
And keep his curls from discomposing air,
Then thus proceeds—
                    "My wonder it is grown

[1]Glass windows in her coach, still a rare luxury.

To find Almeria here, and here alone.
Where are the nymphs that round you used to crowd,
Of your long courted approbation proud,
Learning from you, how to erect their hair,
And in perfection, all their habit wear,
To place a patch in some peculiar way,   60
That may an unmarked smile to sight betray,
And the vast genius of the sex, display?"
   "Pity me then," she cries, "and learn the fate
That makes me porter to a temple gate;
Ardelia came to Town some weeks ago,
Who does on books her rural hours bestow,
And is so rustic in her clothes and mien,
'Tis with her ungenteel but to be seen,
Did not a long acquaintance plead excuse:
Besides, she likes no wit that's now in use,   70
Despises courtly vice, and plainly says,
That sense and nature should be found in plays,
And therefore, none will e'er be brought to see
But those of Dryden, Etherege, or Lee,
And some few authors, old and dull to me.[2]
To her I did engage my coach and day,
And here must wait, while she within does pray.
Ere twelve was struck, she calls me from my bed,
Nor once observes how well my toilet's spread;
Then, drinks the fragrant tea contented up,   80
Without a compliment upon the cup,
Though to the ships for the first choice I steered,
Through such a storm, as the stout bargemen feared;
Lest that a praise, which I have long engrossed,
Of the best china equipage, be lost.[3]
Of fashions now and colors I discoursed,
Detected shops that would expose the worst,
What silks, what lace, what ribbons she must have,
And by my own, an ample pattern gave;
To which, she cold and unconcerned replied,   90
I deal with one that does all these provide,
Having of other cares, enough beside;

---

[2]John Dryden, George Etherege, and Nathaniel Lee were major writers of Restoration drama, a form out of fashion when this poem was written (1690s).
[3]It was fashionable to collect fine imported china.

And in a cheap or an ill chosen gown,
Can value blood that's nobler than my own,
And therefore hope, myself not to be weighed
By gold or silver on my garments laid;
Or that my wit or judgment should be read
In an uncommon color on my head."
  "Stupid! and dull!" the shrugging zany cries;
When, service ended, me he moving spies,   *100*
Hastes to conduct me out, and in my ear
Drops some vile praise, too low for her to hear;
Which to avoid, more than the begging throng,
I reach the coach, that swiftly rolls along,
Lest to Hyde Park[4] we should too late be brought,
And lose ere night, an hour of finding fault.
Arrived, she cries—
             "That awkward creature see,
A fortune born, and would a beauty be
Could others but believe as fast as she."
Round me I look, some monster to descry,   *110*
Whose wealthy acres must a title buy,
Support my Lord, and be, since his have failed,
With the high shoulder, on his race entailed;
When to my sight, a lovely face appears,
Perfect in everything, but growing years;
This I defend, to do my judgment right,
"Can you dispraise a skin so smooth, so white,
That blush, which o'er such well turned cheeks does rise,
That look of youth, and those enlivened eyes?"
She soon replies—   *120*
             "That skin, which you admire,
Is shrunk and sickly, could you view it nigher.
The crimson lining and uncertain light
Reflects that blush and paints her to the sight.
Trust me, the look, which you commend, betrays
A want of sense more than the want of days,
And those wild eyes, that round the circle stray,
Seem as her wits had but mistook their way."
As I did mine, I to myself repeat,
When by this envious side I took my seat:

[4]Fashionable people drove their coaches around a circular drive in Hyde Park ("the circle," line 126; "the ring," lines 167, 211) to see and be seen.

Oh! for my groves, my country walks, and bowers,   *130*
Trees blast not trees, nor flowers envenom flowers,
As beauty here, all beauty's praise devours.
But noble Piso[5] passes—
          "He's a wit.
As some," she says, "would have it, though as yet
No line he in a lady's fan has writ.
Ne'er on their dress, in verse soft things would say,
Or with loud clamor overpowered a play,
And right or wrong, prevented the third day;[6]
To read in public places is not known,
Or in his chariot, here appears alone;   *140*
Bestows no hasty praise on all that's new.
When first this coach came out to public view,
Met in a visit, he presents his hand
And takes me out, I make a willful stand,
Expecting, sure, this would applause invite,
And often turned that way, to guide his sight;
Till finding him wrapped in a silent thought,
I asked, if that the painter well had wrought,
Who then replied, he has in the fable erred,
Covering Adonis with a monstrous beard;   *150*
Made Hercules (who by his club is shown)
A gentler fop than any of the Town,
Whilst Venus from a bog is rising seen,
And eyes asquint are given to beauty's queen.
I had no patience, longer to attend,
And know 'tis want of wit, to discommend."
  Must Piso, then, be judged by such as these!
Piso, who from the Latin, Virgil frees,
Who loosed the bands which old Silenus bound,
And made our Albion rocks repeat the mystic sound,   *160*
"Whilst all he sung was present to our eyes
And as he raised his verse, the poplars seem'd to rise"?
Scarce could I in my breast my thoughts contain,

---

[5]Piso is Wentworth Dillon, Earl of Roscommon, known chiefly for his "Essay on Translated Verse" (1684); he was a personal friend of the Finches, and Anne would also have approved the unusually pure morality of his work. She refers particularly to his translation of Virgil's Sixth Eclogue, 'Silenus," in which two shepherds tie up Silenus to force him to sing for them. Lines 161–62 come, slightly altered, from this translation.
[6]Because the playwright was paid by the net profits of the third night his play was performed, to prevent its running this long would deprive him of pay for his work.

Or for this folly hide my just disdain.
"When see," she says, "observe my best of friends,"
And through the window half her length extends,
Exalts her voice, that all the ring may hear;
How fulsomely she oft repeats "my dear,"
Lets fall some doubtful words, that we may know
There still a secret is, betwixt them two,   *170*
And makes a sign, the small white hand to show.
When, Fate be praised, the coachman slacks the reins,
And o'er my lap, no longer now she leans,
But how her choice I like, does soon enquire?
   "Can I dislike," I cry, "what all admire,
Discreet, and witty, civil and refined,
Nor in her person fairer than her mind,
Is young Alinda, if report be just;
For half the character, my eyes I trust.
What changed, Almeria, on a sudden cold,   *180*
As if I of your friend some tale had told?"
"No," she replies, "but when I hear her praise,
A secret failing does my pity raise,
Damon she loves, and 'tis my daily care
To keep the passion from the public ear,"
I ask, amazed, if this she has revealed.
"No, but 'tis true," she cries, "though much concealed;
I have observed it long, nor would betray
But to yourself, what now with grief I say,
Who this, to none, but confidants must break,   *190*
Nor they to others, but in whispers, speak;
I am her friend and must consult her fame."
More was she saying, when fresh objects came,
"Now what's that thing," she cries, "Ardelia, guess?"
"A woman sure."—
                         "Ay, and a poetess,
They say she writes, and 'tis a common jest."
"Then sure sh' has publicly the skill professed,"
I soon reply, "or makes that gift her pride,
And all the word, but scribblers, does deride;
Sets out lampoons, where only spite is seen,   *200*
Not filled with female wit, but female spleen.[7]

---

[7]Here, "spleen" means ill-nature, spite. (Contrast its meaning in "The Spleen" and "An Apology for My Fearful Temper.")

Her flourished name does o'er a song expose,
Which through all ranks, down to the carman, goes.
Or poetry is on her picture found,
In which she sits, with painted laurel crowned.
If no such flies, no vanity defile
The Heliconian balm, the sacred oil,
Why should we from that pleasing art be tied,
Or like State prisoners, pen and ink denied?
But see, the Sun his chariot home has driven   210
From the vast shining ring of spacious Heaven,
Nor after him celestial beauties stay,
But crowd with sparkling wheels the milky way.
Shall we not then, the great example take
And ours below, with equal speed forsake?
When to your favors, adding this one more,
You'll stop, and leave me thankful, at my door."
"How! ere you've in the drawing-room[8] appeared,
And all the follies there beheld and heard.
Since you've been absent, such intrigues are grown;   220
Such new coquets and fops are to be shown,
Without their sight you must not leave the Town."
"Excuse me," I reply, "my eyes ne'er feast
Upon a fool, though ne'er so nicely dressed.
Nor is it music to my burthened ear
The unripe pratings of our sex to hear,
A noisy girl, who has at fifteen talked more
Than grandmother or mother heretofore,
In all the cautious, prudent years they bore."
"Statesmen there are," she cries, "whom I can show,   230
That bear the kingdom's cares, on a bent brow;
Who take the weight of politics by grains,
And to the least, know what each skull contains,
Who's to be coached, who talked to when abroad,
Who but the smile must have, and who the nod;
And when this is the utmost of their skill,
'Tis not much wonder, if affairs go ill.
Then for the Churchmen—"
                    "Hold, my lodging's here."
Nor can I longer a reproof forbear
When sacred things nor persons she would spare.   240

[8]Fashionable people regularly gathered at the drawing-room, a public reception at Court.

We parted thus, the night in peace I spent,
And the next day, with haste and pleasure went
To the best seat of famed and fertile Kent.[9]
Where let me live from all detraction free
Till thus the world is criticized by me; -
Till friend, and foe, I treat with such despite,
May I no scorn, the worst of ills, excite.

Friendship Between Ephelia and Ardelia

Eph. What *friendship* is, ARDELIA show.
Ard. 'Tis to love, as I love you.
Eph. This account, so short (though kind)
        Suits not my enquiring mind.
        Therefore farther now repeat;
        What is *friendship* when complete?
Ard. 'Tis to share all joy and grief;
        'Tis to lend all due relief
        From the tongue, the heart, the hand;
        'Tis to mortgage house and land;
        For a friend be sold a slave;
        'Tis to die upon a grave,
        If a friend therein do lie.
Eph. This indeed, though carried high,
        This, though more than e'er was done
        Underneath the rolling sun,
        This has all been said before.
        Can ARDELIA say no more?
Ard. Words indeed no more can show:
        But 'tis to love, as I love you.

---

[9]Eastwell Park in Kent, seat of the Earls of Winchilsea. Anne was grateful to the current Earl, Heneage's nephew, for making them welcome there.

The Bird and the Arras

By near resemblance see that bird betrayed
Who takes the well wrought arras for a shade,
There hopes to perch and with a cheerful tune
O'er-pass the scorchings of the sultry noon.
But soon repulsed by the obdurate scene
How swift she turns, but turns alas in vain.
That piece a grove, this shows an ambient sky,
Where imitated fowl their pinions ply,
Seeming to mount in flight and aiming still more high.
All she outstrips, and with a moment's pride
Their understation[1] silent does deride,
Till the dashed ceiling strikes her to the ground,
No intercepting shrub to break the fall is found;
Recovering breath the window next she gains,
Nor fears a stop from the transparent panes.

But we digress and leave th' imprisoned wretch,
Now sinking low, now on a loftier stretch,
Fluttering in endless circles of dismay
Till some kind hand directs the certain way,
Which through the casement an escape affords,
And leads to ample space, the only Heaven of birds.

The Circuit of Apollo[1]

Apollo as lately a circuit he made
Through the lands of the Muses, when Kent he surveyed,
And saw there that poets were not very common,
But most that pretended to verse were the women,
Resolved to encourage the few that he found,
And she that writ best, with a wreath should be crowned.

[1]Lower position.
[1]Finch puns on the (apparent) circuit of the sun through the sky every day and the circuit of a judge as he moves through his district to preside over trials. Apollo, god of the sun and of poetry, has come to judge which poet is best, who deserves the bays or laurel wreath.

A summons sent out, was obeyed but by four,
When Phoebus, afflicted to meet with no more,
And standing where, sadly, he now might descry,
From the banks of the Stour the desolate Wye,   10
He lamented for Behn o'er that place of her birth,[2]
And said amongst Femens[3] was not on the earth
Her superior in fancy, in language, or wit,
Yet owned that a little too loosely she writ;
Since the art of the Muse is to stir up soft thoughts,
Yet to make all hearts beat without blushes or faults.
But now to proceed, and their merits to know,
Before he on any, the bays would bestow,
He ordered them each, in their several[4] way,
To show him their papers, to sing, or to say,   20
Whate'er they thought best, their pretensions might prove,
When Alinda began, with a song upon love.
So easy the verse, yet composed with such art,
That not one expression fell short of the heart;
Apollo himself did their influence obey,
He catched up his lyre, and a part he would play,
Declaring, no harmony else could be found,
Fit to wait upon[5] words of so moving a sound.
The wreath he reached out, to have placed on her head,
If Laura not quickly a paper had read,   30
Wherein she Orinda[6] has praised so high,
He owned it had reached him, while yet in the sky,
That he thought with himself, when it first struck his ear,
Whoe'er could write that, ought the laurel to wear.
Betwixt them he stood, in a musing suspense,
Till Valeria withdrew him a little from thence,
And told him, as soon as she'd got him aside,
Her works, by no other but him should be tried;
Which so often he read, and with still new delight,
That judgment 'twas thought would not pass till 'twas night; 40
Yet at length he restored them, but told her withal,
If she kept it still close, he'd the talent[7] recall.

[2]The Stour is a river in Kent, where Finch lived. Finch added a note that Behn was born in "Wye, a little market town (now much decay'd) in Kent. Actually, Behn's birthplace is not known.
[2]Women.
[4]Individual.
[5]Accompany.
[6]Katherine Philips. Alinda, Laura, and Valeria (line 36) have not been identified.
[7]See Jesus' parable of using and hiding talents, Matthew 25:14–30.

Ardelia came last, as expecting least praise,
Who writ for her pleasure and not for the bays,
But yet, as occasion or fancy should sway,
Would sometimes endeavor to pass a dull day
In composing a song or a scene of a play.
Not seeking for fame, which so little does last
That ere we can taste it, the pleasure is past.
But Apollo replied, though so careless she seemed,   50
Yet the bays, if her share, would be highly esteemed.

And now, he was going to make an oration,
Had thrown by one lock, with a delicate fashion,
Upon the left foot, most genteelly did stand.
Had drawn back the other, and waved his white hand,
When calling to mind, how the prize, although given
By Paris to her who was fairest in Heaven,
Had pulled on the rash, inconsiderate boy
The fall of his house, with the ruin of Troy,[8]
Since in wit, or in beauty, it never was heard,   60
One female could yield t' have another preferred,
He changed his design, and divided his praise,
And said that they all had a right to the bays,
And that t'were injustice, one brow to adorn
With a wreath, which so fitly by each might be worn.
Then smiled to himself, and applauded his art,
Who thus nicely has acted so subtle a part,
Four women to wheedle, but found 'em too many,
For who would please all, can never please any.
In vain then, he thought it, there longer to stay,   70
But told them, he now must go drive on the day,
Yet the case to Parnassus should soon be referred,
And there in a council of Muses be heard,
Who of their own sex, best the title might try,
Since no man upon earth, nor himself in the sky,
Would be so imprudent, so dull, or so blind,
To lose three parts in four from amongst womankind.

---

[8]In Greek legend, Paris, a Trojan prince, was asked by three goddesses to judge who was most beautiful. He chose Aphrodite, and the other two, Hera and Athena, were so incensed that they helped the Greeks to destroy his city, Troy.

Clarinda's Indifference at Parting with Her Beauty

Now, age came on, and all the dismal train
That fright the vicious and afflict the vain.
Departing beauty, now Clarinda spies
Pale in her cheeks, and dying in her eyes;
That youthful air that wanders o'er the face,
That undescribed, that unresisted grace,
Those morning beams, that strongly warm, and shine,
Which men that feel and see, can ne'er define,
Now, on the wings of restless time, were fled,
And evening shades began to rise, and spread,   10
When thus resolved and ready soon to part,
Slighting the short reprieves of proffered art
She spake—
And what, vain beauty, didst thou e'er achieve
When at thy height, that I thy fall should grieve,
When did'st thou e'er successfully pursue?
When did'st thou e'er th' appointed foe subdue?
'Tis vain of numbers or of strength to boast,
In an undisciplined, unguided host,
And love, that did thy mighty hopes deride,   20
Would pay no sacrifice, but to thy pride.
When did'st thou e'er a pleasing rule obtain,
A glorious empire's but a glorious pain.
Thou art indeed but vanity's chief source,
But foil to wit, to want of wit a curse,
For often, by the gaudy signs descried,
A fool, which unobserved, had been untried;
And when thou dost such empty things adorn,
'Tis but to make them more the public scorn,
I know thee well, but weak thy reign would be   30
Did none adore or prize thee more than me.
I see indeed, thy certain ruin near,
But can't afford one parting sigh or tear,
Nor rail at time, nor quarrel with my glass,
But unconcerned, can let thy glories pass.

The Unequal Fetters

Could we stop the time that's flying
  Or recall it when 'tis past,
Put far off the day of dying
  Or make youth for ever last,
To love would then be worth our cost.

But since we must lose those graces
  Which at first your hearts have won
And you seek for in new faces
  When our spring of life is done,
It would but urge our ruin on.

Free as Nature's first intention
  Was to make us, I'll be found,
Nor by subtle man's invention
  Yield to be in fetters bound
By one that walks a freer round.

Marriage does but slightly tie men
  Whilst close prisoners we remain,
They the larger slaves of Hymen
  Still are begging love again
At the full length of all their chain.

The Young Rat and His Dam,
the Cock and the Cat

No cautions of a matron, old and sage,
Young Rattlehead to prudence could engage;
But forth the offspring of her bed would go,
Nor reason gave, but that he *would* do so.
Much counsel was, at parting, thrown away,
Even all that Mother-Rat to Son could say;
Who followed him with utmost reach of sight,
Then, lost in tears and in abandoned plight,
Turned to her mournful cell, and bid the world Good Night.

But *Fortune*, kinder than her boding thought,   10
In little time the vagrant homewards brought,
Raised in his mind, and mended in his dress,
Who the *bel-air*[1] did every way confess,
Had learnt to flour his wig, nor brushed away
The falling meal, that on his shoulders lay;
And from a nutshell, wimbled by a worm,
Took snuff, and could the government reform.
The mother, weeping from maternal love,
To see him thus prodigiously improve,
Expected mighty changes too, within,   20
And wisdom to avoid the cat and gin.
"Whom did you chiefly note, Sweetheart," quoth she,
"Of all the strangers you abroad did see?
Who graced you most, or did your fancy take?"
The younger rat then cursed a noisy rake,
That barred the best acquaintance he could make,
And feared him so, he trembled every part;
Nor to describe him, scarce could have the heart.
"High on his feet," quoth he, "himself he bore,
And terribly, in his own language, swore;   30
A feathered arm came out from either side,
Which loud he clapped, and combatants defied,
And to each leg a bayonet was tied:
And certainly his head with wounds was sore;
For that, and both his cheeks, a sanguine color wore.
Near him there lay the creature I admired,
And for a friend by sympathy desired:
His make like ours, as far as tail and feet,
With coat of fur in parallel do meet;
Yet seeming of a more exalted race,   40
Though humble meekness beautified his face:
A purring sound composed his gentle mind,
Whilst frequent slumbers did his eyelids bind;
Whose soft, contracted paw lay calmly still,
As if unused to prejudice or kill.
I paused a while, to meditate a speech,
And now was stepping just within his reach,
When that rude clown began his hectoring cry,
And made me for my life, and from th' attempt to fly."

[1]Fashionable appearance.

"Indeed 'twas time," the shivering beldam said,   *50*
"To scour the plain, and be of life afraid.
Thou base, degenerate seed of injured rats,
Thou veriest fool," she cried, "of all my brats;
Would'st thou have shaken hands with hostile cats,
And dost not yet thine own, and country's foe,
At this expense of time and travel know?
Alas! that swearing, staring, bullying thing,
That tore his throat and blustered with his wing,
Was but some paltry, dunghill, craven cock,
Who serves the early household for a clock.   *60*
And we his oats and barley often steal,
Nor fear he should revenge the pilfered meal:
Whilst that demure and seeming harmless puss
Herself, and mewing chits regales with us.
If then, of useful sense thou'st gained no more
Than ere thou'dst passed the threshold of my door,
Be here, my son, content to dress and dine,
Steeping the list of beauties in thy wine,
And neighboring vermin with false gloss outshine.
    Amongst mankind a thousand *fops* we see,   *70*
Who in their rambles learn no more than thee;
Cross o'er the Alps and make the Tour of France[2]
To learn a paltry song or antic dance;
Bringing their noddles and valises packed
With mysteries, from shops and tailors wrecked:
But what may prejudice their native land,
Whose troops are raising, or whose fleet is manned,
Ne'er moves their thoughts, nor do they understand.
Thou, my dear Rattlehead, and such as these,
Might keep at home, and brood on sloth and ease;   *80*
Whilst others, more adapted to the age,
May vigorously in warlike feats engage,
And live on foreign spoils, or dying thin the stage.

[2] A tour of Europe, especially France, put the finishing touch on a gentleman's education.

The Spleen[1]

A Pindaric Poem

What art thou, *SPLEEN*, which every thing dost ape?
  Thou Proteus to abused mankind,
  Who never yet thy real cause could find,
Or fix thee to remain in one continued shape.
  Still varying thy perplexing form,
  Now a Dead Sea thou'lt represent,
  A calm of stupid discontent,
Then, dashing on the rocks wilt rage into a storm.
  Trembling sometimes thou dost appear,
  Dissolved into a panic fear;   10
  On sleep intruding dost thy shadows spread,
  Thy gloomy terrors round the silent bed,
And crowd with boding dreams the melancholy head;
  Or, when the midnight hour is told,
  And drooping lids thou still dost waking hold,
  Thy fond delusions cheat the eyes,
  Before them antic Specters dance,
Unusual fires their pointed heads advance,
  And airy phantoms rise.
  Such was the monstrous *vision* seen,   20
When Brutus (now beneath his cares oppressed,
And all Rome's fortunes rolling in his breast,
  Before Philippi's latest field,
Before his fate did to Octavius lead)
  Was vanquished by the *spleen*.[2]

  Falsely, the mortal part we blame
  Of our depressed and ponderous frame,
  Which, till the first degrading sin
  Let thee, its dull attendant, in,

[1]Spleen, also called melancholy or vapors (line 53), is close to what is today called depression and, like depression, could be a normal mood or a neurotic or psychotic condition. It was a fashionable disease at the time and hence was sometimes affected (lines 65ff). Finch's references to rage (line 8) and causeless laughter (line 52) reflect the contemporary failure to differentiate between depressive and manic-depressive disorders.
[2]Finch attributes to spleen Brutus's strangely self-defeating conduct at his fatal battle at Philippi, referring particularly to his vision of the ghost of Julius Caesar, as represented in Shakespeare's *Julius Caesar* IV, iii.

Still with the other did comply,   30
Nor clogged the active soul, disposed to fly,
And range the mansions of its native sky.[3]
    Nor, whilst in his own Heaven he dwelt,
    Whilst man his Paradise possessed,
His fertile garden in the fragrant East,
    And all united odors smelt,
    No armed sweets, until thy reign,
    Could shock the sense, or in the face
    A flushed, unhandsome color place.
Now the Jonquil o'ercomes the feeble brain;   40
We faint beneath the aromatic pain,
Till some offensive scent thy powers appease,
And pleasure we resign for short and nauseous ease.[4]

    In every one thou dost possess,
    New are thy motions and thy dress:
    Now in some grove a listening friend
    Thy false suggestions must attend,
Thy whispered griefs, thy fancied sorrows hear,
Breathed in a sigh, and witnessed by a tear;
    Whilst in the light and vulgar crowd,   50
    Thy slaves, more clamorous and loud,
By laughters unprovoked, thy influence to confess.
In the imperious *wife* thou vapors art,
    Which from o'erheated passions rise
    In clouds to the attractive brain,
    Until descending thence again,
    Through the o'ercast and showering eyes,
    Upon her husband's softened heart,
    He the disputed point must yield,
Something resign of the contested field;   60
Till lordly *man*, born to imperial sway,
Compounds for peace, to make that right away,
And *woman*, armed with *spleen*, does servilely obey.

    The *fool*, to imitate the wits,
    Complains of thy pretended fits,

---

[3]Finch follows a tradition that mind and body were in perfect harmony before the Fall ("the first degrading sin"); thus spleen, which was attributed to physical causes, was not part of God's original plan.
    [4]Unpleasant smells, such as that of burning feathers, were used to allay hysteric fits, one of the symptoms of the spleen.

And dullness, born with him, would lay
Upon thy accidental sway;
Because, sometimes, thou dost presume
Into the ablest heads to come:
That, often, men of thoughts refined,   70
Impatient of unequal sense,
Such slow returns, where they so much dispense,
Retiring from the crowd, are to thy shades inclined.
O'er me alas! thou dost too much prevail:
I feel thy force, whilst I against thee rail;
I feel my verse decay, and my cramped numbers fail.
Through thy black jaundice I all objects see,
As dark and terrible as thee,
My lines decried, and my employment thought
An useless folly, or presumptuous fault: 80
Whilst in the Muses' paths I stray,
Whilst in their groves, and by their secret springs,
My hand delights to trace unusual things,
And deviates from the known and common way;
Nor will in fading silks compose
Faintly th' inimitable rose,
Fill up an ill-drawn bird, or paint on glass
The Sovereign's blurred and undistinguished face,
The threatening Angel, and the speaking ass.[5]

Patron thou art to every gross abuse,   90
The sullen *husband's* feigned excuse,
When the ill humor with his wife he spends,
And bears recruited wit and spirits to his friends.
The Son of Bacchus pleads thy power,
As to the glass he still repairs,
Pretends but to remove thy cares,
Snatch from thy shades one gay and smiling hour,
And drown thy kingdom in a purple shower.
When the coquet, whom every fool admires,
Would in variety be fair,   100
And, changing hastily the scene
From light, impertinent, and vain,
Assumes a soft, a melancholy air,

[5]Ladies were supposed to occupy themselves (and keep away the spleen) with useless
handicrafts such as embroidery and painting on glass, which might portray the King or
Biblical characters like the prophet Balaam and his ass (Numbers 22:22–30).

And of her eyes rebates the wandering fires,
The careless posture and the head reclined,
  The thoughtful and composed face,
Proclaiming the withdrawn, the absent mind,
Allows the fop more liberty to gaze,
Who gently for the tender cause enquires;
The cause, indeed, is a defect in sense,   *110*
Yet is the *spleen* alleged, and still the dull pretense.
  But these are thy fantastic harms,
  The tricks of thy pernicious stage,
  Which do the weaker sort engage;
Worse are the dire effects of thy more powerful charms.
  By thee *Religion*, all we know,
  That should enlighten here below,
  Is veiled in darkness, and perplexed
With anxious doubts, with endless scruples vexed,
And some restraint implied from each perverted text.   *120*
  Whilst *Touch not, Taste not* what is freely given,
Is but thy niggard voice, disgracing bounteous Heaven.
  From speech restrained, by thy deceits abused,
  To deserts banished or in cells reclused,
  Mistaken votaries to the powers divine,
  Whilst they a purer sacrifice design,
Do but the *spleen* obey, and worship at thy shrine.[6]
  In vain to chase thee every art we try,
  In vain all remedies apply,
  In vain the Indian leaf infuse,   *130*
  Or the parched Eastern berry bruise;
Some pass, in vain, those bounds, and nobler liquors use.
  Now *harmony*, in vain, we bring,
  Inspire the flute and touch the string.
  From harmony no help is had;
Music but soothes thee, if too sweetly sad,
And if too light, but turns thee gaily mad.[7]
  Though the physician's greatest gains,
  Although his growing wealth he sees
  Daily increased by ladies' fees,   *140*
  Yet dost thou baffle all his studious pains.

[6]Religious melancholia, leading to overscrupulosity and needless asceticism, was a recognized symptom of the spleen.
[7]Tea (line 130), coffee (line 131), alcohol (line 132), and music were often tried as remedies for the spleen.

Not skilful Lower thy source could find,
Or through the well-dissected body trace
The secret, the mysterious ways,
By which thou dost surprise, and prey upon the mind.
Though in the search, too deep for human thought,
With unsuccessful toil he wrought,
Till thinking thee to've catched, himself by thee was caught,
Retained thy prisoner, thy acknowledged slave.
And sunk beneath thy chain to a lamented grave.[8]   *150*

To the Nightingale

Exert thy voice, sweet harbinger of spring!
This moment is thy time to sing,
This moment I attend to praise,
And set my numbers to thy lays.
Free as thine shall be my song;
As thy music, short, or long.
Poets, wild as thee, were born,
Pleasing best when unconfined,
When to please is least designed,
Soothing but their cares to rest;   *10*
Cares do still their thoughts molest,
And still th' unhappy poet's breast,
Like thine, when best he sings, is placed against a thorn.
She begins, Let all be still!
Muse, thy promise now fulfill!
Sweet, oh! sweet, still sweeter yet
Can thy words such accents fit,
Canst thou syllables refine,
Melt a sense that shall retain
Still some spirit of the brain,   *20*
Till with sounds like these it join.
'Twill not be! then change thy note;

---

[8]Dr. Richard Lower, an eminent medical researcher, yielded to depression and committed
suicide in 1691.

Let division[1] shake thy throat.
Hark! Division now she tries;
Yet as far the Muse outflies.
  Cease then, prithee, cease thy tune;
  Trifler, wilt thou sing till *June?*
Till thy business all lies waste,
And the time of building's past!
  Thus we poets that have speech,   *30*
Unlike what thy forests teach,
  If a fluent vein be shown
  That's transcendent to our own,
Criticize, reform, or preach,
Or censure what we cannot reach.

A Nocturnal Reverie

In such a *Night*, when every louder wind
Is to its distant cavern safe confined;
And only gentle Zephyr fans his wings,
And lonely Philomel, still waking, sings;
Or from some tree, famed for the *owl's* delight,
She, hollowing clear, directs the wanderer right:
In such a *night*, when passing clouds give place,
Or thinly veil the heavens' mysterious face;
When in some river, overhung with green,
The waving moon and trembling leaves are seen; *10*
When freshened grass now bears itself upright,
And makes cool banks to pleasing rest invite,
Whence springs the *woodbind*, and the *bramble-rose*,
And where the sleepy *cowslip* sheltered grows;
Whilst now a paler hue the *foxglove* takes,
Yet checkers still with red the dusky brakes,
When scattered *glow-worms*, but in twilight fine,
Show trivial beauties watch their hour to shine;
Whilst Salisbury[1] stands the test of every light,

---

[1]Florid variation on a melody, featuring runs and trills.
[1]Probably Anne Tufton, Countess of Salisbury, daughter of one of Finch's close friends.

In perfect charms and perfect virtue bright: 20
When odors, which declined repelling day,
Through temperate air uninterrupted stray;
When darkened groves their softest shadows wear,
And falling waters we distinctly hear;
When through the gloom more venerable shows
Some ancient fabric, awful in repose,
While sunburnt hills their swarthy looks conceal,
And swelling haycocks thicken up the vale:
When the loosed *horse* now, as his pasture leads,
Comes slowly grazing through th' adjoining meads,   30
Whose stealing pace and lengthened shade we fear,
Till torn up forage in his teeth we hear:
When nibbling *sheep* at large pursue their food,
And unmolested kine rechew the cud;
When *curlews* cry beneath the village walls,
And to her struggling brood the *partridge* calls;
Their shortlived jubilee the creatures keep,
Which but endures, whilst tyrant *man* does sleep;
When a sedate content the spirit feels,
And no fierce light disturbs, whilst it reveals;   40
But silent musings urge the mind to seek
Something, too high for syllables to speak;
Till the free soul to a composedness charmed,
Finding the elements of rage disarmed,
O'er all below a solemn quiet grown,
Joys in th' inferior world, and thinks it like her own:
In such a *night* let me abroad remain,
Till morning breaks, and all's confused again;
Our cares, our toils, our clamors are renewed,
Or pleasures, seldom reached, again pursued.   50

An Apology for My Fearful Temper, in a Letter in Burlesque upon the Firing of My Chimney at Wye College,[1] March 25, 1702

'Tis true of courage I'm no mistress,
No Boadicea nor Thalestris,
Nor shall I e'er be famed hereafter
For such a Soul as Cato's daughter;
Nor active valor nor enduring,
Nor leading troops nor forts securing,
Like Teckley's wife or Pucelle valiant,[2]
Will e'er be reckoned for my talent,
Who all things fear whilst day is shining
And my own shadow light declining,   *10*
And from the Spleen's prolific fountain
Can of a molehill make a mountain;
And if a coach that was invented
Since Bess on palfrey rode contented,
Threatens to tumble topsy-turvy,
With screeches loud and faces scurvy,
I break discourse whilst some are laughing,
Some fall to cheer me, some to chaffing,
As secretly the driver curses
And whips my fault upon the horses.   *20*
These and ten thousand are the errors
Arising from tumultuous terrors,
Yet can't I understand the merit
In females of a daring spirit,
Since to them never was imparted
A manly strength, though manly hearted.
Nor need that sex be self-defending,
Who charm the most when most depending,
And by sweet plaints and soft distresses

---

[1]The Finches lived for some time at Wye College.
[2]Boadicea was a heroic British queen who died fighting the Romans; Thalestris was a legendary queen of the Amazons; Portia, daughter of the Stoic Cato and wife of the Stoic Brutus, was noted for her fortitude; the warrior Joan of Arc was called La Pucelle (the virgin).

First gain assistance, then addresses,   *30*
As our fourth Edward (beauty suing)
From but relieving fell to wooing,
Who by heroic speech or ranting
Had ne'er been melted to gallanting.[3]
Nor had th' Egyptian Queen defying
Drawn off that fleet she led by flying,
Whilst Caesar and his ship's crew holloed
To see how Tony rowed and followed.[4]
Oh Actium, triumph of the ladies,
And plea for her who most afraid is.   *40*
Then let my conduct work no wonder
When Fame, who cleaves the air asunder
And everything in time discovers,[5]
Nor counsel keeps for kings or lovers,
Yet stoops when tired with states and battles
To gossips' chats and idler tattles,
When she I say has given no knowledge
Of what has happened at Wye College,
Think it not strange to save my person
I gave the family diversion.   *50*
'Twas at an hour when most were sleeping,
Some chimneys clean, some wanted sweeping,
Mine through good fires maintained this winter
(Of which no FINCH was e'er a stinter)
Poured down such flakes not Etna bigger
Throws up as did my fancy figure,
Nor does a cannon rammed with powder
To others seem to bellow louder.
All that I thought or spoke or acted
Can't in a letter be compacted,   *60*
Nor how I threatened those with burning
Who thoughtless on their beds were turning,
As Shakespeare says they served old Priam
When that the Greeks were got too nigh 'em.[6]

[3]When Lady Elizabeth Grey appealed to King Edward IV to restore her dead husband's lands, she charmed the king so effectively that he married her. See Shakespeare's *Henry VI Part 3*, III, ii.
[4]The Egyptian Queen Cleopatra insisted on leading her navy into battle at Actium, but panicked and fled; her lover, Mark Antony, ingloriously followed her. See Shakespeare's *Antony and Cleopatra* III, vii–viii.
[5]Reveals.
[6]See Shakespeare's *Henry IV Part 2*, I, i, 70–73. Hecuba (line 66) was Priam's aged wife.

And such th'effect, in spite of weather,
Our Hecubas all rose together,
I at their head, half clothed and shaking,
Was instantly the house forsaking,
And told them 'twas no time for talking,
But who'd be safe had best be walking.   70
This hasty counsel and conclusion
Seemed harsh to those who had no shoes on
And saw no flames and heard no clatter
But as I had rehearsed the matter
And wildly talked of fire and water,
For sooner than 'thas took to tell it,
Right applications did repel it.
And now my fear our mirth creating,
Affords still subject for repeating,
Whilst some deplore th'unusual folly,   80
Some (kinder) call it melancholy,
Though certainly the spirits sinking
Comes not from want of wit or thinking,
Since Rochester[7] all dangers hated
And left to those were harder pated.

A Supplication for the Joys of Heaven

To the superior world, to solemn peace,
To regions where delights shall never cease,
To living springs and to celestial shade
For change of pleasure not protection made,
To blissful harmony's o'erflowing source,
Which strings or stops can neither bind or force,
But wafting air forever bears along,
Perpetual motion with perpetual song;
On which the Blest in symphonies ascend
And towards the Throne with vocal ardors bend,   10
To radial light o'erspreading boundless space,
To the safe goal of our well ended race,

---

[7]The poet John Wilmot, Earl of Rochester, was lampooned for showing cowardice in a
brawl and a duel (though he is known to have fought bravely in naval combat).

To shelter where the weary shall have rest,
And where the wicked never shall molest,
To that Jerusalem which ours below
Did but in type and faint resemblance show,
To the first born and ransomed Church above,
To seraphim whose whole composure's love,
To active cherubim whom wings surround,
Not made to rest though on immortal ground,   20
But still suspended wait with flaming joy
In swift commands their vigor to employ,
Ambrosial dews distilling from their plumes
Scattering where'er they pass innate perfumes,
To angels of innumerable sorts
Subordinate in the ethereal courts,
To men refined from every gross allay,
Who taught the flesh the spirit to obey,
And keeping late futurity in view,
Do now possess what long they did pursue,   30
To Jesus, founder of the Christian race
And kind dispenser of the Gospel grace,
Bring me my God in my accomplished time,
From weakness freed and from degrading crime,
Fast by the Tree of Life be my retreat,
Whose leaves are medicine and whose fruit is meat.
Healed by the first and by the last renewed,
With all perfections be my soul endued,
My form that has the earthly figure borne
Take the celestial in its glorious turn,   40
My temper frail and subject to dismay
Be steadfast there, spiritualized and gay,
My low poetic tendency be raised
Till the bestower worthily is praised,
Till Dryden's numbers for Cecilia's feast,[1]
Which soothe, depress, inflame, and shake the breast,
Vary the passions with each varying line,
Allowed below all others to outshine,
Shall yield to those above, shall yield to mine
In sound, in sense, in emphasis Divine.   50
Stupendous are the heights to which they rise

---

[1]John Dryden's "Alexander's Feast . . . An Ode in Honor of St. Cecilia's Day" skillfully uses metrical effects to evoke a series of contrasting passions.

Whose anthems match the music of the skies,
Whilst that which art we call when studied here
Is nature there in its sublimest sphere,
And the pathetic[2] now so hard to find
Flows from the grateful transports of the mind.
With poets who supernal voices raise
And here begin their never ending lays,
With those who to the brethren of their Lord
In all distress a warm relief afford,   60
With the heroic spirits of the brave
Who durst be true when threatened with the grave,
And when from evil in triumphant sway
Who e'er departed made himself a prey
To sanguine perils, to penurious care,
To scanty clothing and precarious fare,
To lingering solitude, exhausting thoughts,
Unsuccored losses and imputed faults,[3]
With these let me be joined when Heaven reveals
The judgment which admits of no appeals,   70
And having heard from the deciding throne,
Well have ye suffered, wisely have ye done,
Henceforth the Kingdom of the Blest is yours,
For you unfolds its everlasting doors,
With joyful Alleluias let me hail
The strength that o'er my weakness could prevail,
Upheld me here and raised my feeble clay
To this felicity for which I pray,
Through him whose intercession I implore.
And Heaven once entered, prayer shall be no more;   80
Loud acclamations shall its place supply
And praise, the breath of angels in the sky.

Finished February 6, 1719.

[2]Moving, stirring the emotions.
[3]Those who, like Heneage Finch, refused to swear allegiance to the new sovereigns, William and Mary (usurpers in the Finches' view, representing "evil in triumphant sway"), suffered hardships such as loss of place and income and accusations of disloyalty.

Mary Astell
1666–1731

MARY ASTELL, born into a middle-class family in Newcastle, is thought to have been educated in logic and philosophy by her clergyman uncle. At twenty-two she moved to Chelsea in London, where she remained for the rest of her life, supported apparently by her upper-class friends. In 1694 she published, anonymously, *A Serious Proposal to the Ladies*, in which she deplored the contemporary failure to develop women's minds and proposed a religious-educational institution where women could study, converse, and live together. In 1697 she brought out a second part, outlining a system by which women could train their minds. The *Proposal* attracted considerable attention, much of it respectful, but met the fate Astell feared: no one was sufficiently persuaded to put its principles into practice. The religious retirement reminded people too much of a Roman Catholic convent, and even sympathetic readers thought the dangers of popery outweighed the interests of women. Meanwhile Astell was corresponding on ethics and theology with a clergyman, John Norris; at his instance, this correspondence was published as *Letters Concerning the Love of God* (1695).

In *Some Reflections on Marriage* (1700), which went into several editions, Astell paints a grim picture of what marriage meant for women in the seventeenth and eighteenth centuries, though she does not suggest that the laws of state or church be modified to alleviate conjugal oppression. (She herself avoided it by never marrying.) Apart from her views on women's nature and potential, Astell was highly conservative. She supported the established order in a series of capable, vigorous tracts such as *An Impartial Enquiry into the Causes of Rebellion and Civil War* (1704) and *The Christian Religion as Professed by a Daughter of the Church of England* (1705). Clergymen respected her intellect and valued her contributions in defense of the Church, though one deplored her tendency to be "now and then a little offensive and shocking in her expressions, which I wonder at, because a civil turn of words . . . is what her sex is always mistress of." Astell had many close friendships with women, including Lady Mary Wortley Montagu.

from A Serious Proposal to the Ladies

Let us learn to pride ourselves in something more excellent than the invention of a fashion, and not entertain such a degrading thought of our own *worth*, as to imagine that our souls were given us only for the service of our bodies, and that the best improvement we can make of these, is to attract the eyes of men. We value *them* too much, and *ourselves* too little, if we place any part of our desert in their opinion, and don't think ourselves capable of nobler things than the pitiful conquest of some worthless heart. She who has opportunities of making an interest in Heaven, of obtaining the love and admiration of GOD and angels, is too prodigal of her time, and injurious to her charms, to throw them away on vain insignificant men. She need not make herself so cheap as to descend to court their applauses, for at the greater distance she keeps, and the more she is above them, the more effectually she secures their esteem and wonder. Be so generous then, ladies, as to do nothing unworthy of you; so true to your interest, as not to lessen your empire and depreciate your charms. Let not your thoughts be wholly busied in observing what respect is paid you, but a part of them at least, in studying to deserve it. And after all, remember that goodness is the truest greatness; to be wise for yourselves the greatest wit; and *that* beauty the most desirable which will endure to eternity.

. . . The men perhaps will cry out that I teach you false doctrine, for because by their deductions[1] some amongst us are become very mean and contemptible, they would fain persuade the rest to be as despicable and forlorn as they. We're indeed obliged to them for their management, in endeavoring to make us so, who use all the artifice they can to spoil, and deny us the means of improvement. So that instead of enquiring why all women are not wise and good, we have reason to wonder that there are any so. Were the men as much neglected, and as little care taken to cultivate and improve them, perhaps they would be so far from surpassing those whom they now despise that they themselves would sink into the greatest stupidity and brutality. The preposterous returns that the most of them make to all the

[1] By what they have taken away from us.

care and pains that is bestowed on them, renders this no uncharitable nor improbable conjecture. One would therefore almost
think that the wise disposer of all things, foreseeing how unjustly women are denied opportunities of improvement from
without, has therefore by way of compensation endowed them
with greater propensions to virtue and a natural goodness of
temper *within*, which if duly managed would raise them to the
most eminent pitch of heroic virtue. Hither, ladies, I desire you
would aspire; 'tis a noble and becoming ambition, and to remove
such obstacles as lie in your way is the design of this paper. We
will therefore inquire what it is that stops your flight, that
keeps you groveling here below, like Domitian catching flies
when you should be busied in obtaining empires.[2]

• • •

The incapacity, if there be any, is acquired not natural, and
none of their women's follies are so necessary, but that they
might avoid them if they pleased themselves. Some disadvantages indeed they labor under, and what these are we shall see
by and by and endeavor to surmount; but women need not take
up with mean things, since (if they are not wanting to themselves) they are capable of the best. Neither God nor Nature
have excluded them from being ornaments to their families and
useful in their generation; there is therefore no reason they
should be content to be ciphers in the world, useless at the best,
and in a little time a burden and nuisance to all about them. And
'tis very great pity that they who are so apt to overrate themselves in smaller matters, should, where it most concerns them
to know and stand upon their value, be so insensible of their
own worth. The cause therefore of the defects we labor under is,
if not wholly, yet at least in the first place, to be ascribed to the
mistakes of our education, which like an error in the first con-
coction, spreads its ill influence through all our lives.

The soil is rich and would if well cultivated produce a noble
harvest; if then the unskillful managers not only permit, but
encourage noxious weeds, though we shall suffer by the neglect,
yet they ought not in justice to blame any but themselves, if
they reap the fruit of this their foolish conduct. Women are from

[2]Domitian, a Roman Emperor, "used to spend hours in seclusion every day, doing
nothing but catch flies and stab them" (Suetonius, *Lives of the Caesars*, trans. J. C. Rolfe,
Bk. VIII, paragraph 3).

their very infancy debarred those advantages with the want of
which they are afterwards reproached, and nursed up in those
vices which will hereafter be upbraided to them. So partial are
men as to expect brick where they afford no straw; and so
abundantly civil as to take care we should make good that
obliging epithet of *ignorant*, which out of an excess of good
manners, they are pleased to bestow on us!

· · ·

Thus ignorance and a narrow education lay the foundation of
vice, and imitation and custom rear it up. Custom, that merci-
less torrent that carries all before it, and which indeed can be
stemmed by none but such as have a great deal of prudence and
a rooted virtue. For 'tis but decorous that she who is not
capable of giving better rules, should follow those she sees
before her, lest she only change the instance and retain the
absurdity. 'Twould puzzle a considerate person to account for
all that sin and folly that is in the world (which certainly has
nothing in itself to recommend it) did not custom help to solve
the difficulty. For virtue without question has on all accounts
the preeminence of vice, 'tis abundantly more pleasant in the
act, as well as more advantageous in the *consequences*, as
anyone who will but rightly use her reason, in a serious reflection on herself and the nature of things, may easily perceive, 'Tis
custom, therefore, that tyrant custom, which is the grand motive
to all those irrational choices which we daily see made in the
world, so very contrary to our *present* interest and pleasure, as
well as to our future. We think it an unpardonable mistake not to
do as our neighbors do, and part with our peace and pleasure as
well as our innocence and virtue, merely in compliance with
an unreasonable fashion, and having inured ourselves to folly,
we know not how to quit it; we go on in vice, not because we
find satisfaction in it, but because we are unacquainted with the
joys of virtue.

· · ·

When a poor young lady is taught to value herself on nothing
but her clothes, and to think she's very fine when well accoutered; when she hears say, that 'tis wisdom enough for her to
know how to dress herself, that she may become amiable in his
eyes, to whom it appertains to be knowing and learned; who can
blame her if she lay out her industry and money on such accom-

plishments, and sometimes extends it farther than her misinformer desires she should? When she sees the vain and the gay, making *parade* in the world and attended with the courtship and admiration of the gazing herd, no wonder that her tender eyes are dazzled with the pageantry, and wanting judgment to pass a due estimate on them and their admirers, longs to be such a fine and celebrated thing as they? What though she be sometimes told of another world, she has however a more lively perception of this, and may well think that if her instructors were in earnest when they tell her of *hereafter*, they would not be so busied and concerned about what happens *here*. She is, it may be, taught the principles and duties of religion, but not acquainted with the reasons and grounds of them; being told 'tis enough for her to believe, to examine why and wherefore belongs not to her. And therefore, though her piety may be tall and spreading, yet because it wants foundation and root, the first rude temptation overthrows and blasts it, or perhaps the short-lived gourd decays and withers of its own accord. But why should she be blamed for setting no great value on her soul, whose noblest faculty, her understanding, is rendered useless to her? Or censured for relinquishing a course of life whose prerogatives she was never acquainted with and, though highly reasonable in itself, was put upon the embracing it with as little reason as she now forsakes it? For if her religion itself be taken up as the mode of the country, 'tis no strange thing that she lays it down again in conformity to the fashion. Whereas she whose reason is suffered to display itself, to inquire into the grounds and motives of religion, to make a disquisition[3] of its graces and search out its hidden beauties; who is a Christian out of choice, not in conformity to those among whom she lives; and cleaves to piety because 'tis her wisdom, her interest, her joy, not because she has been accustomed to it; she who is not only eminently and unmovably good, but able to give a reason *why* she is so, is too firm and stable to be moved by the pitiful allurements of sin, too wise and too well bottomed[4] to be undermined and supplanted by the strongest efforts of temptation. Doubtless a truly Christian life requires a clear understanding as well as regular affections, that both together may move the will to a direct choice of good and a steadfast adherence to it. For

---

[3]Diligent investigation.
[4]Firmly established.

though the heart may be honest, it is but by chance that the will is right if the understanding be ignorant and cloudy.

• • •

Now as to the proposal, it is to erect a *Monastery*, or if you will (to avoid giving offense to the scrupulous and injudicious, by names which though innocent in themselves, have been abused by superstitious practices), we will call it a *Religious Retirement*, and such as shall have a double aspect, being not only a retreat from the world for those who desire that advantage, but likewise, an institution and previous discipline, to fit us to do the greatest good in it; such an institution as this (if I do not mightily deceive myself) would be the most probable method to amend the present and improve the future age. For here those who are convinced of the emptiness of earthly enjoyments, who are sick of the vanity of the world and its impertinencies, may find more substantial and satisfying entertainments, and need not be confined to what they justly loathe. Those who are desirous to know and fortify their weak side, first do good to themselves, that hereafter they may be capable of doing more good to others; or for their greater security are willing to avoid *temptation*, may get out of that danger which a continual stay in view of the enemy, and the familiarity and unwearied application of the temptation may expose them to; and gain an opportunity to look into themselves, to be acquainted at home and no longer the greatest strangers to their own hearts. Such as are willing in a more peculiar and undisturbed manner, to attend the great business they came into the world about, the service of GOD and improvement of their own minds, may find a convenient and blissful recess from the noise and hurry of the world. A world so cumbersome, so infectious, that although through the grace of GOD and their own strict watchfulness, they are kept from sinking down into its corruptions, 'twill however damp their flight to Heaven, hinder them from attaining any eminent pitch of virtue.

You are therefore, ladies, invited into a place where you shall suffer no other confinement, but to be kept out of the road of sin: You shall not be deprived of your grandeur but only exchange the vain pomps and pageantry of the world, empty titles and forms of state, for the true and solid greatness of being able to despise them. You will not only quit the chat of insignificant people for an ingenious conversation; the froth of flashy wit for real wisdom; idle tales for instructive discourses. The deceitful flatteries of those who, under pretense of loving and admiring you, really served their *own* base ends, for the seasonable re-proofs and wholesome counsels of your hearty well-wishers and affectionate friends, which will procure you those perfections your feigned lovers pretended you had, and kept you from obtaining. No uneasy task will be enjoined you, all your labor being only to prepare for the highest degrees of that glory, the very lowest of which is more than at present you are able to conceive, and the prospect of it sufficient to outweigh all the pains of religion, were there any in it, as really there are none. All that is required of you, is only to be as happy as possibly you can, and to make sure of a felicity that will fill all the capacities of your souls!

• • •

But because we were not made for ourselves, nor can by any means so effectually glorify GOD, and do good to our own souls, as by doing offices of charity and beneficence to others; and to the intent that every virtue, and the highest degrees of every virtue, may be exercised and promoted the most that may be; your retreat shall be so managed as not to exclude the good works of an *active* from the pleasure and serenity of a *contemplative* life, but by a due mixture of both retain all the advantages and avoid the inconveniences that attend either. It shall not so cut you off from the world as to hinder you from bettering and improving it, but rather qualify you to do it the greatest good, and be a seminary to stock the kingdom with pious and prudent ladies, whose good example, it is to be hoped, will so influence the rest of their sex that women may no longer pass for those little useless and impertinent animals, which the ill conduct of too many has caused 'em to be mistaken for.

We have hitherto considered our retirement only in relation to religion, which is indeed its *main*, I may say its *only* design; nor can this be thought too contracting a word, since religion is the adequate business of our lives and, largely considered, takes in all we have to do, nothing being a fit employment for a rational creature which has not either a *direct* or *remote* tendency to this great and *only* end. But because, as we have all along observed, religion never appears in its true beauty but when it is accompanied with wisdom and discretion; and that without a good understanding, we can scarce be *truly*, but never *eminently* good;

being liable to a thousand seductions and mistakes (for even the men themselves, if they have not a competent degree of knowledge, are carried about with every wind of doctrine). Therefore, one great end of this institution shall be, to expel that cloud of ignorance which custom has involved us in, to furnish our minds with a stock of solid and useful knowledge, that the souls of women may no longer be the only unadorned and neglected things. It is not intended that our *religious* should waste their time and trouble their heads about such unconcerning matters as the vogue of the world has turned up for learning, the impertinency of which has been excellently exposed by an ingenious pen, but busy themselves in a serious enquiry after *necessary* and *perfective* truths, something which it *concerns* them to know, and which tends to their real interest and perfection, and what that is the excellent author just now mentioned will sufficiently inform them.[5] Such a course of study will neither be too troublesome nor out of the reach of a female *virtuoso*,[6] for it is not intended she should spend her hours in learning *words* but *things*, and therefore no more languages than are necessary to acquaint her with useful authors. Nor need she trouble herself in turning over a great number of books, but take care to understand and digest a few well chosen and good ones. Let her but obtain right ideas, and be truly acquainted with the nature of those objects that present themselves to her mind, and then no matter whether or no she be able to tell what fanciful people have said about them: And thoroughly to understand Christianity as professed by the Church of England will be sufficient to confirm her in the truth, though she have not a catalogue of those particular errors which oppose it. Indeed a learned education of the women will appear so unfashionable that I began to startle at the singularity of the proposition, but was extremely pleased when I found a late ingenious author (whose book I met with since the writing of this) agree with me in my opinion. For speaking of the repute that learning was in about 150 years ago, *It was so very modish* (says he) *that the fair sex seemed to believe that Greek and Latin added to their charms: and Plato and Aristotle untranslated, were frequent ornaments of their*

---

[5]The Reverend John Norris, in *Reflections upon the Conduct of Human Life* (1690), as Astell notes. In the following year (1695) appeared *Letters concerning the Love of God*, in which Norris argued that the love of God should exclude all others, and Astell defended the moral and spiritual value of love for human friends. Cf. below, pp. 122–23.
[6]Scholar.

closets. One would think by the effects, that it was a proper way of educating them, since there are no accounts in history of so many great women in any one age, as are to be found between the years 15 and 1600.[7]

For since GOD has given women as well as men intelligent souls, why should they be forbidden to improve them? Since he has not denied us the faculty of thinking, why should we not (at least in gratitude to him) employ our thoughts on himself, their noblest object, and not unworthily bestow them on trifles and gaieties and secular affairs? Being the soul was created for the contemplation of truth as well as for the fruition of good, is it not as cruel and unjust to exclude women from the knowledge of the one as from the enjoyment of the other? Especially since the will is blind, and cannot choose but by the direction of the understanding; or to speak more properly, since the soul always *wills* according as she *understands*, so that if she understands amiss, she wills amiss. And as exercise enlarges and exalts any faculty, so through want of using it becomes cramped and lessened; if therefore we make little or no use of our understandings, we shall shortly have none to use; and the more contracted and unemployed the deliberating and directive power is, the more liable is the elective to unworthy and mischievous choices. What is it but the want of an ingenious education that renders the generality of feminine conversations so insipid and foolish and their solitude so insupportable? Learning is therefore necessary to render them more agreeable and useful in company, and to furnish them with becoming entertainments when alone, that so they may not be driven to those miserable shifts, which too many make use of to put off their time, that precious talent that never lies on the hands of a judicious person.

• • •

There is a sort of learning indeed which is worse than the greatest ignorance: a woman may study plays and romances all her days, and be a great deal more knowing but never a jot the wiser. Such a knowledge as this serves only to instruct and put her forward in the practice of the greatest follies, yet how can they justly blame her who forbid, or at least won't afford opportunity of better? A rational mind *will* be employed, it will never

---

[7]From William Wotton's *Reflections upon Ancient and Modern Learning* (1694), as Astell notes.

be satisfied in doing nothing, and if you neglect to furnish it with good materials, 'tis like to take up with such as come to hand.

We pretend not that women should teach in the Church, or usurp authority where it is not allowed them; permit us only to understand our *own* duty, and not be forced to take it upon trust from others; to be at least so far learned, as to be able to form in our minds a true idea of Christianity, it being so very necessary to fence us against the danger of these *last* and *perilous days*, in which deceivers, a part of whose character is to *lead captive silly women*, need not *creep into houses*, since they have authority to proclaim their errors on the *house top*.[8] And let us also acquire a true practical knowledge, such as will convince us of the absolute necessity of *holy living* as well as of *right believing*, and that no heresy is more dangerous than that of an ungodly and wicked life. And since the French tongue is understood by most ladies, methinks they may much better improve it by the study of philosophy (as I hear the French Ladies do), Descartes, Malebranche[9] and others, than by reading idle *novels* and *romances*. 'Tis strange we should be so forward to imitate their fashions and fopperies, and have no regard to what really deserves our imitation. And why shall it not be thought as genteel to understand *French philosophy*, as to be accoutered in a *French mode*? Let therefore the famous Madam Dacier, Scudéry, &c, and our own incomparable Orinda,[10] excite the emulation of the English ladies.

The ladies, I'm sure, have no reason to dislike this proposal, but I know not how the men will resent it to have their enclosure broke down, and women invited to taste of that tree of knowledge they have so long unjustly *monopolized*. But they must excuse me if I be as partial to my own sex as they are to theirs, and think women as capable of learning as men are, and that it becomes them as well. For I cannot imagine wherein the hurt lies, if instead of doing mischief to one another, by an uncharitable and vain conversation, women be enabled to inform and instruct those of their own sex at least; the Holy Ghost having left it on record, that Priscilla as well as her husband, catechized

---

[8]Quoted and condensed from II Timothy 3:1,6. Astell claims that deceivers need no longer creep, as they did in Biblical times, but may seduce women openly.

[9]René Descartes and Nicolas de Malebranche were seventeenth-century French philosophers.

[10]Anne Dacier (1654–1720), an eminent classical scholar, translated Homer into French. Madeleine de Scudéry (1607–1701) was an intellectual whose heroic romances delighted Europe. For Katherine Philips, "the Matchless Orinda," see p. 373.

the eloquent Apollos and the great Apostle found no fault with her.[11] It will therefore be very proper for our ladies to spend part of their time in this retirement in adorning their minds with useful knowledge.

To enter into the detail of the particulars concerning the government of the *religious*, their offices of devotion, employments, work, etc. is not now necessary. Suffice it at present to signify that they will be more than ordinarily careful to redeem their time, spending no more of it on the body than the necessities of nature require, but by a judicious choice of their employment and a constant industry about it, so improve this invaluable treasure that it may neither be buried in idleness, nor lavished out in unprofitable concerns. For a stated portion of it being daily paid to GOD in prayers and praises, the rest shall be employed in innocent, charitable, and useful business; either in study in learning themselves or instructing others, for it is designed that part of their employment be the education of those of their own sex; or else in spiritual and corporal works of mercy, relieving the poor, healing the sick, mingling charity to the soul with that they express to the body, instructing the ignorant, counseling the doubtful, comforting the afflicted, and correcting those that err and do amiss.

• • •

Farther yet, besides that holy emulation which a continual view of the brightest and most exemplary lives will excite in us, we shall have opportunity of contracting the purest and noblest friendship; a blessing, the purchase of which were richly worth all the world besides! For she who possesses a worthy person, has certainly obtained the richest treasure. A blessing that monarchs may envy, and she who enjoys is happier than she who fills a throne! A blessing which, next to the love of GOD, is the choicest jewel in our celestial diadem; which, were it duly practiced would both fit us for Heaven and bring it down into our hearts whilst we tarry here. For friendship is a virtue which comprehends all the rest; none being fit for this, who is not adorned with every other virtue. Probably one considerable cause of the degeneracy of the present age is the little true friendship that is to be found in it; or perhaps you will rather say that this is the effect of our corruption. The cause and the effect

[11]The Acts of the Apostles 18:24–26.

are indeed reciprocal; for were the world better there would be more friendship, and were there more friendship we should have a better world. But because *iniquity abounds*, therefore the *love of many* is not only *waxen cold*, but quite benumbed and perished.[12] But if we have such narrow hearts, be so full of mistaken self-love, so unreasonably fond of ourselves, that we cannot spare a hearty good-will to one or two choice persons, how can it ever be thought that we should well acquit ourselves of that charity which is due to all mankind? For friendship is nothing else but charity contracted; it is (in the words of an admired author) a kind of revenging ourselves on the narrowness of our faculties, by exemplifying the extraordinary charity on one or two which we are willing, but not able to exercise towards all. And therefore 'tis without doubt the best instructor to teach us our duty to our neighbor, and a most excellent monitor to excite us to make payment as far as our power will reach. It has a special force to dilate our hearts, to deliver them from that vicious *selfishness* and the rest of those sordid passions which express a narrow illiberal temper and are of such pernicious consequence to mankind. That institution therefore must needs be highly beneficial, which both disposes us to be friends ourselves and helps to find them. But by friendship I do not mean anything like those intimacies that are abroad in the world, which are often combinations in evil and at best but insignificant dearnesses, as little resembling true friendship, as modern practice does primitive Christianity. But I intend by it the greatest usefulness, the most refined and disinterested benevolence, a love that thinks nothing within the bounds of power and duty, too much to do or suffer for its beloved; and makes no distinction betwixt its friend and its self, except that in temporals it prefers her interest.

• • •

And if after so many spiritual advantages, it be convenient to mention temporals, here heiresses and persons of fortune may be kept secure from the rude attempts of designing men; And she who has more money than discretion need not curse her stars for being exposed a prey to bold, importunate and rapacious vultures. She will not here be inveigled and imposed on,

[12]Matthew 24:12. Again, Astell claims that the present situation is even worse than that described by the Biblical writer.

will neither be bought nor sold, nor be forced to marry for her own quiet, when she has no inclination to it, but what the being tired out with a restless importunity occasions. Or if she be disposed to marry, here she may remain in safety till a convenient match be offered by her friends,[13] and be freed from the danger of a dishonorable one. Modesty requiring that a woman should not love before marriage, but only make choice of one whom she can love hereafter; she who has none but innocent affections, being easily able to fix them where duty requires.

And though at first I proposed to myself to speak nothing in particular of the employment of the *religious*, yet to give a specimen how useful they will be to the world, I am now inclined to declare, that it is designed a part of their business shall be to give the best education to the children of persons of quality, who shall be attended and instructed in lesser matters by meaner persons deputed to that office, but the forming of their minds shall be the particular care of those of their own rank, who cannot have a more pleasant and useful employment than to exercise and increase their own knowledge by instilling it into these young ones, who are most like to profit under such tutors.

• • •

And when by the increase of their revenue, the *religious* are enabled to do such a work of charity, the education they design to bestow on the daughters of gentlemen who are fallen into decay will be no inconsiderable advantage to the nation. For hereby many souls will be preserved from great dishonors and put in a comfortable way of subsisting, being either received into the house if they incline to it, or otherwise disposed of. It being supposed that prudent men will reckon the endowments they here acquire a sufficient *dowry*, and that a discreet and virtuous gentlewoman will make a better wife than she whose mind is empty though her purse be full.

• • •

If any object against a learned education that it will make women vain and assuming, and instead of correcting increase their pride, I grant that a smattering in learning may, for it has this effect on the men; none so dogmatical and so forward to

---

[13]Family.

show their parts as your little *pretenders* to science. But I would not have the ladies content themselves with the *show*, my desire is that they should not rest till they obtain the *substance*. And then, she who is most knowing will be forward to own with the wise Socrates that she knows nothing: nothing that is matter of pride and ostentation; nothing but what is attended with so much ignorance and imperfection, that it cannot reasonably elate and puff her up. The more she knows, she will be the less subject to talkativeness and its sister vices, because she discerns that the most difficult piece of learning is to know when to use and when to hold one's tongue, and never to speak but to the purpose.

But the men, if they rightly understand their own interest, have no reason to oppose an ingenious education of the women, since 'twould go a great way toward reclaiming the men. Great is the influence we have over them in their childhood, in which time, if a mother be discreet, and knowing as well as devout, she has many opportunities of giving such a *form* and *season* to the tender mind of the child, as will show its good effects through all the stages of his life. But though you should not allow her capable of doing *good*, 'tis certain she may do *hurt:* if she do not *make* the child, she has power to *mar* him, by suffering her fondness to get the better of discreet affection. But besides this, a good and prudent wife would wonderfully work on an ill man; he must be a brute indeed who could hold out against all those innocent arts, those gentle persuasives and obliging methods she would use to reclaim him. Piety is often offensive when it is accompanied with indiscretion; but she who is as wise as good possesses such charms as can hardly fail of prevailing. Doubtless her husband is a much happier man and more likely to abandon all his ill courses than he who has none to come home to but an ignorant, forward and fantastic creature. An ingenious conversation will make his life comfortable, and he who can be so well entertained at home needs not run into temptations in search of diversions abroad. The only danger is that the wife be more knowing than the husband; but if she be 'tis his own fault, since he wants no opportunities of improvement; unless he be a natural *blockhead*, and then such an one will need a wise woman to govern him, whose prudence will conceal it from public observation, and at once both cover and supply his defects. Give me leave therefore to hope that no gentleman who has honorable designs will henceforward decry knowledge and ingenuity in her he would pretend to honor; if he does, it may serve for a test to distinguish the feigned and unworthy from the real lover.

. . .

from Part II of
A Serious Proposal

As for those who think so contemptibly of such a considerable part of GOD's creation as to suppose that we were made for nothing else but to admire and do them service, and to make provision for the low concerns of an animal life, we pity their mistake and can calmly bear their scoffs, for they do not express so much contempt of us as they do of our Maker; and therefore the reproach of such incompetent judges is not an injury but an honor to us.

The ladies I hope pass a truer estimate on themselves and need not be told that they were made for nobler purposes. For though I would by no means encourage pride, yet I would not have them take a mean and groveling spirit for true humility. A being content with ignorance is really but a pretense, for the frame of our nature is such that it is impossible we should be so; even those very pretenders value themselves for some knowledge or other, though it be a trifling or mistaken one. She who makes the most grimace at a woman of sense, who employs all her little skill in endeavoring to render learning and ingenuity ridiculous, is yet very desirous to be thought knowing in a dress, in the management of an intrigue, in coquetry or good houswifery. If then either the nobleness or necessity of our nature unavoidably excites us to desire of advancing, shall it be thought a fault to do it by pursuing the best things? and since we *will* value ourselves on somewhat or other, why should it not be on the most substantial ground? The humblest person that lives has some self-esteem, nor is it either fit or possible that any should be without it. Because we always neglect what we despise, we take no care of its preservation and improvement, and were we thoroughly possessed with a contempt of ourselves, we should abandon all care both of our temporal and eternal concerns, and burst with envy at our neighbors. The only difference therefore between the humble and the proud is this, that whereas the former does not prize herself on some imaginary excellency, or for anything that is not truly valuable; does not ascribe to herself what is her Maker's due, nor esteem herself on any other account but because she is GOD's workmanship, endowed by him with many excellent qualities, and made capable of knowing and enjoying the sovereign and only good; so that her self-esteem does not terminate in *herself* but in GOD, and she values herself only for GOD's sake. The proud on the contrary is mistaken both in her estimate of good and in thinking it is her own; she values herself on things that have no real excellency, or which at least add none to her, and forgets from whose liberality she receives them: she does not employ them in the donor's service; all her care is to raise herself, and she little considers that the most excellent things are distributed to others in an equal, perhaps in a greater measure than to herself, they have opportunities of advancing as well as she, and so long as she's puffed up by this tumor of mind, they do really excel her.

The men therefore may still enjoy their prerogatives for us; we mean not to intrench on any of their lawful privileges; our only contention shall be that they may not outdo us in promoting his glory who is lord both of them and us; and by all that appears the generality will not oppose us in this matter, we shall not provoke them by striving to be better Christians. They may busy their heads with affairs of state and spend their time and strength in recommending themselves to an uncertain master, or a more giddy multitude; our only endeavor shall be to be absolute monarchs in our own bosoms. They shall still if they please dispute about religion, let 'em only give us leave to understand and practice it. And whilst they have unrivaled the glory of speaking as *many* langauges as Babel afforded, we only desire to express ourselves pertinently and judiciously in *one*. We will not vie with them in thumbing over authors, nor pretend to be walking libraries, provided they'll but allow us a competent knowledge of the books of GOD, Nature I mean and the Holy Scriptures: And whilst they accomplish themselves with the knowledge of the world, and experiment[14] all the pleasures and follies of it, we'll aspire no further than to be intimately acquainted with our own hearts. And sure the complaisant and

[14]Experience, feel.

good natured sex will not deny us this; nor can they who are so well assured of their own merit entertain the least suspicion that we shall overtop them. It is upon some other account therefore that they object against our proposal, but what that is I shall not pretend to guess, since they do not think fit to speak out and declare it.

From Some Reflections upon Marriage

THESE *Reflections upon Marriage* were inspired by a defense of herself published by Hortense Mancini, Duchess of Mazarin. Forced by her uncle to marry an odious and unbalanced man, the Duchess eloped from him and embarked on a series of affairs with, among others, King Charles II. Though Astell could not approve of the Duchess's conduct, she blamed it primarily upon "some abuses [of the marital institution], which are not the less because power and prescription seem to authorize them": particularly, forcing people into marriage and marrying for the wrong reasons. The institution itself must be good, because it was ordained by God. Why, then, are there so many unhappy marriages?

• • •

In a word, when we have reckoned up how many look no further than the making of their fortune, as they call it; who don't so much as propose to themselves any satisfaction in the woman to whom they plight their faith, seeking only to be masters of her estate, that so they may have money enough to indulge all their irregular appetites; who think they are as good as can be expected, if they are but, according to the fashionable term, *civil husbands*; when we have taken the number of your giddy lovers, who are not more violent in their passion than they are certain to repent of it; when to these you have added such as marry without any thought at all, further than it is the custom of the world, what others have done before them, that the family must be kept up, the ancient race preserved, and therefore their kind parents and guardians choose as they think convenient, without ever consulting the young one's inclinations, who must be satisfied, or pretend so at least, upon pain of their displeasure, and that heavy consequence of it, forfeiture of their estate: These set aside, I fear there will be but a small remainder to marry out of better considerations; and even amongst the few that do, not one in a hundred takes care to deserve his choice.

But do the women never choose amiss? Are the men only in

fault? That is not pretended, for he who will be just, must be forced to acknowledge that neither sex are always in the right. A woman, indeed, can't properly be said to choose; all that is allowed her is to refuse or accept what is offered. And when we have made such reasonable allowances as are due to the sex, perhaps they may not appear so much in fault as one would at first imagine, and a generous spirit will find more occasion to pity than to reprove.

• • •

And as men have little reason to expect happiness when they marry only for the love of money, wit, or beauty, as has been already shown, so much less can a woman expect a tolerable life, when she goes upon these considerations. Let the business be carried as prudently as it can be on the woman's side, a reasonable man can't deny that she has by much the harder bargain, because she puts herself entirely into her husband's power, and if the matrimonial yoke be grievous, neither law nor custom afford her that redress which a man obtains. He who has sovereign power does not value the provocations of a rebellious subject; he knows how to subdue him with ease, and will make himself obeyed: But patience and submission are the only comforts that are left to a poor people who groan under tyranny, unless they are strong enough to break the yoke, to depose and abdicate, which, I doubt, would not be allowed of here. For whatever may be said against passive obedience in another case, I suppose there's no man but likes it very well in this; how much soever arbitrary power may be disliked on a throne, not Milton,[1] nor B.H.———, nor any of the advocates of resistance, would cry up liberty to poor *female slaves* or plead for the lawfulness of resisting a private tyranny.

If there be a disagreeableness of humors, this, in my mind, is harder to be borne than greater faults, as being a continual plague, and for the most part incurable. Other vices a man may grow weary of, or may be convinced of the evil of them, he may forsake them, or they him, but his humor and temper are seldom, if ever, put off. Ill-nature sticks to him from his youth to

---

[1]John Milton defended the rebellion against King Charles I on the grounds that rulers held their power in trust for the people, who could revoke it if the rulers acted tyrannically (*The Tenure of Kings and Magistrates*, 1649). But he insisted that men had natural dominion over women, for example, in *Paradise Lost* IV lines 295–311, 635–638, X lines 145–156. B. H. may be Benjamin Hoadly, a clergyman who preached and published against absolute authority in government.

his gray hairs, and a boy that's humorous[2] and proud, makes a peevish, positive, and insolent old man. Now if this be the case, and the husband be full of himself, obstinately bent on his own way, with or without reason, if he be one who must be always admired, always humored, and yet scarce knows what will please him; if he has prosperity enough to keep him from considering and to furnish him with a train of flatterers and obsequious admirers; and learning and sense enough to make him a fop in perfection, for a man can never be a complete coxcomb unless he has a considerable share of these to value himself upon; what can the poor woman do? The husband is too wise to be advised, too good to be reformed, she must follow all his paces, and tread in all his unreasonable steps, or there is no peace, no quiet for her; she must obey with the greatest exactness, 'tis in vain to expect any manner of compliance on his side, and the more she complies, the more she may: his fantastical humors grow with her desire to gratify them, for age increases opinionatry[3] in some, as well as it does experience in others.

• • •

If therefore it be a woman's hard fate to meet with a disagreeable temper, and of all others, the haughty, imperious, and self-conceited are the most so, she is as unhappy as any thing in this world can make her. For when a wife's temper does not please, if she makes her husband uneasy, he can find entertainments abroad; he has a hundred ways of relieving himself; but neither prudence nor duty will allow a woman to fly out: her business and entertainment are at home; and though he makes it ever so uneasy to her, she must be content, and make her best on't. She who elects a monarch for life, who gives him an authority she cannot recall, however he misapply it, who puts her fortune and person entirely in his power, nay, even the very desires of her heart, according to some learned casuists, so as that it is not lawful to will or desire any thing but what he approves and allows, had need be very sure that she does not make a fool her head, nor a vicious man her guide and pattern; she had best stay till she can meet with one who has the government of his own passions and has duly regulated his own desires, since he is to have such an absolute power over hers. But he who dotes on a face, he who makes money his idol, he who is

<hr>

[2]Moody, ill-humored.
[3]Obstinacy.

charmed with vain and empty wit, gives no such evidence, either of wisdom or goodness, that a woman of any tolerable sense should care to venture herself to his conduct.

Indeed, your fine gentleman's actions are nowadays such, that did not custom and the dignity of his sex give weight and authority to them, a woman that thinks twice might bless herself and say, Is this the Lord and Master to whom I am to promise love, honor and obedience? What can be the object of love but amiable qualities, the image of the deity impressed upon a generous and godlike mind, a mind that is above this world, to be sure above all the vices, the tricks and baseness of it; a mind that is not full of itself, nor contracted to little private interests, but which, in imitation of that glorious pattern it endeavors to copy after, expands and diffuses itself to its utmost capacity in doing good. But this fine gentleman is quite of another strain, he is the reverse of this in every instance. He is, I confess, very fond of his own dear person, he sees very much in it to admire; his air and mien, his words and actions, every motion he makes, declare it; but they must have a judgment of his size, every whit as shallow, and a partiality as great as his own, who can be of his mind. How then can I love? And if not love, much less honor. Love may arise from pity, or a generous desire to make that lovely which as yet is not so, when we see any hopes of success in our endeavors of improving it; but honor supposes some excellent qualities already, something worth our esteem; but, alas! there is nothing more contemptible than this trifle of a man, this mere outside, whose mind is as base and mean as his external pomp is glittering. His office or title apart, to which some ceremonious observance must be paid for order's sake, there's nothing in him that can command our respect. Strip him of equipage and fortune, and such things as only dazzle our eyes and imaginations, but don't in any measure affect our reason or cause a reverence in our hearts, and the poor creature sinks beneath our notice, because not supported by real worth. And if a woman can neither love nor honor, she does ill in promising to obey, since she is like to have a crooked rule to regulate her actions.

A mere obedience, such as is paid only to authority, and not out of love and a sense of the justice and reasonableness of the command, will be of an uncertain tenure. As it can't but be uneasy to the person who pays it, so he who receives it will be sometimes disappointed when he expects to find it: For that woman must be endowed with a wisdom and goodness much above what we suppose the sex capable of, I fear much greater than any man can pretend to, who can so constantly conquer her passions, and divest herself even of innocent self-love, as to give up the cause when she is in the right, and to submit her enlightened reason to the imperious dictates of a blind will and wild imagination, even when she clearly perceives the ill consequences of it, the imprudence, nay, folly and madness of such a conduct.

And if a woman runs such a risk when she marries prudently, according to the opinion of the world, that is, when she permits herself to be disposed of to a man equal to her in birth, education and fortune, and as good as the most of his neighbors (for if none were to marry, but men of strict virtue and honor, I doubt the world would be thinly peopled), if at the very best her lot is hard, what can she expect who is sold, or any otherwise betrayed into mercenary hands, to one who is in all, or most respects, unequal to her? A lover who comes upon what is called equal terms makes no very advantageous proposal to the lady he courts, and to whom he seems to be an humble servant. For under many sounding compliments, words that have nothing in them, this is his true meaning: He wants one to manage his family, an housekeeper, one whose interest it will be not to wrong him, and in whom therefore he can put greater confidence than in any he can hire for money. One who may breed his children, taking all the care and trouble of their education, to preserve his name and family. One whose beauty, wit, or good humor and agreeable conversation, will entertain him at home when he has been contradicted and disappointed abroad; who will do him that justice the ill-natured world denies him; that is, in anyone's language but his own, soothe his pride and flatter his vanity, by having always so much good sense as to be on his side, to conclude him in the right, when others are so ignorant or so rude as to deny it. Who will not be blind to his merit nor contradict his will and pleasure, but make it her business, her very ambition to content him; whose softness and gentle compliance will calm his passions, to whom he may safely disclose his troublesome thoughts, and in her breast discharge his cares; whose duty, submission and observance will heal those wounds other people's opposition or neglect have given him. In a word, one whom he can entirely govern, and consequently may form her to his will and liking, who must be his for life, and therefore cannot quit his service, let him treat her how he will.

• • •

What then is to be done? How must a man choose, and what qualities must incline a woman to accept, that so our married couple may be as happy as that state can make them? This is no hard question; let the soul be principally considered, and regard had in the first place to a good understanding, a virtuous mind; and in all other respects let there be as much equality as may be. If they are good Christians and of suitable tempers all will be well . . .

But it is not enough to enter wisely into this state, care must be taken of our conduct afterwards. A woman will not want being admonished of her duty; the custom of the world, economy, every thing almost reminds her of it. Governors do not often suffer their subjects to forget obedience through their want of demanding it; perhaps husbands are but too forward on this occasion, and claim their right oftener and more imperiously than either discretion or good manners will justify, and might have both a more cheerful and constant obedience paid them if they were not so rigorous in exacting it. For there is a mutual stipulation, and love, honor, and worship, by which certainly civility and respect at least are meant, are as much the woman's due, as love, honor and obedience are the man's. And being the woman is said to be the weaker vessel, the man should be more careful not to grieve or offend her. Since her reason is supposed to be less, and her passions stronger than his, he should not give occasion to call that supposition in question by his pettish carriage and needless provocations. Since he is the *man*, by which very word custom would have us understand not only greatest strength of body, but even greatest firmness and force of mind, he should not play the *Little Master* so much as to expect to be cockered, nor run over to that side which the woman used to be ranked in; for, according to the wisdom of the Italians, *Will you? is spoken to sick folks.*

Indeed subjection, according to the common notion of it, is not over easy; none of us, whether men or women, but have so good an opinion of our own conduct as to believe we are fit, if not to direct others, at least to govern ourselves. Nothing but a sound understanding and grace, the best improver of natural reason, can correct this opinion, truly humble us, and heartily reconcile us to obedience. This bitter cup therefore ought to be sweetened as much as may be; for authority may be preserved and government kept inviolable without that nauseous ostentation of power, which serves to no end or purpose but to blow up the pride and vanity of those who have it, and to exasperate the spirits of such as must truckle under it.

• • •

Considering the just dignity of man, his great wisdom so conspicuous on all occasions! the goodness of his temper and reasonableness of all his commands, which make it a woman's interest as well as duty to be observant and obedient in all things; that his prerogative is settled by an undoubted right and the prescription of many ages; it cannot be supposed that he should make frequent and insolent claims of an authority so well established and used with such moderation, nor give an impartial bystander (could such an one be found) any occasion from thence to suspect that he is inwardly conscious of the badness of his title; usurpers being always most desirous of recognitions and busy in imposing oaths, whereas a lawful prince contents himself with the usual methods and securities.

And since power does naturally puff up, and he who finds himself exalted, seldom fails to think he *ought* to be so, it is more suitable to a man's wisdom and generosity to be mindful of his great obligations, than to insist on his rights and prerogatives. Sweetness of temper and an obliging carriage are so justly due to a wife that a husband who must not be thought to want either understanding to know what is fit, nor goodness to perform it, can't be supposed not to show them. For setting aside the hazard of her person to keep up his name and family, with all the pains and trouble that attend it, which may well be thought great enough to deserve all the respect and kindness that may be; setting this aside, though 'tis very considerable, a woman has so much the disadvantage in *most*, I was about to say, in *all* things, that she makes a man the greatest compliment in the world when she condescends to take him *for better for worse*. She puts herself entirely in his power, leaves all that is dear to her, her friends and family, to espouse his interests and follow his fortune, and makes it her business and duty to please him! What acknowledgments, what returns can he make? What gratitude can be sufficient for such obligations? She shows her good opinion of him by the great trust she reposes in him, and what a brute must he be who betrays that trust, or acts any way unworthy of it? Ingratitude is one of the basest vices, and if a man's soul is sunk so low as to be guilty of it towards her who has so generously obliged him, and who so entirely depends on him, if he can treat her disrespectfully, who has so fully testified her esteem of him, she must have a stock of virtue which he should blush to discern, if she can pay him that obedience of which he is so unworthy.

• • •

But how can a woman scruple entire subjection, how can she forbear to admire the worth and excellency of the superior sex, if she at all considers it! Have not all the great actions that have been performed in the world been done by men? Have not they founded empires and overturned them? Do not they make laws and continually repeal and amend them? Their vast minds lay kingdoms waste, no bounds or measures can be prescribed to their desires. War and peace depend on them; they form cabals and have the wisdom and courage to get over all the rubs, the petty restraints which honor and conscience may lay in the way of their desired grandeur. What is it they cannot do? They make worlds and ruin them, form systems of universal nature and dispute eternally about them; their pen gives worth to the most trifling controversy; nor can a fray be inconsiderable if they have drawn their swords in't. All that the wise man pronounces is an oracle, and every word the witty speaks, a jest. It is a woman's happiness to hear, admire and praise them, especially if a little ill-nature keeps them at any time from bestowing due applauses on each other! And if she aspires no further, she is thought to be in her proper sphere of action; she is as wise and as good as can be expected from her!

She then who marries ought to lay it down for an indisputable maxim, that her husband must govern absolutely and entirely, and that she has nothing else to do but to please and obey. She must not attempt to divide his authority, or so much as dispute it; to struggle with her yoke will only make it gall the more, but must believe him wise and good, and in all respects the best, at least he must be so to her. She who can't do this is no way fit to be a wife, she may set up for that peculiar coronet the ancient fathers talked of,[4] but is not qualified to receive that great reward which attends the eminent exercise of humility and self-denial, patience and resignation, the duties that a wife is called to.

---

[4] The Fathers of the Christian Church, such as Saints Paul, Jerome, and Augustine, claimed that celibacy was morally preferable to marriage, but assumed that most men and women were not strong enough to abstain from marrying. Celibates were supposed to be rewarded in Heaven with special virgins' crowns or coronets.

But some refractory woman perhaps will say, how can this be? Is it possible for her to believe him wise and good, who by a thousand demonstrations convinces her, and all the world, of the contrary? Did the bare name of husband confer sense on a man, and the mere being in authority infallibly qualify him for government, much might be done. But since a wise man and a husband are not terms convertible, and how loth soever one is to own it, matter of fact won't allow us to deny that the head many times stands in need of the inferior's brains to manage it, she must beg leave to be excused from such high thoughts of her sovereign, and if she submits to his power, it is not so much reason as necessity that compels her.

Now of how little force soever this objection may be in other respects, methinks it is strong enough to prove the necessity of a good education, and that men never mistake their true interest more than when they endeavor to keep women in ignorance. Could they indeed deprive them of their natural good sense at the same time they deny them the true improvement of it, they might compass their end; otherwise natural sense unassisted may run into a false track, and serve only to punish him justly, who would not allow it to be useful to himself or others. If man's authority be justly established, the more sense a woman has, the more reason she will find to submit to it; if according to the tradition of our fathers (who having had *possession* of the pen, thought they had also the best *right* to it), women's understanding is but small, and man's partiality adds no weight to the observation, ought not the more care to be taken to improve them? How it agrees with the justice of men we inquire not, but certainly Heaven is abundantly more equitable than to enjoin women the hardest task and give them at least strength to perform it. And if men, learned, wise and discreet as they are, who have, as is said, all the advantages of nature, and without controversy have, or may have, all the assistance of art, are so far from acquitting themselves as they ought, from living according to that reason and excellent understanding they so much boast of, can it be expected that a woman, who is reckoned silly enough in herself, at least comparatively, and whom men take care to make yet more so; can it be expected that she should constantly perform so difficult a duty as entire subjection, to which corrupt Nature is so averse?

If the great and wise Cato, a man, a man of no ordinary firmness and strength of mind, a man who was esteemed as an oracle, and by the philosophers and great men of his nation equaled even to the gods themselves; if he, with all his stoical principles, was not able to bear the sight of a triumphant conqueror (who perhaps would have insulted, and perhaps would not), but out of a cowardly fear of an insult, ran to death, to secure him from it;[5] can it be thought that an ignorant weak woman should have patience to bear a continual outrage and insolence all the days of her life? Unless you will suppose her a *very ass*, but then remember what the Italians say, to quote them once more, since being *very* husbands[6] they may be presumed to have some authority in this case, *An ass, though slow, if provoked, will kick.*

We never observe, or perhaps make sport, with the ill effects of a bad education, till it comes to touch us home in the ill conduct of a sister, a daughter, or wife. Then the women must be blamed, their folly is exclaimed against, when all this while it was the wise man's fault, who did not set a better guard on those, who, according to him, stand in so much need of one. A young gentleman, as a celebrated author tells us, ought above all things to be acquainted with the state of the world, the ways and humors, the follies, the cheats, the faults of the age he is fallen into; he should by degrees be informed of the vice in fashion, and warned of the application and design of those who will make it their business to corrupt him, should be told the arts they use, and the trains they lay, be prepared to be shocked by some, and caressed by others; warned who are like to oppose, who to mislead, who to undermine, and who to serve him. He should be instructed how to know and distinguish them, where he should let them see, and when dissemble the knowledge of them and their aims and workings.

• • •

And it is not less necessary that a young lady should receive the like instructions; whether or no her temptations be fewer, her reputation and honor however are to be more nicely preserved; they may be ruined by a little ignorance or indiscretion, and then though she has kept her innocence, and so is secured

---

[5]Cato the Younger, enormously admired for his probity and adherence to Stoic principles, fought Julius Caesar in defense of the Roman Republic. He committed suicide rather than surrender to Caesar.

[6]"True" (i.e. tyrannical) husbands. Italian women were, in general, even more restricted than English ones; and contemporary Englishmen constantly harped on the difference.

as to the next world, yet she is in a great measure lost to this. A woman cannot be too watchful, too apprehensive of her danger, nor keep at too great a distance from it, since man, whose wisdom and ingenuity is so much superior to hers! condescends for his interest sometimes, and sometimes by way of diversion, to lay snares for her. For though all men are *virtuosi*, philosophers and politicians, in comparison of the ignorant and illiterate women, yet they don't all pretend to be saints, and 'tis no great matter to them if women, who were born to be their slaves, be now and then ruined for their entertainment.

But according to the rate that young women are educated, according to the way their time is spent, they are destined to folly and impertinence, to say no worse, and, which is yet more inhuman, they are blamed for that ill conduct they are not suffered to avoid, and reproached for those faults they are in a manner forced into; so that if Heaven has bestowed any sense on them, no other use is made of it, than to leave them without excuse. So much, and no more, of the world is shown them, than serves to weaken and corrupt their minds, to give them wrong notions and busy them in mean pursuits; to disturb, not to regulate their passions; to make them timorous and dependent, and, in a word, fit for nothing else but to act a farce for the diversion of their governors.

Even men themselves improve no otherwise than according to the aim they take and the end they propose; and he whose designs are but little and mean, will be the same himself. Though ambition, as 'tis usually understood, is a foolish, not to say a base and pitiful vice, yet the aspirings of the soul after true glory are so much its nature, that it seems to have forgot itself and to degenerate if it can forbear; and perhaps the great secret of education lies in affecting the soul with a lively sense of what is truly its perfection, and exciting the most ardent desires after it.

But, alas! what poor woman is ever taught that she should have a higher design than to get her a husband? Heaven will fall in of course; and if she makes but an obedient and dutiful wife, she cannot miss of it. A husband indeed is thought by both sexes so very valuable, that scarce a man who can keep himself clean and make a bow, but thinks he is good enough to pretend to any woman; no matter for the difference of birth or fortune, a husband in such a wonder-working name as to make an equality, or something more, whenever it is obtained.

• • •

If mankind had never sinned, Reason would always have been obeyed, there would have been no struggle for dominion, and brutal power would not have prevailed. But in the lapsed state of mankind, and now that men will not be guided by their Reason but by their appetites, and do not what they *ought* but what they *can*, the Reason, or that which stands for it, the will and pleasure of the governor, is to be the Reason of those who will not be guided by their own, and must take place for order's sake, although it should not be conformable to right Reason. Nor can there be any society great or little, from empires down to private families, without a last resort, to determine the affairs of that society by an irresistible sentence. Now unless this supremacy be fixed somewhere, there will be a perpetual contention about it, such is the love of dominion, and let the Reason of things be what it may, those who have least force or cunning to supply it, will have the disadvantage. So that since women are acknowledged to have least bodily strength, their being commanded to obey is in pure kindness to them, and for their quiet and security, as well as for the exercise of their virtue. But does it follow, that domestic governors have more sense than their subjects, any more than that other governors have? We do not find that any man thinks the worse of his own understanding because another has superior power; or concludes himself less capable of a post of honor and authority because he is not preferred to it. How much time would lie on men's hands, how empty would the places of concourse be, and how silent most companies, did men forbear to censure their governors, that is, in effect, to think themselves wiser. Indeed, government would be much more desirable than it is, did it invest the possessor with a superior understanding as well as power. And if mere power gives a right to rule, there can be no such thing as usurpation; but a highwayman, so long as he has strength to force, has also a right to require our obedience.

Again, if absolute sovereignty be not necessary in a state, how comes it to be so in a family? Or if in a family why not in a state; since no reason can be alleged for the one that will not hold more strongly for the other? If the authority of the husband, so far as it extends, is sacred and inalienable, why not that of the prince? The domestic sovereign is without dispute elected, and the stipulations and contract are mutual; it is not then partial in

men to the last degree to contend for and practice that arbitrary
dominion in their families which they abhor and exclaim against
in the state? For if arbitrary power is evil in itself, and an
improper method of governing rational and free agents, it ought
not to be practiced anywhere; nor is it less, but rather more
mischievous in families than in kingdoms, by how much 100,000
tyrants are worse than one. What though a husband can't deprive a wife of life without being responsible to the law, he may,
however, do what is much more grievous to a generous mind,
render life miserable, for which she has no redress, scarce pity,
which is afforded to every other complainant, it being thought a
wife's duty to suffer everything without complaint. If *all men
are born free*, how is it that all women are born slaves? As they
must be, if the being subjected to the *inconstant, uncertain,
unknown, arbitrary will* of men, be the *perfect condition of
slavery?* And if the essence of freedom consists, as our masters
say it does, in having a *standing rule to live by?* And why is
slavery so much condemned and strove against in one case, and
so highly applauded, and held so necessary and so sacred in
another?

• • •

I do not propose this [developing women's reason] to prevent
a rebellion, for women are not so well united as to form an
insurrection. They are for the most part wise enough to love
their chains, and to discern how very becomingly they fit. They
think as humbly of themselves as their masters can wish, with
respect to the other sex, but in regard to their own, they have a
spice of masculine ambition; every one would lead, and none
would follow. Both sexes being too apt to envy, and too backward in emulating, and take more delight in detracting from their
neighbor's virtue than in improving their own. And therefore, as
to those women who find themselves born for slavery, and are
so sensible of their own meanness as to conclude it impossible
to attain to anything excellent, since they are, or ought to be
acquainted with their own strength and genius, she's a fool who
would attempt their deliverance or improvement. No, let them
enjoy the great honor and felicity of their tame, submissive and
depending temper! Let the men applaud, and let them glory in
this wonderful humility! Let them receive the flatteries and
grimaces of the other sex, live unenvied by their own, and be as
much beloved as one such woman can afford to love another!

Let them enjoy the glory of treading in the footsteps of their predecessors, and of having the prudence to avoid that audacious attempt of soaring beyond their sphere! Let them huswife[7] or play, dress, and be pretty entertaining company! Or, which is better, relieve the poor to ease their own compassions, read pious books, say their prayers, and go to church, because they have been taught and used to do so, without being able to give a better reason for their faith and practice! Let them not by any means aspire at being women of understanding, because no man can endure a woman of superior sense or would treat a reasonable woman civilly, but that he thinks he stands on higher ground, and that she is so wise as to make exceptions in his favor and to take her measures by his directions; they may pretend to sense, indeed, since mere pretenses only render one the more ridiculous! Let them, in short, be what is called *very* women, for this is most acceptable to all sorts of men; or let them aim at the title of *good devout* women, since some men can bear with this; but let them not judge of the sex by their own scantling: For the great Author of Nature and Fountain of all Perfection never designed that the mean and imperfect, but that the most complete and excellent of his creatures in every kind, should be the standard to the rest.

[7]Act the housewife, manage the household.

Delarivière Manley
1672(?)–1724

DELARIVIÈRE MANLEY was the foremost professional woman author of the Age of Queen Anne. She wrote a wildly successful best-seller, edited the leading government periodical, and associated familiarly with Sir Richard Steele and Jonathan Swift. Her ability earned Swift's respect, and her flamboyant temperament made her a character on the London literary scene.

Her father, Sir Roger Manley, military governor of the isle of Jersey, died in 1687 and left her in the care of a cousin, John Manley, who, like Roderigo in "The Wife's Resentment," duped her into a false marriage and then abandoned her. Pregnant, her reputation blasted, Manley took up her pen as a last resort.

Her first efforts, a comedy and a tragedy, were produced in 1696 but earned no money. Manley then allied herself with John Tilly, chief warden of the Fleet prison; after several years as his mistress, she withdrew when he found a more eligible wife. In 1705 she enjoyed her first writing success: *The Secret History of Queen Zarah and the Zarazians*, an allegorical satire on Sarah, Duchess of Marlborough, and her political associates.

In this work, a combination of *roman à clef*, politics, and sex, Manley found the form and content most congenial to her. She then carried them to triumph in *Secret Memoirs . . . of Several Persons of Quality of Both Sexes, from the New Atlantis* (1709). Both works took advantage of a heated political climate, and Manley, an ardent Tory, delighted in abusing the Whigs, who were then in power. They responded by arresting her for libel but had to release her for lack of evidence. As soon as she was free, she published two more volumes of the *Atlantis*. When the Tories came to power (1710), Manley became Swift's assistant on *The Examiner*, and then his successor, occupying one of the most important political-journalistic positions in England. When the Tory government fell (1714), Manley wrote a fictionalized autobiography (*Adventures of Rivella*, 1714), brought out another play, and remodeled a collection of old romances (*The Power of Love*, 1720). She also became the mistress of John Barber, her publisher.

Manley's posthumous reputation suffered from the (inevitably) disreputable character of her life. Also, like most professional writers in her era, she wrote hastily, addressed the issues of the day, and aimed for immediate effect. Thus her most famous work, the *New Atlantis*, lacks for us the racy excitement it offered its first readers. We can better appreciate her tale "The Wife's Resentment," where she develops the themes of sexual and class exploitation.

The Wife's Resentment[1]

When the Duke of Calabria, son to Frederick King of Aragon, was viceroy of the Kingdom of Valencia, he kept his court in the city of Valencia, which was then the chief and only rampart of that part of Spain, esteemed as the seat of justice, faith and humanity. Among its other ornaments, the beauty of their women was deservedly thought the greatest; to which was joined the reputation of understanding, and such a keenness of wit, that it grew into a proverb, *When a fellow was dull and thought a blockhead, that he must go to Valencia.* In the time of this Viceroy lived Seignior Roderigo, knight of Valencia, descended of the ancient, illustrious and rich family of the Ventimiglia. This noble lord was devoted to his pleasures, and besides a handsome person, had an address and behavior that was pleasing to everybody. He did not love his studies; and there being no war at that time to employ an active mind, for want of better business, according to the custom of Spain, he walked up and down the city, wasting his youth in trifles, music, masquerades, courting of ladies, a form of devotion which was very common, and fit for such pilgrims, designing only to conquer, not to be conquered; for as yet all women were equally indifferent to him, he

[1]In the "Dedication" to *The Power of Love*, Manley writes, "I have attempted, in modern English, to draw [old stories] out of obscurity; with the same design as Mr. [John] Dryden had in his tales from Boccace [Boccaccio] and Chaucer." "The Wife's Resentment" is a retelling of the story of Didaco and Violenta in William Painter's *Palace of Pleasure* (1566). Its origin is a tale by Matteo Bandello (1485–1561), the "Bandwell" of p. 170 below. Although Manley often copies Painter closely, she also cuts long passages that do not advance the story and adds much detail, especially in the first half. Her version, about 2,000 words longer than Painter's, puts more emphasis on motives and the moral meaning of the events.

had no more esteem or tenderness for one than another; his business was mere gallantry, he knew not what it was to love; provided he could but triumph, he valued not the conquest. The whole city rang of his inconstancy, and yet he was so handsome, so rich, and of such eminent quality, that he still found a favorable reception amongst the ladies; each one imagining that her charms were sufficient to make a convert of him. His youth, good mien, gay temper and generosity, introduced him everywhere. Some aspired to gain him for a husband, the already married for a gallant, and they succeeded the best. Thus he never thought of the injury he did others, but led a life of pleasure, unthinking and without principles. His conversation did not lie in the road of such persons who either could or cared to teach him. One must love people a good deal whom one takes pains to convince or instruct. Thus Roderigo daily made the tour of the city of Valencia, to the ruin of many an easy damsel; but that was none of his concern, for amongst all the virtues, he was yet wholly unacquainted with that of remorse.

Seignior Roderigo was ranging the city one holiday, that being the time the ladies show themselves at their doors or windows, when he beheld a face that was entirely new to him; neither had he, till then, seen anything so handsome in Valencia. This young maid suddenly cast her eyes upon the Count; his garb was very rich and distinguishing. She met his looks in such a manner that he thought a pistol had been discharged at his heart; he felt as hot and fatal a fire, and which he had never been sensible of before. This fair creature had the greatest luster, the finest water, as we may call it, in her eyes, that was ever seen; her air was modest; her height, inclining rather to tall; her taper waist and exact symmetry well deserved consideration; she was in a habit rather neat than fine, but there was a *je ne sais quoi* that might very well arrest the curiosity of those that passed along: though, her eyes excepted, there was none of her other features so glorious, unless her complexion, which was varnished by Nature with a gloss shining like polished marble, and whiter than imagination, an uncommon charm in Spain, and would, even in England, be looked upon as a very extraordinary beauty.

Roderigo, disarmed by the flashes of her eyes, stayed some time to gaze on her that had wounded him to so dangerous a degree. The maid, perceiving how intent the Count was in beholding her, with a modest blush retired into the house. He passed and repassed before the door several times in hopes of seeing her again, perceiving that she purposely avoided him; and by that means lost the diversion of gazing on the holiday folks, he absconded behind a corner of the street. After some time that ravishing beauty, having no longer seen the person that had by his admiration caused her to withdraw, returned to the door to entertain herself innocently with looking on the passengers, which on Sundays and holidays is almost the only liberty allowed to the Spanish women, and those too of an inferior degree. Roderigo, having watched her every motion, returned to the attack. Finding her again at the door, by which he again encountered the full luster of her lovely eyes, he made a stop before her, and bowed thrice with that submission and languishment, as was able, in a less intelligent country than Spain, where persons from their infancy speak with their eyes and fingers, to convince her, that that cavalier was surprised by her beauty. The young creature, named Violenta, who had more wit than all the women of Valencia besides, considering her years, beheld with delight the extraordinary mien and application of that stranger; from a fatal presentiment she felt something within that made her wish to engage him. She answered his salute in so graceful and peculiar a manner, that he was more and more confirmed her slave. What was now become of that indifferency, with which he had triumphed over the foible of the greatest ladies in Valencia? He, whose business had hitherto been to give love, rather than take it, was in a moment reduced to be one of the order of lovers; to wish, sigh, and desire, in return of those sighs and desires he had caused in others.

Violenta having done enough to engage Roderigo, and show her native civility, once more withdrew. The night coming on, there was no prospect of her returning again that evening, which caused the Count also to depart; but not without taking full notice of the house, the street, and the ways that led to it. When he came home, he sent for one of his agents in amour, who knew all the persons in Valencia, to enquire of him, by description, of the name and quality of such a young maiden, living in such a street, situated at the corner of such a square, near such a church, opposite to such a palace; by which particular account the engine[2] quickly found how it went with the Count; and that he must have made more than ordinary observation, to be able to give him such a true chart of the coast. This person shook his

[2]Agent.

head, and told the Don, "he knew the maiden very well, but feared she was not for his Lordship's turn, for that no virgin in Valencia had so fair and honest a report; that her wit was more commended than her beauty, for she could both read and write, in which she took extreme delight." An accomplishment which, in those days, few ladies aimed at, since they believed all inferior knowledge, as well as the sciences, was reserved for the other sex. This procurator added, "that her name was Violenta, a poor orphan, kept by her mother, who had been some years a widow, her husband no better than a goldsmith; that he had also left two sons, who followed his trade in great obscurity; that Violenta had the reputation of being extreme modest; and though she was sought by many, yet was she defamed for none."

Count Roderigo was so far gone in love, and his first love too, that if his intelligencer had brought him the most disadvantageous character in the world, it could not have cured him. This favorable report did certainly inflame his passion the more; he resolved to send her a declaration of love, which he did in form, but the maid returned him no answer. However, as the letter had been received and read by her, he did not absolutely despair. The next day he sent her another, more passionate than the former, letting her know the name and quality of her lover, together with the present of a pair of bracelets, valued at five hundred gold ducats. She returned the bracelets, and with it this letter:

To Count Roderigo di Ventimiglia, Knight of Valencia
My Lord,
Your person is handsome, your present very well, your letter is witty and extraordinarily well writ; but what are all these accomplishments to a virgin that values nothing but virtue? That which courage is to your sex, chastity is to ours; and indeed more, since the greatest cowardice is retrievable by one act of valor, but modesty is rarely or never to be regained. Neither my eyes nor my vanity shall be entertained at so vast a hazard: yet, that your Lordship may not think me altogether stupid, I do confess that your addresses have flattered both; my sight by your person, my pride by the offer you make me of your heart. But, illustrious cavalier, 'tis neither by the one nor the other that a maid must conduct herself, who knows the true estimation of virtue, and who would die in the defense of it. This from the humblest of your servants,

Violenta

Roderigo saw the gaining the heart of this fair person must be a work of time; but as he was prodigiously in earnest, and was so far from having any other affair of the heart, that this was the first time his was ever touched, he pursued her with such assiduity that she durst no longer appear either at her windows or door. From thence he traced her to church, where, to be near her, he committed a thousand indecencies. She changed every day the place and hour of her devotions; yet he everywhere found her out, and still it was all the same story: he must perish without her pity, and nothing but her love could preserve him. When he had urged this to her in a letter, with the tautology and true impertinence of a real lover (for when they are really affected, those creatures fly certainly beyond all common sense), she returned him this answer:

To Count Roderigo di Ventimiglia, Knight of Valencia
My Lord,
You very eloquently tell me you shall die if I continue unkind; but I very plainly tell your Lordship, that I must perish if I prove otherwise: since I know it will be impossible for me to live after the loss of my honor. I conjure you to leave me in repose, lest I be obliged to shut myself up in a cloister to avoid your pursuit. I may justly complain of that moment when first I saw you, for if it has made your Lordship unhappy, I am not less miserable; if it has taught you what it is to love, it has not left me insensible; but I neither must nor will indulge either my heart or eyes! I have a mind truly intrepid in the cause of virtue, which neither the preservation of your precious life, nor that of my mother, brothers, or of my own, can ever induce me to forsake: I would see the whole world in a conflagration, and myself in the middle of it, before I could be brought to do anything contrary to the rules of modesty. Wonder not, that a maid so meanly born and educated, should have such exalted ideas of virtue: I have studied her well, all her ways are lovely, peace and honor attend her votaries in this life, a fragrant report when they are dead, and a crown of glory hereafter! How despicable are those advantages which you offer me in exchange? Consider of it, and farewell.

This pursuit lasted six months. At length, all that the Count could obtain was a confession that she loved him within the degrees of honor, but not a jot beyond it. Yet as much in love as Roderigo was, during all that time, he never once thought of marrying her: the disparity between them was so great he had no notion of wedlock. In Spain they have other maxims than in

England; here a person ennobles his wife, there 'tis a reproach for a man of quality and to his descendants, if he chance to mingle with the people. However, Violenta, as her heart was too haughty to speak first of that union, so she resolved he should never have favors of her without it. One day, he had so well ordered his intelligence that he had notice of a visit she had designed to make to a maiden of the same rank. Roderigo, by the force of presents, got leave of that person to conceal himself in her closet till Violenta came; soon after he surprised her with his sight. Being left together, he said to her, with some coldness, "Considering, Madam, the small regard you have given either to my letters or presents, I may compare your subtlety to that of a serpent, who is said to close his ears, for fear of hearing the voice of the charmer; which has made me forbear writing or sending to you; and I wish I had the same power to desist from seeing you, since my mortal enemy could not more cruelly torment me. If love were not involuntary, I could never submit to such usage. What objection have you to the truest lover, to the most passionate adorer that ever was? Were it possible for you to look into my heart and know what I suffer, you could not persist in your tyranny! I die for you! but you will not pity me!"

"My Lord," answered the discreet maid, "I do more than pity you, I sympathize with you in everything; I feel all your pains, I sigh as much, I lament as much, and perhaps I love as much, but with this difference, which makes me more wretched than you can be, that you have your redress in your own power, which, alas! is not in mine; you may be cured whenever you please, but it is quite otherwise with me! I am ready to be commanded by you, but you will not obey me; you think me too far beneath your quality, whilst I wish you were not so much above mine. But since there is no descending for you, nor any exaltation for me, leave me in repose from this moment, and content yourself with having the first place in my heart, which no other shall ever possess; but for the favors your Lordship expects, they are not mine to bestow. I have devoted myself to virtue; all my thoughts, words and actions are dedicated to that goddess! I cannot take the smallest part from her without an immortal offense; therefore do not be displeased if I never see you more!" Here she broke from his arms that would have retained her; and coming home, she made a vow to make no visit, and to go nowhere, unless to church, till she were released of Roderigo's persecutions for fear of meeting him, as she had done that day.

The Count very well understood what Violenta aimed at in her discourse; but he could not bring himself, notwithstanding the extremity of his love, to debase his blood so far as to mingle by marriage with one of her low degree. Observing the small progress that he had made in fifteen months' courtship, and that there was no probability of advancing farther, he resolved to do all that was in his power towards curing himself of so infamous and uneasy a passion. He began to return to his old practice of gallantry; gave balls, treats, music and entertainments to the ladies, who had very much lamented that alteration in his temper, though they knew not the cause; they did all that was possible to keep up his good humor and engage him amongst them, but in vain; he carried within his breast that which poisoned all his delights. A lover who is not yet in the rank of the happy reserves his heart wholly, without any division, for the cruel person to whom destiny has made a present of it. All the favors upon earth from the greatest beauties could have no taste for Roderigo. Satisfied of this cruel circumstance, he found it impossible for him to live any longer in a state of rebellion against his sovereign mistress; wherefore he returned to her with all the contrition imaginable, full of penitence, for having dared to attempt so impossible a thing as breaking the chains she had imposed upon him. That cruel tyrant of the heart, brought him once again to sue, with all the humble arts of flattery, for the least contemptible favor; but that prudent maid told him, there was none such in love, the smallest being of equal value to the greatest: as in a ladder of stairs, the lowest step is as necessary as the highest, though the last lands you at the place where you desire to be, and where you could never have arrived but by those degrees. Which rule well observed, a virgin ought never to permit her lover the smallest favor, not the freedom of her hand or lip, for the lover's touch, nay, his very breath, sullies and takes from modesty its native luster, and destroys the merit of being wholly innocent.

Poor Roderigo was not like to make any great progress amidst these exalted notions; at length he bethought him of another expedient. He resolved to change his battery, and knowing they were pretty poor, he made Donna Camilla a visit, Violenta's mother, in which he confessed his passion for her daughter, and complained of the ineffectual eighteen months' courtship he had paid her. The old gentlewoman, to whom this was no great news, though she affected to be ignorant, answered that Violenta was highly honored by those marks of his respect, but that she was a maid unskilled in courts, rude of fashion, and not used to the conversation of persons of his quality. In the end, he presented her with a thousand ducats toward her occasions, and told her he would assign her daughter a handsome dowry, if she could find any honest man for her husband, where she might be well disposed of, provided she would have some small consideration of his suffering, and afford him a little ease from that intolerable rack he endured! Donna Camilla, whose sense of honor was not inferior to Violenta's, let him know, with all regard to his quality, that she was offended at his proposal; that her house was no place to purchase virtue in, whose price was inestimable! The Count carried back his ducats, which he could not get the good gentlewoman to touch; and fell to debate farther with himself, what was next to be done. He could not abandon the maid, that he had in vain essayed; he could not by diversion drive her out of his thoughts, that was a fruitless project; he could not corrupt her, nor could he live without her! He found he had but lost time in all his enterprises, and prolonged his own torment, which daily augmented: therefore he at last resolved to marry her. And though she was neither of such birth or fortune as his quality deserved, yet her virtue and accomplishments, her beauty and discretion deserved greater advancement! This resolution once taken, he found he was much more at his ease, and even wondered at himself for not coming to the point before. Now he felt mercy and compassion for the maid intrude into his breast, where only self-love had dwelt before. He owned that it was pity so fair an example of virtue should be cast away; that 'twas hard, a life so faultless should be attended with infamy and ruin! and was therefore pleased looking upon himself as a person destined to reward her chastity, raise her abject fortune, and draw forth of obscurity a bright example, which the virgins of the age might imitate. Thus composed, he fell into a slumber, where he thought Violenta appeared to his sight, with her hair flowing! her dress infinitely disordered! her face sullied with tears! and her breast bruised with the blows she had given herself! She struck a dagger to his heart, and told him, that was the reward of treachery and inconstancy! The blow pained him so much, by imagination, that he awakened in a horrible fright, and giving a great shriek, he found himself upon the floor, where he had fallen in his agony: but having no opinion at all of dreams, he applied this to his restless mind, which always carried Violenta's idea. The next morning, he determined to make her a visit in form, and propose to her the accomplishment, as he hoped of both their desires. He found her at her needle, for she was always employed, according to an inscription at the Villa Benediti:

> Donna virtuosa, non sá star otiosa.
> A virtuous lady can never be idle.

Violenta flushed red as scarlet at seeing Don Roderigo enter, then turned pale as ashes, with such an universal trembling, that she was unable to support herself without sitting. "Is this aversion, fair creature, or some kinder passion?" said the Count, "that you are always thus disordered when I see you?"

"Say rather," answered the maid, "it is my better angel that warns, and makes me shudder and shrink from you as my evil genius, as the persecutor of virtue, as a tyrant, that would force from me the only treasure I possess! As one that must either leave me in repose, or take away my life. Something whispers my soul that your passion will be fatal to me; I would fly you as an abhorrence to nature, as a destroyer of chastity."

"As the man you love, fair Violenta," interrupted the Count with a smile, "your disorder and invectives are more glorious for me than the favors of others; you could not be thus affected for a person indifferent to you; since in so soft a creature, hatred could never have so great an ascendant, or work you to such a degree; it must be the kinder passion from which I expect advantageous effects."

"If that were true, my Lord," answered the constant maid, "as I will not pretend to convince you of the contrary, I would starve and die a martyr to my desires, rather than gratify the smallest wish at the expense of my virtue! Yes, Count Roderigo, I do love, and have loved you for a long time. I will not presume to say that I retained my indifferency a minute after I first beheld you; and from that inauspicious moment I felt other sentiments for your Lordship, than I had ever done for any of your sex. When you had abandoned me, to renew the vicious pursuits of your former gallantries, you left a fury in my breast to supply your place, or a worse tormentor; a fiend, that amidst all your sufferings you have been a stranger to. Jealousy, that cruel tyrant! allowed me not a moment's repose; thus, since I have dared to demonstrate that my pains rather exceed yours, and that I am not at all in debt to you for what you have endured let us make a drawn battle of it, both call off our forces at once, and no more trouble one another with our mutual follies; let us try to cure ourselves as well as we can. As to my part, I have determined to do something, but what, I cannot yet resolve; neither ought I to tell your Lordship, lest it should look like threatening, or a desire of being retained; but certainly, my Lord, this is the last time I will ever allow myself the liberty to converse with you. I beseech your Lordship not to be displeased, when you are refused the door; you shall suddenly hear that I have either taken the veil, or have abandoned my mother, brothers, country, and wandered far from Valencia to seek my bread in a foreign clime, distant from your Lordship's cruel persecution.'' She ended this discourse with a shower of tears. Roderigo, unable to stand the torment, fell at her feet, and confessed to her the design that brought him thither, and the resolution that he had taken to marry her.

As we have often beheld the sun break out with sudden glory, in the midst of clouds and rain, so darted from Violenta's eyes, rays of light which restored to every charm its native grace; then the Count discovered how truly lovely she was. She gave a loose to joy, and spoke such transporting things, full of gratitude and passion, that Roderigo confessed the greatest pleasure was in pleasing, and how far the transport of virtuous love exceeded the sophisticated pleasures of the vicious. Violenta telling him that though he exceeded her in all other advantages, yet she could not be outdone in love; that she would be emulous to please him, and hoped by her obedience to make him one day confess he would not exchange her for the noblest lady. At which he thanked her for her good intentions, and plucked a diamond ring from his finger of great value, which he gave her as a pledge of their marriage; and then, and not till then, had he ever presumed to kiss her; so sacred and inviolable had that chaste maid preserved herself, amidst the flames of love that had surrounded her from the Count's passion without, and from her own fires within. A pattern worthy the imitation of young virgins, who, though perhaps virtuous in what they call the main, yet prostitute their modesty too far in suffering the touches of the hand, the neck, and the kisses of men. They may assure themselves, that they lose a great degree of their value, by such unwarrantable freedoms; as the luster wears off the richest silks by handling, and the inimitable blue from the plum, which when once lost, can never be restored. A great many things more might be said against so vile a custom; besides the habit and air of lightness that it gives a virgin, by which she is with much greater facility brought to suffer further liberties, and very often loses her character for those she has granted, under the notion that they are but innocent freedoms, inwardly satisfied with being what they call essentially virtuous.

After the Count and Violenta had interchanged their mutual vows, Roderigo begged her to conceal his happiness for some time, because of the inequality of their condition, till he had taken care to inform his relations and friends gradually of their marriage; however, he permitted her to discover it to her mother and her brothers, bidding her invite them to be there in the evening, and he would bring a priest out of the country, who knew them not, with the first valet of his chamber, whom he could trust, that her maid who was brought up by Donna Camilla from her youth might also be admitted, to make up the number of witnesses six, which was sufficient to attest a marriage, if ever it should come by any unforeseen chance to be disputed. You need not ask whether Violenta were very diligent and careful to put all things in order; she dressed up the nuptial chamber and bed, with all the decency the time and her circumstances allowed her. At length, the long looked-for hour approached, the bridegroom came, and brought along with him a priest and his gentleman. They were married in the presence of Violenta's mother and her two brothers, Ianthe the maid, and the Count's valet, without either pomp or preparation, or any expense requisite for the nuptials of a man of his extraction and great possessions.

Roderigo vouchsafed to sit down to eat with the mother and brothers of his new bride, whom he acknowledged and caressed by those appellations. They had prepared a very handsome supper, and were as happy in their own opinions, as persons suddenly raised from poverty to wealth, or from a mean degree to an exalted state of honor. They conducted the new-married pair to the bride-chamber, and then took their leave, recommending them to the mercy of love, and favor of the night: which I shall no otherways describe, than by a person long laboring under the extremity of thirst, who at length arrives to a place where he can quench that violent distress, where he quaffs at liberty in flowing bowls, and unstinted draughts of pleasure.

In the morning, Violenta, without assuming the airs of a countess, begged her lord, since he was now in possession of what he had so long and vehemently desired, that he would prescribe rules to her conduct, assuring him, that she should be as diligent to observe his orders, and as ambitious to please him in whatever he desired, as the poorest slave, who was most faithful, most dutiful, and affectionate to his master. Roderigo said, "Sweet, charming wife, I beg you to use none of those affected airs of humility to me; I am burdened with them, I beseech you let me hear no more of that; you are now my wife, and so you must conduct yourself; I have no less a value for you, than if you were descended from the noblest family in Spain. Hereafter you will be convinced of this truth; but till I have taken order for my affairs, I require you by the obedience of which you boast yourself, to conceal our marriage; and pray be not displeased, if I am often from you in the daytime, but every night shall be yours. As soon as I go home I will send you two thousand ducats, not to buy your wedding-clothes, it is not yet time for that. When we publish our marriage, I will myself take care to provide you what in all respects shall be fit for my bride: but women need trifles as well as essentials, and I would not have my dear Violenta want anything within my power to grant."

Seignior Roderigo departed thus from his lady's house, who entertained him with such passionate love and sweetness, that for a year's time he never thought himself happy but when he was in the arms of his dear Violenta; omitting not one night from embracing and sleeping with her; which could not be carried so privately, notwithstanding all the caution he used, but the neighbors discovered his resort to Donna Camilla's house, and were prodigiously scandalized at it. They imagined that Violenta was kept by the Count; some of the well-meaning part (as to the others they tattled abroad and at home, and were very glad that they had got a piece of scandal to entertain the town with) reproached Donna Camilla and her sons for tolerating that abuse: they even reprimanded Violenta, lamenting her misfortune, whose reputation had flourished twenty years in honor, and been a fair example to all the virgins of Valencia, that she should now fall by the gripes of poverty, involving her mother and brothers in her sin, a prey to shame and dishonesty; deploring those happy days in which she was thought not only the fairest but chastest maid in all that part of Spain; but now degenerating from her accustomed virtue, her behavior was esteemed light, abandoned to lascivious love, one who was contented, by the price of sin, to support herself and her mother in ease and plenty. Poor Violenta, whose conscience acquitted her from these slanderous reproaches, took less care of their spreading, because she knew her own innocence; yet could not help being very uneasy at the difference she found in the behavior of her friends, the open scoffs and fleers of some of the boldest of them; and which was more sensible, the cold civilities and freezing looks of the better mannered and most charitable. Yet assuring herself that she had an antidote in reserve against all their poison, and that when her marriage was published, it would serve as an excellent moral against the malice of such who were forward to condemn only upon appearances and false opinion. But when those reproaches were most cutting, though her husband were "the Lord of her idolatry"[3] and whom she would much rather die than displease, she could not forbear telling him her sufferings, and begged him very earnestly to take her home to his house, since it was as much to the injury of his reputation, that such infamous reports should be spread of a woman, whom they would one day find had the honor to be his wife.

Count Roderigo knew very well how to delay Violenta's request, having found the great secret of her passion, that she dreaded nothing so much as his displeasure; he could cunningly give her cause to apprehend the effects of it, since she had rather have offended the whole world together, than in the smallest matter displease her lord. Her humble manner of education had not yet given place to a desire of rank or greatness; she knew no ambition but that of retaining Roderigo by her charms and goodness; and whereas she had been slow to receive the fire of love, so much the fiercer and surer it burnt in her heart, which had not the least taste of delight, but in the enjoyment of Roderigo, an eager thirst of virtue being the only thing that could ever rival her lord in her esteem. The Count's observation soon rendered him master of this secret; and seeing there was nothing new for his desires; that he had even surfeited with the delicious banquet; that it was all but a repetition of the same delight; he first began to wonder how he could so eagerly pursue a common pleasure, and then enquired of his memory, which was but too faithful, whether he had ever done so or no? And

[3]Shakespeare, *Romeo and Juliet*, II. ii. 114.

when by melancholy proof he was too well convinced of the state of his affairs, he grew from cool to more cold, from frost to ice, from ice to aversion, and a hatred of his own folly for so unworthily matching himself with the lees of the people. In this fluctuation of his thoughts, he often forbore her bed; which, when he approached, it was rather like a sinner than a husband, to gratify the call of nature, and in which a common strumpet might as easily have assisted, than from the first motive of generous love and husbandly tenderness and affection.

Violenta's duty and sense of gratitude had so far enslaved her will to his pleasure, that she durst not even complain of his neglect; and when, after several days' absence, she presumed to send a letter to him to his palace, to enquire of his health, and the cause why she did not see him, he acted the tyrant to the life; and at their next meeting gave her to understand, that if she any more presumed to enquire into his recesses, he would never forgive, nor own her for his wife. This was as a dagger to pierce the heart of the miserable Violenta. Her complaints rather wearied, than softened him; he looked upon her as a despicable creature, whose reputation being lost, not one of any figure would appear in her defense, or imagine her to be married to him, especially if they should see him married to another. There are many vices which are not believed because of their magnitude; such Roderigo thought would be his double marriage, forgetting that he had ever heard of religion; forgetting the call of his own conscience, for certainly there must be a remorse for betraying so virtuous a creature. He took up his old haunts of gallantry and luxury, which terminated in a violent passion for a fair young creature called Aurelia,[4] the sole daughter and heiress of Don Ramires, one of the chiefest knights and most honorable families in all Valencia.

Count Roderigo was considerable for estate and quality, without any allay but a flirt of youthful pleasure which was imagined would pass away with his youth, if not sooner, should he once marry and settle; and who was incomparably the most advantageous match in the city. Don Ramires quickly came to an accommodation with his proposals, offering a very large dowry with his daughter in present, and the rest of his estate in reversion, after the death of himself and his wife. Count Roderigo settled all things to their satisfaction, and the marriage was

[4]Aurelia, a name that Manley added to Painter's story, comes from Latin *aurum*, gold.

solemnized to the pleasure of all persons concerned, and the good will of those, who having no immediate interest in those nuptials, were delighted with any public occasion of mirth and joy.

The marriage done and ended, the bride and bridegroom continued at Don Ramires's house, where they lived in all the pleasures of the happy, such as new married persons of high rank and prosperous fortunes enjoy, without any remorse for what Violenta might suffer when she should hear the news of his inconstancy. He looked upon her as an idle girl, a creature of low degree, the favorite of an hour, a little mistress with whom he had condescended to squander away some superfluous hours of youth but unworthy his regard when in cooler thoughts, or to expect the continuance of his noble name and family from. In short, he forgot that ever she had been of any consequence to his happiness! He forgot he had married her; and hearing so many people talk of her as a mistress he kept, he imagined it was so, and no more; never fearing, from her excessive love and humble behavior, that he needed to apprehend anything from her resentment; more especially from those mechanics her brothers, who indeed had no part of their sister's spirit or understanding; and who dreamt of no other notions of honor but what they expected to find in their customers. Donna Camilla, her mother, he looked upon as a piece of old household stuff quite out of date; poor and independent as she was, he knew it would be very difficult for her, at that time of day, to find any one to espouse her interests against his in Valencia.

Thus Seignior Roderigo, fearless of the reproaches of Violenta, publicly espoused Donna Aurelia in the face of the sun, in the great church of Valencia; immediately the report of such a fine wedding was carried to all parts of the city. Violenta's brothers were first informed of it, they ran to their mother to let her know the disaster; yet without that honorable resentment which is always found in the well-born. According to the custom of Spain, they should immediately have made the villain's blood atone for the injury he had done their sister, and to which they were witnesses; but their souls were of a piece with their profession, they did not dream of honor and revenge, provided they could sell their plate; nay, they were so sordid as to comply with the orders Roderigo had given his intendant to go to such persons, meaning Violenta's brothers, and bespeak from them all the necessary vessels and utensils, whether of silver, silver-gilt, or gold plate, that was necessary for his degree, to furnish his house and table upon his nuptials with a person of Aurelia's quality and fortune.

Donna Camilla indeed resented the abuse, not only as a person of a high heart, but as one who wept drops of blood for the dishonor of her daughter; she sent for her sons, reproaching them with the pitifulness of their spirit, to take employment from the man they should much sooner destroy. They protested to her that they knew not when the plate was bespoke, but that it was for the publication of their sister's marriage; and afterwards could not go back from their word, the gentleman only designing to oblige them for their sister's sake. Camilla, seeing them to be such stocks and stones, sent them away and was contented to mourn alone. This wretched dame lived in great anguish, because she durst not make her complaint to any, and was ignorant of the name of the priest who had married her daughter; neither would she impart her sorrow to Violenta, imagining she would too soon hear of the fatal disaster that was befallen her.

And indeed, this virtuous lady, only tantalized with the hopes of greatness, with the mock scene or airy idea of grandeur, which like a golden bough hung far out of her reach,[5] was the last in knowing what was now stale news in Valencia. A person of her penetration, however blinded she was by love and Roderigo's continual pretenses, thought there must be something extraordinary to make him absent himself so frequently as he did. At first she used to write him the kindest letters to enquire of his health; but the airs he took to himself, as we have before related, soon gave her enough of presuming to enquire after him. He had carried all things with a high hand; her humble spirit durst not dispute the pleasure of so great a man. He might lie away as long as he thought fit, the joy she had when he came again made her forget the pain she had suffered by his absence. She always received him with smiles, and never with cold looks or reproaches. Having lately used her to stay away several nights together, she did not wonder at it now; but she was not left long in ignorance. Her next neighbors, merely to insult her, asked what she would do for a sweetheart now her lord was

[5]Alluding to the legend of Tantalus, who was condemned to hunger for a bough of fruit he could not reach; Manley seems to conflate it, however, with the golden bough in Virgil's *Aeneid* (Book VI).

married? how came it that she was not at the wedding? especially since it was so public, and the finest that was ever seen in Valencia? Donna Aurelia was a charming bride!

Violenta having very well examined these reports, for she at first regarded them as stories designed by malicious persons only to insult her, when she grew confirmed in the truth, her heart was immediately open to wrath, indignation, madness and revenge. All the furies of hell entered like a torrent into her breast, and in a moment expelled her native softness; Love hid his face and would be seen no more; he took wing with all his train and dependents, and flew forever away from that hospitable heart where he had been so fondled and tenderly entertained. The sense of honor lost, of her virtue demolished, her chastity overthrown, her ruined reputation swelled her to an extremity of resentment; she tore her ornaments, her dress, her hair; she stamped, and traversed her apartment like a raging bacchanal; like Medea,[6] furious in her revenge; like the fiends with fatal torches in their hands, to set the world on fire: she was more than all these, she was herself, that is to say, most miserable and most outrageous. She could not weep, that distress was too soft for her obdurate grief; she could not in a long time speak, even the relief of words were denied her; she could only beat her breast, groan, and puff her breath out, as if flames had come at every blast. At length, nature, unable longer to maintain so cruel a war against itself, suffered this wretched creature to sink down on the carpet for an interval of time, that she might recover strength enough to renew the conflict; essaying several times to rise, she sunk again, and with groans poured forth this torrent of complaints.

"Alas! alas! what inexpressible torture does my poor heart endure without the least prospect of relief? No one creature on the whole earth can give me ease! what ruin do I suffer for no offense of mine? Ah Fortune! Fortune! thou art so totally my enemy, that thou hast not left me so much as the prospect of a friend to revenge my injury. Oh blood! blood! a villain's blood! too small an expiation for ruined chastity! Oh cruel husband! Do not my groans echo in thy ears? Dost thou not hear my voice crying aloud for vengeance? Canst thou regard any other object

---

[6]In Euripides's *Medea*, Medea's loyalty to Jason extends even to committing crimes on his behalf. Nevertheless, he abandons her in order to marry the daughter of Creon, King of Corinth, a more advantageous match. Her revenge is to murder Jason's children. This comparison of Violenta to Medea does not occur in Painter.

but thy first, thy lawful wife? dishonored by thy cruelty, and suffering a thousand furious martyrdoms for thy adulterous crime! Ah ungrateful! Is this, thou monstrous wretch, all the return that thy base heart can make for excessive love, unshaken fidelity and obedient humility? Since this is all that thou canst bestow upon me, I will pay myself, be sure I will. Thy blood shall be the atonement, that I may die with joy, insensible of pain."

Donna Camilla and her sons, with Ianthe, hearing her voice so outrageous, talking loudly to herself like a tempest or a whirlwind, went up to her chamber, where they found her so deformed with rage and fury, that she was almost out of their knowledge; they feared she would run mad, and said whatever they could to reduce her from those violent pangs; but their endeavors increased rather than allayed the storm. Reason was utterly lost upon her, she was insensible to all things but revenge, which she insatiably thirsted after; then, as she said, she should be at rest. Finding they could make no impression upon her obdurate mind, Donna Camilla and her sons withdrew, leaving the old maid Ianthe, whom Violenta loved more than any other, to take care she did herself no hurt. This poor creature had from her childhood, when she was first made a slave, been bred up by Donna Camilla. The slave had brought up Violenta, and so tenderly loved her, that she would have done anything for her relief. After she had flattered and humored her rage awhile, she told her lady, that if she would suspend her fury for a little time, she would go herself and seek out Count Roderigo and hear what he had to say, and she doubted not but to order the matter so well, that she would bring him along with her, where, if he did not give her the satisfaction she desired, she might do with him as she pleased, and wreak upon him her just revenge.

"No! no, Ianthe!" said Violenta, "those are light and small offenses that we can be reasoned out of the sense of; what Roderigo had committed against me, Reason itself supports me in my desire of vengeance! And should my heart give way to any other thoughts, I would with my own hands divide it from this wretched body! Nothing but his life alone can satisfy me! God caused me to be born his instrument of wrath to punish the injury done my honor; what reputation remains to me but that of an abominable whore? Shall he live who has bestowed so vile a quality upon me? Shall he breathe in pleasure whilst I hourly pine away in infamy? That base seducer, that wretch without

principles or honor, who used laughingly to say, as I then thought
in jest, but the villain was too much in earnest, that maids of my
base birth had no pretensions to honor, what had we to do with
such fantastic notions? Virtue and chastity were pretty names
indeed for boors to play with! As if courage were only appropriated to men of quality, or modesty to noble women. Yes,
Roderigo, thou shalt know that my sentiments were worthy the
most exalted birth! Thou shalt feel it by the ardor of thy wife's
resentment! by that height of vengeance with which I will appease and vindicate my honor! and if thou, Ianthe, dost deny to
assist me, I will do the work alone. Thou art a stranger born,
and leadest the life of a poor wretched slave, condemned all thy
days to drudgery; I have here two thousand ducats and several
jewels which that false traitor gave me; they are destined by
Heaven to reward that person who shall assist me in my revenge. I will now put that treasure in thy hands, I will give all to
thee, if thou wilt help me to sacrifice Roderigo to my injured
honor. Too well I know there is but little redress for so mean a
person as I am, to expect by law, against two the most potent
families in Valencia. When the question is, which shall be proved
the wife, and which the whore! most certain, Don Ramires's
daughter must have the honorable and I the infamous appellation. Justice waits upon the great, Interest holds the scale, and
Riches turns the balance. Besides, I know not even the priest
who married us, perhaps he was not a priest, and my ruin was
originally designed; or if he be, Roderigo will take care to keep
him far from my knowledge. Wherefore, my dear Ianthe, if from
my youth thou didst ever love me, or that thou wert ever
sensible of the love I had for thee, show me the effects now,
when thy help is most necessary. If thou dost deny me, I will
execute my purpose alone; the first time I ever behold him, with
these enraged, accursed eyes, I will strike him dead, or murder
him with these two trembling hands, without any other assistance."

Ianthe hearing what Violenta said, and well knowing her undaunted resolution and heroic spirit, after she had revolved and
debated several things in her mind, resolved at length to devote
herself wholly to her mistress's infernal commands, potently
moved at her being defamed and dishonored by the pretense of
marriage; and partly prompted by covetousness and the desire
of liberty, by which she should gain so great a reward; with
which she meant to fly away to her own land, and seek her
kindred and parents, if they were yet alive or to be found. When

she was thoroughly resolved, she embraced Violenta and said to her, "Madam, here I plight my faith and hand to you. Your poor Ianthe shall follow your commands in life and death! I have as great an appetite to revenge your dishonor as yourself can desire; but that we may be sure to effect it, you must disguise your rage, and put on you the habit of dissimulation. You shall write the Count a letter, as you well can do, to invite him hither; as if you only grieved at the loss of his heart, and did not dispute Aurelia's title to his bed. Leave the rest to my management. When we have him here fast, we will send him to rest in a more assured place, where he shall everlastingly continue to curse the time whenever he betrayed poor virgins by the sacred pretense of marriage."

Violenta harkened to her as the oracle that was to resolve her destiny, and feed her bloody and cruel vengeance. That fair prospect, which stood before her, of revenge, caused her, like ebbing seas after the workings of a mighty storm, to sink appeased, though within she stood collected and ready to execute what the most cruel hatred can inspire. She gave herself so much respite as to write him a letter, which fully expressed all she suffered, and what more she was like to suffer; and then she rose into distant threatenings of what a lover forsaken might attempt; yet soon sunk again into the more humble necessities of a lover, who could not live without the sight of the person beloved; which as a reward of all her sufferings she beseeched him to grant her; in an indirect manner, seeming to give up her title to marriage, if she could hope to preserve what she much more valued, that which once she had to his heart.

"Take there, Ianthe," says the afflicted Violenta, "thy passport to Roderigo; if thou canst play thy part as well as I have done mine, we may then assure ourselves that my vengeance will be complete. I may rest satisfied my date of life shall not be long, since life is more insupportable to me than a thousand deaths, and yet I cannot die unrevenged."

Ianthe having the letter, rose early the next morning, and rendered herself with great diligence at the house of Don Ramires, where she waited obsequiously till she could speak with some person belonging to the Count, which was not long after. Ianthe seeing that gentleman who was present at Roderigo's first marriage, he blushed, and would have avoided her, pretending to go about affairs for his master. The old slave, who was not to learn her business at that time of day, bore up briskly to him, whispering him in the ear, asked how the Count did! and if she might be admitted to the honor of speaking with him alone, for her business required privacy? Don Roderigo being soon advertised of this by his servant, came forth, and pointed her towards the street, where he presently followed her; to whom smilingly she said, having made him a feigned courtesy and presented him the letter, "I am a poor slave, my Lord, and can neither write nor read, yet I dare lay my life, there is humble suit made to you in that paper for the sight of your sweet person; and to say the truth, my poor mistress has been very much injured by you—not in the point of marriage, for I never thought Madam Violenta, a beggarly tradesman's daughter, was a fit wife for the great Count Roderigo, but that you will not vouchsafe to visit her, that she may not be miserable all at once; you take no care to cure her dishonor, by providing her a husband in some other place, which would prevent the infamy she will meet with from being a forsaken mistress. She loves you in a lost manner, she is ready to die, and no longer than last night said to me, 'Dear Ianthe, I cannot possibly live without the sight of him; though I must not pretend, after his marriage with the Lady Aurelia, to have him for my husband, I wish he would still regard me as his friend, and provide for me that I fall not into poverty, and would set apart but one day in the week, or rather night, for fear of the neighbors, that I might be happy in his love.' And sure my Lord," added the old impertinent,[7] "you cannot do a better thing, if it were but for the pleasure of telling yourself that you have the fairest wife, and most beautiful mistress of any nobleman in all Spain."

Roderigo listening with profound attention to what the slave said, as gathering from thence the pacific sentiments of her mistress, took and opened the letter, which when he had read, he fell to consider what it contained. The warring passions rose in his breast, as heat and cold meet and jostle together, pent up in the same cloud; love and hatred, compassion and disdain, combatted in his heart, and vexed him with contrarieties. Then pausing upon an answer, he thought it necessary to flatter her despair, till he could see her to take his measures, that she might not by her offensive fondness give any disturbance to his new enjoyments. "My dear friend, Ianthe," said the dissembling Count, "recommend me to the good grace and favor of thy

---

[7]Presumptuous person.

charming mistress; for this time I will write her no answer, but tomorrow night at eight o'clock I will be sure to wait upon her, and give her an account of this ugly matter, and of what has happened since I had the happiness of seeing her last; when I shall have told her the necessity that urged me to what I have done, she will certainly pity rather than condemn me."

Ianthe posted away with her good news to Violenta. They quickly set themselves to prepare all things for Roderigo's reception; whilst he told his new bride he was called away by certain affairs to his villa, where he was obliged to remain a whole night, but he would return the morning after. Then ordering his gentleman of the chamber, who was the confidant of all his amours, he bade him command two horses to be got ready, upon which they rode forth out of the city till it was duskish; then the Count fetched a compass, and entered Valencia by another gate; he ordered his servant to put up the horses in a strange inn, and stay for him there till he returned from Violenta in the morning. When he came to the house, he found Ianthe, with great devotion, waiting his arrival, with a settled purpose to use him according to his deserts. She conveyed him to the chamber of her expecting mistress; their meeting was such as might be well supposed between two persons that had once desperately loved, and now as perfectly hated one another, but who yet with cold and dissembled flattery now sought to deceive each other. Violenta represented to him her despair when she heard of his marriage, the sorrow that she endured, having neither been able to eat nor sleep since the fatal tidings of her dishonor, and the loss of his heart. Roderigo took her in his arms, and protested to her he was still the same, but that the late Count his father had left so vast a debt upon the estate, which was all mortgaged to Don Ramires, that if it had not been in consideration of this marriage with his daughter he would have seized upon his whole inheritance, and then he must have been a beggar, and unable to assist her whom he valued more than his life; for though he were wedded to Aurelia, he loved none but Violenta, assuring her, that after a little time he meant to poison his new wife, and return to end his days with her in love and happiness. He concluded this discourse, which was only framed to appease her, with protestations of his love, and ten thousand vows of constancy, which are easily sworn by those who intend only to deceive. Doubtless, if this miserable woman had credited his words and oaths, and from thence have whispered peace to her deluded heart, he would have changed his mind, and not thought himself tied to the performance of his vows, since he could so manifestly break that which he had made in the sight of Heaven, when in the sacred bands of wedlock he had plighted his faith indissolubly to hers.

The Count was very well satisfied that he found Violenta so well appeased; he thought he need not give himself much trouble about that little maid, a creature of no consequence, whom he might use as he pleased. She was careful not to mention anything of her own marriage, nor a word of revenge for her dishonor. Her complaints were wholly directed to her fears of losing his heart, which he could soothe without much difficulty, since it was her business to believe. After supper, the Count not having taken much rest for several nights before, grew sleepy and ordered his bed to be made ready. We need not enquire whether Violenta and Ianthe obeyed his commands with diligence, in which consisted the good or evil fortune of their enterprise.

Violenta, to show herself most affectionate, went first to bed; as soon as they were laid, Ianthe drew the curtains and took away the Count's sword, his dagger she laid upon a stool by her mistress' bedside; for though they had provided a large knife for that purpose, the slave thought the justice would be more remarkable if he fell by his own weapon, but to make sure work, she placed them both together; then taking away the candles, she feigned to go out of the chamber, but returned again, and locked the door on the inside, as if she had been gone away, and rested herself against the door, waiting for the cruel minute when her mistress would want her assistance. The destined[8] Count thinking himself alone in the chamber with Violenta, began to embrace and kiss her; but she begged him to desist till she awoke again, for having never rested since the news of his fatal marriage, her heart being now somewhat more at ease, she found herself so sleepy she was not able to speak; and then she turned herself away from him to her repose. Roderigo, who had had as little sleep as possible, and perhaps stood more in need of rest, very gladly complied with her request, his designed caresses were more in the prospect of pleasing her than himself; soon after he fell into a profound sleep, which they were very well assured of by the manner of taking his breath.[9] Violenta reached

---

[8]Doomed.
[9]From here to the end, Manley follows Painter almost word for word.

the dagger, and feeling softly for the place where she could most commodiously strike, raising herself in the bed, and transported with wrath, struck the poniard into his throat: Ianthe hearing him groan, leaped briskly upon the bed, and getting upon him with her knees and hands kept him down; he struggled, but Violenta, like another Medea, mad with rage and fury, redoubled her stroke, and thrust the point of the dagger with such force into his throat that she pierced it through on the other side. The wretched Count, thinking to make some resistance against his cruel destiny, received another wound; being held down by Ianthe he could not use hand nor foot. Through the excessive violence of his pain, he had not power to cry out or speak a word. After he had received ten or twelve mortal wounds, his soul flew away from his martyred body, in all probability to a dreadful audit, since he was taken away in the fullness of his sins, without a moment's space for repentance.

Violenta having finished this cruel enterprise, commanded Ianthe to light a candle. She approached with it near the Count's face, and saw that he was without life. "Ah traitor!" said she, "thou oughtest to have been years a-dying, if I had enjoyed power sufficient thou certainly should'st; yet some comfort it is to me to think, though I could not devote thy body to suffer such torments as thou did'st deserve, thy immortal soul is fled without a moment's warning to deprecate the divine vengeance!" Not able to quench her hate, nor satisfy the furious rage that burnt in her breast, with the point of the dagger she tore the eyes out of his head, speaking to them with a hideous voice, as if they were still alive, "Ah traitorous eyes, the interpreters of a villainous mind! come out of your shameful seat for ever! the spring of your false tears is now exhausted and dried up, so that ye shall weep no more! no more deceive chaste virgins with your feigned and falling showers." Her rage rather increased than abated, she seized upon his tongue, which with her bloody hands she plucked from the root; and beholding it with an unrelenting eye, said, as she was tearing it out, "Oh perjured and abominable tongue! false and cruel as thou wert, how many lies didst thou tell, before with the chain-shot[10] of this cursed member, thou could'st make a breach to overthrow my honor? Of which being robbed by thy traitorous means, I must devote myself to death, to which I have now shown thee the way."

[10] A kind of shot particularly effective in sieges.

Then, insatiable of cruelty (like a wolf fleshed upon his prey, irritated the more by the taste of blood), with the knife she violently ripped up his stomach; then launching her daring hands upon his heart tore it from the seat, and gashed it with a thousand wounds, cried, "Ah, vile heart, more obdurate and harder than adamant! upon this cruel anvil was forged the chains that bound up my unlucky destiny! What did I mean by wreaking my vengeance upon the eyes and tongue of this insatiable monster? The heart! This infamous heart of thine was the original of all my misery! It was by this the traitor was taught to flatter and betray! Oh that I could erst have discovered thy base imaginations, as now I do thy material substance, I might then have preserved myself from thy abominable treason and infidelity! yet shall not the hand only have reason to complain that it made no part of my revenge, when it had so great a one in my ruin! Take, cursed instrument," said she, dismembering his right hand from his body, "take thy reward for the faith thou didst dare to plight to me in the face of Heaven! Extreme provocations must have extreme punishment, my only grief is that thou art dead and cannot feel the torture." When she had mangled the body all over, with an infinite number of gashes, she cried out, "Oh infected carrion, once the organ and instrument of a most vile and traitorous mind, now thou are repaid as thy merits did deserve."

Ianthe, with horror and exceeding terror, had immovably beheld her butchery, when she said to her, "Ianthe, now I am at ease! my poor laboring heart is lightened of its burden! Come Death when thou wilt, thou shalt find me able to bear thy strongest assaults! I have daily proved thy torture, lest I should not bring my full revenge to the desired period! Help me then to drag this unworthy wretch out of my father's house, where I was first dishonored, where the odor of my chaste name was exchanged for poisonous infamy! Since my virtue is traduced abroad, my revenge shall be as manifest, and this carcass be exposed as publicly as was my reputation."

Violenta and Ianthe dragged the body to a chamber window and threw it out upon the pavement in the street, with the several parts that she had cut off. That done, she said to Ianthe, "Take this casket, there is in it all my jewels and two thousand ducats in gold, which I promised thee; ship thyself at the next port thou shalt come at, get thee over into Africa to save thy life as speedily as thou canst, and never return into these parts again, nor to any other where thou art known.'' Which Ianthe purposed to have done though Violenta had not counseled her to it. The poor slave, being just ready to depart, embraced and kissed her mistress; she took her leave with a doleful farewell, and went in search of better fortune; and from that time was never heard no more. All the pursuit that was made after her proved ineffectual, since no creature in Valencia could ever recover the least knowledge of the way she had taken.

Soon as day appeared, the first that passed through the street discovered the dead body; one told another of the strange spectacle that lay there to be seen, but no man knew who it was, because the eyes were picked out, and the other members mutilated and deformed. By that time it came to be eight o'clock, there was such a multitude of people assembled that it was almost impossible to come near the body. The generality thought thieves had murdered and stripped the dead person, because he was found in his shirt; others were of a contrary opinion. Violenta, who was at her window, hearing them give their several judgments, came down and with a firm voice said to the multitude, ''Gentlemen, you dispute about a thing which if I were examined by the lawful magistrate, I could give undoubted evidence of. This murder cannot be discovered by any other than by me, without great difficulty.'' Which words her neighbors easily believed, thinking this was a person slain by some of her lovers that were jealous of her; for poor Violenta had lost her former good reputation since the report that Count Roderigo kept her.

These words were carried to the magistrates, who, with their officers of justice, soon came to the place, where they found Violenta more undaunted than any of the spectators! They enquired of her immediately, ''What account she could give of that murder?'' Without fear or hesitation she readily answered, ''My Lords, he that you see here dead is Count Roderigo di Ventimiglia: and because many persons are concerned in his death, as, his father-in-law Don Ramires, his new wife Donna Aurelia, and all his own relations, if your Lordships please, I would, in their presence, before our most noble viceroy the Duke of Calabria, freely declare what I know of this unhappy affair.''

The magistrates, amazed to see so great a man as Roderigo lie there, inhumanly slain and butchered, took Violenta into custody till the viceroy's pleasure was known; who being urged by his own curiosity, and the importunity of Don Ramires, Donna Aurelia his daughter, and the kindred of the deceased, commanded, after dinner, she should be brought to her examination in the great hall of the palace; where the viceroy, the judges, the evidence and all persons being met, there was so great a crowd, that it was not possible to thrust in another creature. Violenta, as if she were conscious of well doing, and glowed with the pride of some worthy action performed, in the presence of them all, with a loud and clear voice, without either rage or passion, first recounted the chaste love between Count Roderigo and herself during the space of eighteen months, though without receiving the returns he expected: that within a while after, quite vanquished with love, he married her secretly in her own house: that the nuptials were solemnized by a priest unknown, in the presence of her mother, brothers, and two servants, whereof one of them was the Count's gentleman, and still in his service: that she had been more than a year his most obedient wife, without the least offense given on her part. Then she repeated to them his second marriage with Donna Aurelia, there present. Adding, that as he had deprived her of her reputation of honor, she had sought means to deprive him of his life; which she had effected by the assistance of her maid Ianthe, who, being filled with remorse, had drowned herself in the sea. "Think not, most noble Duke," added she, "that I have given you this plain relation to move your pity and prolong my life; I could for ever have escaped your justice, if I had so intended! my purpose was to have my honor as publicly cleared as it was aspersed; for a terror to all young virgins, how they receive the addresses of persons so greatly above them; and to warn them how they consent to a clandestine marriage, as I have done, by which I am this day brought to ruin. I hold myself unworthy to live, after being stained with blood; though that blood was shed to wash away my stain. So far am I from desiring life that I cannot endure to live. I beg death of your justice, lest in saving my body you condemn my soul, and force me with my own hands to commit the most unpardonable sin, that of self-murder!"

The Duke, the magistrates, and all the spectators were amazed at the courage and magnanimity of the maid; and that one of so little rank should have so great a sense of her dishonor. The people were so far moved with pity that they wept with luke-warm tears, to think so fair and chaste a creature should meet with such great misfortunes. Detesting the memory of Count Roderigo, they thought his death too small an expiation for a wretch, who, under the pretense of sacred marriage, could enjoy her love, and then traitorously wed himself to another. The viceroy resolving not to give too hasty a judgment, remitted back Violenta to prison; and gave orders for the dead Count to be interred as obscurely as his crime deserved; taking from Violenta all weapons by which she might do herself an injury. They used such diligence, that the priest who married them was sought out and found. The Count's gentleman also deposed what he knew of the nuptials, and his Lord's designed visit to Violenta the night before the murder was committed. All things were so fully proved, that nothing could be more plain, unless they could have had the confession of the dead lord himself. Violenta, notwithstanding the pity of the people, the intercession of the ladies, and the applause her chastity and magnanimity deserved, was condemned to be beheaded; not only for that she had presumed to punish the Count's offense by her own hand, without the help of justice, but for the unexampled cruelty committed afterwards upon the dead body.

Thus the fair and virtuous Violenta ended her life; her mother and brothers being acquitted. She died with the same spirit and resolution with which she had defended her chastity; and was executed in the presence of the Duke of Calabria, who caused this history to be registered, with other things worthy remembrance, that happened at Valencia in his viceroyalty. Bandwell reports that Ianthe was put to death with her mistress, but Paludanus, a noble Spaniard alive at that time, who wrote an excellent history in Latin, positively declares that she was never apprehended; which opinion I have followed, as that which seemed to be the most probable.

Lady Mary Wortley Montagu
1689–1762

LADY MARY PIERREPONT was early introduced to the brightest circles of London society. Before she was eight years old, her father, a leading Whig aristocrat, displayed her wit and beauty to his friends, who included Joseph Addison, Sir Richard Steele, and William Congreve. She was almost entirely self-educated, reading voluminously in her father's library and teaching herself Latin (as later she was to teach herself Turkish).

After a clandestine and troubled courtship, she eloped with Edward Wortley Montagu, a rising politician, in 1712. They had two children, a son who turned out badly and a daughter who married John Stuart, Earl of Bute, who was to become prime minister under George III. While Wortley pursued his career at court, Lady Mary cultivated literature and society. She wrote and circulated essays and poems, and was a close friend of Alexander Pope; they eventually quarreled, however, and Pope's later poems make savage reference to her under the name "Sappho."

In 1716 Wortley was named ambassador to Turkey, and Lady Mary accompanied him across Europe to Constantinople. From letters and notes that she wrote at the time, she later composed a brilliant travel book, leaving it to be published after her death (1763). Her friend Mary Astell wrote its preface (1724), emphasizing its originality and urging readers to "be pleased that a *woman* triumphs." In Turkey she also learned the method of inoculation for smallpox (she had been badly scarred by the disease in 1715), using it on her own children and publicizing it at home despite opposition from the medical profession.

Lady Mary never regarded herself as a professional writer, but in the winter of 1737–1738, provoked by attacks on the Whig government of her friend Sir Robert Walpole, she undertook anonymously a periodical, *The Nonsense of Common Sense*. It ran for nine numbers; Number Six is a feminist essay suggesting the influence of Astell.

At this time she fell deeply in love with a handsome bisexual Italian savant, Count Francesco Algarotti, who was many years her junior.

This passion may have prompted her to end her marriage, which had long been polite but loveless. In 1739 she left England, officially to travel for her health but actually in hope of meeting Algarotti in Venice. Although she did not meet him she remained in Italy and France until Wortley's death (1761).

from Letters

[TO EDWARD WORTLEY MONTAGU]

[March 24, 1711]

Though your letter is far from what I expected, having once promised to answer it with the sincere account of my inmost thoughts, I am resolved you shall not find me worse than my word, which is (whatever you may think) inviolable.

'Tis no affectation to say I despise the pleasure of pleasing people that I despise. All the fine equipages that shine in the Ring[1] never gave me another thought than either pity or contempt for the owners, that could place happiness in attracting the eyes of strangers. Nothing touches me with satisfaction but what touches my heart; and I should find more pleasure in the secret joy I should feel at a kind expression from a friend I esteemed, than at the admiration of a whole playhouse, or the envy of those of my own sex who could not attain to the same number of jewels, fine clothes, etc., supposing I was at the very top of this sort of happiness.

You may be this friend if you please. Did you really esteem me, had you any tender regard for me, I could, I think, pass my life in any station happier with you than in all the grandeur of the world with any other. You have some humors that would be disagreeable to any woman that married with an intention of finding her happiness abroad. That is not my resolution. If I marry, I propose to myself a retirement. There is few of my acquaintance I should ever wish to see again; and the pleasing one, and only one, is the way I design to please myself.

Happiness is the natural design of all the world, and every-

---

[1]A fashionable drive in Hyde Park, London.

thing we see done is meant in order to attain it. My imagination places it in friendship. By friendship I mean an entire communication of thoughts, wishes, interests, and pleasures, being undivided; a mutual esteem, which naturally carries with it a pleasing sweetness of conversation, and terminates in the desire of making one or another happy, without being forced to run into visits, noise, and hurry, which serve rather to trouble than compose the thoughts of any reasonable creature. There are few capable of a friendship such as I have described, and 'tis necessary for the generality of the world to be taken up with trifles. Carry a fine lady or a fine gentleman out of town, and they know no more what to say. To take from them plays, operas, and fashions is taking away all their topics of discourse, and they know not how to form their thoughts on any other subjects. They know very well what it is to be admired, but are perfectly ignorant of what it is to be loved.

I take you to have sense enough not to think this scheme romantic. I rather choose to use the word friendship than love because in the general sense that word is spoke, it signifies a passion rather founded on fancy than reason; and when I say friendship, I mean a mixture of tenderness and esteem, and which a long acquaintance increases, not decays. How far I deserve such a friendship, I can be no judge of myself. I may want the good sense that is necessary to be agreeable to a man of merit, but I know I want the vanity to believe I have; and can promise you shall never like me less upon knowing me better, and that I shall never forget you have a better understanding than myself.

And now let me entreat you to think (if possible) tolerably of my modesty, after so bold a declaration. I am resolved to throw off reserve, and use me ill if you please. I am sensible, to own an inclination for a man is putting one's self wholly in his power; but sure you have generosity enough not to abuse it. After all I have said, I pretend no tie but on your heart. If you do not love me, I shall not be happy with you; if you do, I need add no farther. I am not mercenary, and would not receive an obligation that comes not from one that loves me.

I do not desire my letter back again. You have honor, and I dare trust you. I am going to the same place I went last spring. I shall think of you there; it depends upon you in what manner.

[TO PHILIPPA MUNDY]

[10 Jan. 1713]

You will be convinced, my dear Phil, that absence and distance can make no alteration in my heart, or diminution of your power there, by my sudden answer to your obliging letter, notwithstanding the impediments to writing, arising from company or my own indisposition, which renders it almost always uneasy to me.

You ask my advice in a matter too difficult, but since you ask it, my friendship obliges me to give it to the best of my understanding. You have not made your case very clear, but I think you ask whether it would conduce most to your happiness to comply with your relations, in taking a man whose person you dislike, or to dispose of yourself according to your inclination. By that expression of a thorough contempt of the pomps and vanities of this wicked world, I suppose your inclination is in favor of one unequal in point of fortune to him proposed by your father. I know there is nothing more natural than for a heart in love to imagine nothing more easy than to reduce all expenses to a very narrow compass. If you like a man of a £500 per annum, I am sure you imagine you can live without one thought of equipage, or that proportion of attendance, new clothes, etc., that you have been used to. But, my dear, can you be very sure of this? The cares, the self-denial, and the novelty that you will find in that manner of living, will it never be uneasy to you? Accidental losses, thousands of unforeseen chances, may make you repent a hasty action, never to be undone. When time and cares have changed you to a downright housekeeper, will you not try,

> Though then, alas, that trial be too late,
> To find your father's hospitable gate,
> And seats where ease and plenty brooding sate,
> Those seats which long excluded you may mourn,
> That gate forever barred to your return?[2]

My dear Phil, my kindness for you makes me carry it very far, and beg you to look a little on the other side. If the gentleman

---

[2]This and the quotation below are from Matthew Prior's "Henry and Emma," lines 378–382 and 310–311.

proposed to you has really no other fault but a disagreeable person, if his conversation is to be liked, his principles to be esteemed, and there is nothing loathsome in his form, nor no disproportion in your ages, if all your dislike is founded on a displeasing mixture of features, it cannot last long. There is no figure that after the eyes have been accustomed to, does not become pleasing, or at least not otherwise. I fancy it is him that I danced with at N.; if so, I cannot commend his person; but if his understanding is to be valued, the progress from esteem to love is shorter and easier than it is generally imagined.

However, after all I have said, if the difference between your choice and your father's is only between a great estate and a competency, 'tis better to be privately happy than splendidly miserable. The reputation of having acted prudently will be no comfort. Follow your inclination, but in the first place remember, though 'tis easy to be without superfluities, 'tis impossible to be without necessaries, and as the world is made (and I see no prospect of its being reformed) there are some superfluities become necessaries. You can be without 6 horses, you can't be without a coach; you can be without laced liveries, you can't be without footmen. Consider over these things calmly, but if you have a beloved lover with an easy fortune, consider also 'tis possible to be very happy without the rank and show of Mr. Ch[ester]'s wife, and (as an experienced person) I advise you to consult chiefly and firstly if you can be pleased, and secondly the world. But if both is impossible, please yourself, and believe from my experience there is no state so happy as with a man you like.—I should not be so free in giving my opinion, dear Phil, but through an entire zeal for your happiness, which I heartily wish for, and conclude my letter with a seasonable remembrance,

> Now is your hour, or to comply or shun,
> Better not do the deed, than weep it done.

If you would avoid Mr. C. only because he is not well made, don't avoid him; if you would marry another only because you like him, don't marry him.

One word of your little friend, and I have done. If you was to meet, she would be as fond as ever. There are some people no more made for friends than politicians.

[TO THE LADY R(ICH)][3]

Vienna, Sept. 20, O.S. [1716]

I am extremely pleased, but not at all surprised, at the long delightful letter you have had the goodness to send me. I know that you can think of an absent friend even in the midst of a court, and that you love to oblige where you can have no view of a return; and I expect from you that you should love me and think of me when you don't see me.

I have compassion for the mortifications that you tell me befall our little friend, and I pity her much more since I know that they are only owing to the barbarous customs of our country. Upon my word, if she was here she would have no other fault but being something too young for the fashion, and she has nothing to do but to transplant hither about seven years hence, to be again a young and blooming beauty. I can assure you that wrinkles or a small stoop in the shoulders, nay, gray hair itself, is no objection to the making new conquests. I know you can't easily figure to yourself a young fellow of five-and-twenty ogling my Lady Suff[olk] with passion, or pressing to lead the Countess of O[xfor]d from an opera, but such are the sights I see every day, and I don't perceive anybody surprised at 'em but myself. A woman till five-and-thirty is only looked upon as a raw girl, and can possibly make no noise in the world till about forty. I don't know what your ladyship may think of this matter; but 'tis a considerable comfort to me to know there is upon earth such a paradise for old women, and I am content to be insignificant at present, in the design of returning when I am fit to appear nowhere else.

I cannot help lamenting upon this occasion the pitiful case of so many good English ladies long since retired to prudery and ratafia, who, if their stars had luckily conducted them hither, would still shine in the first rank of beauties; and then that perplexing word "reputation" has quite another meaning here than what you give it at London; and getting a lover is so far from losing, that 'tis properly getting reputation, ladies being much more respected in regard to the rank of their lovers, than that of their husbands.

---

[3]This and the next five are Embassy letters: See headnote. "O.S." in the date means "Old Style" (i.e., according to the Julian calendar then used in England). It was eleven days behind the Gregorian calendar. They have been revised by Montagu with an eye to eventual publication.

But what you'll think very odd, the two sects that divide our whole nation of petticoats are utterly unknown. Here are neither coquettes nor prudes. No woman dares appear coquette enough to encourage two lovers at a time; and I have not seen any such prudes as to pretend fidelity to their husbands, who are certainly the best-natured set of people in the world, and they look upon their wives' gallants as favorably as men do upon their deputies, that take the troublesome part of their business off of their hands; though they have not the less to do, for they are generally deputies in another place themselves. In one word, 'tis the established custom for every lady to have two husbands, one that bears the name, and another that performs the duties; and these engagements are so well known, that it would be a downright affront, and publicly resented, if you invited a woman of quality to dinner without at the same time inviting her two attendants of lover and husband, between whom she always sits in state with great gravity. These sub-marriages generally last twenty years together, and the lady often commands the poor lover's estate even to the utter ruin of his family, though they are as seldom begun by any passion as other matches. But a man makes but an ill figure that is not in some commerce of this nature, and a woman looks out for a lover as soon as she's married, as part of her equipage, without which she could not be genteel; and the first article of the treaty is establishing the pension, which remains to the lady though the gallant should prove inconstant; and this chargeable point of honor I look upon as the real foundation of so many wonderful instances of constancy. I really know several women of the first quality whose pensions are as well known as their annual rents, and yet nobody esteems them the less. On the contrary, their discretion would be called in question if they should be suspected to be mistresses for nothing, and a great part of their emulation consists in trying who shall get most; and having no intrigue at all is so far a disgrace that, I'll assure you, a lady who is very much my friend here told me but yesterday, how much I was obliged to her for justifying my conduct in a conversation on my subject, where it was publicly asserted that I could not possibly have common sense that had been about town above a fortnight and had made no steps towards commencing an amour. My friend pleaded for me that my stay was uncertain, and she believed that was the cause of my seeming stupidity; and this was all she could find to say in my justification.

But one of the pleasantest adventures I ever met in my life was last night, and which will give you a just idea after what delicate manner the *belles passions*[4] are managed in this country. I was at the assembly of the Countess of ——, and the young Count of —— led me downstairs, and he asked me how long I intended to stay here. I made answer that my stay depended on the emperor, and it was not in my power to determine it. Well, madam (said he), whether your time here is to be long or short, I think you ought to pass it agreeably, and to that end you must engage in a little affair of the heart.—My heart (answered I gravely enough) does not engage very easily, and I have no design of parting with it. I see, madam (said he sighing), by the ill nature of that answer, that I am not to hope for it, which is a great mortification to me that am charmed with you. But, however, I am still devoted to your service; and since I am not worthy of entertaining you myself, do me the honor of letting me know whom you like best among us, and I'll engage to manage the affair entirely to your satisfaction.—You may judge in what manner I should have received this compliment in my own country; but I was well enough acquainted with the way of this to know that he really intended me an obligation, and thanked him with a grave courtesy for his zeal to serve me, and only assured him that I had no occasion to make use of it.

Thus you see, my dear, gallantry and good breeding are as different in different climates, as morality and religion. Who have the rightest notions of both, we shall never know till the day of judgment, for which great day of *éclaircissement*, I own there is very little impatience in your, etc.

[TO LADY ——]

Adrianople, April 1, O.S. [1717]

I am now got into a new world, where everything I see appears to me a change of scene; and I write to your ladyship with some content of mind, hoping at least that you will find the charm of novelty in my letters and no longer reproach me that I tell you nothing extraordinary.

I won't trouble you with a relation of our tedious journey; but I must not omit what I saw remarkable at Sophia, one of the

---

[4]The polite passions; affairs of love.

most beautiful towns in the Turkish empire and famous for its hot baths, that are resorted to both for diversion and health. I stopped here one day on purpose to see them. Designing to go incognita, I hired a Turkish coach. These voitures[5] are not at all like ours, but much more convenient for the country, the heat being so great that glasses would be very troublesome. They are made a good deal in the manner of the Dutch coaches, having wooden lattices painted and gilded, the inside being painted with baskets and nosegays of flowers, intermixed commonly with little poetical mottoes. They are covered all over with scarlet cloth, lined with silk and very often richly embroidered and fringed. This covering entirely hides the persons in them, but may be thrown back at pleasure, and the ladies peep through the lattices. They hold four people very conveniently, seated on cushions, but not raised.

In one of these covered wagons I went to the bagnio[6] about ten o'clock. It was already full of women. It is built of stone, in the shape of a dome, with no windows but in the roof, which gives light enough. There was five of these domes joined together, the outmost being less than the rest and serving only as a hall, where the portress stood at the door. Ladies of quality generally give this woman the value of a crown or ten shillings, and I did not forget that ceremony. The next room is a very large one, paved with marble, and all round it, raised, two sofas of marble, one above another. There were four fountains of cold water in this room, falling first into marble basins and then running on the floor in little channels made for that purpose, which carried the streams into the next room, something less than this, with the same sort of marble sofas, but so hot with steams of sulphur proceeding from the baths joining to it, 'twas impossible to stay there with one's clothes on. The two other domes were the hot baths, one of which had cocks of cold water turning into it, to temper it to what degree of warmth the bathers have a mind to.

I was in my travelling habit, which is a riding dress, and certainly appeared very extraordinary to them. Yet there was not one of 'em that showed the least surprise or impertinent curiosity, but received me with all the obliging civility possible. I know no European court where the ladies would have behaved themselves in so polite a manner to a stranger.

---

[5]Carriages. "Glasses" (below) means glass windows.
[6]Baths.

I believe in the whole there were two hundred women, and yet none of those disdainful smiles or satiric whispers that never fail in our assemblies when anybody appears that is not dressed exactly in fashion. They repeated over and over to me, "Uzelle, pék uzelle," which is nothing but Charming, very charming. The first sofas were covered with cushions and rich carpets, on which sat the ladies; and on the second, their slaves behind them, but without any distinction of rank by their dress, all being in the state of nature, that is, in plain English, stark naked, without any beauty or defect concealed. Yet there was not the least wanton smile or immodest gesture amongst 'em. They walked and moved with the same majestic grace which Milton describes of our general mother.[7] There were many amongst them as exactly proportioned as ever any goddess was drawn by the pencil of Guido or Titian, and most of their skins shiningly white, only adorned by their beautiful hair divided into many tresses hanging on their shoulders, braided either with pearl or ribbon, perfectly representing the figures of the Graces.

I was here convinced of the truth of a reflection I had often made, that if 'twas the fashion to go naked, the face would be hardly observed. I perceived that the ladies with the finest skins and most delicate shapes had the greatest share of my admiration, though their faces were sometimes less beautiful than those of their companions. To tell you the truth, I had wickedness enough to wish secretly that Mr. Jervas[8] could have been there invisible. I fancy it would have very much improved his art to see so many fine women naked in different postures, some in conversation, some working, others drinking coffee or sherbet, and many negligently lying on their cushions while their slaves (generally pretty girls of seventeen or eighteen) were employed in braiding their hair in several pretty manners. In short, 'tis the women's coffee-house, where all the news of the town is told, scandal invented, etc. They generally take this diversion once a week, and stay there at least four or five hours without getting cold by immediate coming out of the hot bath into the cool room, which was very surprising to me. The lady that seemed the most considerable amongst them entreated me to sit by her, and would fain have undressed me for the bath. I excused

[7]Eve, as described in *Paradise Lost* IV. 304–320; "our general mother" is line 492. Guido (Reni, 1575–1642) and Titian, below, were Italian painters.
[8]Charles Jervas (1675?–1739), a painter celebrated for his portraits of women.

myself with some difficulty, they being all so earnest in persuading me. I was at last forced to open my skirt and show them my stays; which satisfied them very well, for I saw they believed I was so locked up in that machine that it was not in my own power to open it, which contrivance they attributed to my husband. I was charmed with their civility and beauty, and should have been very glad to pass more time with them; but Mr. W[ortley] resolving to pursue his journey the next morning early, I was in haste to see the ruins of Justinian's church, which did not afford me so agreeable a prospect as I had left, being little more than a heap of stones.

Adieu, madam. I am sure I have now entertained you with an account of such a sight as you never saw in your life, and what no book of travels could inform you of. 'Tis no less than death for a man to be found in one of these places.

[TO LADY MAR]

Adrianople, April 1, O.S. [1717]

I wish to God, dear sister, that you was as regular in letting me have the pleasure of knowing what passes on your side of the globe, as I am careful in endeavoring to amuse you by the account of all I see that I think you care to hear of. You content yourself with telling me over and over that the town is very dull. It may possibly be dull to you, when every day does not present you with something new; but for me that am in arrear at least two months' news, all that seems very stale with you would be fresh and sweet here; pray let me into more particulars. I will try to awaken your gratitude by giving you a full and true relation of the novelties of this place, none of which would surprise you more than a sight of my person as I am now in my Turkish habit, though I believe you would be of my opinion that 'tis admirably becoming. I intend to send you my picture; in the meantime accept of it here.

The first piece of my dress is a pair of drawers, very full, that reach to my shoes, and conceal the legs more modestly than your petticoats. They are of a thin rose-color damask brocaded with silver flowers, my shoes of white kid leather embroidered with gold. Over this hangs my smock, of a fine white silk gauze edged with embroidery. This smock has wide sleeves hanging half way down the arm, and is closed at the neck with a diamond button; but the shape and color of the bosom very well to be distinguished through it. The *antery* is a waistcoat made close to the shape, of white and gold damask, with very long sleeves falling back and fringed with deep gold fringe, and should have diamond or pearl buttons. My *caftan*, of the same stuff with my drawers, is a robe exactly fitted to my shape, and reaching to my feet, with very long straight falling sleeves. Over this is the girdle of about four fingers broad, which all that can afford have entirely of diamonds or other precious stones. Those that will not be at that expense have it of exquisite embroidery on satin, but it must be fastened before with a clasp of diamonds. The *curdee* is a loose robe they throw off or put on according to the weather, being of a rich brocade (mine is green and gold), either lined with ermine or sables; the sleeves reach very little below the shoulders. The head-dress is composed of a cap called *talpock*, which is in winter of fine velvet embroidered with pearls or diamonds, and in summer of a light shining silver stuff. This is fixed on one side of the head, hanging a little way down with a gold tassel, and bound on, either with a circle of diamonds (as I have seen several) or a rich embroidered handkerchief. On the other side of the head, the hair is laid flat; and here the ladies are at liberty to show their fancies, some putting flowers, others a plume of heron's feathers, and, in short, what they please; but the most general fashion is a large bouquet of jewels, made like natural flowers; that is, the buds of pearl, the roses of different colored rubies, the jessamines of diamonds, jonquils of topazes, etc., so well set and enameled, 'tis hard to imagine anything of that kind so beautiful. The hair hangs at its full length behind, divided into tresses braided with pearl or ribbon, which is always in great quantity.

I never saw in my life so many fine heads of hair. I have counted a hundred and ten of these tresses of one lady's, all natural; but it must be owned that every beauty is more common here than with us. 'Tis surprising to see a young woman that is not very handsome. They have naturally the most beautiful complexions in the world, and generally large black eyes. I can assure you with great truth that the court of England (though I believe it the fairest in Christendom) cannot show so many beauties as are under our protection here. They generally shape their eyebrows; and the Greeks and Turks have a custom of putting round their eyes (on the inside) a black tincture that, at a distance or by candlelight, adds very much to the blackness of them. I fancy many of our ladies would be overjoyed to know this secret, but 'tis too visible by day. They dye their nails rose-color; I own I cannot enough accustom myself to this fashion to find any beauty in it.

As to their morality or good conduct, I can say, like Harlequin, 'tis just as 'tis with you,[9] and the Turkish ladies don't commit one sin the less for not being Christians. Now I am a little acquainted with their ways, I cannot forbear admiring either the exemplary discretion or extreme stupidity of all the writers that have given accounts of 'em.[10] 'Tis very easy to see they have more liberty than we have, no woman, of what rank soever, being permitted to go in the streets without two muslins, one that covers her face all but her eyes, and another that hides the whole dress of her head and hangs halfway down her back; and their shapes are wholly concealed by a thing they call a *ferigée*, which no woman of any sort appears without. This has straight sleeves that reach to their fingers ends, and it laps all round 'em, not unlike a riding-hood. In winter 'tis of cloth, and in summer plain stuff or silk. You may guess how effectually this disguises them, that there is no distinguishing the great lady from her slave; 'tis impossible for the most jealous husband to know his wife when he meets her, and no man dare either touch or follow a woman in the street.

This perpetual masquerade gives them entire liberty of following their inclinations without danger of discovery. The most usual method of intrigue is to send an appointment to the lover to meet the lady at a Jew's shop, which are as notoriously convenient as our Indian houses,[11] and yet, even those who don't make that use of 'em do not scruple to go to buy pennyworths and tumble over rich goods, which are chiefly to be found amongst that sort of people. The great ladies seldom let their gallants know who they are, and 'tis so difficult to find it out that they can very seldom guess at her name they have corresponded with above half a year together. You may easily imagine the number of faithful wives very small in a country where they have nothing to fear from their lovers' indiscretion, since we see

[9]Alluding to Behn, *The Emperor of the Moon* (1687), III.i., where Harlequin says that lunar morality is the same as terrestrial.

[10]Halsband cites Jean Dumont, *A New Voyage to the Levant* (4th ed., 1705), and Aaron Hill, *A Full . . . Account of . . . the Ottoman Empire* (1709) as examples; they claimed that Turkish women were strictly confined.

[11]Shops where East Indian goods were sold.

so many that have the courage to expose themselves to that in this world, and all the threatened punishment of the next, which is never preached to the Turkish damsels. Neither have they much to apprehend from the resentment of their husbands; those ladies that are rich having all their money in their own hands, which they take with 'em upon a divorce, with an addition which he is obliged to give 'em.

Upon the whole, I look upon the Turkish women as the only free people in the empire. The very Divan pays a respect to 'em; and the Grand Signior himself, when a pasha is executed, never violates the privileges of the harem (or women's apartment), which remains unsearched entire to the widow. They are queens of their slaves, which the husband has no permission so much as to look upon, except it be an old woman or two that his lady chooses. 'Tis true their law permits them four wives; but there is no instance of a man of quality that makes use of this liberty, or of a woman of rank that would suffer it. When a husband happens to be inconstant (as those things will happen), he keeps his mistress in a house apart and visits her as privately as he can, just as 'tis with you. Amongst all the great men here, I only know the *tefterdar* (i.e. treasurer) that keeps a number of she slaves for his own use (that is, on his own side of the house; for a slave once given to serve a lady is entirely at her disposal), and he is spoke of as a libertine, or what we should call a rake, and his wife won't see him, though she continues to live in his house.

Thus you see, dear sister, the manners of mankind do not differ so widely as our voyage writers would make us believe. Perhaps it would be more entertaining to add a few surprising customs of my own invention; but nothing seems to me so agreeable as truth, and I believe nothing so acceptable to you. I conclude with repeating the great truth of my being,

Dear sister, etc.

[TO SARAH CHISWELL]

Adrianople, April 1, O.S. [1717]

In my opinion, dear S., I ought rather to quarrel with you for not answering my Nimeguen letter of August till December, than to excuse my not writing again till now. I am sure there is on my side a very good excuse for silence, having gone such tiresome land journeys, though I don't find the conclusion of 'em so bad as you seem to imagine. I am very easy here, and not in the solitude you fancy me; the great quantity of Greek, French, English, and Italians that are under our protection make their court to me from morning till night, and, I'll assure you, are many of 'em very fine ladies; for there is no possibility for a Christian to live easily under this government but by the protection of an ambassador, and the richer they are, the greater their danger.

Those dreadful stories you have heard of the plague have very little foundation in truth. I own I have much ado to reconcile myself to the sound of a word which has always given me such terrible ideas, though I am convinced there is little more in it than a fever, as a proof of which we passed through two or three towns most violently infected. In the very next house where we lay (in one of them), two persons died of it. Luckily for me, I was so well deceived that I knew nothing of the matter; and I was made believe that our second cook who fell ill there had only a great cold. However, we left our doctor to take care of him, and yesterday they both arrived here in good health; and I am now let into the secret that he has had the plague. There are many that 'scape of it; neither is the air ever infected. I am persuaded it would be as easy to root it out here as out of Italy and France; but it does so little mischief, they are not very solicitous about it, and are content to suffer this distemper instead of our variety, which they are utterly unacquainted with.

A propos of distempers, I am going to tell you a thing that I am sure will make you wish yourself here. The smallpox, so fatal[12] and so general amongst us, is here entirely harmless by the invention of *ingrafting* (which is the term they give it). There is a set of old women who make it their business to perform the operation. Every autumn, in the month of September, when the great heat is abated, people send to one another to know if any of their family has a mind to have the smallpox. They make parties for this purpose, and when they are met (commonly fifteen or sixteen together), the old woman comes with a nut-shell full of the matter of the best sort of smallpox, and asks what veins you please to have opened. She immediately rips open that you offer to her with a large needle (which gives you no more pain than a common scratch), and puts into the vein as

[12]Lady Mary's brother had died of it, and she had barely survived it.

much venom as can lie upon the head of her needle, and after
binds up the little wound with a hollow bit of shell; and in this
manner opens four or five veins. The Grecians have commonly
the superstition of opening one in the middle of the forehead, in
each arm, and on the breast, to mark the sign of the cross; but
this has a very ill effect, all these wounds leaving little scars,
and is not done by those that are not superstitious, who choose to
have them in the legs, or that part of the arm that is concealed.
The children or young patients play together all the rest of the
day, and are in perfect health till the eighth. Then the fever
begins to seize 'em, and they keep their beds two days, very
seldom three. They have very rarely above twenty or thirty in
their faces, which never mark; and in eight days' time they are
as well as before their illness. Where they are wounded there
remains running sores during the distemper, which I don't doubt
is a great relief to it. Every year thousands undergo this operation; and the French ambassador says pleasantly that they take
the smallpox here by way of diversion, as they take the waters
in other countries. There is no example of anyone that has died
in it; and you may believe I am very well satisfied of the safety
of the experiment, since I intend to try it on my dear little son.

I am patriot enough to take pains to bring this useful invention
into fashion in England; and I should not fail to write to some of
our doctors very particularly about it, if I knew any one of 'em
that I thought had virtue enough to destroy such a considerable
branch of their revenue for the good of mankind. But that
distemper is too beneficial to them not to expose to all their
resentment the hardy wight that should undertake to put an end
to it. Perhaps, if I live to return, I may, however, have courage
to war with 'em.[13] Upon this occasion admire the heroism in the
heart of your friend, etc.

[TO THE COUNTESS OF ——]

[1718]

I am now preparing to leave Constantinople, and perhaps you
will accuse me of hypocrisy when I tell you 'tis with regret; but I
am used to the air, and have learnt the language. I am easy

---

[13]For her "war" with the doctors see Halsband, "New Light on Lady Mary Wortley
Montagu's Contribution to Inoculation," *Journal of the History of Medicine* 8 (1953): 390–405.

here; and as much as I love traveling, I tremble at the inconveniences attending so great a journey with a numerous family and a little infant hanging at the breast. However, I endeavor upon this occasion to do as I have hitherto done in all the odd turns of my life, turn 'em, if I can, to my diversion. In order to this, I ramble every day, wrapped up in my *ferigée* and *asmák*, about Constantinople, and amuse myself with seeing all that is curious in it.

I know you'll expect this declaration should be followed with some account of what I have seen, but I am in no humor to copy what has been writ so often over. To what purpose should I tell you that Constantinople was the ancient Byzantium; that 'tis at present the conquest of a race of people supposed Scythians; that there are five or six thousand mosques in it; that Santa Sophia was founded by Justinian, etc.? I'll assure you 'tis not [for] want of learning that I forbear writing all these bright things. I could also, with little trouble, turn over Knolles and Sir Paul Rycaut, to give you a list of Turkish emperors; but I will not tell you what you may find in every author that has writ of this country.[14]

I am more inclined, out of a true female spirit of contradiction, to tell you the falsehood of a great part of what you find in authors; as, for example, the admirable Mr. Hill, who so gravely asserts that he saw in Santa Sophia a sweating pillar, very balsamic for disordered heads. There is not the least tradition of any such matter, and I suppose it was revealed to him in vision during his wonderful stay in the Egyptian catacombs, for I am sure he never heard of any such miracle here. 'Tis also very pleasant to observe how tenderly he and all his brethren voyage-writers lament the miserable confinement of the Turkish ladies, who are (perhaps) freer than any ladies in the universe, and are the only women in the world that lead a life of uninterrupted pleasure exempt from cares, their whole time being spent in visiting, bathing, or the agreeable amusement of spending money and inventing new fashions. A husband would be thought mad that exacted any degree of economy from his wife, whose expenses are no way limited but by her own fancy. 'Tis his business to get money, and hers to spend it; and this noble prerogative extends itself to the very meanest of the sex. Here is a fellow

---

[14]Justinian was emperor, 527–565 A.D.; Richard Knolles wrote a *History of the Turks* (1603), and Sir Paul Rycaut continued it to 1700. For Hill (below), see n. 10.

that carries embroidered handkerchiefs upon his back to sell, as miserable a figure as you may suppose such a mean dealer, yet I'll assure you his wife scorns to wear anything less than cloth of gold; has her ermine furs, and a very handsome set of jewels for her head. They go abroad when and where they please. 'Tis true they have no public places but the bagnios, and there can only be seen by their own sex; however, that is a diversion they take great pleasure in. . . .

. . . The Turkish ladies have at least as much wit and civility, nay, liberty, as ladies amongst us. 'Tis true, the same customs that give them so many opportunities of gratifying their evil inclinations (if they have any) also put it very fully in the power of their husbands to revenge them if they are discovered, and I don't doubt but they suffer sometimes for their indiscretions in a very severe manner. About two months ago there was found at daybreak, not very far from my house, the bleeding body of a young woman, naked, only wrapped in a coarse sheet, with two wounds with a knife, one in her side and another in her breast. She was not yet quite cold, and so surprisingly beautiful that there were very few men in Pera that did not go to look upon her; but it was not possible for anybody to know her, no woman's face being known. She was supposed to be brought in [the] dead of night from the Constantinople side and laid there. Very little enquiry was made about the murderer, and the corpse privately buried without noise. Murder is never pursued by the king's officers as with us. 'Tis the business of the next relations to revenge the dead person; and if they like better to compound the matter for money (as they generally do), there is no more said of it. One would imagine this defect in their government should make such tragedies very frequent, yet they are extremely rare; which is enough to prove the people not naturally cruel, neither do I think in many other particulars they deserve the barbarous character we give them.

I am well acquainted with a Christian woman of quality who made it her choice to live with a Turkish husband, and is a very agreeable, sensible lady. Her story is so extraordinary I cannot forbear relating it, but I promise you it shall be in as few words as I can possibly express it. She is a Spaniard, and was at Naples with her family when that kingdom was part of the Spanish dominion. Coming from thence in a felucca, accompanied by her brother, they were attacked by the Turkish admiral, boarded, and taken—and now, how shall I modestly tell you the rest of her adventure? The same accident happened to her that happened to the fair Lucretia so many years before her,[15] but she was too good a Christian to kill herself, as that heathenish Roman did. The admiral was so much charmed with the beauty and long-suffering of the fair captive, that, as his first compliment, he gave immediate liberty to her brother and attendants, who made haste to Spain, and in a few months sent the sum of four thousand pounds sterling as a ransom for his sister. The Turk took the money, which he presented to her, and told her she was at liberty, but the lady very discreetly weighed the different treatment she was likely to find in her native country. Her Catholic relations, as the kindest thing they could do for her in her present circumstances, would certainly confine her to a nunnery for the rest of her days. Her infidel lover was very handsome, very tender, fond of her, and lavished at her feet all the Turkish magnificence. She answered him very resolutely that her liberty was not so precious to her as her honor; that he could no way restore that but by marrying her. She desired him to accept the ransom as her portion, and give her the satisfaction of knowing no man could boast of her favors without being her husband. The admiral was transported at this kind offer and sent back the money to her relations, saying he was too happy in her possession. He married her and never took any other wife, and (as she says herself) she never had any reason to repent the choice she made. He left her some years after one of the richest widows in Constantinople. But there is no remaining honorably a single woman, and that consideration has obliged her to marry the present captain pashá (i.e., admiral), his successor. I am afraid you'll think that my friend fell in love with her ravisher; but I am willing to take her word for it that she acted wholly on principles of honor, though I think she might be reasonably touched at his generosity, which is very often found amongst the Turks of rank.

'Tis a degree of generosity to tell the truth, and 'tis very rare that any Turk will assert a solemn falsehood. I don't speak of the lowest sort, for as there is a great deal of ignorance, there is very little virtue amongst them; and false witnesses are much cheaper than in Christendom, those wretches not being punished (even when they are publicly detected) with the rigor they ought to be.

---

[15]The Roman matron Lucretia, raped by Sextus, committed suicide.

Now I am speaking of their law, I don't know whether I have ever mentioned to you one custom peculiar to this country. I mean adoption, very common amongst the Turks and yet more amongst the Greeks and Armenians. Not having it in their power to give their estates to a friend or distant relation, to avoid its falling into the Grand Signior's treasury, when they are not likely to have children of their own they choose some pretty child of either sex amongst the meanest people, and carry the child and its parents before the cadi,[16] and there declare they receive it for their heir. The parents at the same time renounce all future claim to it; a writing is drawn and witnessed, and a child thus adopted cannot be disinherited. Yet I have seen some common beggars that have refused to part with their children in this manner to some of the richest amongst the Greeks; so powerful is the instinctive fondness natural to parents! though the adopting fathers are generally very tender to these children of their souls, as they call them. I own this custom pleases me much better than our absurd following our name.[17] Methinks 'tis much more reasonable to make happy and rich an infant whom I educate after my own manner, brought up (in the Turkish phrase) upon my knees, and who has learned to look upon me with a filial respect, than to give an estate to a creature without other merit or relation to me than by a few letters. Yet this is an absurdity we see frequently practiced. . . .

[TO ALEXANDER POPE]

Dover, Nov. 1 [1718]

I have this minute received a letter of yours sent me from Paris. I believe and hope I shall very soon see both you and Mr. Congreve,[18] but as I am here in an inn, where we stay to regulate our march to London, bag and baggage, I shall employ some of my leisure time in answering that part of yours that seems to require an answer.

I must applaud your good nature in supposing that your pastoral lovers (vulgarly called haymakers) would have lived in everlasting joy and harmony, if the lightning had not interrupted

[16]The village judge.
[17]Willing property to a person who bears our surname, however remote a relative.
[18]William Congreve (1670–1729), playwright, an early friend of Lady Mary.

their scheme of happiness.[19] I see no reason to imagine that John Hughes and Sarah Drew were either wiser or more virtuous than their neighbors. That a well-set man of twenty-five should have a fancy to marry a brown woman of eighteen is nothing marvelous; and I cannot help thinking that had they married, their lives would have passed in the common track with their fellow parishioners. His endeavoring to shield her from the storm was a natural action, and what he would have certainly done for his horse if he had been in the same situation. Neither am I of opinion that their sudden death was a reward of their mutual virtue. You know the Jews were reproved for thinking a village destroyed by fire more wicked than those that had escaped the thunder. Time and chance happen to all men.[20] Since you desire me to try my skill in an epitaph, I think the following lines perhaps more just, though not so poetical as yours:

Here lie John Hughes and Sarah Drew;
Perhaps you'll say, what's that to you?
Believe me, friend, much may be said
On this poor couple that are dead.
On Sunday next they should have married,
But see how oddly things are carried.
On Thursday last it rained and lightened;
These tender lovers, sadly frightened,
Sheltered beneath the cocking hay
In hopes to pass the storm away.
But the bold thunder found them out
(Commissioned for that end, no doubt),
And, seizing on their trembling breath,
Consigned them to the shades of death.
Who knows if 'twas not kindly done?
For had they seen the next year's sun,
A beaten wife and cuckold swain
Had jointly cursed the marriage chain.
Now they are happy in their doom,
For P[ope] has wrote upon their tomb.

[19]Pope's letter (1 Sept. 1718) told the story of two rural lovers, "as constant as ever were found in romance," who had been killed by lightning. John's body was found "with one arm about his Sarah's neck, and the other held over her face as if to screen her from the lightning. They were struck dead . . . in this tender posture." A monument was erected to them, for which Pope wrote two epitaphs emphasizing their supposed virtue: "Victims so pure Heav'n saw well-pleased, / And snatched them in celestial fire." Finally, Pope asked Lady Mary to write an epitaph also; "I think 'twas what you could not have refused me on so moving an occasion."
[20]Ecclesiastes 9:11.

I confess these sentiments are not altogether so heroic as yours, but I hope you will forgive them in favor of the two last lines. You see how much I esteem the honor you have done them; though I am not very impatient to have the same, and had rather continue to be your stupid living humble servant than be celebrated by all the pens in Europe.

I would write to Mr. C[ongreve], but suppose you will read this to him if he enquires after me.

[TO LADY MAR][21]

October 31 [1723]

I write to you at this time piping hot from the birth-night, my brain warmed with all the agreeable ideas that fine clothes, fine gentlemen, brisk tunes, and lively dances can raise there. 'Tis to be hoped that my letter will entertain you; at least you will certainly have the freshest account of all passages on that glorious day. First, you must know that I led up the ball, which you'll stare at; but what's more, I think in my conscience I made one of the best figures there. To say truth, people are grown so extravagantly ugly that we old beauties are forced to come out on show-days, to keep the court in countenance. I saw Mrs. Murray there, through whose hands this epistle is to be conveyed. I don't know whether she'll make the same complaint to you that I do. Mrs. West was with her, who is a great prude, having but two lovers at a time; I think those are Lord Haddington and Mr. Lindsay, the one for use, the one for show.

The world improves in one virtue to a violent degree—I mean plain-dealing. Hypocrisy being, as the Scripture declares,[22] a damnable sin, I hope our publicans and sinners will be saved by the open profession of the contrary virtue. I was told by a very good author, who is deep in the secret, that at this very minute there is a bill cooking up at a hunting-seat in Norfolk,[23] to have "not" taken out of the commandments and clapped into the

---

[21]Lady Mar, Lady Mary's sister, lived in France with her exiled husband. She suffered from severe depression; Lady Mary's letters were efforts to cheer her up. The birth-night (below) was the evening of the Prince of Wales's birthday, October 30.

[22]Matthew 23.

[23]Norfolk was the home county of Sir Robert Walpole, prime minister 1721–1742; at this time he was entertaining "a hunting party of his political cronies" (Halsband). Yonge and Dodington (below) were among those cronies.

creed, the ensuing session of parliament. This bold attempt for
the liberty of the subject is wholly projected by Mr. Walpole,
who proposed it to the secret committee in his parlor. Will
Yonge seconded it, and answered for all his acquaintance voting
right to a man. Dodington very gravely objected that the obstinacy of human nature was such, that he feared when they had
positive commandments so to do, perhaps people would not commit adultery and bear false witness against their neighbors with
the readiness and cheerfulness they do at present. This objection
seemed to sink deep into the minds of the greatest politicians at
the board; and I don't know whether the bill won't be dropped,
though 'tis certain it might be carried with great ease, the world
being entirely *revenue du bagatelle*,[24] and honor, virtue, reputation, etc., which we used to hear of in our nursery, is as much
laid aside and forgotten as crumpled riband. To speak plainly, I
am very sorry for the forlorn state of matrimony, which is as
much ridiculed by our young ladies as it used to be by young
fellows; in short, both sexes have found the inconveniences of
it, and the appellation of rake is as genteel in a woman as a man
of quality. 'Tis no scandal to say "Miss——, the maid of honor,
looks very well now she's up again, and poor Biddy Noel has
never been quite well since her last flux." You may imagine we
married women look very silly; we have nothing to excuse
ourselves but that 'twas done a great while ago, and we were
very young when we did it.

This is the general state of affairs; as to particulars, if you
have any curiosity for things of that kind, you have nothing to
do but to ask me questions, and they shall be answered to the
best of my understanding; my time never being passed more
agreeably than when I am doing something obliging to you.
This is truth, in spite of all the beaus, wits, and witlings in Great
Britain.

[TO LADY POMFRET]

[March, 1739]

I am so well acquainted with the lady you mention, that I am not
surprised at any proof of her want of judgment; she is one of

---

[24]"Given over to trifles."

those who has passed upon the world vivacity in the place of understanding; for me, who think with Boileau,

> Rien n'est beau que le vrai, le vrai seul est aimable,[25]

I have always thought those geniuses much inferior to the plain sense of a cookmaid, who can make a good pudding and keep the kitchen in good order.

Here is no news to be sent you from this place, which has been for this fortnight and still continues overwhelmed with politics, and which are of so mysterious a nature, one ought to have some of the gifts of Lilly or Partridge to be able to write about them; and I leave all those dissertations to those distinguished mortals who are endowed with the talent of divination; though I am at present the only one of my sex who seems to be of that opinion, the ladies having shown their zeal and appetite for knowledge in a most glorious manner. At the last warm debate in the House of Lords, it was unanimously resolved there should be no crowd of unnecessary auditors; consequently the fair sex were excluded, and the gallery destined to the sole use of the House of Commons. Notwithstanding which determination, a tribe of dames resolved to show on this occasion that neither men nor laws could resist them. These heroines were Lady Huntingdon, the Duchess of Queensberry, the Duchess of Ancaster, Lady Westmoreland, Lady Cobham, Lady Charlotte Edwin, Lady Archibald Hamilton and her daughter, Mrs. Scott, and Mrs. Pendarves, and Lady Frances Saunderson. I am thus particular in their names, since I look upon them to be the boldest asserters, and most resigned sufferers for liberty, I ever read of. They presented themselves at the door at nine o'clock in the morning, where Sir William Saunderson respectfully informed them the Chancellor had made an order against their admittance. The Duchess of Queensberry, as head of the squadron, pished at the ill-breeding of a mere lawyer, and desired him to let them upstairs privately. After some modest refusals, he swore by G— he would not let them in. Her grace, with a noble warmth, answered, by G— they would come in, in spite of the Chancellor and the whole House. This being reported, the Peers resolved to starve them out; an order was made that the doors should not be opened till they had raised their siege.

---

[25]"Nothing but truth is beautiful, truth alone is lovely" (Nicholas Boileau, *Epistle* IX). Lilly and Partridge (below) were astrologers.

These Amazons now showed themselves qualified for the duty even of foot soldiers; they stood there till five in the afternoon, without either sustenance or evacuation, every now and then playing volleys of thumps, kicks, and raps against the door, with so much violence that the speakers in the House were scarce heard. When the Lords were not to be conquered by this, the two duchesses (very well apprised of the use of stratagems in war) commanded a dead silence of half an hour; and the Chancellor, who thought this a certain proof of their absence (the Commons also being very impatient to enter), gave order for the opening of the door; upon which they all rushed in, pushed aside their competitors, and placed themselves in the front rows of the gallery. They stayed there till after eleven, when the House rose; and during the debate gave applause, and showed marks of dislike, not only by smiles and winks (which have always been allowed in these cases), but by noisy laughs and apparent contempts; which is supposed the true reason why poor Lord Hervey spoke miserably.[26] I beg your pardon, dear madam, for this long relation; but 'tis impossible to be short on so copious a subject; and you must own this action very well worthy of record, and I think not to be paralleled in any history, ancient or modern. I look so little in my own eyes (who was at that time ingloriously sitting over a tea-table), I hardly dare subscribe myself even,

Yours.

[TO LADY BUTE]

Gottolengo, July 10 [1748]

Dear Child,—I received yours of May the 12th but yesterday, July the 9th. I am surprised you complain of my silence. I have never failed answering yours the post after I received them; but I fear, being directed to Twickenham (having no other direction from you), your servants there may have neglected them.

I have been this six weeks, and still am, at my dairy-house, which joins to my garden. I believe I have already told you it is a long mile from the castle, which is situate in the midst of a

---

[26]The debate, on March 1, concerned war with Spain. Mrs. Mary Pendarves, afterward Delany, one of the leaders of this action, wrote a somewhat different account of it (Delany, *Correspondence*, 2:44–45). Lady Mary stayed home (below) probably because, as Halsband suggests, she supported Walpole and these women were all in the Opposition.

very large village (once a considerable town, part of the walls
still remaining) and has not vacant ground enough about it to
make a garden, which is my greatest amusement; and it being
now troublesome to walk, or even go in the chaise till the
evening, I have fitted up in this farmhouse a room for myself—
that is to say, strewed the floor with rushes, covered the chimney with moss and branches, and adorned the room with basins
of earthenware (which is made here to great perfection) filled
with flowers, and put in some straw chairs and a couch bed,
which is my whole furniture.

This spot of ground is so beautiful I am afraid you will scarce
credit the description, which, however, I can assure you shall be
very literal, without any embellishment from imagination. It is
on a bank forming a kind of peninsula, raised from the river
Oglio fifty foot, to which you may descend by easy stairs cut in
the turf, and either take the air on the river, which is as large as
the Thames at Richmond, or by walking an avenue two hundred
yards on the side of it, you find a wood of a hundred acres,
which was already cut into walks and ridings when I took it. I
have only added fifteen bowers in different views, with seats of
turf. They were easily made, here being a large quantity of
underwood, and a great number of wild vines, which twist to the
top of the highest trees, and from which they make a very good
sort of wine they call *brusco*. I am now writing to you in one of
these arbors, which is so thick shaded, the sun is not troublesome, even at noon. Another is on the side of the river, where I
have made a camp kitchen, that I may take the fish, dress and
eat it immediately, and at the same time see the barks which
ascend or descend every day to or from Mantua, Guastalla, or
Pont de Vic, all considerable towns. This little wood is carpeted,
in their succeeding seasons, with violets and strawberries, inhabited by a nation of nightingales, and filled with game of all
kinds, excepting deer and wild boar, the first being unknown
here, and not being large enough for the other.

My garden was a plain vineyard when it came into my hands
not two year ago, and it is, with a small expense, turned into a
garden that (apart from the advantage of the climate) I like
better than that of Kensington.[27] The Italian vineyards are not
planted like those in France, but in clumps, fastened to trees
planted in equal ranks (commonly fruit trees), and continued in

---

[27]The gardens of Kensington Palace in London.

festoons from one to another, which I have turned into covered galleries of shade, that I can walk in the heat without being incommoded by it. I have made a dining room of verdure, capable of holding a table of twenty covers. The whole ground is three hundred seventeen feet in length, and two hundred in breadth. You see it is far from large; but so prettily disposed (though I say it) that I never saw a more agreeable rustic garden, abounding with all sort of fruit, and produces a variety of wines. I would send you a piece if I did not fear the customs would make you pay too dear for it. I believe my description gives you but an imperfect idea of my garden.

Perhaps I shall succeed better in describing my manner of life, which is as regular as that of any monastery. I generally rise at six, and as soon as I have breakfasted put myself at the head of my weeder women, and work with them till nine. I then inspect my dairy and take a turn amongst my poultry, which is a very large inquiry. I have at present two hundred chicken, besides turkeys, geese, ducks, and peacocks. All things have hitherto prospered under my care. My bees and silkworms are doubled, and I am told that, without accidents, my capital will be so in two years' time. At eleven o'clock I retire to my books. I dare not indulge myself in that pleasure above an hour. At twelve I constantly dine, and sleep after dinner till about three. I then send for some of my old priests, and either play at piquet or whist till 'tis cool enough to go out. One evening I walk in my wood, where I often sup, take the air on horseback the next, and go on the water the third. The fishery of this part of the river belongs to me, and my fisherman's little boat (where I have a green lutestring awning) serves me for a barge. He and his son are my rowers, without any expense, he being very well paid by the profit of the fish, which I give him on condition of having every day one dish for my table. Here is plenty of every sort of fresh-water fish excepting salmon, but we have a large trout so like it that I, that have almost forgot the taste, do not distinguish it.

We are both placed properly in regard to our different times of life: you amidst the fair, the gallant, and the gay, I in a retreat where I enjoy every amusement that solitude can afford. I confess I sometimes wish for a little conversation; but I reflect that the commerce of the world gives more uneasiness than pleasure, and quiet is all the hope that can reasonably be indulged at my age.

My letter is of an unconscionable length. I should ask your

pardon for it, but I had a mind to give you an idea of my passing
my time. Take it as an instance of the affection of, dear child,

Your most affectionate mother.

[TO LADY BUTE]

Nov. 27, N.S. [1749]

Dear Child,—By the account you give me of London, I think it
very much reformed. At least you have one sin the less, and it
was a very reigning one in my time: I mean scandal. It must be
literally reduced to a whisper, since the custom of living all
together. I hope it has also banished the fashion of talking all at
once, which was very prevailing when I was in town, and may
perhaps contribute to brotherly love and unity, which was so
much declined in my memory that it was hard to invite six
people that would not, by cold looks or piquing reflections,
affront one another. I suppose parties are at an end, though I
fear it is the consequence of the old almanac prophecy, "Poverty brings peace"; and I fancy you really follow the French
mode, and the lady keeps an assembly that the assembly may
keep the lady, and card money pay for clothes and equipage as
well as cards and candles. I find I should be as solitary in
London as I am here in the country, it being impossible for me
to submit to live in a drum,[28] which I think so far from a cure of
uneasinesses that it is, in my opinion, adding one more to the
heap. There are so many attached to humanity, 'tis impossible
to fly from them all; but experience has confirmed to me (what I
always thought), that the pursuit of pleasure will be ever attended
with pain, and the study of ease be most certainly accompanied
with pleasures.

I have had this morning as much delight in a walk in the sun
as ever I felt formerly in the crowded Mall,[29] even when I
imagined I had my share of the admiration of the place, which
was generally soured before I slept by the informations of my
female friends, who seldom failed to tell me it was observed I
had showed an inch above my shoe-heels, or some other criticism of equal weight, which was construed affectation, and
utterly destroyed all the satisfaction my vanity had given me. I

[28]A private evening party.
[29]A promenade along St. James's Park, London.

have now no other but in my little housewifery, which is easily
gratified in this country, where, by the help of my receipt book, I
make a very shining figure among my neighbors by the introduction of custards, cheesecakes, and minced pies, which were entirely unknown in these parts, and are received with universal
applause and I have reason to believe will preserve my memory even to future ages, particularly by the art of butter-making,
in which I have so improved them that they now make as good
as in any part of England.

My paper is at an end, which I do not doubt you are glad of. I
have hardly room for my compliments to Lord Bute, blessing to
my grandchildren, and to assure you that I am ever

Your most affectionate mother.

[TO LADY BUTE]

July 22, N.S. [1752]

When I wrote to you last, my dear child, I told you I had a great
cold, which ended in a very bad fever, which continued a fortnight without intermission, and you may imagine has brought me
very low. I have not yet left my chamber. My first care is to
thank you for yours of May 8.

I have not yet lost all my interest in this country by the death
of the Doge, having another very considerable friend, though I
cannot expect to keep him long, he being near fourscore. I mean
the Cardinal Querini,[30] who is archbishop of this diocese, and
consequently of great power, there being not one family, high or
low, in this province that has not some ecclesiastic in it, and
therefore all of them have some dependence on him. He is of one
of the first families of Venice, vastly rich of himself, and has
many great benefices beside his archbishopric; but these advantages are little in his eyes, in comparison of being the first author
(as he fancies) at this day in Christendom; and indeed, if the
merit of books consisted in bulk and number, he might very
justly claim that character. I believe he has published yearly
several volumes for above fifty years, besides corresponding with
all the literati of Europe, and amongst these several of the senior

---

[30]Angelo Maria Querini (1680–1755), Librarian of the Vatican. The list of his works totals
eighty (Halsband). He is mentioned again on p. 208 below.

fellows at Oxford, and some members of the Royal Society[31] that neither you nor I ever heard of, whom he is persuaded are the most eminent men in England. He is at present employed in writing his own life, of which he has already printed the first tome; and if he goes on in the same style, it will be a most voluminous performance. He begins from the moment of his birth, and tells us that in that day he made such extraordinary faces, the midwife, chambermaids, and nurses all agreed that there was born a shining light in church and state.

You'll think me very merry with the failings of my friend. I confess I ought to forgive a vanity to which I am obliged for many good offices, since I do not doubt it is owing to that, that he professes himself so highly attached to my service, having an opinion that my suffrage is of great weight in the learned world, and that I shall not fail to spread his fame at least all over Great Britain. He sent me a present last week of a very uncommon kind, even his own picture, extremely well done, but so flattering it is a young old man, with a most pompous inscription under it. I suppose he intended it for the ornament of my library, not knowing it is only a closet. However, these distinctions he shows me give me a figure in this town, where everybody has something to hope from him; and it was certainly in a view to that they would have complimented me with a statue, for I would not have you mistake so far as to imagine there is any set of people more grateful or generous than another. Mankind is everywhere the same: like cherries or apples, they may differ in size, shape, or color, from different soils, climates, or culture, but are still essentially the same species; and the little black wood cherry is not nearer akin to the dukes that are served at great tables, than the wild naked negro to the fine figures adorned with coronets and ribands. This observation might be carried yet farther: all animals are stimulated by the same passions, and act very near alike, as far as we are capable of observing them.

The conclusion of your letter has touched me very much. I sympathize with you, my dear child, in all the concern you express for your family. You may remember I represented it to you before you was married; but that is one of the sentiments it is impossible to comprehend till it is felt. A mother only knows a mother's fondness. Indeed, the pain so overbalances the pleasure, that I believe, if it could be thoroughly understood, there

[31]For the advancement of science (founded 1660).

would be no mothers at all. However, take care that your anxiety for the future does not take from you the comforts you may enjoy in the present hour. It is all that is properly ours; and yet such is the weakness of humanity, we commonly lose what is, either by regretting the past, or disturbing our minds with fear of what may be. You have many blessings: a husband you love and who behaves well to you, agreeable, hopeful children, a handsome, convenient house with pleasant gardens, in a good air and fine situation; which I place amongst the most solid satisfactions of life. The truest wisdom is that which diminishes to us what is displeasing, and turns our thoughts to the advantages we possess.

I can assure you I give no precepts I do not daily practice. How often do I fancy to myself the pleasure I should take in seeing you in the midst of your little people! And how severe do I then think my destiny, that denies me that happiness! I endeavor to comfort myself by reflecting that we should certainly have perpetual disputes (if not quarrels) concerning the management of them. The affection of a grandmother has generally a tincture of dotage. You would say I spoilt them, and perhaps not be much in the wrong. Speaking of them calls to my remembrance the token I have so long promised my goddaughter. I am really ashamed of it. I would have sent it by Mr. Anderson if he had been going immediately to London, but as he proposed a long tour I durst not press it upon him. It is not easy to find anyone who will take the charge of a jewel for a long journey. It may be the value of it in money, to choose something for herself, would be as acceptable. If so, I will send you a note upon Child.[32] Ceremony should be banished between us. I beg you would speak freely upon that, and all other occasions, to

Your most affectionate mother.

[TO LADY BUTE]

Jan. 28, N.S. [1753]

Dear Child,—You have given me a great deal of satisfaction by your account of your eldest daughter. I am particularly pleased to hear she is a good arithmetician; it is the best proof of understanding. The knowledge of numbers is one of the chief

---

[32]Samuel Child, her London banker.

distinctions between us and brutes. If there is anything in blood, you may reasonably expect your children should be endowed with an uncommon share of good sense. Mr. Wortley's family and mine have both produced some of the greatest men that have been born in England. I mean Admiral Sandwich, and my great-grandfather, who was distinguished by the name of Wise William.[33] I have heard Lord Bute's father mentioned as an extraordinary genius, though he had not many opportunities of showing it; and his uncle, the present Duke of Argyll, has one of the best heads I ever knew.

I will therefore speak to you as supposing Lady Mary not only capable, but desirous of learning. In that case, by all means let her be indulged in it. You will tell me I did not make it a part of your education. Your prospect was very different from hers, as you had no defect either in mind or person to hinder, and much in your circumstances to attract, the highest offers. It seemed your business to learn how to live in the world, as it is hers to know how to be easy out of it. It is the common error of builders and parents to follow some plan they think beautiful (and perhaps is so), without considering that nothing is beautiful that is misplaced. Hence we see so many edifices raised that the raisers can never inhabit, being too large for their fortunes. Vistas are laid open over barren heaths, and apartments contrived for a coolness very agreeable in Italy, but killing in the north of Britain. Thus every woman endeavors to breed her daughter a fine lady, qualifying her for a station in which she will never appear, and at the same time incapacitating her for that retirement to which she is destined. Learning, if she has a real taste for it, will not only make her contented but happy in it. No entertainment is so cheap as reading, nor any pleasure so lasting. She will not want new fashions, nor regret the loss of expensive diversions or variety of company, if she can be amused with an author in her closet. To render this amusement extensive, she should be permitted to learn the languages. I have heard it lamented that boys lose so many years in mere learning of words. This is no objection to a girl, whose time is not so precious. She cannot advance herself in any profession, and has therefore more hours to spare; and as you say her memory is good, she will be very agreeably employed this way.

[33]Admiral Sandwich was Edward Montagu (1625–1672), first Earl of Sandwich; "Wise William" was William Pierrepont (1608–1678), politician. Lady Mary exaggerates their greatness.

There are two cautions to be given on this subject: first, not to think herself learned when she can read Latin, or even Greek. Languages are more properly to be called vehicles of learning than learning itself, as may be observed in many schoolmasters, who, though perhaps critics in grammar, are the most ignorant fellows upon earth. True knowledge consists in knowing things, not words. I would wish her no farther a linguist than to enable her to read books in their originals, that are often corrupted and always injured by translations. Two hours' application every morning will bring this about much sooner than you can imagine, and she will have leisure enough besides to run over the English poetry, which is a more important part of a woman's education than it is generally supposed. Many a young damsel has been ruined by a fine copy of verses, which she would have laughed at if she had known it had been stolen from Mr. Waller.[34] I remember when I was a girl, I saved one of my companions from destruction, who communicated to me an epistle she was quite charmed with. As she had a natural good taste, she observed the lines were not so smooth as Prior's or Pope's, but had more thought and spirit than any of theirs. She was wonderfully delighted with such a demonstration of her lover's sense and passion, and not a little pleased with her own charms, that had force enough to inspire such elegancies. In the midst of this triumph I showed her they were taken from Randolph's poems, and the unfortunate transcriber was dismissed with the scorn he deserved. To say truth, the poor plagiary was very unlucky to fall into my hands; that author, being no longer in fashion, would have escaped anyone of less universal reading than myself.[35] You should encourage your daughter to talk over with you what she reads; and as you are very capable of distinguishing, take care she does not mistake pert folly for wit and humor, or rhyme for poetry, which are the common errors of young people, and have a train of ill consequences.

The second caution to be given her (and which is most absolutely necessary) is to conceal whatever learning she attains, with as much solicitude as she would hide crookedness or lameness. The parade of it can only serve to draw on her the envy, and consequently the most inveterate hatred, of all he and she fools, which will certainly be at least three parts in four of all her

[34]Edmund Waller (1606–1687), noted for his flattering verses.
[35]Thomas Randolph, author of *Poems* (1638), was virtually unknown.

acquaintance. The use of knowledge in our sex, besides the amusement of solitude, is to moderate the passions and learn to be contented with a small expense, which are the certain effects of a studious life and, it may be, preferable even to that fame which men have engrossed to themselves and will not suffer us to share. You will tell me I have not observed this rule myself, but you are mistaken; it is only inevitable accident that has given me any reputation that way. I have always carefully avoided it, and ever thought it a misfortune.

The explanation of this paragraph would occasion a long digression, which I will not trouble you with, it being my present design only to say what I think useful for the instruction of my granddaughter, which I have much at heart. If she has the same inclination (I should say passion) for learning that I was born with, history, geography, and philosophy will furnish her with materials to pass away cheerfully a longer life than is allotted to mortals. I believe there are few heads capable of making Sir I. Newton's calculations, but the result of them is not difficult to be understood by a moderate capacity. Do not fear this should make her affect the character of Lady ——, or Lady ——, or Mrs. ——. Those women are ridiculous, not because they have learning, but because they have it not. One thinks herself a complete historian after reading Echard's Roman History; another a profound philosopher having got by heart some of Pope's unintelligible essays; and a third an able divine on the strength of Whitefield's sermons.[36] Thus you hear them screaming politics and controversy.

It is a saying of Thucydides, ignorance is bold, and knowledge reserved. Indeed, it is impossible to be far advanced in it without being more humbled by a conviction of human ignorance, than elated by learning.

At the same time I recommend books, I neither exclude work nor drawing. I think it as scandalous for a woman not to know how to use a needle, as for a man not to know how to use a sword. I was once extreme fond of my pencil, and it was a great mortification to me when my father turned off my master, having made a considerable progress for a short time I learnt. My overeagerness in the pursuit of it had brought a weakness on my

---

[36]Lawrence Echard's *Roman History* (1695–1698), Pope's *Essay on Man*, and the emotional sermons of George Whitefield (Methodist preacher, 1714–1770) were all intended for general, not learned, audiences. "A saying of Thucydides" (below) alludes to the *Peloponnesian War*, II.xl.3 (Halsband).

eyes that made it necessary to leave it off; and all the advantage I got was the improvement of my hand.[37] I see by hers that practice will make her a ready writer. She may attain it by serving you for a secretary when your health or affairs make it troublesome to you to write yourself, and custom will make it an agreeable amusement to her. She cannot have too many for that station of life which will probably be her fate. The ultimate end of your education was to make you a good wife (and I have the comfort to hear that you are one); hers ought to be, to make her happy in a virgin state. I will not say it is happier but it is undoubtedly safer than any marriage. In a lottery where there is (at the lowest computation) ten thousand blanks to a prize, it is the most prudent choice not to venture.

I have always been so thoroughly persuaded of this truth that, notwithstanding the flattering views I had for you (as I never intended you a sacrifice to my vanity), I thought I owed you the justice to lay before you all the hazards attending matrimony. You may recollect I did so in the strongest manner. Perhaps you may have more success in the instructing your daughter. She has so much company at home she will not need seeking it abroad, and will more readily take the notions you think fit to give her. As you were alone in my family, it would have been thought a great cruelty to suffer you no companions of your own age, especially having so many near relations, and I do not wonder their opinions influenced yours. I was not sorry to see you not determined on a single life, knowing it was not your father's intention, and contented myself with endeavoring to make your home so easy that you might not be in haste to leave it.

I am afraid you will think this a very long and insignificant letter. I hope the kindness of the design will excuse it, being willing to give you every proof in my power that I am

Your most affectionate mother.

[TO LADY BUTE]

[March 6, 1753]

I cannot help writing a sort of apology for my last letter, foreseeing that you will think it wrong, or at least Lord Bute will be

---

[37]Handwriting. "Pencil" (above) refers to painting and drawing.

extremely shocked at the proposal of a learned education for daughters, which the generality of men believe as great a profanation as the clergy would do if the laity should presume to exercise the functions of the priesthood. I desire you would take notice I would not have learning enjoined them as a task, but permitted as a pleasure if their genius leads them naturally to it. I look upon my granddaughters as a sort of lay nuns. Destiny may have laid up other things for them, but they have no reason to expect to pass their time otherwise than their aunts do at present; and I know by experience it is in the power of study not only to make solitude tolerable, but agreeable. I have now lived almost seven years in a stricter retirement than yours in the Isle of Bute,[38] and can assure you I have never had half an hour heavy on my hands for want of something to do.

Whoever will cultivate their own mind will find full employment. Every virtue does not only require great care in the planting, but as much daily solicitude in cherishing, as exotic fruits and flowers; the vices and passions (which I am afraid are the natural product of the soil) demand perpetual weeding. Add to this the search after knowledge (every branch of which is entertaining), and the longest life is too short for the pursuit of it; which, though in some regards confined to very strait limits, leaves still a vast variety of amusements to those capable of tasting them, which is utterly impossible for those that are blinded by prejudices, which are the certain effect of an ignorant education. My own was one of the worst in the world, being exactly the same as Clarissa Harlowe's;[39] her pious Mrs. Norton so perfectly resembling my governess, who had been nurse to my mother, I could almost fancy the author was acquainted with her. She took so much pains, from my infancy, to fill my head with superstitious tales and false notions, it was none of her fault I am not at this day afraid of witches and hobgoblins, or turned Methodist.

Almost all girls are bred after this manner. I believe you are the only woman (perhaps I might say, person) that never was either frighted or cheated into anything by your parents. I can truly affirm I never deceived anybody in my life, excepting (which I confess has often happened undesignedly) by speaking

[38]"Because of their small means, the Butes lived in the [isolated] Isle of Bute for ten years after their marriage in 1736" (Halsband).
[39]Mrs. Norton in Samuel Richardson's *Clarissa* (1748) has raised the heroine to be conventionally good, but Richardson does not represent her as superstitious.

plainly. As Earl Stanhope used to say (during his ministry), he always imposed on the foreign ministers by telling them the naked truth, which, as they thought impossible to come from the mouth of a statesman, they never failed to write informations to their respective courts directly contrary to the assurances he gave them; most people confounding the ideas of sense and cunning, though there are really no two things in nature more opposite. It is in part from this false reasoning, the unjust custom prevails of debarring our sex from the advantages of learning, the men fancying the improvement of our understandings would only furnish us with more art to deceive them, which is directly contrary to the truth. Fools are always enterprising, not seeing the difficulties of deceit or the ill consequences of detection. I could give many examples of ladies whose ill conduct has been very notorious, which has been owing to that ignorance which has exposed them to idleness, which is justly called the mother of mischief.

There is nothing so like the education of a woman of quality as that of a prince. They are taught to dance, and the exterior part of what is called good breeding, which, if they attain, they are extraordinary creatures in their kind, and have all the accomplishments required by their directors. The same characters are formed by the same lessons, which inclines me to think (if I dare say it) that nature has not placed us in an inferior rank to men, no more than the females of other animals, where we see no distinction of capacity; though I am persuaded, if there was a commonwealth of rational horses (as Doctor Swift has supposed),[40] it would be an established maxim amongst them that a mare could not be taught to pace. I could add a great deal on this subject, but I am not now endeavoring to remove the prejudices of mankind. My only design is to point out to my granddaughters the method of being contented with that retreat to which probably their circumstances will oblige them, and which is perhaps preferable to all the show of public life. It has always been my inclination. Lady Stafford (who knew me better than anybody else in the world, both from her own just discernment, and my heart being ever as open to her as myself) used to tell me my true vocation was a monastery; and I now find by experience more sincere pleasures with my books and garden, than all the flutter of a court could give me.

[40] In *Gulliver's Travels* (1726), Book IV.

If you follow my advice in relation to Lady Mary, my correspondence may be of use to her; and I shall very willingly give her those instructions that may be necessary in the pursuit of her studies. Before her age I was in the most regular commerce with my grandmother, though the difference of our time of life was much greater, she being past forty-five when she married my grandfather. She died at ninety-six, retaining to the last the vivacity and clearness of her understanding, which was very uncommon. You cannot remember her, being then in your nurse's arms. I conclude with repeating to you, I only recommend, but am far from commanding, which I think I have no right to do. I tell you my sentiments because you desired to know them, and hope you will receive them with some partiality, as coming from

Your most affectionate mother.

[TO LADY BUTE]

[October 10, 1753]

This letter will be very dull or very peevish (perhaps both). I am at present much out of humor, being on the edge of a quarrel with my friend and patron the C[ardinal]. He is really a good-natured and generous man, and spends his vast revenue in (what he thinks) the service of his country. Besides contributing largely to the building a new cathedral, which, when finished, will stand in the first rank of fine churches (where he has already the comfort of seeing his own busto[41] finely done both within and without), he has founded a magnificent college for one hundred scholars, which I don't doubt he will endow very nobly, and greatly enlarged and embellished his episcopal palace. He has joined to it a public library, which, when I saw it, was a very beautiful room. It is now finished and furnished, and open twice in a week with proper attendance.

Yesterday here arrived one of his chief chaplains, with a long compliment, which concluded with desiring I would send him my works. Having dedicated one of his cases to English books, he intended my labors should appear in the most conspicuous place. I was struck dumb for some time with this astonishing request. When I recovered my vexatious surprise (foreseeing the

[41]Bust.

consequence), I made answer, I was highly sensible of the honor designed me, but upon my word I had never printed a single line in my life.[42] I was answered in a cold tone, his eminence could send for them to England, but they would be a long time coming, and with some hazard; and that he had flattered himself I would not refuse him such a favor, and I need not be ashamed of seeing my name in a collection where he admitted none but the most eminent authors. It was to no purpose to endeavor to convince him. He would not stay dinner, though earnestly invited, and went away with the air of one that thought he had reason to be offended. I know his master will have the same sentiments, and I shall pass in his opinion for a monster of ingratitude, while 'tis the blackest of vices in my opinion, and of which I am utterly incapable. I really could cry for vexation.

Sure nobody ever had such various provocations to print as myself. I have seen things I have wrote so mangled and falsified, I have scarce known them. I have seen poems I never read published with my name at length, and others that were truly and singly wrote by me, printed under the names of others. I have made myself easy under all these mortifications by the reflection I did not deserve them, having never aimed at the vanity of popular applause; but I own my philosophy is not proof against losing a friend, and, it may be, making an enemy of one to whom I am obliged.

I confess I have often been complimented, since I have been in Italy, on the books I have given the public. I used at first to deny it with some warmth; but, finding I persuaded nobody, I have of late contented myself with laughing whenever I heard it mentioned, knowing the character of a learned woman is far from being ridiculous in this country, the greatest families being proud of having produced female writers, and a Milanese lady[43] being now professor of mathematics in the university of Bologna, invited thither by a most obliging letter wrote by the present Pope, who desired her to accept of the chair not as a recompense for her merit, but to do honor to a town which is under his protection.

To say truth, there is no part of the world where our sex is treated with so much contempt as in England. I do not complain

---

[42]That is, she had never presented herself as an author. Her published poems and essays had all been anonymous or unauthorized.

[43]Maria Gaetana Agnesi (1718–1799).

of men for having engrossed the government. In excluding us from all degrees of power, they preserve us from many fatigues, many dangers, and perhaps many crimes. The small proportion of authority that has fallen to my share (only over a few children and servants) has always been a burden and never a pleasure, and I believe everyone finds it so who acts from a maxim (I think an indispensable duty), that whoever is under my power is under my protection. Those who find a joy in inflicting hardships and seeing objects of misery may have other sensations, but I have always thought corrections, even when necessary, as painful to the giver as to the sufferer, and am therefore very well satisfied with the state of subjection we are placed in.

But I think it the highest injustice to be debarred the entertainment of my closet, and that the same studies which raise the character of a man should hurt that of a woman. We are educated in the grossest ignorance, and no art omitted to stifle our natural reason; if some few get above their nurses' instructions, our knowledge must rest concealed and be as useless to the world as gold in the mine. I am now speaking according to our English notions, which may wear out, some ages hence, along with others equally absurd. It appears to me the strongest proof of a clear understanding in Longinus (in every light acknowledged one of the greatest men among the ancients), when I find him so far superior to vulgar prejudices as to choose his two examples of fine writing from a Jew (at that time the most despised people upon earth) and a woman.[44] Our modern wits would be so far from quoting, they would scarce own they had read the works of such contemptible creatures, though perhaps they would condescend to steal from them, at the same time they declared they were below their notice.

This subject is apt to run away with me; I will trouble you with no more of it. My compliments to Lord Bute and blessing to all yours, which are truly dear to

Your most affectionate mother.

[44]In Chap. 9 of *On the Sublime* (1st cent. A.D.) Longinus instances Moses; in Chap. 10, Sappho.

[TO LADY BUTE]

Lovere, July 23 [1754]

My dear Child,—I have promised you some remarks on all the books I have received. I believe you would easily forgive my not keeping my word; however, I shall go on. The Rambler is certainly a strong misnomer. He always plods in the beaten road of his predecessors, following the Spectator (with the same pace a pack-horse would do a hunter) in the style that is proper to lengthen a paper. These writers may perhaps be of service to the public, which is saying a great deal in their favor. There are numbers of both sexes who never read anything but such productions, and cannot spare time from doing nothing to go through a sixpenny pamphlet. Such gentle readers may be improved by a moral hint which, though repeated over and over from generation to generation, they never heard in their lives. I should be glad to know the name of this laborious author.[45]

H. Fielding has given a true picture of himself and his first wife in the characters of Mr. and Mrs. Booth, some compliment to his own figure excepted; and I am persuaded several of the incidents he mentions are real matters of fact. I wonder he does not perceive Tom Jones and Mr. Booth are sorry scoundrels. All these sort of books have the same fault, which I cannot easily pardon, being very mischievous. They place a merit in extravagant passions, and encourage young people to hope for impossible events to draw them out of the misery they choose to plunge themselves into, expecting legacies from unknown relations, and generous benefactors to distressed virtue, as much out of nature as fairy treasures.[46] Fielding has really a fund of true humor, and was to be pitied at his first entrance into the world, having no choice, as he said himself, but to be a hackney writer or a hackney coachman. His genius deserved a better fate; but I cannot help blaming that continued indiscretion (to give it the softest name) that has run through his life, and I am afraid still remains. I guessed R. Random to be his, though without his

<hr>

[45]Samuel Johnson's *The Rambler* (1750–1752), published anonymously, is a less lively work than Addison and Steele's *The Spectator*, but it has a dignified wisdom that Lady Mary does not recognize.

[46]Henry Fielding's *Amelia* (1751), which centers on the Booths, and *Tom Jones* (1749), have implausibly happy endings. Below: *Roderick Random* (1748) and *Ferdinand Count Fathom* (1753) are by Tobias Smollett; so is *Peregrine Pickle* (p. 213).

name. I cannot think Fathom wrote by the same hand; it is every way so much below it.

Sally [Fielding] has mended her style in her last volume of D. Simple; which conveys a useful moral, though she does not seem to have intended it: I mean, shows the ill consequences of not providing against casual losses, which happen to almost everybody. Mrs. Orgueil's character is well drawn, and is frequently to be met with.[47] The Art of Tormenting, the Female Quixote, and Sir C. Goodville are all sale work. I suppose they proceed from her pen, and heartily pity her, constrained by her circumstances to seek her bread by a method I do not doubt she despises. Tell me who is that accomplished countess she celebrates. I left no such person in London; nor can I imagine who is meant by the English Sappho mentioned in Betsy Thoughtless, whose adventures, and those of Jenny Jessamy, gave me some amusement. I was better entertained by the Valet, who very fairly represents how you are bought and sold by your servants. I am now so accustomed to another manner of treatment, it would be difficult for me to suffer them. His adventures have the uncommon merit of ending in a surprising manner.

The general want of invention which reigns amongst our writers inclines me to think it is not the natural growth of our island, which has not sun enough to warm the imagination; the press is loaded by the servile flock of imitators. (Lord B[olingbroke] would have quoted Horace in this place.[48]) Since I was born, no original has appeared excepting Congreve, and Fielding, who would, I believe, have approached nearer to his excellences if not forced by necessity to publish without correction, and throw many productions into the world he would have thrown into the fire if meat could have been got without money, or money without scribbling. The greatest virtue, justice, and the most distinguishing prerogative of mankind, writing, when duly executed do honor to human nature, but when degenerated into

[47]In Sarah Fielding's *David Simple* (1753), Mrs. Orgueil is cruel and hypocritical. Below: *An Essay on the Art of Ingeniously Tormenting* (1753) is by Jane Collier; *The Female Quixote* (1752) by Charlotte Lennox; *Sir Charles Goodville* (1753) is anonymous. The "accomplished countess" appears in *The Female Quixote*, Book VIII, Chap. 5; the "English Sappho" is quoted in *Betsy Thoughtless* (1751) by Eliza Haywood, who also wrote *Jemmy and Jenny Jessamy* (1753). "The Valet" is the author of *Adventures of a Valet* (1752).

[48]Henry St. John, Viscount Bolingbroke (1678–1751), historical and political writer; he would have quoted Horace, *Epistles*, I.xix.19: "O imitatores, servum pecus" ("the servile flock of imitators").

trades are the most contemptible ways of getting bread. I am sorry not to see any more of P. Pickle's performances; I wish you would tell me his name.

I can't forbear saying something in relation to my granddaughters, who are very near my heart. If any of them are fond of reading, I would not advise you to hinder them (chiefly because it is impossible) seeing poetry, plays, or romances; but accustom them to talk over what they read, and point to them, as you are very capable of doing, the absurdity often concealed under fine expressions, where the sound is apt to engage the admiration of young people. I was so much charmed at fourteen with the dialogue of Henry and Emma, I can say it by heart to this day, without reflecting on the monstrous folly of the story in plain prose, where a young heiress to a fond father is represented falling in love with a fellow she had only seen as a huntsman, a falconer, and a beggar, and who confesses, without any circumstances of excuse, that he is obliged to run his country, having newly committed a murder. She ought reasonably to have supposed him, at best, a highwayman; yet the virtuous virgin resolves to run away with him to live among the banditti, and wait upon his trollop if she had no other way of enjoying his company. This senseless tale is, however, so well varnished with melody of words and pomp of sentiments, I am convinced it has hurt more girls than ever were injured by the lewdest poems extant.[49]

I fear this counsel has been repeated to you before; but I have lost so many letters designed for you, I know not which you have received. If you would have me avoid this fault, you must take notice of those that arrive, which you very seldom do.

My dear child, God bless you and yours. I am ever your most affectionate mother.

[TO SIR JAMES STEUART]

Venice, Jan. 13 [1759]

I have indulged myself some time with daydreams of the happiness I hoped to enjoy this summer in the conversation of Lady

---

[49]Lady Mary's derisive plot summary of Matthew Prior's "Henry and Emma" is accurate. Nevertheless she had loved the poem; she quotes it on pp. 174 and 175 above.

Fanny and Sir James S[teuart];[50] but I hear such frightful stories of precipices and hovels during the whole journey, I begin to fear there is no such pleasure allotted me in the book of fate. The Alps were once molehills in my sight when they interposed between me and the slightest inclination; now age begins to freeze, and brings with it the usual train of melancholy apprehensions. Poor human-kind! We always march blindly on; the fire of youth represents to us all our wishes possible; and, that over, we fall into despondency that prevents even easy enterprises: a stove in winter, a garden in summer, bounds all our desires, or at least our undertakings. If Mr. Steuart would disclose all his imaginations, I dare swear he has some thoughts of emulating Alexander or Demosthenes, perhaps both;[51] nothing seems difficult at his time of life, everything at mine. I am very unwilling, but am afraid I must submit to the confinement of my boat and my easy-chair, and go no farther than they can carry me. Why are our views so extensive and our power so miserably limited? This is among the mysteries which (as you justly say) will remain ever unfolded to our shallow capacities. I am much inclined to think we are no more free agents than the queen of clubs when she victoriously takes prisoner the knave of hearts; and all our efforts (when we rebel against destiny) as weak as a card that sticks to a glove when the gamester is determined to throw it on the table. Let us then (which is the only true philosophy) be contented with our chance, and make the best of that very bad bargain of being born in this vile planet; where we may find, however (God be thanked!), much to laugh at, though little to approve.

I confess I delight extremely in looking on men in that light. How many thousands trample under foot honor, ease, and pleasure, in pursuit of ribands of certain colors, dabs of embroidery on their clothes, and gilt wood carved behind their coaches in a particular figure! Others breaking their hearts till they are distinguished by the shape and color of their hats; and, in general, all people earnestly seeking what they do not want, while they neglect the real blessings in their possession—I mean the innocent gratification of their senses, which is all we can properly

---

[50]The Steuarts, Sir James and Lady Frances, were exiled Jacobites whom Lady Mary had met at Venice. They were now living at Tübingen, Germany, where their son (Mr. Steuart, below) attended the university.

[51]Alexander the Great (356-323 BC), conqueror of Greece and Asia Minor; Demosthenes (384-322 BC), famous Greek orator.

call our own. For my part, I will endeavor to comfort myself for the cruel disappointment I find in renouncing Tubingen, by eating some fresh oysters on the table. I hope you are sitting down with dear Lady F[anny] to some admirable red partridges, which I think are the growth of that country. Adieu! Live happy, and be not unmindful of your sincere distant friend, who will remember you in the tenderest manner while there is any such faculty as memory in the machine called

M.W. Montagu.

The Lover: A Ballad

At length, by so much importunity pressed,
Take, Molly,[1] at once the inside of my breast.
This stupid indifference so often you blame,
Is not owing to nature, to fear, or to shame;
I am not as cold as a virgin in lead,[2]
Nor is Sunday's sermon so strong in my head.
I know but too well how time flies along,
That we live but few years, and yet fewer are young.

But I hate to be cheated, and never will buy
Long years of repentance for moments of joy.   10
Oh! was there a man (but where shall I find
Good sense and good nature so equally joined?)
Would value his pleasure, contribute to mine;
Not meanly would boast, nor lewdly design;
Not over severe, yet not stupidly vain,
For I would have the power, though not give the pain.

No pedant, yet learned; not rakehelly[3] gay,
Or laughing because he has nothing to say;
To all my whole sex obliging and free,
Yet never be fond of any but me;   20
In public preserve the decorum that's just,
And show in his eyes he is true to his trust!

[1] Molly Skerrett, Lady Mary's best friend in the 1720s, when the poem was written.
[2] Lead was used as a lining for coffins.
[3] In the manner of a rakehell.

Then rarely approach, and respectfully bow,
But not fulsomely pert, nor yet foppishly low.

But when the long hours of public are past,
And we meet with champagne and a chicken at last,
May every fond pleasure that hour endear;
Be banished afar both discretion and fear!
Forgetting or scorning the airs of the crowd,
He may cease to be formal, and I to be proud,   30
Till lost in the joy we confess that we live,
And he may be rude, and yet I may forgive.

And that my delight may be solidly fixed,
Let the friend and the lover be handsomely mixed;
In whose tender bosom my soul might confide,
Whose kindness can soothe me, whose counsel could guide.
From such a dear lover as here I describe,
No danger should fright me, no millions should bribe;
But till this astonishing creature I know,
As I long have lived chaste, I will keep myself so.   40

I never will share with the wanton coquette,
Or be caught by a vain affectation of wit.
The toasters and songsters may try all their art,
But never shall enter the pass of my heart.
I loathe the lewd rake, the dressed fopling[4] despise:
Before such pursuers the nice virgin flies;
And as Ovid has sweetly in parable told,
We harden like trees, and like rivers grow cold.[5]

[4]A petty fop.
[5]Alluding to the stories of Daphne (turned to a laurel) and Arethusa (transformed to a stream) in the *Metamorphoses*.

The Reasons that Induced
Dr. S[wift] to Write a Poem Called
"The Lady's Dressing-Room"[1]

The Doctor, in a clean starched band,
His golden snuff-box in his hand,
With care his diamond ring displays,
And artful shows its various rays;
While grave he stalks down—— Street,
His dearest Betty——[2] to meet.
 Long had he waited for this hour,
Nor gained admittance to the bower;
Had joked, and punned, and swore, and writ,[3]
Tried all his gallantry and wit;   *10*
Had told her oft what part he bore
In Oxford's schemes in days of yore;[4]
But bawdy, politics, nor satyr[5]
Could move this dull hard-hearted creature.
 Jenny, her maid, could taste a rhyme,
And grieved to see him lose his time,
Had kindly whispered in his ear,
"For twice two pounds you enter here;
My lady vows without that sum,
It is in vain you write or come."   *20*
 The destined offering now he brought,
And in a paradise of thought,
With a low bow approached the dame,
Who smiling heard him preach his flame.
His gold she took (such proofs as these

---

[1]In "The Lady's Dressing Room" (1732) Swift imagines the filth and disorder out of which "haughty Celia" composes her ravishing beauty. His emphasis on Celia's excretions (as in the line, "Oh! Celia, Celia, Celia shits!") and dirty linen can be construed as misogynistic. Lady Mary's reply (one of several) retaliates not only by assigning a motive for Swift's malice but also by mocking the style and themes of other Swift poems—and the mannerisms of Swift himself, in lines 1–4.
[2]Betty in Swift's poem is Celia's maid.
[3]In Swift's *Cadenus and Vanessa*, Cadenus "Had sighed and languished, vowed and writ, / For pastime, or to show his wit" (lines 542–543).
[4]The high point of Swift's political career, of which he was thought to be vain, had been his role as chief propagandist for the Tory government under the Earl of Oxford, 1710–1714.
[5]Obsolete form of *satire*; pronounced "sater," it rhymed exactly with *creature* ("crater").

Convince most unbelieving she's)
And in her trunk rose up to lock it
(Too wise to trust it in her pocket),
And then, returned with blushing grace,
Expects the Doctor's warm embrace.   *30*
   But now this is the proper place
Where morals stare me in the face;
And for the sake of fine expression,
I'm forced to make a small digression.[6]
   Alas! for wretched humankind,
With learning mad, with wisdom blind!
The ox thinks he's for saddle fit
(As long ago friend Horace writ);[7]
And men their talents still mistaking,
The stutterer fancies his is speaking.   *40*
   With admiration oft we see
Hard features heightened by toupee;
The beau affects the politician,
Wit is the citizen's ambition;
Poor P[ope] philosophy displays on,
With so much rhyme and little reason;
And though he argues ne'er so long
That *all is right*, his head is wrong.[8]
None strive to know their proper merit,
But strain for wisdom, beauty, spirit,   *50*
And lose the praise that is their due,
While they've th'impossible in view.
   [So have I seen the injudicious heir,
To add one window, the whole house impair.]
   Instinct the hound does better teach,
Who never undertook to preach;
The frighted hare from dogs does run,
But not attempts to bear a gun—
Here many noble thoughts occur,
But I prolixity abhor;   *60*
And will pursue th'instructive tale,

---

[6]The digression is a common Swift device.

[7]In Epistles I.xiv.43. Line 39 below echoes "The Beasts' Confession to the Priest, on Observing How Most Men Mistake their Own Talents" (1738, but written in 1732). In another Swift poem, "On Poetry" (1733), the idea of mistaken talent is illustrated by examples similar to Lady Mary's in lines 53–56 below.

[8]Alluding to *Essay on Man* (1733), I.294: "Whatever is, is right."

To show the wise in some things fail.
  The reverend lover with surprise,
Peeps in her bubbies[9] and her eyes,
And kisses both—and tries—and tries.
The evening in this hellish play,
Besides his guineas thrown away,
Provoked the priest to that degree,
He swore, "*The fault is not in me.*
Your damned close-stool so near my nose,   70
Your dirty smock, and stinking toes[10]
Would make a Hercules as tame
As any beau that you can name."
  The nymph grown furious, roared, "By God,
The blame lies all in sixty-odd;"[11]
And scornful, pointing to the door,
Cried, "*Fumbler, see my face no more.*"
"With all my heart I'll go away,
But nothing done, I'll nothing pay;
Give back the money"—"How," cried she,   80
"Would you palm such a cheat on me?
I locked it in the trunk stands there,
And break it open if you dare;
For poor four pounds to roar and bellow,
Why sure you want some new prunella?[12]
What if your verses have not sold,
Must therefore I return your gold?
Perhaps you have no better luck in
The knack of rhyming than of_____.
I won't give back one single crown,
To wash your band, or turn your gown."   90
  "I'll be revenged, you saucy quean,"
(Replies the disappointed Dean)
"I'll so describe your *dressing room*,
The very *Irish* shall not come."[13]
She answered short, "I'm glad you'll write,
You'll furnish paper when I shite."

---

[9]Breasts.
[10]All details in "The Lady's Dressing Room." A close-stool is a chamber pot set in a chair.
[11]Swift was sixty-five in 1732.
[12]Prunella was the cloth used to make clergyman's gowns. Isobel Grundy has found that it was also the name of an amorous grocer's daughter in *Prunella, an Interlude* (1708) by Richard Estcourt.
[13]The English customarily sneered at the Irish for dirtiness and barbarity.

The Nonsense
of Common-Sense:
Number 6

Tuesday, January 24, 1738

I have always, as I have already declared, professed myself a friend, though I do not aspire to the character of an admirer, of the fair sex; and as such, I am warmed with indignation at the barbarous treatment they have received from the *Common-Sense* of January 14, and the false advice that he gives them.[1] He either knows them very little, or like an interested quack, prescribes such medicines as are likely to hurt their constitutions. It is very plain to me, from the extreme partiality with which he speaks of operas and the rage with which he attacks both tragedy and comedy, that the author is a performer in the opera; and whoever reads his paper with attention will be of my opinion. Nothing else alive would assert at the same time the innocence of an entertainment contrived wholly to soften the mind and soothe the sense, without any pretense to a moral, and so vehemently declaim against plays, whose end is to show the fatal consequences of vice and warn the innocent against the snares of a well-bred, designing Dorimant.[2] You see there to what insults a woman of wit, beauty, and quality is exposed, that has been seduced by the artificial tenderness of a vain, agreeable gallant; and I believe that very comedy has given more checks to ladies in pursuit of present pleasures so closely attended with shame and sorrow, than all the sermons they have ever heard in their lives.

But this author does not seem to think it possible to stop their propensity to gallantry by reason or reflection; he only desires them to fill up their time with all sorts of other trifles: In short, he recommends to them gossiping, scandal, lying, and a whole troop of follies instead of it, as the only preservatives for their virtue.

[1]*Common-Sense* was a Tory periodical that attacked Sir Robert Walpole's administration. Its issue of January 14 advised women how to avoid temptation: opera is safe to attend because it "admit[s] of no application," whereas stage plays "soften the heart and inflame the imagination" (Halsband).

[2]The unscrupulous hero of George Etherege's comedy *The Man of Mode*, who baits his cast-off mistress, Loveit.

I am for treating them with more dignity, and as I profess myself a protector of all the oppressed, I shall look upon them as my peculiar care. I expect to be told this is downright Quixotism, and that I am venturing to engage the strongest part of mankind with a paper helmet upon my head. I confess it an undertaking where I cannot foresee any considerable success, and according to an author I have read somewhere,

> The world will still be ruled by knaves,
> And fools contending to be slaves.[3]

But however, I keep up to the character I have assumed, of a moralist, and shall use my endeavors to relieve the distressed and defeat vulgar prejudices, whatever the event may be. Amongst the most universal errors I reckon that of treating the weaker sex with a contempt which has a very bad influence on their conduct. How many of them think it excuse enough to say, they are women, to indulge any folly that comes into their heads? This renders them useless members of the commonwealth, and only burdensome to their own families, where the wise husband thinks he lessens the opinion of his own understanding if he at any time condescends to consult his wife's. Thus what reason nature has given them is thrown away, and a blind obedience expected from them by all their ill-natured masters; and on the other side, as blind a complaisance shown by those that are indulgent, who say often that women's weakness must be complied with, and it is a vain troublesome attempt to make them hear reason.

I attribute a great part of this way of thinking, which is hardly ever controverted, either to the ignorance of authors, who are many of them heavy collegians that have never been admitted to politer conversations than those of their bed-makers, or to the design of selling their works, which is generally the only view of writing, without any regard to truth or the ill consequences that attend the propagation of wrong notions. A paper smartly wrote, though perhaps only some old conceits dressed in new words, either in rhyme or prose: I say *rhyme* for I have seen no *verses* wrote of many years. Such a paper, either to ridicule or declaim against the ladies, is very welcome to the coffee-houses, where there is hardly one man in ten but fancies he hath some reason or other to curse some of the sex most heartily. Perhaps his

---

[3]John How, imitation of Horace, *Odes* II.2, in *The History of Adolphus, Prince of Russi . . . with a Collection of Songs and Love-Verses*, 1691 (Halsband).

sisters' fortunes are to run away with the money that would be better bestowed at the groom-porter's;[4] or an old mother, good for nothing, keeps a jointure from a hopeful son, that wants to make a settlement on his mistress; or a handsome young fellow is plagued with a wife, that will remain alive to hinder his running away with a great fortune, having two or three of them in love with him. These are serious misfortunes, that are sufficient to exasperate the mildest tempers to a contempt of the sex; not to speak of lesser inconveniences, which are very provoking at the time they are felt.

How many pretty gentlemen have been unmercifully jilted by pert hussies, after having curtsied to them at *half a dozen operas*; nay, permitted themselves to be led out[5] *twice:* yet after these encouragements, which amount very near to an engagement, have refused to read their *billets-doux*, and perhaps married other men under their noses. How welcome is a couplet or two in scorn of womankind to such a disappointed lover; and with what comfort he reads in many profound authors, that they are never to be pleased but by coxcombs, and consequently he owes his ill success to the brightness of his understanding, which is beyond female comprehension! The country 'squire is confirmed in the elegant choice he has made, in preferring the conversation of his hounds to that of his wife; and the kind keepers,[6] a numerous sect, find themselves justified in throwing away their time and estates on a parcel of jilts, when they read that neither birth nor education can make any of the sex rational creatures, and they can have no value but what is to be seen in their faces.

Hence springs the applause with which such libels are read; but I would ask the applauders if these notions, in their own nature, are likely to produce any good effect towards reforming the vicious, instructing the weak, or guiding the young? I would not every day tell my footmen, if I kept any, that their whole fraternity were a pack of scoundrels; that lying and stealing were such inseparable qualities to their cloth, that I should think myself very happy in them if they confined themselves to innocent lies, and would only steal candles' ends. On the contrary, I would say in their presence that birth and money were accidents of fortune that no man was to be seriously despised for

---

[4]"Fortunes" were the dowries that had to be given with sisters when they married; the groom porter was an officer in charge of gambling at court.
[5]Led in a dance.
[6]Of mistresses.

wanting; that an honest faithful servant was a character of more value than an insolent corrupt lord; that the real distinction between man and man lay in his integrity, which in one shape or other generally met with its reward in the world, and could not fail of giving the highest pleasure by a consciousness of virtue, which every man feels that is so happy to possess it.

With this gentleness would I treat my inferiors, with much greater esteem would I speak to that beautiful half of mankind who are distinguished by petticoats. If I was a divine, I would remember that in their first creation they were designed a help for the other sex, and nothing was ever made incapable of the end of its creation. 'Tis true, the first lady had so little experience that she hearkened to the persuasions of an impertinent dangler;[7] and if you mind the story, he succeeded by persuading her that she was not so wise as she should be, and I own I suspect something like this device under the railleries that are so freely applied to the fair sex.

Men that have not sense enough to show any superiority in their arguments, hope to be yielded to by a faith that, as they are men, all the reason that has been allotted to humankind has fallen to their share. I am seriously of another opinion. As much greatness of mind may be shown in submission as in command; and some women have suffered a life of hardships with as much philosophy as Cato traversed the deserts of Africa,[8] and without that support the view of glory offered him, which is enough for the human mind that is touched with it to go through any toil or danger. But this is not the situation of a woman, whose virtue must only shine to her own recollection, and loses that name when it is ostentatiously exposed to the world. A lady who has performed her duty as a daughter, a wife, and a mother, raises in me as much veneration as Socrates or Xenophon; and much more than I would pay either to Julius Cæsar or Cardinal Mazarine, though the first was the most famous enslaver of his country, and the last the most successful plunderer of his master.[9]

A woman really virtuous, in the utmost extent of this expression, has virtue of a purer kind than any philosopher has ever

[7]Alluding to Eve and the serpent (Genesis 3:1–6); a *dangler* is a man who hovers around women.

[8]In Addison's *Cato*, III.265ff., the stoic Cato recalls this arduous journey.

[9]Socrates was renowned as a philosopher and martyr, Xenophon as an ethical teacher, Julius Caesar as a conqueror, and Mazarin, prime minister of France, as a powerful politician.

shown; since she knows, if she has sense, and without it there can be no virtue, that mankind is too much prejudiced against her sex to give her any degree of that fame which is so sharp a spur to their greatest actions. I have some thoughts of exhibiting a set of pictures of such meritorious ladies, where I shall say nothing of the fire of their eyes or the pureness of their complexions, but give them such praises as befits a rational sensible being: virtues of choice, and not beauties of accident. I beg they would not so far mistake me as to think I am undervaluing their charms: a beautiful mind in a beautiful body is one of the finest objects shown us by Nature. But I would not have them place so much value on a quality that can be only useful to one, as to neglect that which may be of benefit to thousands by precept or by example. There will be no occasion of amusing them with trifles, when they consider themselves capable of making not only the most amiable but the most estimable figures in life. Begin then, ladies, by paying those authors with scorn and contempt who, with a sneer of affected admiration, would throw you below the dignity of the human species.

Hester Thrale Piozzi
1741–1821

HESTER LYNCH SALUSBURY was brought up to be intellectual. In childhood she was tutored in languages, history, and geography; in her teens Dr. Arthur Collier taught her Latin, logic, and rhetoric. Her first identified publications, poems sent to newspapers, appeared in 1762. This incipient writing career was halted, however, when her family compelled her to marry (1763) Henry Thrale, a brewer. To him, during the next fifteen years, she bore twelve children, of whom eight died young.

In 1765 occurred what now seems the great event of her life: her meeting with Samuel Johnson. They were soon close friends. Through Johnson the Thrales met most of the leading intellectuals and artists of the day; among their frequent guests at Streatham Park were Oliver Goldsmith, Charles and Frances Burney, Sir Joshua Reynolds, David Garrick, and Edmund Burke. Thrale attained such eminence as a salonière that she was held to rival the "Queen of the Bluestockings," Elizabeth Montagu.

Her celebrity turned to scandal, however, when, after Mr. Thrale's death, she took for her second husband (1784) Gabriel Piozzi. An Italian, a Roman Catholic, and a professional musician, Piozzi was considered thoroughly unsuitable for an upper middle-class Englishwoman; it was even more unsuitable for a widow of forty-three to make what was patently a love match. The Piozzis retired to Italy, where she resumed her writing career by collecting ideas for a travel book and contributing poems to the *Florence Miscellany* (1785). Hearing of Johnson's death, she wrote *Anecdotes of the Late Samuel Johnson* (1786); on returning home she undertook the first edition of Johnson's letters (1788). Then came her travel book, *Observations and Reflections Made in the Course of a Journey through France, Italy, and Germany* (1789). In *British Synonymy* (1794) she produced the first original English dictionary of synonyms. *Retrospection* (1801), a history of the Christian era designed to assert royalist principles against the French Revolution, was a critical disaster. Its failure ended Piozzi's career.

She lived for twenty years more, enshrined as a relic of the Age of Johnson. After her death she acquired a new reputation as a diarist, consolidated by the appearance in 1942 of *Thraliana*. As a commentator on Johnson she has always been recognized as the chief rival of James Boswell. Boswell's attack on her in the *Life of Johnson* is an unwilling tribute to a competitor whom she feared.

Thraliana is the name given by Henry Thrale to a set of six blank books he presented to Hester as an anniversary gift. She wrote in them off and on for almost thirty years. "Diary" is a misnomer for what she wrote; the character of *Thraliana* is best described by her prefatory entry.

from Thraliana

It is many years since Doctor Samuel Johnson advised me to get a little book, and write in it all the little anecdotes which might come to my knowledge, all the observations I might make or hear, all the verses never likely to be published, and in fine everything which struck me at the time. Mr. Thrale has now treated me with a repository—and provided it with the pompous title of Thraliana; I must endeavor to fill it with nonsense new and old. 15 September 1776.

• • •

[20 Nov. 1776]

Doctor Collier has been mentioned several times in these few pages, one should naturally wish of course to give his character; but I must do it with caution if at all, because when I was but two and twenty our intimacy ended, and a girl of that age is not likely to know much of mankind.

He was however as far as I could judge a man of sound religion, pure morality, and endued with much learning; kind in his disposition, gentle in his manners— soft though not polite in his address, and cheerful in his general tenor of behavior beyond any man I ever knew: though disputation was all his delight, I never heard him loud and clamorous, nor ever saw him insolent and assuming. He had indeed much the air of a gentleman and was even scrupulously clean in his dress, which was always black, but with ruffles—to distinguish himself from a clergyman. His sight was very bad, worse I think than that of Johnson, but glasses gave him some assistance and he always wore spectacles for that reason. He was a person of a most assimilating temper, could live in any family, conform to any hours, and take his share in any conversation; he had such a taste of general knowledge, that he was not nice in his choice of company, and would make talk with anyone rather than be alone; yet Collier was no melancholy man, no hypochondriac, and made less bustle about real calamities than the people I have since lived amongst do with imaginary ones. Yet to many, nay to most people the Doctor was no agreeable companion; he loved to talk better than to hear, and to dispute better than to please; his conversation too was always upon such subjects as the rest of mankind seem by one consent to avoid. Duration and eternity, matter and motion, Whig and Tory, faith and works were his favorite topics;[1] and upon these or other metaphysical disquisitions would he be perpetually forcing his company—while by his superiority in logic, and constant exercise in all the arts of ratiocination, he delighted to drive them into absurdities they were desirous to keep clear of, and then laugh at the ridiculous figures that they made. All this, however, being done with an air of great civility made him more a painful than an offensive companion, and people generally left the room with a high opinion of that gentleman's parts and a confirmed resolution to avoid his society.

To perplex and disappoint was indeed so much his disposition that he seemed to converse for scarcely any other purpose; so that if a man had expressed a desire of talking with him on some critical or metaphysical subject, he would that day purposely expatiate on the skill of curing hams, or making minced pies, or say what pains he had taken to invent an universal pickle.

By such like artifices—and who can wonder—he was ever surrounded by enemies whom his charity was ready to forgive, and his benevolence to assist; for I have not yet seen a man so free from malice or rancor as Doctor Collier, nor a man whom malice and rancor were more sedulously employed to defame. . . .

[June 1777]

As this is *Thraliana*—in good time—I will now write Mr. *Thrale's* character in it: it is not because I am in good or ill humor with him or he with me, for we are not capricious people, but have I believe the same opinion of each other at all places and times.

---

[1]They are topics in philosophy, physics, politics, and theology, respectively.

Mr. Thrale's person is manly, his countenance agreeable, his eyes steady and of the deepest blue: his look neither soft nor severe, neither sprightly nor gloomy, but thoughtful and intelligent. His address is neither caressive nor repulsive, but unaffectedly civil and decorous; and his manner more completely free from every kind of trick or particularity than I ever saw any person's—he is a man wholly, as I think, out of the power of mimicry. He loves money and is diligent to obtain it; but he loves liberality too, and is willing enough both to give generously and spend fashionably. His passions either are not strong, or else he keeps them under such command that they seldom disturb his tranquillity or his friends, and it must I think be something more than common which can affect him strongly either with hope, fear, anger, love or joy. His regard for his father's memory is remarkably great, and he has been a most exemplary brother; though when the house of his favorite sister was on fire, and we were alarmed with the account of it in the night, I well remember that he never rose, but bidding the servant who called us go to her assistance, quietly turned about and slept to his usual hour. I must give another trait of his tranquillity on a different occasion; he had built great casks holding 1000 hogsheads each, and was much pleased with their profit and appearance. One day however he came down to Streatham as usual to dinner, and after hearing and talking of a hundred trifles—"but I forgot," says he, "to tell you how one of my great casks is burst and all the beer run out."

Mr. Thrale's sobriety, and the decency of his conversation, being wholly free from all oaths, ribaldry and profaneness, make him a man exceedingly comfortable to live with, while the easiness of his temper and slowness to take offense add greatly to his value as a domestic man. Yet I think his servants do not much love him, and I am not sure that his children feel much affection for him; low people almost all indeed agree to abhor him, as he has none of that officious and cordial manner which is universally required by them—nor any skill to dissemble his dislike of their coarseness. With regard to his wife, though little tender of her person, he is very partial to her understanding—but he is obliging to *nobody*; and *confers* a favor less pleasingly than many a man *refuses* to confer one. This appears to me to be as just a character as can be given of the man with whom I have now lived thirteen years, and though he is extremely reserved and uncommunicative, yet one *must* know something of him after so long acquaintance.

• • •

[18 September 1777]

In order to . . . delight myself by committing to paper the regard I have for Mr. Johnson, I shall begin this book by mentioning such little anecdotes concerning his life, his character, and his conversation, as I have been able to collect. All my friends reproach me with neglecting to write down such things as drop from him almost perpetually, and often say how much I shall sometime regret that I have not done 't with diligence ever since the commencement of our acquaintance. They say well, but ever since that time I have been the mother of children, and little do these wise men know or feel, that the crying of a young child, or the perverseness of an elder, or the danger, however trifling, of any one—will soon drive out of a female parent's head a conversation concerning wit, science or sentiment, however she may appear to be impressed with it at the moment: besides that to a *mère de famille*[2] doing something is more necessary and suitable than even hearing something; and if one is to listen all evening and write all morning what one has heard, where will be the time for tutoring, caressing, or what is still more useful, for having one's children about one? I therefore charge all my neglect to my young ones' account, and feel myself at this moment very miserable that I have at last, after being married fourteen years and bringing eleven children, leisure to write a *Thraliana* forsooth—though the second volume *does* begin with Mr. Johnson.[3]

[Sept.–Nov. 1777]

[When] poor Miss Owen said meekly enough one day, "I am sure my aunt was exceedingly sorry when the report was raised of Mr. Thrale's death,"[4] "Not sorrier I suppose," replied Mr. Johnson, "than the horse is when the cow miscarries." If in short anyone, or even himself, had bestowed more praise on a person or thing than he thought they deserved he would instantly rough them, and that in a manner brutal enough to be sure; at Sir Robert Cotton's table I once inadvertently commended the peas

---

[2]Mother of a family.
[3]The anecdotes of Johnson in *Thraliana* derive partly from a collection of "Johnsoniana" Thrale had started c. 1768 (she had in fact been "writing such things as drop from him"); they are the materials from which she composed *Anecdotes of Johnson*.
[4]"An April Fool jest of 1777" (Balderston).

. . . adding, "Taste these peas Mr. Johnson do, are not they charming?" "Yes, Madam," replied he, "for a pig."

It was at Streatham however, and before Murphy, Baretti, Lyttelton and *multis aliis*,[5] that he served Sir Joshua Reynolds saucily enough. The conversation turned upon painting—"I am sorry," says our Doctor, "to see so much mind laid out on such perishable materials—canvas is so slight a substance, and your art deserves to be recorded on more durable stuff, why do you not paint oftener upon copper?" Sir Joshua urged the difficulty of getting a plate large enough for historical subjects and was going on to raise further objections, when Mr. Johnson, fretting that he had so inflamed his friend's vanity I suppose—suddenly and in a surly tone replied, "What's here to do with such foppery? Has not Thrale here got a thousand tun of copper? you may paint it all round if you will, it will be no worse for him to brew in—afterwards." On the other hand, if he had unawares spoken harshly to a modest man, he would strive to make him amends as in the following case. A young fellow of great fortune, as he was sitting with a book in his hand at our house one day, called to him rather abruptly—and he fancied disrespectfully—"Mr. Johnson," says the man, "would you advise me to marry?" "I would advise *no man* to marry," answered he, bouncing from his chair and leaving the room in a fret, "that is not likely to propagate understanding." The young fellow looked confounded and had barely begun to recover his spirits when the Doctor returned with a smiling countenance, and joining in the general prattle of the party, turned it insensibly to the subject of marriage; where he laid himself out in a conversation so entertaining, instructive and gay that nobody remembered the offense except to rejoice in its consequences. Nothing indeed seems to flatter him more than to observe a person struck with his conversation whom he did not expect to be so; and this happened to him particularly in company with the famous Daniel Sutton,[6] who at that time inoculated one of my children and who was a fellow of very quick parts I think, though as ignorant as dirt both with regard to books and the world. The following thoughts I remember made the man stare as we call it, and seemed to throw a new light upon his mind. Money chanced to be the topic

[5] Arthur Murphy (1727–1805), playwright, who had introduced Johnson to Thrale; Joseph Baretti (1719–1789), Italian scholar and author; William Henry Lyttelton, 1st Baron Westcote; "and many others."

[6] A specialist in smallpox inoculation.

of the morning talk, and Mr. Johnson observed that it resembled poison, as a small quantity would often produce fatal effects; but given in large doses, though it might sometimes prove destructive to a weak constitution, yet it might often be found to work itself off, and leave the patient well. He took notice in the course of the same conversation that all expense was a kind of game, wherein the skillful player catches and keeps what the unskillful suffers to slip out of his hands. Sutton listened and grinned and gaped and said at last—half out of breath, "I never kept such company before and cannot tell how to set about leaving it now." The compliment though awkward pleased our Doctor much, and no wonder; it was likely to please both vanity and virtue.

[Nov. 1777]

We were speaking of Young as a poet: "Young's works," cried Johnson, "are like a miry road, with here and there a stepping stone or so; but you must always so dirty your feet before another clean place appears, that nobody will often walk that way." "In this, however," said I, "as well as in his general manner of writing he resembles your favorite Dryden"—and to this no answer was made. The next morning we were drawing spirits over a lamp, and the liquor bubbled in the glass retort; "There," says Mr. Johnson—"Young bubbles and froths in his descriptions like this spirit; but Dryden foams like the sea we saw in a storm the other day at Brighthelmstone."[7] Of Brighthelmstone itself he said, "This is a country so truly desolate, that one's only comfort is to think if one *had* a mind to hang oneself, no tree could be found on which to tie the rope."

[Nov.–Dec. 1777]

The vacuity of life had at some early period of his life perhaps so struck upon the mind of Mr. Johnson, that it became by repeated impression his favorite hypothesis, and the general tenor of his reasonings commonly ended in that. The things therefore which other philosophers attribute to various and contradictory causes, appeared to him uniform enough; all was done to fill up the time upon his principle. One man for example was profligate, followed the girls or the gaming table: "Why life

---

[7]The long-winded poems of Edward Young (1683–1765) were admired by many, including Thrale. Drawing spirits was an operation in chemistry. Brighthelmstone, or Brighton, was (and is) a seaside resort.

must be filled up, Madam, and the man was capable of nothing less sensual." Another was active in the management of his estate and delighted in domestic economy: "Why a man *must do something*, and what so easy to a narrow mind as hoarding halfpence till they turn into silver?" A third was conspicuous for maternal tenderness, and spent her youth in caressing or instructing her children: "Enquire however before you commend," cries he, "and you will probably perceive that either her want of health or fortune prevented her from tasting the pleasures of the world." I once talked to him of a gentleman who loved his friend: "He has nothing else to do," replies Johnson; "make him prime minister, and see how long his friend will be remembered." Little Mr. Evans of Southwark had preached one Sunday, and being struck with the discourse I commended it to our Doctor. "What was it about?" said he. "Friendship," replied I. "And what does the blockhead preach about friendship in a busy place like this where no one can ever be thinking of it?" "Why what are they *thinking* of?" said I. "Why the men," replied Johnson, "are thinking of their money, and the women are thinking of their mops."

• • •

There was another tenet of our Doctor's well worth recording: "Reject," says he to somebody, "no positive good: the spirit of such rejection proceeds only from a mean affectation of the power to penetrate consequences. Thus a man of this character will not marry a wife of high birth lest her pride should prove offensive, and is afraid of a beauty lest she should expose him by coquetry; my *prudent* friend therefore picks up an animal whose coarseness disgusts him, whose ignorance distresses, and whose narrowness perplexes him; and thinks it amazing that so *dispassionate* a choice produces so little felicity. There is in life," says Mr. Johnson, "so very little felicity to be possessed with innocence, that we ought surely to catch diligently all that can be had without the hazard of virtue." Something like this same principle was always discoverable in Mr. Johnson's thoughts on education: he hated the cruel prudence by which childhood is made miserable that manhood may become insensible to misery by frequent repetition. Yet no one more delighted in that general discipline by which children were restrained from tormenting their grown-up friends, nor more despised the imbecility of parents who are contented to profess their want of power to govern: "How," says he, "is an army governed?" Old people, I have often heard him observe, were very unfit to manage children; for being most commonly idle themselves they filled up their time, as he said, by tormenting the young folks with prohibitions not meant to be obeyed and questions not intended to be answered. His own parents had it seems teased him so to exhibit his knowledge etc. to the few friends they had, that he used to run up a tree when company was expected, that he might escape the plague of being showed off to them. He was in his turn extremely indulgent to children, not because he loved them, for he loved them not, but because he feared extremely to disoblige them: "A child," says he, "is capable of resentment much earlier than is commonly supposed, and I never could endure my father's caresses after he had once rendered them displeasing to me by mingling them with caresses I did not care to comply with."[8] As he was always on the side of the husband against the wife, so he was always on the side of the children against the old folks. "Old people," says he, "have no honor, no delicacy; the world has blunted their sensibility, and appetite or avarice governs the last stage." This was our talk one morning at breakfast, when a favorite spaniel stole our muffin which stood by the fire to keep hot; "Fie, Belle," said I, "you used to be upon honor." "Yes, Madam," replied Johnson, "but *Belle grows old*." . . .

Although Mr. Johnson would say the roughest and most cruel things, he always wished for the praise of good breeding, which however he did not obtain except from Dr. Barnard, who once asserted—I know not why—that Johnson was the civilest person in the world. True it is, that he was more ceremonious than many men; he would not sit forward or on your right hand in a coach, though he would take up so much room in it you could not sit yourself; he would not go to dinner till you arrived if he was ever so hungry, or the hour ever so late; would not displace an infant if sitting in the chair he chose, and always said he was more attentive to others than anybody was to him—and yet, says he, *People call me rude*.

. . . My mother and he did not like one another much the first two or three years of their acquaintance; the truth was each thought I loved the other better than I needed; as both however were excellent people, they grew insensibly to have great friend-

---

[8]The second "caresses" seems an error. In *Anecdotes* this reads, "he . . . loathed his father's caresses, because he knew they were sure to precede some unpleasing display of his early abilities."

ship; and nothing could be more solemn or striking than his last leave of her on the fatal eighteenth of June 1773. When I called him to her deathbed, and he feeling her pulse observed it did not yet intermit; but seeing the too visible alteration in her countenance, and drawing still nearer, he gave her the final kiss; and said in his peculiarly emphatic manner, "God bless you dearest Madam! for Jesus Christ's sake, and receive your soul to salvation!"

I can write no more just now! I will go on with Johnson on the other side.

[December 1777]

Nothing seemed to disgust Johnson so greatly as hyperbole; he loved not to hear of sallies[9] of excellence; "heroic virtues," said he one day, "are the *bons mots* of life, they seldom appear and are therefore, when they do appear—much talked of; but life is made up of little things, and that character is best which does little but continued acts of beneficence; as that conversation is the best which consists in little but elegant and pleasing thoughts expressed in easy, natural and pleasing terms."

"With regard to my notions of moral virtue, I hope I have not lost my sensibility of wrong, but I hope likewise that I have seen sufficient of the world to prevent my expecting to find any action whose motives, and all its parts are good." This last expression fell from him this day.

He had in his youth been a great reader of Mandeville,[10] and was very watchful for the stains of original corruption both in himself and others. I mentioned an event which might have greatly injured Mr. Thrale once! and said—"if it had happened now," said I—"how sorry you would have been!"—"I *hope*," replies he gravely, and after a pause—"that I should have been *very* sorry." He was indeed no great sorrower for events he had himself no share in; I told him one day of an acquaintance who had hanged himself—he was an old beau—"Foolish rascal," says Johnson, "why, he had better have been airing his clothes." . . .

Mr. Johnson has more tenderness for poverty than any other man I ever knew; and less for other calamities. The person who loses a parent, child or friend he pities but little—"these," says he, "are the distresses of sentiment—which a man who is *indeed*

[9]Outbursts; sudden departures from the customary.
[10]Bernard Mandeville (1670–1733), author of *The Fable of the Bees*; he was regarded by some as a rigid moralist and by others as a cynic. See pp. 245–46.

to be pitied—has no leisure to feel. The want of food and raiment is so common to London," adds Johnson, "that one who lives there has no compassion to spare for the wounds given only to vanity or softness."

. . . But to return to his notions concerning the poor; he really loved them as nobody else does—with a desire they should be happy. "What signifies," says somebody, "giving money to common beggars? They lay it out only in gin or tobacco." "And why should they not?" says our Doctor. "Why should everybody else find pleasure necessary to their existence and deny the poor every possible avenue to it? Gin and tobacco are the only pleasures in their power—let them have the enjoyments within their reach without reproach." Mr. Johnson's own pleasures—except those of conversation—were all coarse ones: he loves a good dinner dearly—eats it voraciously, and his notions of a good dinner are nothing less than delicate—a leg of pork boiled till it drops from the bone almost, a veal pie with plums and sugar, and the outside cut of a buttock of beef are his favorite dainties, though he loves made dishes, soups etc: souses his plum pudding with melted butter, and pours sauce enough into every plate to drown all taste of the victuals. With regard to drink his liking is for the *strongest*, as it is not the flavor but the effect of wine which he even professes to desire, and he used often to pour capillaire[11] into his glass of port when it was his custom to drink wine, which he has now left wholly off. To make himself amends for this concession, he drinks chocolate liberally, and puts in large quantities of butter or of cream. He loves fruit exceedingly, and though I have seen him eat of it immensely, he says he never had his bellyful of fruit but twice—once at our house and once at Ombersly, the seat of my Lord Sandys.

I was saying this morning that I did not love goose much, "one smells it so," says I—"But you, Madam," replies Johnson, "have always had your hunger forestalled by indulgence, and do not know the pleasure of smelling one's meat beforehand." "A pleasure," answered I—"that is to be had in perfection by all who walk through *Porridge Island* of a morning!"—"Come come," says the Doctor gravely, "let us have done laughing at what is serious to so many. Hundreds of your fellow creatures,

[11]A syrup flavored with orange-flower water.

dear Lady, turn another way that they may not be tempted by the luxuries of *Porridge Island*[12] to hope for gratifications they are not able to obtain."

• • •

Mr. Johnson's bodily strength and figure has not yet been mentioned; his height was five foot eleven without shoes, his neck short, his bones large and his shoulders broad; his leg and foot eminently handsome, his hand handsome too, in spite of dirt, and of such deformity as perpetual picking his fingers necessarily produced. His countenance was rugged, though many people pretended to see a benignity of expression when he was in good humor. Garrick tells a story how at a strolling play in some country town, a young fellow took away Johnson's chair, which he had quitted for five minutes, and seated himself in it on the stage; when the original possessor returned, he desired him to leave his chair, which he refused, and claimed it as his own. Johnson did not offer to dispute the matter, but lifting up man and chair, and all together in his arms, took and threw them at one jerk into the pit. Beauclerk tells a story of him that he had two large pointers brought into the parlor on some occasion to show his company, and they immediately fastening on one another alarmed the people present not a little with their ferocity, till Johnson gravely laying hold on each dog by the scuft[13] of the neck, held them asunder at arms' length, and said, "Come, gentlemen, where is your difficulty? Put one of them out at one door and t'other out of the other; and let us go on with our conversation." He confirmed these two stories himself to me before I would write them down. I saw him myself once throw over a bathing tub full of water, which two of the footmen had tried in vain to overturn, but says he, "these fellows have no more strength than cats." As an instance of his activity I will only mention, that one day after riding very hard for fifty miles after Mr. Thrale's foxhounds—they were sitting and talking over the chase when dinner was done in our blue room at Streatham; I mentioned some leap they spoke of as difficult; "no more," says Johnson, "than leaping over that stool." (It was a cabriolet[14] that stood between the windows.) "Which," says I, "would

---

[12]"Porridge Island is an alley in Covent Garden . . . where there are numbers of ordinary cooks' shops to supply the low working people with meat at all hours" (Thrale).
[13]Scruff.
[14]Cabriole (a small armchair).

not be a very easy operation to you, I believe, after fifty miles' galloping—and in boots too.'' He said no more, but jumped fairly over it, and so did Mr. Thrale, who is however full twenty years younger than the Doctor. Johnson loved a frolic or a joke well enough, though he had strange serious rules about them too, and very angry was he always at poor me for being merry at improper times and places. "You care for nothing," says he, "so you can crack your joke." One day to be sure I was saucy in that way and he was very much affronted: my friend Mrs. Strickland and he were entered into a dispute whose dress was most expensive—a gentleman's or a lady's. Mrs. Strickland instanced Lady Townsend's extravagance, and said she knew of her having a new cloak of eight guineas' value every three months. "A cloak, Madam!" cries Johnson, and was going to make a serious answer; "why Lord bless me what does a young girl marry an old Lord *for*," said I—"but for a *cloak*?" He did not like to be served so.

[April–May 1778][15]

. . . Our courtship (if such it might be called) was always carried on under the eye of my mother, whose project it originally was; and this so completely, that except for *one* five minutes only by mere accident, I never had had a tête-à-tête with my husband in my whole life till quite the evening of the wedding day.

We were married at St. Ann's Church, Soho, and came hither to Streatham to celebrate our nuptials; my mother, my uncle, my husband and myself. The next day after many tears of kindness between Sir Thomas and I, he took his leave, and I remember my mother rejoicing in his absence. We remained here till January as the town house was not ready for us I think; but I know I never *saw* the town house all the while, nor was ever consulted about any alterations in it. My mother lived with me and I was content; I read to her in the morning, played at backgammon with her at noon, and worked carpets with her in the evening. Mr. Thrale professed his aversion to a *neighborhood*, in which my mother perfectly agreed with him, so we visited nobody; he sometimes brought a friend from London, and that she had more wit than to oppose, though she did not

---

[15]During April and May 1778 Thrale entered her autobiography in *Thraliana*. This is her account of her marriage to Henry Thrale. Sir Thomas (below) is her uncle.

encourage it. His sisters each came once in a formal way, my mother charged me not to be free or intimate with 'em, and none of them pleased me enough to make me *wish* to break her injunction. Meantime my husband went every day to London and returned either to dinner or tea, said he always found two agreeable women ready to receive him, and thus we lived on terms of great civility and politeness, if not of strong alliance and connection . . . As I never was a fond wife, so I certainly never was a jealous one; I soon saw that I was married from prudential motives, as a passive, though well born and educated girl; who would be contented to dwell in the Borough,[16] which other women had refused to do . . .

Meantime my uncle was wedded to the widow, who soon weaned his affections away from me, whom he now never saw but in a way merely formal. My mother and he too lived on still worse terms; her jointure was not paid, she said; and if I offered to think of paying him a visit or a compliment of any sort, she would be out of humor and cry for whole days, a thing it was quite contrary to my duty to endure, and even to my interest; as she was the only creature that I saw; and if she was not in spirits, what a life I must lead! Mr. Thrale was in his counting house all morning, at Carlisle House perhaps, or the opera, or some public place all evening, and if I did not keep my mother in good humor what chance had I for comfort? . . . Lying-in time now approached though, and I must needs perform that ceremony in Southwark sorely against my will—if any will I had. My eldest daughter's birth was an event of seemingly great joy, for Mr. Thrale had somehow a notion we were to have no children, and even doubted of my pregnancy till it became quite past all question. He was therefore very glad to see his little girl, his beautiful daughter as he called her; as for poor me, I believe he might visit my chamber two or three times a week in a sort of formal way, which my mother said was *quite right*—and therefore I appeared to think so too.

After my month[17] was up, my mother returned to Dean St. and I to my occupation of daddling after her, carrying the child with me, as I had the honor of suckling it till I became a perfect shadow; and they were forced for very shame to let me off that duty, and get me an ass to suck myself. It was now time to *teach*

[16]Southwark, an unfashionable part of London.
[17]After childbirth.

the little girl, my mother said, and bring her forward as she had done by me; I was reproached with want of attention to my daughter, and told that I had now—*or ought* to have, something to amuse me without visiting or fooling at places of public resort, like fashionable wives and parents. I therefore did buckle hard to my business, taught this poor infant twenty pretty tricks she was no better for learning, and so my time was employed.

I now first had the pleasure of getting acquainted with Johnson, who after our acquaintance ripened into friendship, began opening my eyes to my odd kind of life. One day that I mentioned Mr. Thrale's cold carriage to me, though with no resentment, for it occasioned in me no dislike; he said in reply, "Why how for heaven's sake, dearest Madam, should any man delight in a wife that is to him neither use nor ornament? He cannot talk to you about his business, which you do not understand; nor about his pleasures, which you do not partake; if you have wit or beauty you show them nowhere, so he has none of the reputation; if you have economy or understanding you employ neither in attention to his property. You divide your time between your mamma and your babies, and wonder you do not by that means become agreeable to your husband." This was so plain I could not fail to comprehend it, and gently hinted to my mother that I had some curiosity about the trade, which I would maybe one day get Mr. Thrale to inform *me* about as well as the *Jacksons*[18] who I observed had all his confidence. But she saw no need, she said, for me to care *who* was in his confidence, that I had my children to nurse and to teach, and that she thought that was better employment than turning into *My Lady Mashtub.* Those were her words, and well do I remember them; so I went on in the old way, brought a baby once a year, lost some of them and grew so anxious about the rest, that I now fairly cared for nothing else, but them and her; and not a little for Johnson, who I felt to be my true friend, though I could not break through my chains to take his advice as it would only have helped to kill my poor mother, whose health now began to decline, and who was jealous enough of Mr. Johnson's influence as it was.

[May 1778]
The person of her who writes these memoirs is so little that

---

[18]The Jacksons, Henry and Humphrey, were experimenters with the use of isinglass in brewing (Balderston).

the description of it ought by no means to be large: the height four feet eleven only, and the waist, though not a taper one, quite in proportion. The neck rather longish, and remarkably white—so much so as to create suspicions of its being painted—this however is particular only because the woman is a brown one, with chestnut hair and eyebrows of the same color strongly marked over a pair of large—but light gray eyes. The complexion however is perfectly clear—the red very bright, and the white eminently good and clean. So much for color; *expression* there is *none* I think,[19] and the grace—which resembles that of foreigners—is more acquired than natural; for strength and not delicacy was the original characteristic of the figure. By keeping genteel company however, and looking much at paintings, learning to dance almost incessantly, and choosing foreign models, not English misses as patterns of imitation, some grace has been acquired: and if any accident has hindered her speaking among strangers who do not know her—the first question is when she quits the room, "does not that lady come from abroad, pray?"—and I fear the answer is too often—"*no doubt on't*; do not you see how she is painted?" The character of her mind however is almost wholly Italian, or rather Welsh perhaps; for her temper is warm even to irascibility; affectionate and tender, but claiming such returns to her tenderness and affection, as busy people have no time to pay, and coarse people have no pleasure in paying. She is a diligent and active friend, who spares neither money nor pains to oblige, but who is soon disgusted if the person obliged does not express the sense of obligation—by nature a rancorous and revengeful enemy, but having conquered that quality through God's grace, she is now apt *really* and *bona fide* to forget when and how she was offended. Though rather avaricious to procure money, she inclines to profusion in the spending it; yet is no carer about trifles respecting either great matters or small—for there may be trifles in great matters. Her knowledge of ancient languages is superficial enough, in modern ones she is rather skillful; and her comprehension of universal grammar is perhaps somewhat uncommon.[20] Geography and astronomy were her early studies, and she had a love for poetry, which often drove her into the absurdity of making bad

---

[19]"The eyes are so pale-colored there cannot be much expression" (Thrale).

[20]"How few . . . must be those who know grammar universal; that grammar which . . . only respects those principles that are essential to them all?" (James Harris, *Hermes, or, A Philosophical Inquiry Concerning Universal Grammar*, 1751).

verses, and sometimes of publishing them. She took up an odd whim of writing in the newspapers when she was a girl of 14 and sent her letters slyly, no friend suspecting her of such employment, till she herself informed her mother of her tricks, as she had no reserves from *her*, and hated from her cradle a clandestine disposition. And now there was no controversy about a bridge, an exhibition, or any such bauble but Miss Salusbury's letters on the occasion were printed under various names and signatures; so various, that she has long ago forgot them all: except her first essay as a political writer in good time! which was signed Thomas, and called itself the history I think, or Memoirs of the Albion Manor; it was published . . . at the very beginning of this king's reign, when Lord Bute was just come, or coming into power.[21] This letter was answered and buffeted about very comically . . . Another jeu d'esprit was well received by the public—but I have no copy of that neither; I mean an American eclogue—imitating the style of Fingal. The fable from the French of Mademoiselle Bernard was still more admired; and printed in the magazines of the month, from whence I have seen it in boarding schools given to girls for a copy. This I have by me, and shall write it out in the next volume of this farrago—should I live to begin the next.

[July 1778]

Was I to make a scale of novel writers I should put Richardson first, then Rousseau; after them, but at an immeasurable distance—Charlotte Lennox, Smollett and Fielding.[22] *The Female Quixote* and *Count Fathom* I think far before *Tom Jones* or *Joseph Andrews* with regard to body of story, height of coloring, or general powers of thinking. Fielding however knew the shell of life—and the kernel is but for a few.[22] I was showed a little novel t'other day which I thought pretty enough and set Burney to read it, little dreaming it was written by his second daughter, Fanny, who certainly must be a girl of good parts and some knowledge of the world too, or she could not be the author of

[21]"Albion Manor" appeared in 1762; for Bute see Montagu headnote. Below: The "American eclogue"—her first identified publication—appeared in February 1762; "Fingal" was James Macpherson (1736–1796), whose *Fingal* imitated ancient oral epic. The fable from Mlle. Bernard was "Imagination's Search after Happiness" (1763).

[22]Samuel Richardson and Jean-Jacques Rousseau wrote novels of passion and sentiment, notably *Clarissa* (1748) and *La Nouvelle Héloïse* (1761). Charlotte Lennox's *The Female Quixote* (1752), Tobias Smollett's *Ferdinand Count Fathom* (1753), and Henry Fielding's *Joseph Andrews* (1742) and *Tom Jones* (1749) are pictures of society.

Evelina—flimsy as it is, compared with the books I've just mentioned. Johnson says Harry Fielding never did anything equal to the 2nd vol. of *Evelina*.[23]

[14 January 1779]

People have a strange power of making their own characters; commended in youth or even in childhood perhaps, for some particular quality—they drive the thing forward by that delight which everyone naturally takes in talking of himself—"Yes *I* was always mischievous"; or "*I* was always a good-natured fool—the dupe to my playmates, who often had not *half my sense*," etc. Parents and people who are employed about youth might make advantage of this reflection, and be more cautious than they commonly are of giving children's characters before them; "He is so wild," say they—or "She is so sly"—the boy and girl quickly resolve to realize this nonsense, chiefly for the pleasure of hearing it over again too—

"I will run across the ice to the island—Mamma will say, 'George is *so wild*' "; and "I'll go and tell tales of him," says Miss to herself—"Papa'll cry how *sly* a slut she is!" One would not however at first suppose this *could* go on to manhood, but when one hears Johnson tell how *he* was always a *sullen dog* that never tried to please another; how he was twenty years old before ever he could charge himself with any *intention to oblige*; how he was always an *idle dog*, and never would go to business till he was forced to't by necessity: when one hears Seward[24] say how *sickly* he has been from his childhood, and sees him go through long courses of unnecessary medicine to keep up his character of a hypochondriac; when one hears Mr. Thrale boast the coldness of his heart, and the little power his friends' misfortunes *always* had, of making him uneasy; when in consequence of this *original* disposition he tells the man who is sick that he wants nothing but a *horse whip*, and the lady . . . that if she is bad today, she'll be better tomorrow—one must be careful not to take up a character, or contribute to the giving one to another.—

[10 Feb. 1779]

Mr. Thrale is making me a cold bath; I am very fond of bathing, and think it an extremely beneficial thing to general

[23]See Burney headnote. Most of this paragraph was written before Thrale had heard Johnson's opinion (Balderston).
[24]William Seward (1747–1799), anecdotist, a family friend of the Thrales.

health, though more fit for many women than for me. The lax-fibered ladies who are seized with a purging whenever they are vexed, or cry whenever they are contradicted, should certainly be often plunged into the coldest water—and women who are subject to miscarry would doubtless be greatly strengthened by its use; but I who am rather plethoric, am to blame sometimes for indulging myself too much in the habit of it. There are however so many temptations! 'tis such a friend to beauty and to love! smoothing the skin, illuminating the complexion, exciting ideas of such perfect cleanliness, bracing up everything that frequent pregnancy relaxes—I only wonder the women use it so little, and that the men can be pleased with those who never use it at all. . . .

I am sorry Mr. Thrale has such a spirit of alteration; it vexes me to see the old seats my mother used to sit in taken away, and the mount poor Harry used to crawl up leveled with the ground; the place may look finer for aught I know, but I can associate no ideas to it in its present state. The pleasure of recollecting past conversations endears even mute objects to one's mind, and I love the dwarf apple trees my mother planted better than all the woods of Fontainebleau.[25]

I never offer to cross my master's fancy however unless on some truly serious occasion, nor do I think any occasion serious enough to excuse contradiction unless virtue, life, or fortune are concerned. Was I to die tomorrow I could swear I never opposed his inclination three times in the fifteen years we have been married.

It has often been my admiration to observe how many people, and particularly women, delight in contest when they know beforehand they shall be defeated; always fighting the battle with their husbands and always losing the victory; 'tis comical to see how strangely insensible they must be to refusal or rejection. Was I to propose a journey Mr. Thrale would refuse to let me take; or desire a tree to be cut down or planted, and he should—as he most undoubtedly would—give me a coarse reply and abrupt negative, it would make *me* miserable. To have one's own unimportance presented suddenly to one's sight, and one's own qualities insolently undervalued by those who do not even *pretend* to possess them—is sufficiently mortifying; yet I every day see people putting themselves unnecessarily in the way on't.

[25]Which she had visited in 1775. Harry was the eldest Thrale son (d. 1776).

I am therefore among the few who make it a general rule never
to object, and seldom to propose.[26]—I always mean to make
exceptions in questions concerning fortune, life or morality.

[July 1779]

Our new-fangled politics have indeed brought us to a miserable pass; the King has just issued out a proclamation in case of
the Kingdom being invaded,[27] and everybody seems expecting
and preparing for the worst; an estate of £200 a year—*two
hundred* a year, was yesterday sold for only three thousand
pounds to the same man who offered seven thousand five hundred for it just seven years since. This fact was told me not ten
minutes ago by Doctor Wetherell, Dean of Hereford, and Master
(I think) of University College, Oxford. The sugars we gave nine
pence a pound for in the year 1770, are now at sixteen and
seventeen pence a pound; coals too are supposed to be dreadfully dear—in this weather God knows they may be as dear as
they will, but what's to be done in the winter? Taxed beyond
endurance, our resources almost exhausted, a despicable ministry, a feeble government—what will? what *can* be the end? I
think the French would be wiser to delay their visit till *all* our
money, men and spirits were drained off by this cursed American War: should they come this summer, our militia might repel
them, they had better strike the blow at Jamaica now, and
invade England next year when 'tis still more enfeebled.

[August 1779]

. . . The other day . . . after long continued threats of a
miscarriage had confined me to the house and even to my
chamber, some mismanagement among the Borough clerks[28]
obliged me to go thither and set things straight; Mr. Thrale
wished me to go, nay insisted on it, but seemed somewhat
concerned too, as he was well apprised of the risk I should run.
I went however, and after doing the business I went to do,
begged him to make haste home, as I was apprehensive bad
consequences might very quickly arise from the jolting etc.—He
would not be hurried—the probable consequences *did* begin to
arise, I pressed him to order the coach—he could not be hurried—I

---

[26] "See how differently pride operates in different constitutions" (Thrale).

[27] In March 1778 France had joined the American colonies in their war against England.

[28] At Mr. Thrale's brewery. Thrale had long since made good her resolution to interest
herself in the trade.

told his valet my danger, and begged him to hasten his master; no pain, no entreaties of mine could make him set out one *moment* before the appointed hour—so I lay along in the coach all the way from London to Streatham in a state not to be described, nor endured—*but by me*: and being carried to my chamber the instant I got home, miscarried in the utmost agony before they could get me into bed, after fainting five times.

Now though Mr. Thrale's heart never much run over with tenderness towards me God knows—yet common humanity might have had a place here; no *feelings* however, no *shame* could induce him—to put himself in a hurry!

[7 Dec. 1779]

I have an odd power of working myself up into artificial spirits. One day in the first week of April 1777 when I was vexed and frighted out of my wits because of the accident—if one may call it such—that befell our business, when Mr. Thrale was agonizing with apprehension, and I was within a month or two of lying in, . . . I remember Boswell dining here:[29] we talked, we rattled, we flashed, we made extempore verses, we did so much that at last Mr. Boswell said, "Why Mrs. Thrale (says he) you are in most riotous spirits today." "So I am," replied I gaily. and actually ran out of the room to cry—his observation went so to my heart.

[January 1780]

What a fine book is Law's *Serious Call*! Written with such force of thinking, such purity of style, and such penetration into human nature; the characters too so neatly, nay so highly finished. Yet nobody reads it I think, from the notion of its being a religious work most probably. Johnson has however studied it hard I am sure, and many of the *Ramblers* apparently took their rise from that little volume,[30] as the Nile flows majestically from a source difficult to be discovered or even discerned.

I have often mentioned how extremes meet. Law and Mandeville are not only of the same opinion, but even use each other's expressions in speaking of pride and humility; each splits upon the same rock too, for failing to define luxury or temperance,

[29]James Boswell (1740–1795), biographer of Johnson. To *flash* (below) means "to break out into wit, merriment, or bright thought" (Johnson, *Dictionary*).
[30]In William Law's *Serious Call to a Devout and Holy Life* (1729), fictional character sketches illustrate moral ideas, a technique used also by Johnson in *The Rambler*.

they both leave their readers uninformed whether anything but acorns and water are allowable to people of strict virtue, which Mandeville holds to be perpetual self-denial, and says how many trades are exercised to obtain for man the *luxury of small beer*. Law, who was more delicate, considered *friendship* as too luscious a treat for a Christian and commands us to contract no particular kindness for any one or more persons, but to love all mankind alike, and in the same degree—forgetting that our Blessed Savior *wept* for his friend, and *loved* Lazarus and his sisters with very particular and tender regard.[31]

[8 August 1780]

Piozzi is become a prodigious favorite with me; he is so intelligent a creature, so discerning, one can't help wishing for his good opinion. His singing surpasses everybody's for taste, tenderness, and true elegance; his hand on the fortepiano too is so soft, so sweet, so delicate, every tone goes to one's heart I think; and fills the mind with emotions one would not be without, though inconvenient enough sometimes—I made him sing yesterday, and though he says his voice is gone, I cannot somehow or other get it out of my ears—odd enough!

[Monday, 29 January 1781]

One page more I see ends the 3rd volume of Thraliana! strange farrago as it is of sense, nonsense, public, private follies—but chiefly my own—and *I* the little hero etc. Well! but who should be the hero of an *ana*? Let me vindicate my own vanity if it be with my last pen. This volume will be finished at Streatham and be left there . . .

[1 May 1781]

Miss Owen and Miss Burney asked me if I had never been in love; "with myself," said I, "and most passionately." When any man likes me I never am surprised, for I think how should he help it? When any man does *not* like me, I think him a blockhead, and there's an end of the matter.

[7 July 1781]

Dr. Burney did not like his daughter should learn Latin even of

---

[31]Thrale alludes to Mandeville's *Fable*, Remark P (see n. 10); to Law, Chap. 20 ("A love which is not universal may indeed have tenderness and affection, but it hath nothing of righteousness or piety in it"); and to the Bible (John 11:5 and 35).

Johnson, who offered to teach her for friendship, because then she would have been as wise as himself forsooth, and Latin was too masculine for misses—a narrow-souled goose-cap[32] the man must be at last; *agreeable* and *amiable* all the while too beyond almost any other human creature. Well! Mortal man is but a paltry animal! the best of us have *such* drawbacks both upon virtue, wisdom and knowledge.

[Streatham, 17 April 1782]

I am returned to Streatham, pretty well in health, and *very* sound of heart, notwithstanding the watchers and the wager-layers:[33] who think more of the charms of their sex by half than I who know them better. Love and friendship are distinct things; and I would go through fire to serve many a man, whom nothing less than fire would force me to go to bed to. Somebody mentioned my going to be married t'other day, and Johnson was joking about it—"I suppose Sir," said I, "they think they are doing me *honor* with these imaginary matches, when perhaps the man does not *exist*, who would do me honor by marrying me." This indeed was said in the wild and insolent spirit of Baretti,[34] yet 'tis nearer truth than one would think for. A woman of passable person, ancient family, respectable character, uncommon talents, and three thousand a year, has a right to think herself any man's *equal*; and has nothing to seek but return of affection from whatever partner she pitches on. To marry for *love* would therefore be rational in me, who want no advancement of birth or fortune, and till I am in love, I will not marry—*nor perhaps then*.

[1 Oct. 1782]

. . . I am going to leave Streatham for three years, where I lived—never happily indeed, but always easily: the more so perhaps from the total absence of love and ambition

> Else those two passions by the way
> Might chance to show us scurvy play.

Now! that little dear discerning creature Fanny Burney says I'm in love with Piozzi—very likely! He is so amiable, so honorable, so much above his situation by his abilities, that if

[32]Fool.

[33]Thrale had now been widowed for a year, and was returning to Streatham from a stay in London. Her plans were the subject of incessant newspaper gossip.

[34]Joseph Baretti (n. 5), well known for hot-tempered arrogance.

> Fate hadn't fast bound her
> With Styx nine times round her
> Sure music and love were victorious.[35]

But if he is ever so worthy, ever so lovely, he is *below me* forsooth. In what is he below me? In virtue—I would I were above him; in understanding—I would mine were from this instant under the guardianship of his. In birth—to be sure he is below me in birth, and so is almost every man I know, or have a chance to know;—but he is below me in fortune. Is mine sufficient for us both? More than amply so. Does he deserve it by his conduct, in which he has always united warm notions of honor with cool attention to economy, the spirit of a gentleman with the talents of a professor? How shall any man deserve fortune if he does not? But I am the guardian of five daughters by Mr. Thrale, and must not disgrace *their* name and family. Was then the man my mother chose for me of higher extraction than him I have chosen for myself? No. But his fortune was higher. I wanted fortune *then* perhaps, do I want it *now*? Not at all. But I am not to think about myself; I married the first time to please my mother, I must marry the second time to please my daughter—I have always sacrificed my own choice to that of others, so I must sacrifice it again. But why? Oh because I am a woman of superior understanding, and must not for the world degrade myself from my situation in life. But if I *have* superior understanding, let me at least make use of it for once; and rise to the rank of a human being conscious of its own power to discern good from ill—the person who has uniformly acted by the will of others, has hardly that dignity to boast. But once again, I am guardian to five girls; agreed—will this connection prejudice their bodies, souls, or purse? My marriage may assist *my* health, but I suppose it will not injure *theirs*. Will his company or companions corrupt their morals? God forbid, if I did not believe him one of the best of our fellow beings I would reject him instantly. Can it injure their fortunes? And could he impoverish (if he would) five women to whom their father left £20,000 each—independent almost of possibilities?

To what then am I guardian? To their pride and prejudice? and is anything else affected by the alliance?

Now for more solid objections. Is not the man of whom I

[35]Matthew Prior, *Alma*, III.547–548, and Alexander Pope, *Ode on St. Cecilia's Day*, lines 90–92.

desire protection a foreigner? Unskilled in the laws and language of our country certainly. Is he not as the French say *arbitre de mon sort?*[36] and from the hour he possesses my person and fortune have I any power of decision how or where I may continue or end my life? Is not the man upon the continuance of whose affection my whole happiness depends—*younger* than myself,[37] and is it wise to place one's happiness on the continuance of *any* man's affection? Would it not be painful to owe his appearance of regard more to his honor than his love? and is not my person already faded, likelier to fade soon[er] than his? On the other hand, is *his* life a good one? and would it not be lunacy even to risk the wretchedness of losing all situation in the world for the sake of living with a man one loves, and then to lose both companion and consolation? When I lost Mr. Thrale, everyone was officious to comfort and to soothe me: but which of my children or quondam friends would look with kindness upon Piozzi's widow? If I bring children by him must they not be Catholics, and must not I live among people, the *ritual* part of whose religion I disapprove?

These are *my* objections, these *my* fears: not those of being censured by the world as it is called—a composition of vice and folly. Though 'tis surely no good joke to be talked of

> By each affected she that tells my story
> And blesses her good stars that *she* was prudent.[38]

These objections would increase in strength too, if my present state was a happy one. But it really is not: I live a quiet life, but not a pleasant one: My children govern without loving me, my servants devour and despise me, my friends caress and censure me, my money wastes in expenses I do not enjoy, and my time in trifles I do not approve. Everyone is made insolent, and no one comfortable. My reputation unprotected, my heart unsatisfied, my health unsettled. . . .

[2 July 1784]

The happiest day of my whole life I think—Yes, *quite* the happiest; my Piozzi came home[39] yesterday and dined with me. But my spirits were too much agitated, my heart too much

---

[36]"Master of my fate."
[37]"He was half a year *older* when our registers were both examined" (Thrale).
[38]Nicholas Rowe, *The Fair Penitent* (1703), II.i.35–36 (Balderston).
[39]From Italy. They were married three weeks later.

dilated, I was too painfully happy *then*, my sensations are more quiet today, and my felicity less tumultuous. I have spent the night as I ought, in prayer and thanksgiving—Could I have slept I had not deserved such blessings. May the Almighty but preserve them to me!

[25 Jan. 1785]

I have recovered myself sufficiently to think what will be the consequence to me of Johnson's death, but must wait the event as all thoughts on the future in this world are vain.[40]

Six people have already undertaken to write his life I hear, of which Sir John Hawkins, Mr. Boswell, Tom Davies and Dr. Kippis are four. Piozzi says he would have me add to the number, and so I would; but that I think my anecdotes too few, and am afraid of saucy answers if I send to England for others— the saucy answers *I* should disregard, but my heart is made vulnerable by my late marriage, and I am certain that to spite me, they would insult my husband. Poor Johnson! I see they will leave *nothing untold* that I labored so long to keep secret; and I was so very delicate in trying to conceal his fancied insanity, that I retained no proofs of it—or hardly any—nor ever mentioned it in these books, lest by dying first *they* might be printed and the secret (for such I thought it) discovered.[41]

I used to tell him in jest that his biographers would be at a loss concerning some orange peel he used to keep in his pocket, and many a joke we had about the lives that would be published. "Rescue me out of all their hands, my dear, and do it *yourself*," said he: "Taylor, Adams and Hector will furnish you with juvenile anecdotes, and Baretti will give you all the rest that you have not already—for I think Baretti is a liar only when he speaks of himself."[42] "Oh!" said I, "Baretti told me yesterday that you got by heart six pages of Machiavel's History once, and repeated 'em thirty years afterwards word for word." "O, why this indeed is a *gross* lie," says Johnson—"I never read the book at all." "Baretti too told me of *you* (said I) that you once kept 16

---

[40]Johnson died December 13, 1784; Piozzi has just heard of it. Of the people she lists, Hawkins and Boswell did and Davies and Andrew Kippis did not write lives of Johnson.

[41]Johnson's fear of insanity was known to his close friends. The first memoirist to mention it was Thomas Tyers (1784). For the orange peel mentioned below, see also Boswell, *Life of Johnson*, April 1, 1775 and April 18, 1783.

[42]John Taylor and Edmund Hector were Johnson's oldest friends; Dr. William Adams was his tutor at Oxford. Below: the *History of Florence* by Niccolo Machiavelli (1469–1527).

cats in your chamber, and that they scratched your legs to such a degree, you were forced to use mercurial plasters for some time after." "Why this (replied Johnson) is an unprovoked lie indeed: I thought the fellow would not have broken through divine and human laws thus, to make Puss his heroine—but I see I was mistaken."

[7 Jan. 1788 Hanover Square]
I diverted my friend Mrs. Lewis while at Reading with reviewing my own book, and imitating the style of those I expect to abuse it. Here is the performance, and I question whether my enemies will do better.

MONTHLY REVIEW FOR APRIL OR MAY 1788
Letters to and from Dr. Johnson
published by H.L. Piozzi.

The care and attention with which we have reviewed this work was rather excited by our long expectation of it, than repaid by the instruction or amusement it affords; let it not however be consigned to oblivion without a few remarks on its excellencies and defects, which to say truth are neither of them numerous, and we should do the public double injury in covering much paper with criticism upon what the Rambler himself would call *pages of inanity*.[43] For who can it benefit, or who can it please, to hear in one letter that poor Mrs. Salusbury has had a bad night, and that little Sophy's head ached all yesterday? If our fair editress published this correspondence to show with how much insipidity people famed for their wit and their learning might maintain a twenty years' intercourse by letter and conversation, she has succeeded admirably. . . .
The world will . . . be probably but little interested concerning the slippery bowels of an old pious lady long since dead; perhaps the *strong* or *weakly* constitutions of the living Miss Thrales may be of more importance to some men, but our reviewers are unluckily not among the number. We shall conclude by confessing that the correspondence bears every mark of being genuine, that Mrs. Piozzi appears very confident of success, and careless of what may be said concerning her publication; that there are

[43]"The Rambler" is Johnson. Below: Mrs. Salusbury, Thrale's mother, died of cancer. Sophy was a Thrale daughter. The "old pious lady" is Hill Boothby; Johnson's letters to her are printed in *Letters*.

some brilliant passages, and some solid reflections scattered up and down the book, but that upon the whole we find eight or ten shillings very ill bestowed upon a few loosely-printed pages stamped with Johnson's name, which after all can no more render them current than can the Druid on the Paris mine penny,[44] it may like that penny be laid up as curious by some collectors, but must never hope to circulate as either useful or common.

[May 1789]

How the women do shine of late! Miss Williams's Ode on Otaheite, Madame Krumpholtz' tasteful performance on the harp, Madame Gautherot's wonderful execution on the fiddle;[45] "But," say the critics, "a violin is not an instrument for *ladies* to manage." Very likely! I remember when they said the same thing of a *pen*.

I wonder if my executors will burn the Thraliana!

[25 January 1794]

Boswell—

Who tells whate'er you think—whate'er you say,
And if he lies not—must at least betray,[46]

has cleared a thousand guineas by his book: the world is surely not in its dotage alone, but its anec*dotage*.

[Streatham Park 10 August 1795]

Pauca fecit, plura scripsit; fœmina tamen magna fuit.[47] I should like that line upon my tombstone mightily—it is not *too* presuming—is it?

[5 May 1799]

Unequaled—unexampled Spring! If Spring it may be called

When Winter ling'ring chills the lap of May.[48]

I have looked back to see how it was in 1795—but *that*

---

[44]Paris Mine in Anglesey, north Wales, produced copper from which coins were struck.
[45]Helen Maria Williams (1762–1827): her "Ode on Otaheite" was published in 1786. Mme. Krumpholtz, harpist, was the wife of Johann Baptist Krumpholtz, Bohemian composer. Mme. Gautherot is unidentified.
[46]Pope, *Epistle to Dr. Arbuthnot*, lines 297–298. Boswell's *Life of Johnson* cleared over £1,500 on the first edition.
[47]"She did little, she wrote more; still, she was a great woman."
[48]Oliver Goldsmith, *The Traveller*, line 172.

weather was heavenly to *this*. No grass grows at all, sharp cutting frosts and steady continuance of cold operates so that no duck will sit—no bird will sing. The poor farmers' horses drop down dead in the carts, unable to drag weight for want of food—cattle perish, and sheep run from their lambs—100 ewes perished in the neighborhood of Abergelley from the severity of this unparalleled season—What will become of us? Mr. Pitt cares not—he has a majority in the House—indeed in the Nation, for carrying on the war[49] . . . and we expect a victory abroad if we *do* starve at home. Well! I am of King David's mind: anything rather than flee before our enemies—let us, as he says, fall into the hands of God, not into the hands of men[50]—but I really expect a famine. These long days with howling winds like November and no leaves out—no, not a horse chestnut—no, not an apple blossom—is so terrifying, my courage begins to give way.—I did see 3 swallows skimming over the water in Llannerk Park one day last week, but never more swallow nor cuckoo did I hear. The primroses and violets peep out—and the tacamahacs try to push—but nothing else makes the *smallest attempt*. There will not be *one oak leaf out* on the 29th if it goes on so.[51] A bad omen for kings!!! But I must mind my big book—keep my own poor round about here from dying before our eyes if I can, and finish my *Retrospection*; the time is drawing on.

[Brynbella[52] 7 April 1801]

. . . Famine stares us in the face with hollow eyes; and Thraliana has to record its writer's eating bread in 1801 at 2 *shillings and* 4[d]—*the quartern loaf*. Eggs four for one shilling only in Bath Market, and beef, mutton etc., the *coarse pieces*, 9[d] o' pound—veal at 11[d]½—God mend all!!!

. . . Green geese,[53] dry-picked, beautiful, fit for the first nobleman's table, were to be bought this year in *February* (I saw them) of Heming the poulterer in Wade's Passage, Bath, at *five shillings each*. Sea kale and laver—once high priced dainties—were exceedingly moderate, and asparagus—for which in old days I have given 15[s] o' hundred—would scarce fetch 7. Lamb—

[49]William Pitt the Younger, prime minister 1784–1801; his government made war on the French Republic.

[50]2 Samuel 24:14.

[51]May 29, the date of Charles II's death, commemorated by wearing oak leaves (Balderston). She had determined to publish *Retrospection* (below) on the first day of 1801.

[52]Her estate, near Denbigh in north Wales.

[53]Young geese.

house lamb worth a guinea the quarter in 1770, might this Spring
be had for 8 shillings only—January roses half a crown apiece—I
remember my own bouquet 20 years ago being valued at five
guineas. "What does Mrs. Piozzi infer from all this?" exclaims
the reader of these anecdotes.

She infers the increase of luxury and ruin of the poor—when
everything is made smooth to the *rich*, and everything made
rough to *them*: when articles of voluptuous enjoyment are grown
plenty, and the necessaries of life are grown scarce:

What inference would you have her make?

Here is Miss Thrale's birthday come round again, 17 September 1803. The weather beautiful, and I hope my heart grateful
for having lived to see my eldest child 39 years old—and just
now not unkind at all.[54] She has written once or twice this year,
and in the last letters some compassion was expressed for Mr.
Piozzi's sufferings—they are indeed very great. Well! God bless
her, and *him*. A new vault has been constructed under the altar
at Dymerchion for *his* and *my* last cold residence and narrow
apartment—poor dear old Lucy Salusbury, my admirable pro-
genetrix and mother to my father, was found crumbling in dust;
her skull only whole, and the black ribbon pinned round it, that I
suppose bound her head in its last agony—there was no Act then
extant for burying in woollen.

My father, being wrapped in lead, was easily discerned from
his brothers, and dear *Mama*—as he called her to the last. They
had never found money to make themselves a vault, so their
poor bones have been gathered up now by Mr. Piozzi, and placed
decently in our new repository, where ours will shortly accompany them no doubt. . . .

[23 September 1804 Brynbella]

We have been once more for sea-bathing at Prestatyn[55] . . .
No improvement has taken place during my three years' absence, but ever wild and savage and solitary remain all that we
left behind—not wholly unaccompanied by danger—just enough
for the *Sublime*, I think, is the act of dipping in these rough
billows at the equinox—for scarce a machine can resist the fury

---

[54]Relations between Thrale and her eldest daughter were strained by the marriage to
Piozzi. Mr. Piozzi's sufferings (below) were caused by gout.
[55]A village on the northern coast of Wales.

of such northwesters as we saw and *felt* driving old Ocean[56] before them this, and yesterday morning. Nor was our journey *home* a *safe* one (as we made it), crossing the ford at Rhydlan, where the two rivers tried—but in vain—to lose themselves out in the Irish Channel; while the high-flowing tide set in so fierce against them, that our new carriage filled apace with salt water; and but for strong cattle and courageous drivers, we had been surely *lost*.[57] Well! our escape serves us to chat about; and so when conversation's stream runs low, we may recur—not to the passage of the Rhine—but to the crossing of the ford at Rhydlan; where Mr. Piozzi swears we suffered a much nearer approach to drowning.

It may be so, but I was not afraid.

[18 February 1808 Brynbella]

Another long, cruel fit of gout with immense cretaceous abscesses in foot and fingers began upon my wretched husband Sunday night 7 February 1808 and sent him to bed, whence he is not yet risen—and whence God only knows when he will be able to rise. Mrs. Mostyn[58] has sent her boys to school, and came here to escape the solitude of Segroid; it was comfortable to me certainly. These long nights and dismal days are dreadful even to *both of us* when together, how horrible the endurance when separate! Sickness within—and *a blockading*[59] snow without, which precludes all power of calling physicians. What shall we do? Never was season so intensely cold, with fog and frost like Lapland.

[April 1808]

I have lived wholly out of the world this year, so I sent for the *novels of the day* to instruct me how the world *goes*—and they *do* instruct me: not the romance things, or as Colman says—

A hovel:
Clanking of chains, a gallery, a light,
Old armor and a phantom all in white,
And that's a *novel*[60]

—which tells and teaches nothing; but the little *Summer at*

---

[56]A Miltonic phrase: *Paradise Lost*, IV.165. A machine (above) was a coach that conveyed bathers into the water.

[57]" '*Is* anybody ever lost here, pray?' said Dr. Myddelton to a cottager of that neighborhood. 'No sure, Sir,' was the reply; 'we always *find* the dead folks on shore safe enough when the tide is gone out' " (Piozzi).

[58]Piozzi's youngest daughter.

[59]Alluding to the blockade of Europe by Napoleon's fleets.

[60]George Colman the Younger, *My Night-Gown and Slippers*, 1797 (Balderston). Below: *A Summer at Weymouth* (1808) by Mary Julia Young.

Weymouth or such trash—they do my business better; it is about
my Lord Fan-Fly and my Lady Buttercup that I want to be
hearing: and it is curious to observe that there is an admiral and
a masquerade in every story. The *story* a consequence of the
French Revolution of course: the dialogue copied from conversation. These little books are mighty useful as portraits of the
manners—Watteau and Sévigné began these delineations, Hogarth
and Fielding continued 'em.[61] I have forgot the modern painters'
names, the writers desire only pay—they cannot, and they *do*
not wish to be remembered—but if degeneration goes much
deeper—I do think society must *dig* for it.

[February 1809]

No birthday kept, no pleasure, no comfort: poor Piozzi seems
merely kept alive by opium and brandy; if we leave *them* off—
spasms and sickness ensue: if we follow them up, something
dreadful will I fear ensue—*must* ensue.

[30 March 1809]

Everything most dreaded *has* ensued—all is over; and my
second husband's death is the last thing recorded in my first
husband's present! Cruel Death!

The Three Warnings
A Tale[1]

The tree of deepest root is found
   Least willing still to quit the ground;[2]
'Twas therefore said by ancient sages
   That love of life increased with years
So much, that in our latter stages,
When pains grow sharp, and sickness rages,
   The greatest love of life appears.

---

[61]Antoine Watteau (1684–1721), French painter, associated with the Rococo taste for
nature and abandonment of classicism; Marie de Sévigné (1626–1696), noted for her letters,
in which she talks of daily life at court; William Hogarth (1697–1764), painter, and Henry
Fielding, novelist, both famous for scenes of low life.

[1]About the versification of this poem Thrale wrote, "this wild irregular measure is a sort
of favorite with me, I learnt it in [Sir John] Vanbrugh's *Aesop* [a stage comedy]" (*Thraliana*,
December 1778).

[2]From a note by Louis Racine to his *Épître I sur l'Homme* (1747), which Thrale had
translated c. 1760. Racine cites Euripides' *Alcestis*.

This great affection to believe,
Which all confess, but few perceive,
If old assertions can't prevail,   *10*
Be pleased to hear a modern tale.

When sports went round, and all were gay
On neighbor Dobson's wedding day,
Death called aside the jocund groom
With him into another room:
And looking grave, "You must," says he,
"Quit your sweet bride, and come with me."
"With you, and quit my Susan's side!
With you!" the hapless husband cried:
"Young as I am, 'tis monstrous hard!   *20*
Besides, in truth, I'm not prepared:
My thoughts on other matters go,
This is my wedding night, you know."

What more he urged I have not heard,
His reasons could not well be stronger;
  So Death the poor delinquent spared,
And left to live a little longer.
Yet calling up a serious look,
His hour-glass trembled while he spoke,
"Neighbor," he said, "farewell. No more   *30*
Shall Death disturb your mirthful hour,
And further to avoid all blame
Of cruelty upon my name,
To give you time for preparation,
And fit you for your future station,
Three several warnings you shall have
Before you're summoned to the grave.
Willing for once I'll quit my prey,
  And grant a kind reprieve;
In hopes you'll have no more to say,   *40*
But when I call again this way
  Well-pleased the world will leave."

To these conditions both consented,
And parted, perfectly contented.

What next the hero of our tale befell,
How long he lived, how wise, how well,
How roundly he pursued his course,
And smoked his pipe and stroked his horse,
  The willing Muse shall tell:

He chaffered then, he bought, he sold,   50
Nor once perceived his growing old,
    Nor thought of Death as near;
His friends not false, his wife no shrew,
Many his gains, his children few,
    He passed his hours in peace;
But while he viewed his wealth increase,
While thus along life's dusty road
The beaten track content he trod,
Old Time, whose haste no mortal spares,
Uncalled, unheeded, unawares,   60
    Brought on his eightieth year.

    And now one night in musing mood,
        As all alone he sate,
Th' unwelcome messenger of Fate
    Once more before him stood.

    Half killed with anger and surprise,
"So soon returned!" old Dobson cries.
    "So soon, d'ye call it!" Death replies:
"Surely, my friend, you're but in jest.
        Since I was here before   70
'Tis six-and-thirty years at least,
    And you are now fourscore."

    "So much the worse," the clown rejoined.
"To spare the aged would be kind.
However, see your search be legal;
And your authority—Is't regal?
Else you are come on a fool's errand,
With but a secretary's warrant.[3]
Besides, you promised me Three Warnings,
Which I have looked for nights and mornings.   80
But for that loss of time and ease,
I can recover damages."

    "I know," cries Death, "that at the best,
I seldom am a welcome guest;
But don't be captious, friend, at least:
I little thought you'd still be able
To stump about your farm and stable;
Your years have run to a great length,
I wish you joy, though, of your strength."

---

[3]That is, inferior authority.

"Hold," says the farmer, "not so fast,   *90*
I have been lame these four years past."

"And no great wonder," Death replies,
"However, you still keep your eyes,
And sure to see one's loves and friends,
For legs and arms would make amends."

"Perhaps," says Dobson, "so it might,
But latterly I've lost my sight."

"This is a shocking story, faith,
Yet there's some comfort still," says Death;
"Each strives your sadness to amuse,   *100*
I warrant you hear all the news."

"There's none," cries he, "and if there were,
I'm grown so deaf I could not hear."

"Nay then," the specter stern rejoined,
"These are unjustifiable yearnings;
If you are lame, and deaf, and blind,
   You've had your three sufficient warnings.
So come along, no more we'll part,"
He said, and touched him with his dart;
And now old Dobson turning pale,   *110*
Yields to his fate—so ends my tale.

[On the Death of Elizabeth Carter in 1806][1]

Must Carter's form fade from this changeful scene
   Unnoticed by the busy crowds below?
And is there no leaf left, of dusky green,
   To bind round ancient Learning's withered brow?

None: where contend the rich, the bold, the young,
   Wisdom's pale votarist unheeded dies;
But memory's daughters[2] will repair such wrong
   To her who called them from their native skies.

[1]See Carter headnote.
[2]The Muses.

Anna Laetitia Barbauld
1743–1825

ANNA LAETITIA AIKIN was the daughter of a Dissenting minister and schoolmaster. A child prodigy, she received at home a classical education as well as a thorough grounding in English literature. In 1758 her father joined the faculty of Warrington Academy, where his associates included Joseph Priestley, the scientist and founder of Unitarianism, and John Howard, reformer of the prison system.

Urged by her brother John, Aikin wrote and published *Poems* (1773), to immediate acclaim. She next collaborated with him on *Miscellaneous Pieces in Prose* (1773). Having secured a literary reputation, Aikin turned her back on it: she married (1774) Rochemont Barbauld, with whom she opened a boarding school. For ten years, she taught small boys the rudiments of language and science. Her next publications were by-products of that labor: *Lessons for Children* (1778) and *Hymns in Prose* (1781).

Liberal in politics, the Barbaulds welcomed the American and French revolutions. They also welcomed a movement in Parliament, during 1787–1790, to repeal seventeenth-century laws that forbade all but members of the Established Church to hold public office, attend Oxford or Cambridge, and enjoy other rights of citizenship. When, in March 1790, Parliament reaffirmed those laws, Barbauld responded with a brilliant, impassioned pamphlet, *An Address to the Opposers of the Repeal of the Corporation and Test Acts*. It was published anonymously but soon known as hers. Reviewers were shocked that so biting a piece had been written by a woman; "that virago Barbauld," Horace Walpole called her. Three years later, when England declared war on the French Republic, Barbauld wrote her second great polemic, *Sins of Government, Sins of the Nation*, a sermon on the responsibility of citizens to resist immoral acts by their governments. She was active also in the movement to abolish the slave trade.

Barbauld's friends included Hannah More and other Bluestockings, and Maria Edgeworth; her work was admired by Walter Scott and William Wordsworth. Her domestic life, however, became a torment.

Rochemont Barbauld, always unstable, grew into a violent paranoid; twice she escaped being killed by him only by jumping from a window. His eventual suicide (1808) left her badly shaken.

Her later years were devoted largely to editing: the letters of the novelist Samuel Richardson (1804), selections from the *Tatler* and *Spectator* (1804), a fifty-volume set of *The British Novelists* with a distinguished critical essay on the novel (1810), and an anthology of verse and prose for girls, *The Female Speaker* (1811). In her last publication, a long poem, *Eighteen Hundred and Eleven* (1812), she prophesied the death of English culture and its transmigration to America.

Washing-Day

. . . . .and their voice,
Turning again towards childish treble, pipes
And whistles in its sound.——[1]

The Muses are turned gossips; they have lost
The buskined step,[2] and clear high-sounding phrase,
Language of gods. Come then, domestic Muse,
In slipshod measure loosely prattling on
Of farm or orchard, pleasant curds and cream,
Or drowning flies, or shoe lost in the mire
By little whimpering boy, with rueful face;
Come, Muse, and sing the dreaded Washing-Day.
Ye who beneath the yoke of wedlock bend,
With bowèd soul, full well ye ken the day   *10*
Which week, smooth sliding after week, brings on
Too soon—for to that day nor peace belongs
Nor comfort; ere the first gray streak of dawn,
The red-armed washers come and chase repose.
Nor pleasant smile, nor quaint device of mirth,
E'er visited that day: the very cat,
From the wet kitchen scared and reeking hearth,
Visits the parlor—an unwonted guest.
The silent breakfast-meal is soon dispatched;
Uninterrupted, save by anxious looks   *20*
Cast at the lowering sky, if sky should lower.

[1]Shakespeare, *As You Like It*, II.vii.161–163.
[2]Tragic (generally, lofty) style.

From that last evil, O preserve us, heavens!
For should the skies pour down, adieu to all
Remains of quiet: then expect to hear
Of sad disasters—dirt and gravel stains
Hard to efface, and loaded lines at once
Snapped short—and linen-horse[3] by dog thrown down,
And all the petty miseries of life.
Saints have been calm while stretched upon the rack,
And Guatimozin smiled on burning coals;[4]   *30*
But never yet did housewife notable
Greet with a smile a rainy washing-day.
—But grant the welkin fair, require not thou
Who call'st thyself perchance the master there,
Or study swept, or nicely dusted coat,
Or usual 'tendance; ask not, indiscreet,
Thy stockings mended, though the yawning rents
Gape wide as Erebus; nor hope to find
Some snug recess impervious: shouldst thou try
The 'customed garden walks, thine eye shall rue   *40*
The budding fragrance of thy tender shrubs,
Myrtle or rose, all crushed beneath the weight
Of coarse checked apron—with impatient hand
Twitched off when showers impend: or crossing lines
Shall mar thy musings, as the wet cold sheet
Flaps in thy face abrupt. Woe to the friend
Whose evil stars have urged him forth to claim
On such a day the hospitable rites!
Looks, blank at best, and stinted courtesy,
Shall he receive. Vainly he feeds his hopes   *50*
With dinner of roast chicken, savory pie,
Or tart or pudding: pudding he nor tart
That day shall eat; nor, though the husband try,
Mending what can't be helped, to kindle mirth
From cheer deficient, shall his consort's brow
Clear up propitious: the unlucky guest
In silence dines, and early slinks away.
I well remember, when a child, the awe
This day struck into me; for then the maids,
I scarce knew why, looked cross, and drove me from them: *60*

[3]A frame on which washing is hung to dry.
[4]Guatimozin, last Aztec emperor of Mexico; his stoicism under torture (by Cortez) had become legendary in Europe.

Nor soft caress could I obtain, nor hope
Usual indulgences; jelly or creams,
Relic of costly suppers, and set by
For me their petted one; or buttered toast,
When butter was forbid; or thrilling tale
Of ghost or witch, or murder—so I went
And sheltered me beside the parlor fire:
There my dear grandmother, eldest of forms,
Tended the little ones, and watched from harm,
Anxiously fond, though oft her spectacles   *70*
With elfin cunning hid, and oft the pins
Drawn from her ravelled stocking, might have soured
One less indulgent.
At intervals my mother's voice was heard,
Urging dispatch: briskly the work went on,
All hands employed to wash, to rinse, to wring,
To fold, and starch, and clap, and iron, and plait.
Then would I sit me down, and ponder much
Why washings were. Sometimes through hollow bowl
Of pipe amused we blew, and sent aloft   *80*
The floating bubbles; little dreaming then
To see, Montgolfier,[5] thy silken ball
Ride buoyant through the clouds—so near approach
The sports of children and the toils of men.
Earth, air, and sky, and ocean, hath its bubbles,
And verse is one of them—this most of all.

Address to the Opposers

OF THE

Repeal of the Corporation and Test Acts[1]

GENTLEMEN,
Had the question of yesterday been decided in a manner more
favorable to our wishes, which however the previous intimations

---

[5]Joseph Michel (1740–1810) and Jacques Étienne (1745–1799) Montgolfier, balloonists, who first demonstrated their invention in 1783.

[1]The Corporation (1661) and Test (1673) Acts required that holders of civil and military offices take the sacrament in the Anglican Church. After 1689, however, many non-Anglican Protestants (Dissenters) were legally permitted to practice their faith—a fact to which Barbauld alludes on p. 266 below.

of your temper in the business left us little room to expect, we should have addressed our thanks to you on the occasion. As it is, we address to you our thanks for much casual light thrown upon the subject, and for many incidental testimonies of your esteem (whether voluntary or involuntary we will not stop to examine) which in the course of this discussion you have favored us with. We thank you for the compliment paid the Dissenters, when you suppose that the moment they are eligible to places of power and profit, all such places will at once be filled with them. Not content with confounding, by an artful sophism, the right of eligibility with the right to offices, you again confound that right with the probable fact, and then argue accordingly. Is the Test Act, your boasted bulwark, of equal necessity with the dykes in Holland; and do we wait, like an impetuous sea, to rush in and overwhelm the land? Our pretensions, gentlemen, are far humbler. We had not the presumption to imagine that, inconsiderable as we are in numbers, compared to the established church; inferior too in fortune and influence; laboring, as we do, under the frown of the court, and the anathema of the orthodox; we should make our way so readily into the secret recesses of royal favor; and of a sudden, like the frogs of Egypt, swarm about your barns, and under your canopies, and in your kneading troughs, and in the chamber of the king.[2] We rather wished this act as the removal of a stigma than the possession of a certain advantage, and we might have been cheaply pleased with the acknowledgment of the right, though we had never been fortunate enough to enjoy the emolument.

Another compliment for which we offer our acknowledgments may be extracted from the great ferment which has been raised by this business all over the country. What stir and movement has it occasioned among the different orders of men! How quick the alarm has been taken, and sounded from the church to the senate, and from the press to the people; while fears and forebodings were communicated like an electric shock! The old cry of "The church is in danger" has again been made to vibrate in our ears. Here too, if we gave way to impressions of vanity, we might suppose ourselves of much greater importance in the political scale than our numbers and situation seem to indicate. It shows at least we are feared, which to some minds would be the next grateful thing to being beloved. We, indeed,

[2]Exodus 8:1–4.

should only wish for the latter; nor should we have ventured to
suppose, but from the information you have given us, that your
Church *was* so weak. What! fenced and guarded as she is with
her exclusive privileges and rich emoluments, stately with her
learned halls and endowed colleges, with all the attraction of her
wealth, and the thunder of her censures, all that the orator calls
"the majesty of the church" about her—and does she, resting in
security under the broad buckler of the state, does she tremble
at the naked and unarmed sectary? him, whose early connections and phrase uncouth, and unpopular opinions, set him at
distance from the means of advancement; him, who in the inter-
courses of neighborhood and common life, like new settlers,
finds it necessary to clear the ground before him, and is ever
obliged to root up a prejudice before he can plant affection? He
is not of the world, gentlemen; and the world loveth her own.[3]
All that distinguishes him from other men to common observation, operates in his disfavor. His very advocates, while they
plead his cause, are ready to blush for their client; and in justice
to their own character think it necessary to disclaim all knowledge of his obscure tenets. And is it from his hand you expect
the demolition of so massy an edifice? Does the simple removal
of the Test Act involve its destruction? These were not our
thoughts. We had too much reverence for your establishment to
imagine that the structure was so loosely put together, or so
much shaken by years, as that the removal of so slight a pin
should endanger the whole fabric—or is the Test Act the talisman
which holds it together, that, when it is broken, the whole must
fall to pieces like the magic palace of an enchanter? Surely no
species of regular architecture can depend upon so slight a support.
—After all, what is it we have asked?—to share in the rich
benefices of the established church? to have the gates of her
schools and universities thrown open to us? No: let her keep her
golden prebends, her scarfs, her lawn, her miters. Let her digni-
taries be still associated to the honors of legislation; and in our
courts of executive justice, let her inquisitorial tribunals continue to thwart the spirit of a free constitution by a heteroge-
neous mixture of priestly jurisdiction.[4] Let her still gather into
barns, though she neither sows nor reaps. We desire not to

[3]John 8:23 and 15:19.
[4]Anglican bishops sat in the House of Lords, the upper chamber of Parliament. The
English legal system included an ecclesiastical court with jurisdiction over marriages,
divorces, and wills.

share in her good things. We know it is the children's bread, which must not be given to dogs. But having these good things, we could wish to hear her say with the generous spirit of Esau, "I have enough, my brother."[5] We could wish to be considered as children of the state, though we are not so of the church. She must excuse us if we look upon the alliance between her and the state as an ill-assorted union, and herself as a mother-in-law who, with the too frequent arts of that relation, is ever endeavoring to prejudice the state, the common father of us all, against a part of his offspring, for the sake of appropriating a larger portion to her own children. We claim no share in the dowry of her who is not our mother, but we may be pardoned for thinking it hard to be deprived of the inheritance of our father.

But it is objected to us that we have sinned in the manner of making our request, we have brought it forward as a claim instead of asking it as a favor. We should have sued, and crept, and humbled ourselves. Our preachers and our writers should not have dared to express the warm glow of honest sentiment, or even in a foreign country glance at the downfall of a haughty aristocracy.[6] As we were suppliants, we should have behaved like suppliants, and then perhaps—No, gentlemen, we wish to have it understood that we *do* claim it as a right. It loses otherwise half its value. We claim it as men, we claim it as citizens, we claim it as good subjects. We are not conscious of having brought the disqualification upon ourselves by a failure in any of these characters.

But we already enjoy a complete toleration—It is time, so near the end of the eighteenth century, it is surely time to speak with precision, and to call things by their proper names. What you call toleration, we call the exercise of a natural and inalienable right. We do not conceive it to be toleration, first to strip a man of all his dearest rights, and then to give him back a part; or even if it were the whole. You tolerate us in worshiping God according to our consciences—and why not tolerate a man in the use of his limbs, in the disposal of his private property, the contracting his domestic engagements, or any other the most acknowledged privileges of humanity? It is not to these things that the word "toleration" is applied with propriety. It is applied, where from lenity or prudence we forbear doing all which

---

[5]Matthew 6:26 and 15:26; Genesis 33:9

[6]An allusion to the French Revolution. Further allusions to it occur on p. 274 ("a mighty empire breaking from bondage," "a sister nation").

in justice we might do. It is the bearing with what is confessedly an evil, for the sake of some good with which it is connected. It is the Christian virtue of long-suffering; it is the political virtue of adapting measures to times and seasons and situations. Abuses are tolerated, when they are so interwoven with the texture of the piece, that the operation of removing them becomes too delicate and hazardous. Unjust claims are tolerated, when they are complied with for the sake of peace and conscience. The failings and imperfections of those characters in which there appears an evident preponderancy of virtue, are tolerated. These are the proper objects of toleration, these exercise the patience of the Christian and the prudence of the statesman; but if there be a power that advances pretensions which we think unfounded in reason or scripture, that exercises an empire within an empire, and claims submission from those naturally her equals; and if we, from a spirit of brotherly charity, and just deference to public opinion, and a salutary dread of innovation, acquiesce in these pretensions; let her at least be told that the virtue of forbearance should be transferred, and that it is we who tolerate her, not she who tolerates us.

But this, it is again imputed to us, is no contest for religious liberty, but a contest for power, and place, and influence. We want civil offices—And why should citizens *not* aspire to civil offices? Why should not the fair field of generous competition be freely opened to everyone? A contention for power—It is not a contention for power between churchmen and Dissenters, nor is it as Dissenters we wish to enter the lists; we wish to bury every name of distinction in the common appellation of citizen. We wish not the name of Dissenter to be pronounced, except in our theological researches and religious assemblies. It is you, who by considering us as aliens, make us so. It is you who force us to make our dissent a prominent feature in our character. It is you who give relief, and cause to come out upon the canvas what we modestly wished to have shaded over, and thrown into the background. If we are a party, remember it is you who force us to be so. We should have sought places of trust—by no unfair, unconstitutional methods should we have sought them, but in the open and honorable rivalship of virtuous emulation; by trying to deserve well of our king and our country. Our attachment to both is well known.

Perhaps, however, we have all this while mistaken the matter, and what we have taken for bigotry and a narrow-minded spirit is after all only an affair of calculation and arithmetic. Our fellow-subjects remember the homely proverb, "the fewer the better cheer," and, very naturally, are glad to see the number of candidates lessened for the advantages they are themselves striving after. If so, we ask their excuse, their conduct is quite simple; and if, from the number of concurrents,[7] government were to strike out all above or under five feet high, or all whose birthdays happened before the summer solstice, or, by any other mode of distinction equally arbitrary and whimsical, were to reduce the number of their rivals, they would be equally pleased, and equally unwilling to admit an alteration. We are a mercantile people, accustomed to consider chances, and we can easily perceive that in the lottery of life, if a certain proportion are by some means or other excluded from a prize, the adventure is exactly so much the better for the remainder. If this indeed be the case, as I suspect it may, we have been accusing you wrongfully. Your conduct is founded upon principles as sure and unvarying as mathematical truths; and all further discussion is needless. We drop the argument at once. Men have now and then been reasoned out of their prejudices, but it were a hopeless attempt to reason them out of their interest.[8]

We likewise beg leave to apologize to those of the clergy whom we have unwillingly offended by endeavoring to include them as parties in our cause. "Pricked to it by foolish honesty and love,"[9] we thought that what appeared so grievous to us could not be very pleasant to them: but we are convinced of our mistake, and sorry for our officiousness. We own it, sirs, it was a fond imagination that because we should have felt uneasy under the obligation imposed upon you, it should have the same effect upon yourselves. It was weak to impute to you an idle delicacy of conscience, which perhaps can only be preserved at a distance from the splendid scenes which you have continually in prospect. But you will pardon us. We did not consider the force of early discipline over the mind. We are not accustomed to those salvos, and glosses, and accommodating modes of reasoning with which you have been long familiarized. You have the happy art of making easy to yourselves greater things than this. You are regularly disciplined troops, and understand every

[7]Competitors.
[8]Self-interest.
[9]Shakespeare, *Othello*, III.iii.412.

nice maneuver and dexterous evolution[10] which the nature of the ground may require. We are like an unbroken horse; hard-mouthed, and apt to start at shadows. Our conduct towards you in this particular we acknowledge may fairly provoke a smile at our simplicity. Besides, upon reflection, what should you startle at? The mixture of secular and religious concerns cannot to you appear extraordinary; and in truth nothing is more reasonable than that, as the state has been drawn in to the aggrandizement of your church, your church should in return make itself subservient to the convenience of the state. If we are wise, we shall never again make ourselves uneasy about your share of the grievance.

But we were enumerating our obligations to you, gentlemen, who have thwarted our request; and we must take the liberty to inform you that if it be any object of our ambition to exist and attract notice as a separate body, you have done us the greatest service in the world. What we desired, by blending us with the common mass of citizens, would have sunk our relative importance, and consigned our discussions to oblivion. You have refused us; and by so doing, you keep us under the eye of the public, in the interesting point of view of men who suffer under a deprivation of their rights. You have set a mark of separation upon us, and it is not in our power to take it off; but it is in our power to determine whether it shall be a disgraceful stigma or an honorable distinction. If, by the continued peaceableness of our demeanor, and the superior sobriety of our conversation—a sobriety for which we have not yet quite ceased to be distinguished; if, by our attention to literature, and that ardent love of liberty which you are pretty ready to allow us, we deserve esteem, we shall enjoy it. If our rising seminaries should excel in wholesome discipline and regularity, if they should be schools of morality, and yours, unhappily, should be corrupted into schools of immorality, you will entrust us with the education of your youth, when the parent, trembling at the profligacy of the times, wishes to preserve the blooming and ingenuous child from the degrading taint of early licentiousness. If our writers are solid, elegant, or nervous,[11] you will read our books and imbibe our sentiments, and even your preachers will not disdain, occasionally, to *illustrate* our morality. If we enlighten the world by

---

[10]The disposition of a body of troops.
[11]Sinewy or strong.

philosophical discoveries,[12] you will pay the involuntary homage due to genius, and boast of our names when, amongst foreign societies, you are inclined to do credit to your country. If your restraints operate towards keeping us in that middle rank of life where industry and virtue most abound, we shall have the honor to count ourselves among that class of the community which has ever been the source of manners, of population, and of wealth. If we seek for fortune in that track which you have left most open to us, we shall increase your commercial importance. If, in short, we render ourselves worthy of respect, you cannot hinder us from being respected—you cannot help respecting us—and in spite of all names of opprobrious separation, we shall be bound together by mutual esteem and the mutual reciprocation of good offices.

One good office we shall most probably do you is rather an invidious one, and seldom meets with thanks. By laying us under such a marked disqualification, you have rendered us—we hope not uncandid—we hope not disaffected—may the God of love and charity preserve us from all such acrimonious dispositions! But you certainly have, as far as in you lies, rendered us quick-sighted to encroachment and abuses of all kinds. We have the feelings of men; and though we should be very blameable to suffer ourselves to be biased by any private hardships, and hope that, as a body, we never shall, yet this you will consider, that we have at least no bias on the other side. We have no favors to blind us, no golden padlock on our tongues, and therefore it is probable enough, that, if cause is given, we shall cry aloud and spare not. But in this you have done yourselves no disservice. It is perfectly agreeable to the jealous spirit of a free constitution that there should be some who will season the mass with the wholesome spirit of opposition. Without a little of that bitter leaven there is great danger of its being corrupted.

With regard to ourselves, you have by your late determination given perhaps a salutary, perhaps a seasonable check to that spirit of worldliness, which of late has gained but too much ground amongst us.[13] Before you—before the world—we have a right to bear the brow erect, to talk of rights and services; but there is a place and a presence where it will become us to make no boast. We, as well as you, are infected. We, as well as you,

---

[12]Alluding to the scientific work of Joseph Priestley.
[13]During most of the eighteenth century the Dissenters, no longer actively persecuted, had prospered. Many grew rich in trade, bought land, and entered Parliament.

have breathed in the universal contagion: a contagion more noxious, and more difficult to escape, than that which on the plains of Cherson has just swept from the world the martyr of humanity.[14] The contagion of selfish indifference and fashionable manners has seized us; and our languishing virtue feels the debilitating influence. If you were more conversant in our assemblies than your prejudices will permit you to be, you would see indifference, where you fancy there is an overproportion of zeal: you would see principles giving way, and families melting into the bosom of the church under the warm influence of prosperity. You would see that establishments, without calling coercive measures to their aid, possess attraction enough severely to try the virtue and steadiness of those who separate from them. You need not strew thorns, or put bars across our path; your golden apples are sufficient to make us turn out of the way.[15] Believe me, gentlemen, you do not know us sufficiently to aim your censure where we should be most vulnerable.

Nor need you apprehend from us the slightest danger to your own establishment. If you will needs have it that it is in danger, we wish you to be aware that the danger arises from among yourselves. If ever your creeds and formularies become as grievous to the generality of your clergy as they already are to many delicate and thinking minds amongst them; if ever any material articles of your professed belief should be generally disbelieved, or that order which has been accustomed to supply faithful pastors and learned inquirers after truth should become a burden upon a generous public, the cry for reformation would then be loud and prevailing. It would be heard. Doctrines which will not stand the test of argument and reason will not always be believed; and when they have ceased to be generally believed, they will not long be articles of belief. If, therefore, there is any weak place in your system, anything which you are obliged to gloss over and touch with a tender hand, anything which shrinks at investigation—look ye to it, its extinction is not far off. Doubts and difficulties, that arise first amongst the learned, will not stop there; they inevitably spread downwards from class to class: and if the people should ever find that your articles[16] are

[14]The prison reformer John Howard (1726–1790) had just died of camp fever while attending the sick at Cherson, near the Black Sea.
[15]In Ovid's *Metamorphoses* (Book X), Hippomenes beats the huntress Atalanta in a foot race by dropping golden apples in her way; she is slowed down when she stops to gather them.
[16]The Thirty-Nine Articles embody the Anglican creed.

generally subscribed as articles of peace, they will be apt to remember that they are articles of expense too. If all the Dissenters in the kingdom, still believing as Dissenters do, were this moment, in order to avoid the reproach of schism, to enter the pale of your church, they would do you mischief; they would hasten its decline: and if all who in their hearts dissent from your professions of faith were to cease making them, and throw themselves amongst the Dissenters, you would stand the firmer for it. Your church is in no danger because we are of a different church; they might stand together to the end of time without interference: but it will be in great danger whenever it has within itself many who have thrown aside its doctrines, or even, who do not embrace them in the simple and obvious sense. All the power and policy of man cannot continue a system long after its truth has ceased to be acknowledged, or an establishment long after it has ceased to contribute to utility. It is equally vain as to expect to preserve a tree whose roots are cut away. It may look as green and flourishing as before for a short time; but its sentence is passed, its principle of life is gone, and death is already within it. If then you think the church in danger, be not backward to preserve the sound part by sacrificing the decayed.

To return to ourselves and our feelings on the business lately in agitation: You will excuse us if we do not appear with the air of men baffled and disappointed. Neither do we blush at our defeat; we may blush, indeed, but it is for our country: but we lay hold on the consoling persuasion, that reason, truth and liberality must finally prevail. We appeal from Philip intoxicated to Philip sober.[17] We know you will refuse us while you are narrow-minded, but you will not always be narrow-minded. You have too much light and candor not to have more. We will no more attempt to pluck the green unripe fruit. We see in you our future friends and brethren, eager to confound and blend with ours your interests and your affections. You will grant us all we ask. The only question between us is, whether you will do it today; tomorrow you certainly will. You will even entreat us, if need were, to allow you to remove from your country the stigma of illiberality. We appeal to the certain, sure operation of increasing light and knowledge, which it is no more in your power to stop, than to repel the tide with your naked hand, or to wither

---

[17]Usually, "appeal from Philip *drunk* to Philip sober." From a classical legend in which King Philip of Macedon, drunk, unjustly condemned a woman to punishment; she declared that she would appeal to him sober.

with your breath the genial influence of vegetation. The spread
of that light is in general gradual and imperceptible; but there are
periods when its progress is accelerated, when it seems with a
sudden flash to open the firmament, and pour in day at once.
Can ye not discern the signs of the times? The minds of men are
in movement from the Borysthenes[18] to the Atlantic. Agitated
with new and strong emotions, they swell and heave beneath
oppression, as the seas within the polar circle, when, at the
approach of spring, they grow impatient to burst their icy chains;
when what, but an instant before, seemed so firm—spread for
many a dreary league like a floor of solid marble—at once with a
tremendous noise gives way, long fissures spread in every direction, and the air resounds with the clash of floating fragments,
which every hour are broken from the mass. The genius of
Philosophy is walking abroad, and with the touch of Ithuriel's
spear is trying the establishments of the earth. The various
forms of Prejudice, Superstition, and Servility start up in their
true shapes, which had long imposed upon the world under the
revered semblances of Honor, Faith, and Loyalty.[19] Whatever is
loose must be shaken, whatever is corrupted must be lopped
away; whatever is not built on the broad basis of public utility
must be thrown to the ground. Obscure murmurs gather, and
swell into a tempest; the spirit of Inquiry, like a severe and
searching wind, penetrates every part of the great body politic;
and whatever is unsound, whatever is infirm, shrinks at the
visitation. Liberty, here with the lifted crosier in her hand, and
the crucifix conspicuous on her breast; there, led by Philosophy,
and crowned with the civic wreath, animates men to assert their
long-forgotten rights. With a policy, far more liberal and comprehensive than the boasted establishments of Greece and Rome,
she diffuses her blessings to every class of men; and even
extends a smile of hope and promise to the poor African, the
victim of hard, impenetrable avarice. Man, as man, becomes an
object of respect. Tenets are transferred from theory to practice.
The glowing sentiment and the lofty speculation no longer serve
"but to adorn the pages of a book;"[20] they are brought home to

[18]The classical name for the river Dnieper in Russia; an allusion to the enlightened
government of the empress Catherine the Great.
[19]In Milton's *Paradise Lost* (IV.810–814) the angel Ithuriel discovers Satan in the form of
a toad: "Him thus intent Ithuriel with his spear / Touched lightly; for no falsehood can
endure / Touch of ethereal temper, but returns / Of force to its own likeness. . . ."
[20]Perhaps a loose paraphrase of Johnson's *Vanity of Human Wishes*, line 222: "To point a
moral, or adorn a tale." The next clause quotes Francis Bacon's "Dedication" (1625) to his
Essays.

men's business and bosoms; and, what some centuries ago it was daring but to think, and dangerous to express, is now realized and carried into effect. Systems are analyzed into their first principles, and principles are fairly pursued to their legitimate consequences. The enemies of reformation, who palliate what they cannot defend, and defer what they dare not refuse; who, with Festus, put off to a more convenient season what, only because it is the present season, is inconvenient,[21] stand aghast, and find they have no power to put back the important hour when nature is laboring with the birth of great events. Can ye not discern—But you do discern these signs; you discern them well, and your alarm is apparent. You see a mighty empire breaking from bondage, and exerting the energies of recovered freedom: and England—which was used to glory in being the asserter of liberty and refuge of the oppressed—England, who with generous and respectful sympathy, in times not far remote from our own memory, afforded an asylum to so many of the subjects of that very empire, when crushed beneath the iron rod of persecution; and, by so doing, circulated a livelier abhorrence of tyranny within her own veins—England, who has long reproached her with being a slave, now censures her for daring to be free. England, who has held the torch to her, is mortified to see it blaze brighter in her hands. England, for whom, and for whose manners and habits of thinking, that empire has, for some time past, felt even an enthusiastic predilection; and to whom, as a model of laws and government, she looks up with affectionate reverence—England, nursed at the breast of liberty, and breathing the purest spirit of enlightened philosophy, views a sister nation with affected scorn and real jealousy, and presumes to ask whether she yet exists.[22] Yes, all of her exists that is worthy to do so. Her dungeons indeed exist no longer, the iron doors are forced, the massy walls are thrown down; and the liberated specters, trembling between joy and horror, may now blazon the infernal secrets of their prison house. Her cloistered monks no longer exist, nor does the soft heart of sensibility beat behind the grate of a convent; but the best affections of the

[21]Not Festus but Felix, the Roman governor of Palestine who delayed releasing Paul (Acts 24).

[22]Barbauld reproaches the English government for its hostility to the French Revolution, a hostility not consistent with England's traditional support of political liberty. Her next sentences allude to the capture of the Bastille and release of its captives (14 July 1789) and the closing of the monasteries by the French National Assembly. The "generous nation" addressed below is France.

human mind, permitted to flow in their natural channel, diffuse their friendly influence over the brightening prospect of domestic happiness. Nobles, the creatures of kings, exist there no longer: but man, the creature of God, exists there. Millions of men exist there, who only now truly begin to exist, and hail with shouts of grateful acclamation the better birthday of their country. Go on, generous nation, set the world an example of virtues as you have of talents. Be our model, as we have been yours. May the spirit of wisdom, the spirit of moderation, the spirit of firmness, guide and bless your counsels! Overcome our wayward perverseness by your steadiness and temper. Silence the scoff of your enemies, and the misgiving fears of your timorous well-wishers. Go on to destroy the empire of prejudices, that empire of gigantic shadows, which are only formidable while they are not attacked. Cause to succeed to the mad ambition of conquest the peaceful industry of commerce, and the simple, useful toils of agriculture. Instructed by the experience of past centuries, and by many a sad and sanguine page in your own histories, may you no more attempt to blend what God has made separate; but may religion and civil polity, like the two necessary but opposite elements of fire and water, each in its province do service to mankind, but never again be forced into discordant union. Let the wandering pilgrims of every tribe and complexion, who in other lands find only an asylum, find with you a country; and may you never seek other proof of the purity of your faith than the largeness of your charity. In your manners, your language, and habits of life, let a manly simplicity, becoming the intercourse of equals with equals, take the place of overstrained refinement and adulation. Let public reformation prepare the way for private. May the abolition of domestic tyranny introduce the modest train of household virtues, and purer incense be burned upon the hallowed altar of conjugal fidelity. Exhibit to the world the rare phenomenon of a patriot minister, of a philosophic senate. May a pure and perfect system of legislation proceed from their forming hands, free from those irregularities and abuses, the wear and tear of a constitution, which in a course of years are necessarily accumulated in the best-formed states; and like the new creation in its first gloss and freshness, yet free from any taint of corruption, when its Maker blessed and called it good.[23] May you never lose sight of

[23]Genesis 1:31.

the great principle you have held forth—the natural equality of men. May you never forget that without public spirit there can be no liberty; that without virtue there may be a confederacy, but cannot be a community. May you, and may we, consigning to oblivion every less generous competition, only contest who shall set the brightest example to the nations; and may its healing influence be diffused, till the reign of Peace shall spread

> . . . . .from shore to shore,
> Till wars shall cease, and slavery be no more.[24]

Amidst causes of such mighty operation, what are we, and what are our petty, peculiar interests? Triumph or despondency at the success or failure of our plans would be treason to the large, expanded, comprehensive wish which embraces the general interests of humanity. Here then we fix our foot with undoubting confidence, sure that all events are in the hands of Him, who from seeming evil

> . . . . .is still educing good;
> And better thence again, and better still,
> In infinite progression.

In this hope we look forward to the period when the name of Dissenter shall no more be heard of than that of Romanist or Episcopalian; when nothing shall be venerable but truth, and nothing valued but utility.

A DISSENTER

March 3, 1790

---

[24]Quoted, not quite accurately, from Pope, "Windsor Forest," lines 407–408. The lines below these may derive from *Paradise Lost* XII.469–471.

Frances Burney d'Arblay
1752–1840

NOVELIST, diarist, and closet playwright, Frances Burney was born into a talented family. Her father, Dr. Charles Burney, was a rising musician who would make his mark as a historian of music; her brother James was to write the history of Pacific exploration; all six Burney children were early exposed to poetry and theater. For Frances that exposure served in place of formal education; at age eight she could not yet read, but her memory for oral speech was already exceptional. So was her power of mimicry, inspired by the example of a family friend, the actor David Garrick. The young Burneys were also avid scribblers. No sooner did Frances learn to read than she began to write. At sixteen she began the journals that she was to carry on for the rest of her life. Initially a private diary, they later became journal-letters addressed to family members, chiefly her sister Susanna.

In 1778 she published, anonymously, her novel *Evelina*. To avert parental disapproval she had written it in secret. It was an immediate best-seller, and Burney found herself a celebrity—to her dismay, for she suffered intensely from shyness and a dread of "doing wrong."

The fame of *Evelina* gave Burney entrance into the Johnson-Thrale circle. She continued writing: "The Witlings" (a comedy, unproduced) and the novel *Cecilia* (1782). Her success, however, had brought no money; to provide for her, Dr. Burney urged her to accept an invitation to serve as Second Keeper of the Robes to Queen Charlotte. She did so reluctantly, enduring for five years (1786–1791) the tiresome rigor of life at the court of George III.

Soon after her resignation she met and married (1793) Alexandre d'Arblay, a penniless exile from the French Revolution. The marriage was passionately happy despite Dr. Burney's disapproval and troubles created by General d'Arblay's later activities as an opponent of Napoleon. Her third novel, *Camilla* (1796), was extraordinarily profitable. In her later years she published her last novel, *The Wanderer* (1814) and a biography of her father (1832), and edited her journals for publication after her death.

Burney's fame as a forerunner of Jane Austen has long been secure, but her achievement is impressive apart from its influence on later fiction. *Evelina* is not only brilliant satire, it is also a compelling representation of a woman's experience. As a diarist Burney easily bears comparison with James Boswell—as will be seen by anyone who compares them on the subject they have in common, Samuel Johnson. In rendering her perception of the world she creates a blend of comedy and terror that is uniquely her own.

from Journals

Poland Street, London, March 27 [1768]

To have some account of my thoughts, manners, acquaintance and actions, when the hour arrives in which time is more nimble than memory, is the reason which induces me to keep a journal. A journal in which I must confess my *every* thought, must open my whole heart! But a thing of this kind ought to be addressed to somebody—I must imagine myself to be talking—talking to the most intimate of friends—to one in whom I should take delight in confiding, and remorse in concealment. But who must this friend be? To make choice of one in whom I can but *half* rely, would be to frustrate entirely the intention of my plan. The only one I could wholly, totally confide in, lives in the same house with me, and not only never *has*, but never *will*, leave me one secret to tell her.[1] To *whom*, then, *must* I dedicate my wonderful, surprising and interesting adventures?—to *whom* dare I reveal my private opinion of my nearest relations? my secret thoughts of my dearest friends? my own hopes, fears, reflections, and dislikes? Nobody!

To Nobody, then, will I write my journal! since to Nobody can I be wholly unreserved—to Nobody can I reveal every thought, every wish of my heart, with the most unlimited confidence, the most unremitting sincerity to the end of my life! For what chance, what accident can end my connections with Nobody? No secret *can* I conceal from Nobody, and to Nobody can I be *ever* unreserved. Disagreement cannot stop our affection, Time itself has no power to end our friendship. The love, the esteem I entertain for Nobody, Nobody's self has not power

[1] Her sister Susanna.

to destroy. From Nobody I have nothing to fear, the secrets sacred to friendship Nobody will not reveal when the affair is doubtful, Nobody will not look towards the side least favorable.

I will suppose you, then, to be my best friend (though God forbid you ever should!), my dearest companion—and a romantic girl, for mere oddity may perhaps be more sincere—more tender—than if you were a friend in propria persona—in as much as imagination often exceeds reality. In your breast my errors may create pity without exciting contempt; may raise your compassion, without eradicating your love. From this moment, then, my dear girl—but why, permit me to ask, must a *female* be made Nobody? Ah! my dear, what were this world good for, *were* Nobody a female? And now I have done with preambulation.

[King's Lynn] July 17

Such a set of tittle tattle, prittle prattle visitants! Oh dear! I am so sick of the ceremony and fuss of these fall lall people! So much dressing—chit chat—complimentary nonsense—in short—a country town is my detestation—all the conversation is scandal, all the attention, dress, and *almost* all the heart, folly, envy, and censoriousness. A city or a village are the only places which I think, can be comfortable, for a country town, I think has all the bad qualities, without one of the good ones, of both.

We live here, generally speaking, in a very regular way—we breakfast always at 10, and rise as much before as we please—we dine precisely at 2, drink tea about 6—and sup exactly at 9. I make a kind of rule, never to indulge myself in my two *most* favorite pursuits, reading and writing, in the morning—no, like a very good girl I give that up wholly, accidental occasions and preventions excepted, to needle work, by which means my reading and writing in the afternoon is a pleasure I cannot be blamed for by my mother, as it does not take up the time I ought to spend otherwise. I never pretend to be so superior a being as to be above having and indulging a *hobby horse*,[2] and while I keep mine within due bounds and limits, nobody, I flatter myself, would wish to deprive me of the poor animal: to be sure, he is not formed for labor, and is rather lame and weak, but then the dear creature is faithful, constant, and loving, and though he sometimes prances, would not kick anyone into the mire, or hurt

[2] A favorite pastime.

a single soul for the world—and I would not part with him for one who could win the greatest prize that ever *was* won at any races.

[Saturday, July]

And so I suppose you are staring at the torn paper and unconnected sentence—I don't much wonder—I'll tell you what happened. Last Monday I was in the little parlor, which room my papa generally dresses in—and writing a letter to my grandmama. You must know I always have the last sheet of my journal in my pocket, and when I have wrote it half full I join it to the rest, and take another sheet—and so on. Now I happened unluckily to take the last sheet out of my pocket with my letter—and laid it on the piano forte, and there, negligent fool!—I left it. . . . Well, as ill fortune would have it, papa went into the room—took my poor journal—read, and pocketed it. Mama came up to me and told me of it. O Dear! I was in a sad distress—I could not for the life of me ask for it—and so *dawdled* and fretted the time away till Tuesday evening. Then, gathering courage, "Pray papa," I said, "have you got—any *papers* of mine?"

"Papers of yours?" said he—"how should *I* come by papers of yours?"

"I'm sure—I don't know—but"—

"Why do you leave your papers about the house?" asked he, gravely.

I could not say another word—he went on playing on the piano forte. Well, to be sure, thought I, these same dear journals are most shocking plaguing things—I've a good mind to resolve never to write a word more. However, I stayed still in the room, working, and looking wistfully at him for about an hour and half. At last, he rose to dress—again I looked wistfully at him—he laughed—"What, Fanny," said he, kindly, "are you in sad distress?" I half laughed. "Well—I'll give it you, now I see you are in such distress—but take care, my dear, of leaving your writings about the house again—suppose anybody else had found it—I declare I was going to read it loud—Here, take it—but if ever I find any more of your journals, I vow I'll stick them up in the market place." And then he kissed me *so* kindly— never was parent so *properly*, so *well*-judgedly affectionate! I was so frightened that I have not had the heart to write since, till now, I should not but that—in short, but that I cannot help it! As to the *paper*, I destroyed it the moment I got it. . . .

[10 o'clock.]

Well, I shall have to undress in the dark if I scribble any longer, and so I must petition for leave to bid you adieu; Granted.

Certainly I have the most complaisant friend in the world—ever ready to comply with my wishes—never hesitating to oblige, never averse to my concluding, yet never wearied with my beginning—charming creature.

And pray, my dear Miss Fanny, *who* is this?

Nobody.

Alas, alas! what then is to become of Everybody?

How should I know? Let everybody manage themselves and others as well as I do Nobody, and they will be "much the same as God made them." And now adieu my charmer. . . . . Adieu then, my fair friend—that's one comfort, that I can make you fair or brown at pleasure—just what I will—a creature of my own forming.

I am now reading the *Iliad*—I cannot help taking notice of one thing in the 3rd Book which has provoked me for the honor of the sex. Venus tempts Helen with every delusion in favor of her darling, in vain—riches—power—honor—love—all in vain—the enraged Deity threatens to deprive her of her own beauty, and render her to the level of the most common of her sex. Blushing and trembling, Helen immediately yields her hand. Thus has Homer proved his opinion of our poor sex—that the love of beauty is our most prevailing passion. It really grieves me to think that there certainly must be some reason for this insignificant opinion the greatest men have of women—at least I fear there must. But I don't in fact believe it.

[London] August [1771]

Dr. King has been with me all this afternoon, amusing himself with spouting Shakespeare, Pope, and others. Though I say amusing himself I must, however, own that it was the only way he had any chance of amusing me; but his visit was unconscionably long, and as I happened to be alone, I had the whole weight of it. For the first time, however, I did not regret Miss Allen's absence, for she sees the ridiculous part of this man's character in so strong a light, that she cannot forbear showing that she despises him every moment. The strongest trait of her own character is sincerity, one of the most noble of virtues, and perhaps, without any exception, *the most* uncommon. But, if it is possible, she is too sincere: she pays too little regard to the world; and indulges herself with too much freedom of raillery and pride of disdain towards those whose vices and follies offend her. Were this a *general* rule of conduct what real benefit might it bring to society; but being *particular* it only hurts and provokes individuals. But yet I am unjust to my own opinion in censuring the first who shall venture, in a good cause, to break through the confinement of custom, and at least show the way to a new and open path. I mean but to blame severity to *harmless* folly, which claims pity and not scorn, though I cannot but acknowledge it to be infinitely tiresome, and for any length of time even almost disgustful.

[1774]

I have had the honor, not long since, of being in company with Mr. Keate, author of an account of Geneva, "Ferney," and some other things, chiefly poetical. He is an author *comme il faut*, for he is in affluent circumstances, and writes at his leisure and for his amusement. It was at the house of six old maids, all sisters, and all above sixty, that I met him. These votaries of Diana are exceedingly worthy women of the name of Blake; and I heartily wish that I, who mean to devote myself to the same goddess, should I be as ancient, may be as good.

Mr. Keate did not appear to me to be very brilliant; his powers of conversation are not of a shining cast; and one disadvantage to his speeches is, his delivery of them; for he speaks in a slow and *sluggish* voice. But what principally banished him from my good graces was, the conceited manner in which he introduced a discourse upon his own writings.

"Do you know, Mrs. Blake," (addressing himself to the senior virgin) "I have at last ventured upon building, in spite of my resolution, and in spite of my Ode?"

Mrs. Blake fell into his plot, without being sensible that he had laid one. "O! Mrs. Burney" (cried she to mama), "that Ode was the prettiest thing! I wish you could see it!"

"Why I had determined, and indeed promised," said he, "that when I went into my new house, I would either give a ball or write an ode—and so I found the ode was the more easy to me; but I protested in the poem, that I would never undertake to *build*." All the sisters then poured forth the incense of praise upon this Ode, to which he listened with the utmost *nonchalance,* reclining his person upon the back of his chair, and kicking his foot now over, and now under, a gold-headed cane.

When these effusions of civility were vented, the good old

ladies began another subject; but, upon the first cessation of
speech, Mr. Keate broke the silence he had kept, and said to
mama, "But the worst thing to me was, that I was obliged to
hang a carpenter in the course of my poem."

"O dear, aye," cried Mrs. Blake, "that part was vastly pretty!
Lord! I wish I could remember it. Dear Mrs. Burney, I wish you
could see it! Mr. Keate, it's a pity it should not be seen—"

"Why surely" (cried he, affectedly), "you would not have me
publish it?"

"O! as to that—I don't know," answered with the utmost
simplicity, Mrs. Blake, "*you* are the best judge of that. But I *do*
wish you could see it, Mrs. Burney."

"No; faith!" added he, "I think that, if I *was* to collect my
other brats, I should not, I believe, put this among them."

"If we may judge," said mama, "of the family *unseen* by those
in the world, we must certainly wish for the pleasure of knowing
them all."

Having now set the conversation upon this favorite topic
again, he resumed his posture and his silence, which he did not
again break, till he had again the trouble of renewing himself the
theme, to which his ear delighted to listen; else he only

> Sat attentive to his own applause.[3]

[Chessington,[4] Sept. 1774]

I have almost, though very undesignedly, occasioned a *grand
fracas* in the house, by a ridiculous joke which I *sported* for the
amusement of Miss Simmons and Kitty. We had been laughing
at some of poor Mrs. Moore's queer phrases, and then I mentioned some of Kitty's own.[5] Her cousin joined in laughing
violently; and as I proceeded from one absurd thing to another, I
took Miss Simmons herself to task upon some speeches she had
made; and in conclusion I told them I intended to write *A
Treatise upon Politeness* for their edification. All this was taken
as it was said, in sport, and we had much laughing in consequence of my scheme, which I accompanied by a thousand
flighty speeches. After this, upon all indecorums, real or fanciful, I referred Miss Simmons and Kitty to my book for instruction, and it became a sort of standard joke among us, to which

---

[3]Pope, *Epistle to Dr. Arbuthnot*, line 210.
[4]Home of a close family friend, Samuel Crisp, whom the Burneys were visiting.
[5]Such as "Chiss," below, and subsequent vulgarisms of grammar and pronunciation.

we made everything that passed applicable, and Miss Simmons, who enjoyed hearing me *run on* as she called it, introduced the subject perpetually. Indeed, the chief amusement I have made myself when with the two cousins, has been indulging myself in that kind of rhodomontade discourse, that it will be easy to you to recollect some instances of. . . . All this did very well among ourselves; but the day after the Simmonses left us, while we were at dinner, Kitty blundered out, "Good people, I tell you what—*she's* going to write something about politeness, *and that*, and it's to be for all of you, here at *Chiss,* to mind your manners."

"I'm sure," cried Mlle. Courvoisyois, "we shall be very much *oblige* to the lady."

"I'll subscribe to the book with all my heart," cried Mlle. Rosat. "I beg leave to bespeak the first copy. I am sure it will be a very useful work."

"She's to tell you all what you're to do," resumed Kitty, "and how you're to do this—and all that."

"Exceedingly well defined, Kate," said Mr. Crisp; "but pray, Fannikin, what shall you *particularly* treat of?"

"O Sir," cried I, "all parts of life! it will be a very comprehensive work; and I hope you'll all have a book."

"Pray, what will it cost?" demanded Mrs. Moore, seriously.

"A guinea a volume," answered I, "and I hope to comprise it in nine volumes."

"O lud!" exclaimed she, "I sha'nt give *no such money* for it."

"*I* will have two copies," said Mlle. Rosat, "let it cost what it will. I am sure it will be exceeding well executed."

"I don't doubt *in least*," cried Mlle. Courvoisyois, "of politeness of Miss Burney; but I should like to see the book, to see if I should *sought* the same."

"Will it be like Swift's 'Polite Conversation'?"[6] said Mr. Crisp.

"I intend to dedicate it to Miss Notable," answered I; "it will contain all the *newest fashioned* regulations. In the first place, you are never again to cough."

"Not to *cough*?" exclaimed everyone at once; "but how are you to help it?"

---

[6]*A Complete Collection of Genteel and Ingenious Conversation, According to the most Polite Mode and Method now Used* (1738)—a mock courtesy book composed of trifling and vulgar conversation. Its heroine, Miss Notable (below), is sharp-tongued and coarse.

"As to *that*," answered I, "I am not very clear about it myself, as I own I am guilty sometimes of doing it; but it is as much a mark of ill breeding, as it is to *laugh;* which is a thing that Lord Chesterfield has stigmatized."[7]

"Lud! well, for my part," said Mrs. Moore, "I think there's no fun without it."

"Not for to *laugh*," exclaimed Courvoisyois, with hands uplifted, "well, I declare I *did* not *sought* of such a *sing*."

"And pray," said Mr. Crisp, making a fine affected face, "may you *simper?*"

"You may *smile*, Sir," answered I; "but to *laugh* is quite abominable; though not quite so bad as *sneezing*, or *blowing the nose*."

"Why, if you don't blow it," cried Kitty, taking me literally, "what *are* you to do with it, don't you think it nastier to let it run, out of politeness?"

I pretended to be too much shocked to answer her.

"But pray, is it permitted," said Mr. Crisp, very dryly, "to *breathe?*"

"*That* is not yet, I believe, quite exploded," answered I; "but I shall be more exact about it in my book, of which I shall send you *six* copies. I shall only tell you in general, that whatever is natural, plain, or easy, is entirely banished from polite circles."

"And all is *sentiment* and *delicacy*, hey, Fannikin?"

"No, Sir; not so," replied I with due gravity; "*sentiments* and *sensations* were the *last* fashion; they are now done with; they were *laughed* out of use, just before laughing was abolished. The present *ton* is *refinement;* nothing *is to be,* that *has been;* all things are to be *new polished* and *highly finished*. I shall explain this fully in my book."

"Well; for my part," cried Mrs. Moore, who, I believe, took every word I said seriously; "I don't desire to read *no* such *tiddling* books. I'm very well as I am."

It's well you think so, thought I.

"Pray, Ma'am," said Mlle. Rosat, "is it within the rules of politeness to *pick the teeth?*"

"Provided you have a little *glass* to look in before you," answered I, and rose to go upstairs to my father.

"Pray, Ma'am," cried she again, "is it polite, when a person

---

[7]"Having mentioned laughing, I must particularly warn you against it. . . . In my mind, there is nothing so illiberal, and so ill-bred, as audible laughter" (*Letters to His Son* [1774], 9 March 1748).

talks, if you don't understand them, to look at another, as if you said, 'What nonsense she says.' "

"I should imagine not," answered I, moving off to the door, as I found these questions were *pointed* against poor Kitty.

"Pray, is it polite, Ma'am," cried Mlle. Rosat again, "to make *signs* and *to whisper?*"

"I suppose not," cried I, opening the door.

"And *pray*," cried Kitty, coloring, "is it *polite* to be *touchy?* and *has* people any business to suspect *and* to be suspicious?"

"O!" cried I, "these are things that don't come into my cognizance"—and away I ran.

My father, however, sent me down again, to ask Mr. Crisp upstairs to play at backgammon. I found them all silent. Mr. Crisp went up immediately, and presently everybody went out, but Kitty, Courvoisyois, and me. I told Kitty, who I saw was swelling with anger, that I began to be sorry she had mentioned the book. "Oh! it does not signify," cried she, bursting into a violent fit of tears. "I don't mind, if people will be cross; it's nothing to me. I'm sure I'm as obliging as I can—and if people don't like me they must let it alone."

[London, June 1775][8]

Notwithstanding I was at once sorry and provoked at perceiving how sanguine this youth chose to be, I was not absolutely concerned at receiving this second letter, because I regarded it as a fortunate opportunity of putting an unalterable conclusion to the whole affair. However.... I thought it my duty to speak to my father before I sent an answer, never doubting his immediate concurrence.

... I went upstairs into the study, and told my father I had received another epistle from Mr. Barlow, which I could only attribute to my not answering, as I had wished, his first. I added that I proposed, with his leave, to write to Mr. Barlow the next morning.

My father looked grave, asked me for the letter, put it in his pocket unread, and wished me good night.

I was seized with a kind of *panic*. I trembled at the idea of his espousing, however mildly, the cause of this young man. I

[8]While visiting an aunt in May, Burney had met a young man named Thomas Barlow, who instantly fell in love with her. Although she gave him no encouragement, he had now written her two ardent letters.

passed a restless night, and in the morning dared not write without his permission, which I was now half afraid to ask.

About 2 o'clock, while I was dawdling in the study, and waiting for an opportunity to speak, we heard a rap at the door and soon after John came in and said—"A gentleman is below, who asks for Miss Burney: Mr. Barlow." I think I was never more distressed in my life—to have taken pains to avoid a private conversation so highly disagreeable to me, and at last to be forced into it at so unfavorable a juncture, for I had now *two* letters from him, both unanswered, and consequently open to his conjectures. I exclaimed—"Lord! how provoking! what shall I do?"

My father looked uneasy and perplexed: he said something about not being hasty, which I did not desire him to explain. Terrified lest he should hint at the advantage of an early establishment—like Mr. Crisp—quick from the study—but slow enough afterwards—I went downstairs. I saw my mother pass from the front into the back parlor; which did not add to the *graciousness* of my reception of poor Mr. Barlow, who I found alone in the front parlor. I was not sorry that none of the family were there, as I now began to seriously dread any protraction of this affair.

He came up to me with an air of *tenderness* and satisfaction, began some anxious enquiries about my health; but I interrupted him with saying—"I fancy, Sir, you have not received a letter I—I——"

I stopped, for I could not say which I had *sent!*

"A letter?—No, Ma'am!"

"You will have it, then, tomorrow, Sir."

We were both silent for a minute or two, when he said—"In consequence I presume, Ma'am, of the one I——"

"Yes, Sir," cried I.

"And pray—Ma'am—Miss Burney!—may I—beg to ask the contents?—that is—the—the—." He could not go on.

"Sir—I—it was only—it was merely—in short, you will see it tomorrow."

"But if you would favor me with the contents now, I could perhaps answer it at once?"

"Sir, it requires no answer!"

A second silence ensued. I was really distressed myself to see *his* distress, which was very apparent. After some time he stammered out something of *hoping*, and *beseeching*—which, gathering more firmness, I answered—"I am much obliged to you, Sir, for the too good opinion you are pleased to have of me—but I should be very sorry you should lose any more time upon my account—as I have no thoughts of changing my situation and abode."

He seemed to be quite overset; having, therefore, so freely explained myself, I then asked him to sit down, and began to talk of the weather. When he had a little recovered himself, he drew a chair close to me and began making most ardent professions of respect and regard, and so forth. I interrupted him as soon as I could, and begged him to rest satisfied with my answer.

"*Satisfied?*" repeated he, "my dear Ma'am—is that possible?"

"Perhaps, Sir," said I, "I ought to make some apologies for not answering your first letter—but really I was so much surprised—upon so short an acquaintance."

He then began making excuses for having written; but as to *short acquaintance,* he owned it was a reason for *me*—but for *him*—fifty years could not have more convinced him of my, etc. etc.

"You have taken a sudden, and far too partial idea of my character," answered I. "If you look round among your older acquaintance, I doubt not but you will very soon be able to make a better choice."

He shook his head: "I have seen, Madam, a great many ladies, it is true—but never——"

"You do me much honor," cried I, "but I must desire you would take no further trouble about me—for I have not at present the slightest thoughts of ever leaving this house."

"*At present?*" repeated he, eagerly. "No, I would not expect it—I would not wish to precipitate—but in future——"

"Neither now or ever, Sir," returned I, "have I any view of changing my condition."

"But surely, surely this can never be! so severe a resolution—you cannot mean it—it would be wronging all the world!"

"I am extremely sorry, Sir, that you did not receive my letter, because it might have saved you this trouble."

He looked very much mortified, and said in a dejected voice—"If there is anything in me—in my connections—or in my situation in life, which you wholly think unworthy of you—and beneath you—or if my character, or disposition meet with your disapprobation—I will immediately forgo all—I will not—I would not——"

"No, indeed, Sir," cried I, "I have neither seen or heard of anything of you that was to your disadvantage—and I have no doubts of your worthiness—"

He thanked me, and seemed reassured; but renewed his solicitations in the most urgent manner. He repeatedly begged my permission to acquaint my family of the state of his affairs, and to abide by their decision; but I would not let him say two words following upon that subject. I told him that my answer was a final one, and begged him to take it as such.

He remonstrated very earnestly. "This is the severest decision! . . . . Surely you must allow that the *social state* is what we were all meant for?—that we were created for one another? —that to form such a resolution is contrary to the design of our being?"—

"All this may be true," said I, "I have nothing to say in contradiction to it—but you know there are many odd characters in the world—and I am one of them."

"O, no, no, no,—that can never be! but is it possible that you can have so bad an opinion of the Married State? It seems to me the *only* state for happiness!"

"Well, Sir, *you* are attracted to the married life—I am to the single—therefore *every man in his humor*—do *you* follow *your* opinion—and let *me* follow *mine.*"

"But, surely—is not this *singular?*"

"I give you leave, Sir," cried I, laughing, "to think me singular—odd—queer—nay, even whimsical, if you please."

"But, my *dear* Miss Burney, only——"

"I entreat you, Sir, to take my answer—you really pain me by being so urgent."

"That would not I do for the world!—I only beg you to suffer me—perhaps in future——"

"No, indeed, I shall never change—I do assure you you will find me very obstinate!"

He began to lament his own destiny. I grew extremely tired of so often saying the same thing; but I could not absolutely turn him out of the house; and, indeed, he seemed so dejected and unhappy, that I made it my study to soften my refusal as much as I could without leaving room for future expectations.

About this time my mother came in. We both rose. I was horridly provoked at my situation.

"I am only come in for a letter," cried she, "pray don't let me disturb you." And away she went. . . .

This could not but be encouraging to him, for she was no sooner gone than he began again the same story, and seemed determined not to give up his cause. He hoped, at least, that I would allow him to enquire after my health?

"I must beg you, Sir, to send me no more letters."

He seemed much hurt, and looked down in silence.

"You had better, Sir, think of me no more, if you study your own happiness——"

"I *do* study my own happiness—more than I have ever had any probability of doing before!"

"You have made an unfortunate choice, Sir, but you will find it easier to forget it than you imagine. You have only to suppose that I was not at Mr. Burney's on May Day—and it was a mere chance my being there—and then you will be——"

"But, if I *could*—could I also forget seeing you at old Mrs. Burney's?—and if I did—can I forget that I see you now?"

"O yes! In three months' time you may forget you ever saw me. You will not find it so difficult as you suppose."

"You have heard, Ma'am, of an old man being ground young? Perhaps you believe *that*? But you will not deny me leave to sometimes see you?"

"My father, Sir, is seldom, hardly ever, indeed, at home."

"I have never seen the Doctor—but I hope he would not refuse me the permission to enquire after your health? I have no wish without his consent."

"Though I acknowledge myself to be *singular* I would not have you think me either affected or *trifling*—and therefore I must assure you I am *fixed* in the answer I have given you—*unalterably* fixed."

His entreaties grew now extremely . . . distressing to me. He besought me to take more time, and said it should be the study of his life to make me happy. "Allow me, my *dear* Miss Burney, only to hope that my future conduct——"

"I shall always think myself obliged, nay, honored by your good opinion—and you are entitled to my best wishes for your health and happiness—but, indeed, the less we meet the better."

"What—what can I do?" cried he very sorrowfully.

"Why—go and *ponder* upon this affair for about half an hour. Then say—what an odd, queer, strange creature she is—and then—think of something else."

"O no, no!—you cannot suppose all that? I shall think of

nothing else; *your* refusal is more pleasing than any other lady's acceptance—"

He said this very simply, but too seriously for me to laugh at. Just then, Susette came in—but did not stay two minutes. It would have been shocking to be thus left purposely as if with a declared lover, and then I was not sorry to have an opportunity of preventing future doubts and expectations.

I rose and walked to the window thinking it high time to end a conversation already much too long; and then he again began to entreat me not to be so *very severe*. I told him that I was *sure* I should never alter the answer I made at first; that I was very happy at home; and not at all inclined to try my fate elsewhere. I then desired my compliments to Mrs. O'Connor and Miss Dickenson, and made a *reverence* by way of leave taking.

"I am extremely sorry to detain you so long, Ma'am," said he, in a melancholy voice. I made no answer. He then walked about the room; and then again besought my leave to ask me how I did some other time. I absolutely, though civilly refused it, and told him frankly that, fixed as I was it was better that we should not meet.

He then took his leave—returned back—took leave—and returned again. I now made a more formal reverence of the head, at the same time expressing my good wishes for his welfare, in a sort of way that implied I expected never to see him again. He would fain have taken a more *tender* leave of me—but I repulsed him with great surprise and displeasure. I did not, however, as he was so terribly sorrowful refuse him my hand, which he had made sundry attempts to take in the course of conversation. When I withdrew it, as I did presently, I rang the bell to prevent his again returning from the door.

Though I was really sorry for the unfortunate and misplaced attachment which this young man professes for me, yet I could almost have *jumped* for joy when he was gone, to think that the affair was thus finally over.

Indeed I think it hardly possible for a woman to be in a more irksome situation than when rejecting a worthy man, who is all humility, respect, and submission, and who throws himself and his fortune at her feet.[9]

---

[9]Burney's father put her into a terror by advising her to entertain Barlow's suit lest she have no other opportunity. Because she could not have resisted his will, it was fortunate that, in the end, he did not insist on her accepting Barlow.

[August 1778]

I have now to write an account of the most consequential day I have spent since my birth: namely, my Streatham visit.

Our journey to Streatham was the least pleasant part of the day, for the roads were dreadfully dusty, and I was really in the fidgets from thinking what my reception might be, and from fearing they would expect a less awkward and backward kind of person than I was sure they would find.

Mr. Thrale's house is white, and very pleasantly situated, in a fine paddock. Mrs. Thrale was strolling about, and came to us as we got out of the chaise.

"Ah," cried she, "I hear Dr. Burney's voice! And you have brought your daughter?—well, now you are good!"

She then received me, taking both my hands, and with mixed politeness and cordiality welcoming me to Streatham. She led me into the house, and addressed herself almost wholly for a few minutes to my father, as if to give me an assurance she did not mean to regard me as a show, or to distress or frighten me by drawing me out. Afterwards she took me upstairs, and showed me the house, and said she had very much wished to see me at Streatham, and should always think herself much obliged to Dr. Burney for his goodness in bringing me, which she looked upon as a very great favor.

But though we were some time together, and though she was so very civil, she did not *hint* at my book, and I love her much more than ever for her delicacy in avoiding a subject which she could not but see would have greatly embarrassed me. . . .

Soon after, Mrs. Thrale took me to the library; she talked a little while upon common topics, and then, at last, she mentioned *Evelina*.

"Yesterday at supper," said she, "we talked it all over, and discussed all your characters; but Dr. Johnson's favorite is Mr. Smith. He declares the fine gentleman *manqué* was never better drawn; and he acted him all the evening, saying he was 'all for the ladies!' He repeated whole scenes by heart. I declare I was astonished at him. Oh you can't imagine how much he is pleased with the book; he 'could not get rid of the rogue,' he told me. But was it not droll," said she, "that I should recommend it to Dr. Burney? and tease him, so innocently, to read it?"

I now prevailed upon Mrs. Thrale to let me amuse myself, and she went to dress. I then prowled about to choose some book, and I saw, upon the reading table, *Evelina*. I had just fixed upon a new translation of Cicero's *Lælius*[10] when the library door was opened, and Mr. Seward entered. I instantly put away my book, because I dreaded being thought studious and affected. He offered his service to find anything for me, and then, in the same breath, ran on to speak of the book with which I had myself "favored the world!"

The exact words he began with I cannot recollect, for I was actually confounded by the attack; and his abrupt manner of letting me know he was *au fait*[11] equally astonished and provoked me. How different from the delicacy of Mr. and Mrs. Thrale!

When we were summoned to dinner, Mrs. Thrale made my father and me sit on each side of her. I said that I hoped I did not take Dr. Johnson's place; for he had not yet appeared.

"No," answered Mrs. Thrale, "he will sit by you, which I am sure will give him great pleasure."

Soon after we were seated, this great man entered. I have so true a veneration for him, that the very sight of him inspires me with delight and reverence, notwithstanding the cruel infirmities to which he is subject; for he has almost perpetual convulsive movements, either of his hands, lips, feet, or knees, and sometimes of all together.

Mrs. Thrale introduced me to him, and he took his place. We had a noble dinner, and a most elegant dessert. Dr. Johnson, in the middle of dinner, asked Mrs. Thrale what was in some little pies that were near him.

"Mutton," answered she, "so I don't ask you to eat any, because I know you despise it."

"No, madam, no," cried he; "I despise nothing that is good of its sort; but I am too proud now to eat of it. Sitting by Miss Burney makes me very proud today!"

"Miss Burney," said Mrs. Thrale, laughing, "you must take great care of your heart if Dr. Johnson attacks it; for I assure you he is not often successless."

"What's that you say, madam?" cried he; "are you making mischief between the young lady and me already?"

A little while after he drank Miss Thrale's health and mine, and then added:

[10]*Laelius: An Essay on Friendship*, translated by William Melmoth, 1777 (Dobson). Seward (below) was a friend of the Thrales.
[11]Current, "tuned in."

" 'Tis a terrible thing that we cannot wish young ladies well, without wishing them to become old women!''

"But some people," said Mr. Seward, "are old and young at the same time, for they wear so well that they never look old."

"No, sir, no," cried the Doctor, laughing; "that never yet was; you might as well say they are at the same time tall and short. I remember an epitaph to that purpose, which is in——''

(I have quite forgot what, and also the name it was made upon, but the rest I recollect exactly:)

> "——lies buried here;
> So early wise, so lasting fair,
> That none, unless her years you told,
> Thought her a child, or thought her old."

Mrs. Thrale then repeated some lines in French, and Dr. Johnson some more in Latin. An epilogue of Mr. Garrick's to *Bonduca*[12] was then mentioned, and Dr. Johnson said it was a miserable performance, and everybody agreed it was the worst he had ever made.

"And yet," said Mr. Seward, "it has been very much admired; but it is in praise of English valor, and so I suppose the subject made it popular."

"I don't know, sir," said Dr. Johnson, "anything about the subject, for I could not read on till I came to it; I got through half a dozen lines, but I could observe no other subject than eternal dullness. I don't know what is the matter with David; I am afraid he is grown superannuated, for his prologues and epilogues used to be incomparable."

"Nothing is so fatiguing," said Mrs. Thrale, "as the life of a wit: he and Wilkes[13] are the two oldest men of their ages I know; for they have both worn themselves out, by being eternally on the rack to give entertainment to others."

"David, madam," said the Doctor, "looks much older than he is; for his face has had double the business of any other man's; it is never at rest; when he speaks one minute, he has quite a different countenance to what he assumes the next; I don't believe he ever kept the same look for half an hour together, in the whole course of his life; and such an eternal, restless, fatigu-

---

[12]*Bonduca*, adapted from Beaumont and Fletcher by George Colman the Elder. Actually it was Garrick's prologue (Dobson).

[13]John Wilkes (1727–1797), politician, notorious for appealing to the "mob."

ing play of the muscles, must certainly wear out a man's face before its real time."

"Oh yes," cried Mrs. Thrale, "we must certainly make some allowance for such wear and tear of a man's face."

The next name that was started, was that of Sir John Hawkins:[14] and Mrs. Thrale said, "Why now, Dr. Johnson, he is another of those whom you suffer nobody to abuse but yourself; Garrick is one, too; for if any other person speaks against him, you browbeat him in a minute!"

"Why, madam," answered he, "they don't know when to abuse him, and when to praise him; I will allow no man to speak ill of David that he does not deserve; and as to Sir John, why really I believe him to be an honest man at the bottom: but to be sure he is penurious, and he is mean, and it must be owned he has a degree of brutality, and a tendency to savageness, that cannot easily be defended."

We all laughed, as he meant we should, at this curious manner of speaking in his favor, and he then related an anecdote that he said he knew to be true in regard to his meanness. He said that Sir John and he once belonged to the same club, but that as he eat no supper after the first night of his admission, he desired to be excused paying his share.

"And was he excused?"

"Oh yes; for no man is angry at another for being inferior to himself! we all scorned him, and admitted his plea. For my part I was such a fool as to pay my share for wine, though I never tasted any. But Sir John was a most *unclubable* man!"

How delighted was I to hear this master of languages so unaffectedly and sociably and good-naturedly make words, for the promotion of sport and good-humor.

"And this," continued he, "reminds me of a gentleman and lady with whom I traveled once; I suppose I must call them gentleman and lady, according to form, because they traveled in their own coach and four horses. But at the first inn where we stopped, the lady called for—a pint of ale! and when it came, quarreled with the waiter for not giving full measure. Now, Madame Duval[15] could not have done a grosser thing!"

Oh, how everybody laughed! and to be sure I did not glow at all, nor munch fast, nor look on my plate, nor lose any part of

---

[14](1719–1789): Charles Burney's rival in writing music history, and later Johnson's biographer.

[15]A character in *Evelina*, originally a tavern waitress. The Branghtons (below), also in *Evelina*, are a vulgar city family.

my usual composure! But how grateful do I feel to this dear Dr. Johnson, for never naming me and the book as belonging one to the other, and yet making an allusion that showed his thoughts led to it, and, at the same time, that seemed to justify the character as being natural! But, indeed, the delicacy I met with from him, and from all the Thrales, was yet more flattering to me than the praise with which I have heard they have honored my book.

[Streatham, 23 August]

Now for this morning's breakfast.

Dr. Johnson, as usual, came last into the library; he was in high spirits, and full of mirth and sport. I had the honor of sitting next to him: and now, all at once, he flung aside his reserve, thinking, perhaps, that it was time I should fling aside mine.

Mrs. Thrale told him that she intended taking me to Mr. T——'s.

"So you ought, madam," cried he; " 'tis your business to be cicerone to her."

Then suddenly he snatched my hand, and kissing it,

"Ah!' he added, "they will little think what a tartar you carry to them!"

"No, that they won't!" cried Mrs. Thrale; "Miss Burney looks so meek and so quiet, nobody would suspect what a comical girl she is; but I believe she has a great deal of malice at heart."

"Oh, she's a toad!" cried the Doctor, laughing—"a sly young rogue! with her Smiths and her Branghtons!"

[Saturday morning]

And now let me try to recollect an account he gave us of certain celebrated ladies of his acquaintance: an account which, had you heard from himself, would have made you die with laughing, his manner is so peculiar, and enforces his humor so originally.

It was begun by Mrs. Thrale's apologizing to him for troubling him with some question she thought trifling—Oh, I remember! We had been talking of colors, and of the fantastic names given to them, and why the palest lilac should be called a *soupir étouffé*; and when Dr. Johnson came in she applied to him.

"Why, madam," said he with wonderful readiness, "it is called a stifled sigh because it is checked in its progress, and only half a color."

I could not help expressing my amazement at his universal readiness upon all subjects, and Mrs. Thrale said to him,

"Sir, Miss Burney wonders at your patience with such stuff; but I tell her you are used to me, for I believe I torment you with more foolish questions than anybody else dares do."

"No, madam," said he, "you don't torment me; you tease me, indeed, sometimes."

"Ay, so I do, Dr. Johnson, and I wonder you bear with my nonsense."

"No, madam, you never talk nonsense; you have as much sense, and more wit, than any woman I know!"

"Oh," cried Mrs. Thrale, blushing, "it is my turn to go under the table this morning, Miss Burney!"

"And yet," continued the Doctor, with the most comical look, "I have known all the wits, from Mrs. Montagu down to Bet Flint!"[16]

"Bet Flint!" cried Mrs. Thrale; "pray who is she?"

"Oh, a fine character, madam! She was habitually a slut and a drunkard, and occasionally a thief and a harlot."

"And, for Heaven's sake, how came you to know her?"

"Why, madam, she figured in the literary world, too! Bet Flint wrote her own life, and called herself Cassandra, and it was in verse; it began:

"When Nature first ordained my birth,
A diminutive I was born on earth:
And then I came from a dark abode,
Into a gay and gaudy world.

"So Bet brought me her verses to correct; but I gave her half-a-crown, and she liked it as well. Bet had a fine spirit; she advertised for a husband, but she had no success, for she told me no man aspired to her! Then she hired very handsome lodgings and a footboy; and she got a harpsichord, but Bet could not play; however, she put herself in fine attitudes, and drummed."

Then he gave an account of another of these geniuses, who called herself by some fine name, I have forgotten what.

"She had not quite the same stock of virtue," continued he, "nor the same stock of honesty as Bet Flint; but I suppose she envied her accomplishments, for she was so little moved by the

---

[16]Elizabeth Montagu (1720–1800), eminent intellectual and society hostess.

power of harmony, that while Bet Flint thought she was drumming very divinely, the other jade had her indicted for a nuisance!"

"And pray what became of her, sir?"

"Why, madam, she stole a quilt from the man of the house, and he had her taken up,[17] but Bet Flint had a spirit not to be subdued; so when she found herself obliged to go to jail, she ordered a sedan chair, and bid her footboy walk before her. However, the boy proved refractory, for he was ashamed, though his mistress was not."

"And did she ever get out of jail again, sir?"

"Yes, madam; when she came to her trial the judge acquitted her. 'So now,' she said to me, 'the quilt is my own, and now I'll make a petticoat of it.' Oh, I loved Bet Flint!"

Oh, how we all laughed! Then he gave an account of another lady, who called herself Laurinda, and who also wrote verses and stole furniture; but he had not the same affection for her, he said, though she too "was a lady who had high notions of honor."

Then followed the history of another, who called herself Hortensia, and who walked up and down the park repeating a book of Virgil.

"But," said he, "though I know her story, I never had the good fortune to see her."

After this he gave us an account of the famous Mrs. Pinkethman.[18] "And she," he said, "told me she owed all her misfortunes to her wit; for she was so unhappy as to marry a man who thought himself also a wit, though I believe she gave him not implicit credit for it, but it occasioned much contradiction and ill-will."

"Bless me, sir!" cried Mrs. Thrale, "how can all these vagabonds contrive to get at *you*, of all people?"

"Oh the dear creatures!" cried he, laughing heartily, "I can't but be glad to see them!"

"Why, I wonder, sir, you never went to see Mrs. Rudd among the rest?"

"Why, madam, I believe I should," said he, "if it was not for the newspapers; but I am prevented many frolics that I should like very well, since I am become such a theme for the papers."

[17]Arrested.
[18]Probably an error for Pilkington (Laetitia, 1700–1750), well known for her memoirs (Dobson). Below: Margaret Caroline Rudd, tried (but acquitted) for forgery, 1775; Kitty Fisher, eminent prostitute; Anna Williams (1706–1783), blind poet, who lived with Johnson.

Now would you ever have imagined this? Bet Flint, it seems, once took Kitty Fisher to see him, but to his no little regret he was not at home. "And Mrs. Williams," he added, "did not love Bet Flint, but Bet Flint made herself very easy about that."

How Mr. Crisp would have enjoyed this account! He gave it all with so droll a solemnity, and it was all so unexpected, that Mrs. Thrale and I were both almost equally diverted.

[London, January 4, 1783]

Young Mr. Cambridge[19] need not complain of my taciturnity, whatever his father may do. Who, indeed, of all my new acquaintances, has so well understood me? The rest all talk of *Evelina* and *Cecilia,* and turn every other word into some compliment; while he talks of Chessington, or Captain Phillips, and pays me, not even by implication, any compliments at all. He neither looks at me with any curiosity, nor speaks to me with any air of expectation; two most insufferable honors, which I am continually receiving. He is very properly conscious he has at least as much to say as to hear, and he is above affecting a ridiculous deference to which he feels I have no claim. If I met with more folks who would talk to me upon such rational terms—considering, like him, their own dignity of full as much value as my ladyship's vanity—with how infinitely more ease and pleasure should I make one in those conversations!

[Windsor] Friday, Dec, 16 [1785]

[In 1783 Burney had met Mrs. Mary Delany, aristocrat and bluestocking, and they became friends. (For more on Delany, see Montagu, Letters, n. 26.) Delany was intimate with the royal family and lived near them at Windsor; she had warned Burney to expect to meet them at her house.]

After dinner . . . Mr. B. Dewes, his little daughter, Miss Port,[20] and myself, went into the drawing room. And here, while, to pass the time, I was amusing the little girl with teaching her some Christmas games, in which her father and cousin joined, Mrs. Delany came in. We were all in the middle of the room, and in some confusion; but she had but just come up to us to inquire what was going forwards, and I was disentangling

[19]George Owen Cambridge, for whom Burney suffered a long and frustrated love. Captain Phillips (below) was her brother-in-law.
[20]Mary Ann Port, Delany's great-grandniece, who lived with her.

myself from Miss Dewes, to be ready to fly off if anyone
knocked at the street-door, when the door of the drawing room
was again opened, and a large man, in deep mourning, appeared
at it, entering and shutting it himself without speaking.

A ghost could not more have scared me, when I discovered,
by its glitter on the black, a star! The general disorder had
prevented his being seen, except by myself, who was always on
the watch, till Miss P——, turning round, exclaimed, "The King!
—Aunt, the King!"

Oh, mercy! thought I, that I were but out of the room! which
way shall I escape? and how pass him unnoticed? There is but
the single door at which he entered, in the room! Everyone
scampered out of the way:[21] Miss P——, to stand next the door;
Mr. Bernard Dewes to a corner opposite it; his little girl clung to
me; and Mrs. Delany advanced to meet His Majesty, who, after
quietly looking on till she saw him, approached, and inquired
how she did.

He then spoke to Mr. Bernard, whom he had already met two
or three times here.

I had now retreated to the wall, and purposed gliding softly,
though speedily, out of the room; but before I had taken a single
step, the King, in a loud whisper to Mrs. Delany, said, "Is that
Miss Burney?"—and on her answering, "Yes, sir," he bowed,
and with a countenance of the most perfect good humor, came
close up to me.

A most profound reverence on my part arrested the progress
of my intended retreat.

"How long have you been come back, Miss Burney?"

"Two days, sir."

Unluckily he did not hear me, and repeated his question; and
whether the second time he heard me or not, I don't know, but
he made a little civil inclination of his head, and went back to
Mrs. Delany.

He insisted she should sit down, though he stood himself, and
began to give her an account of the Princess Elizabeth, who
once again was recovering, and trying, at present, James's Pow-
ders. She had been blooded, he said, twelve times in this last
fortnight, and had lost seventy-five ounces of blood, besides
undergoing blistering and other discipline. He spoke of her ill-

---

[21]". . . The etiquette always observed upon his entrance . . . is to fly off to distant
quarters" (*Diary and Letters* 2:340–341).

ness with the strongest emotion, and seemed quite filled with concern for her danger and sufferings.

Mrs. Delany next inquired for the younger children. They had all, he said, the whooping cough, and were soon to be removed to Kew.[22]

"Not," added he, "for any other reason than change of air for themselves; though I am pretty certain I have never had the distemper myself, and the Queen thinks she has not had it either: we shall take our chance. When the two eldest had it, I sent them away, and would not see them till it was over; but now there are so many of them that there would be no end to separations, so I let it take its course."

Mrs. Delany expressed a good deal of concern at his running this risk, but he laughed at it, and said, he was much more afraid of catching the rheumatism, which has been threatening one of his shoulders lately. However, he added, he should hunt the next morning, in defiance of it. . . .

During this discourse, I stood quietly in the place where he had first spoken to me. His quitting me so soon, and conversing freely and easily with Mrs. Delany, proved so delightful a relief to me, that I no longer wished myself away; and the moment my first panic from the surprise was over, I diverted myself with a thousand ridiculous notions of my own situation.

The Christmas games we had been showing Miss Dewes it seemed as if we were still performing, as none of us thought it proper to move, though our manner of standing reminded one of Puss in the corner. Close to the door was posted Miss P——; opposite her, close to the wainscot, stood Mr. Dewes; at just an equal distance from him, close to a window, stood myself; Mrs. Delany, though seated, was at the opposite side to Miss P——; and His Majesty kept pretty much in the middle of the room. The little girl, who kept close to me, did not break the order, and I could hardly help expecting to be beckoned, with a puss! puss! puss! to change places with one of my neighbors.

This idea, afterwards, gave way to another more pompous. It seemed to me we were acting a play. There is something so little like common and real life, in everybody's standing, while talking, in a room full of chairs, and standing, too, so aloof from each other, that I almost thought myself upon a stage, assisting in the representation of a tragedy—in which the King played his

[22]A royal residence west of London, on the Thames.

own part, of the king; Mrs. Delany that of a venerable confidante; Mr. Dewes, his respectful attendant; Miss P——, a suppliant virgin, waiting encouragement to bring forward some petition; Miss Dewes, a young orphan, intended to move the royal compassion; and myself—a very solemn, sober, and decent mute. . . .

When the discourse upon health . . . was over, the King went up to the table, and looked at a book of prints, from Claude Lorrain, which had been brought down for Miss Dewes; but Mrs. Delany, by mistake, told him they were for me. He turned over a leaf or two, and then said,

"Pray, does Miss Burney draw, too?"

The *too* was pronounced very civilly.

"I believe not, sir," answered Mrs. Delany; "at least, she does not tell?"

"Oh!" cried he, laughing, "that's nothing! she is not apt to tell; she never does tell, you know! Her father told me that himself. He told me the whole history of her *Evelina*. And I shall never forget his face when he spoke of his feelings at first taking up the book!—he looked quite frightened, just as if he was doing it that moment! I never can forget his face while I live!"

Then coming up close to me, he said,

"But what?—what?—how was it?"

"Sir?" cried I, not well understanding him.

"How came you—how happened it—what?—what?"

"I—I only wrote, sir, for my own amusement—only in some odd, idle hours."

"But your publishing—your printing—how was that?"

"That was only, sir—only because——"

I hesitated most abominably, not knowing how to tell him a long story, and growing terribly confused at these questions; besides, to say the truth, his own "what? what?" so reminded me of those vile *Probationary Odes*,[23] that, in the midst of all my flutter, I was really hardly able to keep my countenance.

The *What!* was then repeated, with so earnest a look, that, forced to say something, I stammeringly answered,

"I thought—sir—it would look very well in print!"

I do really flatter myself this is the silliest speech I ever made! I am quite provoked with myself for it; but a fear of laughing

[23]*Probationary Odes for the Laureateship*, satires by various authors occasioned by the death of the Poet Laureate, William Whitehead (1785). Burney remembers the lines, "Methinks I hear, / In accents clear, / Great Brunswick's [i.e. George III's] voice still vibrate on my ear: / 'What?—What?—What?' "

made me eager to utter anything, and by no means conscious, till
I had spoken, of what I was saying.

He laughed very heartily himself—well he might—and walked
away to enjoy it, crying out,

"Very fair indeed! that's being very fair and honest!"

Then, returning to me again, he said,

"But your father—how came you not to show him what you
wrote?"

"I was too much ashamed of it, sir, seriously."

Literal truth that, I am sure.

"And how did he find it out?"

"I don't know myself, sir. He never would tell me."

Literal truth again, my dear father, as you can testify.

"But how did you get it printed?"

"I sent it, sir, to a bookseller my father never employed, and
that I never had seen myself, Mr. Lowndes, in full hope by that
means he never would hear of it."

"But how could you manage that?"

"By means of a brother, sir."

"Oh!—you confided in a brother, then?"

"Yes, sir—that is, for the publication."

"What entertainment you must have had from hearing people's
conjectures, before you were known! Do you remember any of
them?"

"Yes, sir, many."

"And what?"

"I heard that Mr. Baretti[24] laid a wager it was written by a
man; for no woman, he said, could have kept her own counsel."

This diverted him extremely.

"But how was it," he continued, "you thought most likely for
your father to discover you?"

"Sometimes, sir, I have supposed I must have dropped some of
the manuscript; sometimes, that one of my sisters betrayed me."

"Oh! your sister?—what, not your brother?"

"No, sir; he could not, for——"

I was going on, but he laughed so much I could not be heard,
exclaiming,

"Vastly well! I see you are of Mr. Baretti's mind, and think
your brother could keep your secret, and not your sister? . . .
But you have not kept your pen unemployed all this time?"

[24]Joseph Baretti, a friend of the Thrales.

"Indeed I have, sir."

"But why?"

"I—I believe I have exhausted myself, sir."

He laughed aloud at this, and went and told it to Mrs. Delany, civilly treating a plain fact as a mere *bon mot*.

Then, returning to me again, he said, more seriously, "But you have not determined against writing any more?"

"N—o, sir——"

"You have made no vow—no real resolution of that sort?"

"No, sir."

"You only wait for inclination?" . . .

"No, sir."

A very civil little bow spoke him pleased with this answer, and he went again to the middle of the room, where he chiefly stood, and, addressing us in general, talked upon the different motives of writing, concluding with,

"I believe there is no constraint to be put upon real genius; nothing but inclination can set it to work. Miss Burney, however, knows best." And then, hastily returning to me, he cried, "What? what?"

"No, sir, I—I—believe not, certainly," quoth I, very awkwardly, for I seemed taking a violent compliment only as my due; but I knew not how to put him off as I would another person.

He then made some inquiries concerning the pictures with which the room is hung, and which are all Mrs. Delany's own painting; and a little discourse followed, upon some of the masters whose pictures she has copied.

This was all with her; for nobody ever answers him without being immediately addressed by him.

He then came to me again, and said,

"Is your father about anything at present?"

"Yes, sir, he goes on, when he has time, with his history."[25]

"Does he write quick?"

"Yes, sir, when he writes from himself; but in his history, he has so many books to consult, that sometimes he spends three days in finding authorities for a single passage."

"Very true; that must be unavoidable."

He pursued these inquiries some time, and then went again to his general station before the fire, and Mrs. Delany inquired if

[25]Charles Burney's *History of Music*; its final volume appeared in 1789.

he meant to hunt the next day. "Yes," he answered; and, a little pointedly, Mrs. Delany said,

"I would the hunted could but feel as much pleasure as the hunter."

The King understood her, and with some quickness, called out, "Pray what did you hunt?"

Then, looking round at us all—

"Did you know," he said, "that Mrs. Delany once hunted herself?—and in a long gown, and a great hoop?"

It seems she had told His Majesty an adventure of that sort which had befallen her in her youth, from some accident in which her will had no share.

While this was talking over, a violent thunder was made at the door. I was almost certain it was the Queen. Once more I would have given anything to escape; but in vain. I had been informed that nobody ever quitted the royal presence, after having been conversed with, till motioned to withdraw.

Miss P——, according to established etiquette on these occasions, opened the door which she stood next, by putting her hand behind her, and slid out, backwards, into the hall, to light the Queen in. The door soon opened again, and Her Majesty entered.

Immediately seeing the King, she made him a low curtsey. . . .

Instantly after, I felt her eye on my face. I believe, too, she curtsied to me; but though I saw the bend, I was too nearsighted to be sure it was intended for me. I was hardly ever in a situation more embarrassing; I dared not return what I was not certain I had received, yet considered myself as appearing quite a monster, to stand stiff-necked, if really meant.

Almost at the same moment, she spoke to Mr. Bernard Dewes, and then nodded to my little clinging girl.

I was now really ready to sink, with horrid uncertainty of what I was doing, or what I should do—when His Majesty, who I fancy saw my distress, most good-humoredly said to the Queen something, but I was too much flurried to remember what, except these words—"I have been telling Miss Burney——"

Relieved from so painful a dilemma, I immediately dropped a curtsey. She made one to me in the same moment, and, with a very smiling countenance, came up to me; but she could not speak, for the King went on talking, eagerly, and very gaily, repeating to her every word I had said during our conversation upon *Evelina*, its publication, etc. etc.

Then he told her of Baretti's wager, saying, "But she heard of a great many conjectures about the author, before it was known, and of Baretti, an admirable thing!—he laid a bet it must be a man, as no woman, he said, could have kept her own counsel!"

The Queen, laughing a little, exclaimed,

"Oh, that is quite too bad an affront to us! Don't you think so?" addressing herself to me, with great gentleness of voice and manner.

I assented; and the King continued his relation, which she listened to with a look of some interest . . . and when he had finished his narration the Queen took her seat.

She made Mrs. Delany sit next her, and Miss P——brought her some tea.

The King, meanwhile, came to me again, and said, "Are you musical?"

"Not a performer, sir."

Then, going from me to the Queen, he cried, "She does not play."

I did not hear what the Queen answered; she spoke in a low voice, and seemed much out of spirits. . . .

The King then returned to me, and said, "Are you sure you never play?—never touch the keys at all?"

"Never to acknowledge it, sir."

"Oh! that's it!" cried he; and flying to the Queen, cried, "She does play—but not to acknowledge it!"

I was now in a most horrible panic once more; pushed so very home, I could answer no other than I did, for these categorical questions almost constrain categorical answers; and here, at Windsor, it seems an absolute point that whatever they ask must be told, and whatever they desire must be done. Think but, then, of my consternation, in expecting their commands to perform! My dear father, pity me!

The eager air with which he returned to me fully explained what was to follow. I hastily, therefore, spoke first, in order to stop him, crying—"I never, sir, played to anybody but myself! never!"

"No?" cried he, looking incredulous; "what, not to——"

"Not even to me, sir!" cried my kind Mrs. Delany, who saw what was threatening me.

"No?—are you sure?" cried he, disappointed; "but—but you'll——"

"I have never, sir," cried I, very earnestly, "played in my

life, but when I could hear nobody else—quite alone, and from a mere love of any musical sounds."

He repeated all this to the Queen, whose answers I never heard; but when he once more came back, with a face that looked unwilling to give it up, in my fright I had recourse to dumb show, and raised my hands in a supplicating fold, with a most begging countenance to be excused. This, luckily, succeeded; he understood me very readily, and laughed a little, but made a sort of desisting, or rather complying, little bow, and said no more about it. . . .

Afterwards, there was some talk upon sermons, and the Queen wished the Bishop of Chester would publish another volume.

"No, no," said the King, "you must not expect a man, while he continues preaching, to go on publishing. Every sermon printed, diminishes his stock for the pulpit."

"Very true," said the Queen; "but I believe the Bishop of Chester has enough to spare."

The King then praised Carr's sermons, and said he liked none but what were plain and unadorned.

"Nor I neither," said the Queen; "but for me, ît is, I suppose, because the others I don't understand."

The King then, looking at his watch, said, "It is eight o'clock, and if we don't go now, the children will be sent to the other house."

"Yes, your Majesty," cried the Queen, instantly rising.

Mrs. Delany put on Her Majesty's cloak, and she took a very kind leave of her. She then curtsied separately to us all, and the King handed her to the carriage.

It is the custom for everybody they speak to to attend them out, but they would not suffer Mrs. Delany to move. Miss P——, Mr. Dewes, and his little daughter, and myself, all accompanied them, and saw them in their coach, and received their last gracious nods.

When they were gone, Mrs. Delany confessed she had heard the King's knock at the door before she came into the drawing room, but would not avow it, that I might not run away. Well! being over was so good a thing, that I could not but be content.

[Kew, Sunday, January 25, 1789]

I have not mentioned a singular present which has been sent me from Germany this month: it is an almanac, in German, containing for its recreative part an abridgment of *Cecilia,* in

that language; and every month opens with a cut from some part
of her history. It is sent me by M. Henouvre, a gentleman in
some office in the King's establishment at Hanover. I wish I
could read it—but I have only written it!

[Monday, February 2]

[In October 1788, George III showed disturbing signs of illness.
He talked hoarsely, rapidly, and incessantly; he grew sleepless,
stubborn, and unreasonable. In November he became violent. It
was decided to move him from Windsor to Kew and to call in
specialists—the Drs. Willis, mentioned below. In February 1789
Parliament was on the point of declaring a regency when, abruptly,
the king began to recover. By that time the grueling court
routine had undermined Burney's health.]

What an adventure had I this morning! one that has occasioned me the severest personal terror I ever experienced in my
life.

Sir Lucas Pepys[26] still persisting that exercise and air were
absolutely necessary to save me from illness, I have continued
my walks, varying my gardens from Richmond to Kew, according to the accounts I received of the movements of the King.
For this I had Her Majesty's permission, on the representation
of Sir Lucas.

This morning, when I received my intelligence of the King
from Dr. John Willis, I begged to know where I might walk in
safety. "In Kew Gardens," he said, "as the King would be in
Richmond."

"Should any unfortunate circumstance," I cried, "at any time,
occasion my being seen by His Majesty, do not mention my
name, but let me run off without call or notice."

This he promised. Everybody, indeed, is ordered to keep out
of sight.

Taking, therefore, the time I had most at command, I strolled
into the gardens. I had proceeded, in my quick way, nearly half
the round, when I suddenly perceived, through some trees, two
or three figures. Relying on the instructions of Dr. John, I
concluded them to be workmen and gardeners; yet tried to look
sharp, and in so doing, as they were less shaded, I thought I saw
the person of His Majesty!

[26]A court doctor.

Alarmed past all possible expression, I waited not to know more, but turning back, ran off with all my might. But what was my terror to hear myself pursued!—to hear the voice of the King himself loudly and hoarsely calling after me, "Miss Burney! Miss Burney!"

I protest I was ready to die. I knew not in what state he might be at the time; I only knew the orders to keep out of his way were universal; that the Queen would highly disapprove any unauthorized meeting, and that the very action of my running away might deeply, in his present irritable state, offend him. Nevertheless, on I ran, too terrified to stop, and in search of some short passage, for the garden is full of little labyrinths, by which I might escape.

The steps still pursued me, and still the poor hoarse and altered voice rang in my ears; more and more footsteps resounded frightfully behind me—the attendants all running, to catch their eager master, and the voices of the two Dr. Willises loudly exhorting him not to heat himself so unmercifully.

Heavens, how I ran! I do not think I should have felt the hot lava from Vesuvius—at least not the hot cinders—had I so run during its eruption. My feet were not sensible that they even touched the ground.

Soon after, I heard other voices, shriller, though less nervous, call out, "Stop! stop! stop!"

I could by no means consent: I knew not what was purposed, but I recollected fully my agreement with Dr. John that very morning, that I should decamp if surprised, and not be named.

My own fears and repugnance, also, after a flight and disobedience like this, were doubled in the thought of not escaping; I knew not to what I might be exposed, should the malady be then high, and take the turn of resentment. Still, therefore, on I flew; and such was my speed, so almost incredible to relate or recollect, that I fairly believe no one of the whole party could have overtaken me, if these words, from one of the attendants, had not reached me, "Dr. Willis begs you to stop!"

"I cannot! I cannot!" I answered, still flying on, when he called out, "You must, ma'am; it hurts the King to run."

Then, indeed, I stopped—in a state of fear really amounting to agony. I turned round, I saw the two Doctors had got the King between them, and three attendants of Dr. Willis's were hovering about. They all slackened their pace, as they saw me stand still; but such was the excess of my alarm, that I was wholly insensible to the effects of a race which, at any other time, would have required an hour's recruit.[27]

As they approached, some little presence of mind happily came to my command: it occurred to me that, to appease the wrath of my flight, I must now show some confidence: I therefore faced them as undauntedly as I was able, only charging the nearest of the attendants to stand by my side.

When they were within a few yards of me, the King called out, "Why did you run away?"

Shocked at a question impossible to answer, yet a little assured by the mild tone of his voice, I instantly forced myself forward, to meet him, though the internal sensation which satisfied me this was a step the most proper, to appease his suspicions and displeasure, was so violently combated by the tremor of my nerves, that I fairly think I may reckon it the greatest effort of personal courage I have ever made.

The effort answered: I looked up, and met all his wonted benignity of countenance, though something still of wildness in his eyes. Think, however, of my surprise, to feel him put both his hands round my two shoulders, and then kiss my cheek!

I wonder I did not really sink, so exquisite was my affright when I saw him spread out his arms! Involuntarily, I concluded he meant to crush me: but the Willises, who have never seen him till this fatal illness, not knowing how very extraordinary an action this was from him, simply smiled and looked pleased, supposing, perhaps, it was his customary salutation!

I believe, however, it was but the joy of a heart unbridled, now, by the forms and proprieties of established custom and sober reason. To see any of his household thus by accident, seemed such a near approach to liberty and recovery, that who can wonder it should serve rather to elate than lessen what yet remains of his disorder!

He now spoke in such terms of his pleasure in seeing me, that I soon lost the whole of my terror; astonishment to find him so nearly well, and gratification to see him so pleased, removed every uneasy feeling, and the joy that succeeded, in my conviction of his recovery, made me ready to throw myself at his feet to express it.

What a conversation followed! When he saw me fearless, he grew more and more alive, and made me walk close by his side,

[27]Rest.

away from the attendants, and even the Willises themselves, who, to indulge him, retreated. I own myself not completely composed, but alarm I could entertain no more.

Everything that came uppermost in his mind he mentioned; he seemed to have just such remains of his flightiness as heated his imagination without deranging his reason, and robbed him of all control over his speech, though nearly in his perfect state of mind as to his opinions.

What did he not say! He opened his whole heart to me—expounded all his sentiments, and acquainted me with all his intentions. . . .

He assured me he was quite well—as well as he had ever been in his life; and then inquired how I did, and how I went on? and whether I was more comfortable?

If these questions, in their implication, surprised me, imagine how that surprise must increase when he proceeded to explain them! He asked after the coadjutrix,[28] laughing, and saying, "Never mind her!—don't be oppressed—I am your friend! don't let her cast you down!—I know you have a hard time of it—but don't mind her!"

Almost thunderstruck with astonishment, I merely curtsied to his kind "I am your friend," and said nothing.

Then presently he added, "Stick to your father—stick to your own family—let them be your objects."

How readily I assented!

Again he repeated all I have just written, nearly in the same words, but ended it more seriously: he suddenly stopped, and held me to stop too, and putting his hand on his breast, in the most solemn manner, he gravely and slowly said, "I will protect you! I promise you that—and therefore depend upon me!"

I thanked him; and the Willises, thinking him rather too elevated, came to propose my walking on. "No, no, no!" he cried, a hundred times in a breath; and their good-humor prevailed, and they let him again walk on with his new companion.

He then gave me a history of his pages, animating almost into a rage, as he related his subjects of displeasure with them, particularly with Mr. Ernst, who he told me had been brought up by himself. I hope his ideas upon these men are the result of the mistakes of his malady.

Then he asked me some questions that very greatly distressed

[28]Elizabeth Schwellenberg, Burney's tyrannical senior colleague as Keeper of the Robes.

me, relating to information given him in his illness, from various motives, but which he suspected to be false, and which I knew he had reason to suspect: yet was it most dangerous to set anything right, as I was not aware what might be the views of their having been stated wrong. I was as discreet as I knew how to be, and I hope I did no mischief; but this was the worst part of the dialogue.

He next talked to me a great deal of my dear father, and made a thousand inquiries concerning his *History of Music*. This brought him to his favorite theme, Handel; and he told me innumerable anecdotes of him, and particularly that celebrated tale of Handel's saying of himself, when a boy, "While that boy lives, my music will never want a protector." And this, he said, I might relate to my father.[29]

Then he ran over most of his oratorios, attempting to sing the subjects of several airs and choruses, but so dreadfully hoarse that the sound was terrible.

Dr. Willis, quite alarmed at this exertion, feared he would do himself harm, and again proposed a separation. "No! no! no!" he exclaimed, "not yet; I have something I must just mention first."

Dr. Willis, delighted to comply, even when uneasy at compliance, again gave way.

The good King then greatly affected me. He began upon my revered old friend, Mrs. Delany; and he spoke of her with such warmth—such kindness! "She was my friend!" he cried, "and I loved her as a friend! I have made a memorandum when I lost her—I will show it you."

He pulled out a pocketbook, and rummaged some time, but to no purpose.

The tears stood in his eyes—he wiped them, and Dr. Willis again became very anxious. "Come, sir," he cried, "now do you come in and let the lady go on her walk—come, now you have talked a long while—so we'll go in—if your Majesty pleases."

"No, no!" he cried, "I want to ask her a few questions; I have lived so long out of the world, I know nothing!"

This touched me to the heart. We walked on together, and he inquired after various persons, particularly Mrs. Boscawen, because she was Mrs. Delany's friend! Then, for the same reason, after Mr. Frederick Montagu, of whom he kindly said, "I know

---

[29]No modern biography of Handel mentions this anecdote.

he has a great regard for me, for all he joined the opposition." ...

He then told me he was very much dissatisfied with several of his state officers, and meant to form an entire new establishment. He took a paper out of his pocketbook, and showed me his new list.

This was the wildest thing that passed; and Dr. John Willis now seriously urged our separating; but he would not consent; he had only three more words to say, he declared, and again he conquered.

He now spoke of my father, with still more kindness, and told me he ought to have had the post of Master of the Band, and not that little poor musician Parsons, who was not fit for it.[30] "But Lord Salisbury," he cried, "used your father very ill in that business, and so he did me! However, I have dashed out his name, and I shall put your father's in—as soon as I get loose again!"

This again—how affecting was this!

"And what," cried he, "has your father got, at last? nothing but that poor thing at Chelsea? Oh fie! fie! fie! But never mind! I will take care of him! I will do it myself!"

Then presently he added, "As to Lord Salisbury, he is out already, as this memorandum will show you, and so are many more. I shall be much better served; and when once I get away, I shall rule with a rod of iron!"

This was very unlike himself, and startled the two good doctors, who could not bear to cross him, and were exulting at my seeing his great amendment, but yet grew quite uneasy at his earnestness and volubility.

Finding we now must part, he stopped to take leave, and renewed again his charges about the coadjutrix. "Never mind her!" he cried, "depend upon me! I will be your friend as long as I live!—I here pledge myself to be your friend!" And then he saluted me again just as at the meeting, and suffered me to go on.

What a scene! how variously was I affected by it! but, upon the whole, how inexpressibly thankful to see him so nearly himself—so little removed from recovery!

[30]William Parsons had been Charles Burney's successful rival for the court post of Master of the Band. The "poor thing at Chelsea" (below) was the post of organist at Chelsea College, which Burney had obtained in 1783.

[Windsor, October 1790]

And now for a scene a little surprising.

The beautiful chapel of St. George, repaired and finished by the best artists at an immense expense, which was now opened after a very long shutting up for its preparations, brought innumerable strangers to Windsor, and, among others, Mr. Boswell.[31]

This I heard, in my way to the chapel, from Mr. Turbulent, who overtook me, and mentioned having met Mr. Boswell at the Bishop of Carlisle's the evening before. He proposed bringing him to call upon me; but this I declined, certain how little satisfaction would be given here by the entrance of a man so famous for compiling anecdotes. But yet I really wished to see him again, for old acquaintance' sake, and unavoidable amusement from his oddity and good humor, as well as respect for the object of his constant admiration, my revered Dr. Johnson. I therefore told Mr. Turbulent I should be extremely glad to speak with him after the service was over.

Accordingly, at the gate of the choir, Mr. Turbulent brought him to me. We saluted with mutual glee: his comic-serious face and manner have lost nothing of their wonted singularity; nor yet have his mind and language, as you will soon confess.

"I am extremely glad to see you indeed," he cried, "but very sorry to see you here. My dear ma'am, why do you stay?—it won't do, ma'am! you must resign!—we can put up with it no longer. I told my good host the Bishop so last night; we are all grown quite outrageous!"

Whether I laughed the most, or stared the most, I am at a loss to say; but I hurried away from the cathedral, not to have such treasonable declarations overheard, for we were surrounded by a multitude.

He accompanied me, however, not losing one moment in continuing his exhortations: "If you do not quit, ma'am, very soon, some violent measures, I assure you, will be taken. We shall address Dr. Burney in a body; I am ready to make the harangue myself. We shall fall upon him all at once."

I stopped him to inquire about Sir Joshua; he said he saw him very often, and that his spirits were very good. I asked about Mr. Burke's book.[32] "Oh," cried he, "it will come out next

---

[31]Author of the *Life of Johnson* (1791). "Mr. Turbulent" (below) is Burney's private name for the Rev. Charles de Guiffardière, French reader to the Queen.
[32]*Reflections on the Revolution in France*, published in November 1790. Sir Joshua (above) is Reynolds, the painter.

week: 'tis the first book in the world, except my own, and that's coming out also very soon; only I want your help."

"My help?"

"Yes, madam; you must give me some of your choice little notes of the Doctor's; we have seen him long enough upon stilts; I want to show him in a new light. Grave Sam, and great Sam, and solemn Sam, and learned Sam—all these he has appeared over and over. Now I want to entwine a wreath of the graces across his brow; I want to show him as gay Sam, agreeable Sam, pleasant Sam; so you must help me with some of his beautiful billets to yourself."

I evaded this by declaring I had not any stores at hand. He proposed a thousand curious expedients to get at them, but I was invincible.

Then I was hurrying on, lest I should be too late. He followed eagerly, and again exclaimed, "But, ma'am, as I tell you, this won't do—you must resign off-hand! Why, I would farm you out myself for double, treble the money! I wish I had the regulation of such a farm—yet I am no farmer-general.[33] But I should like to farm you, and so I will tell Dr. Burney. I mean to address him; I have a speech ready for the first opportunity."

He then told me his *Life of Dr. Johnson* was nearly printed, and took a proof sheet out of his pocket to show me; with crowds passing and repassing, knowing me well, and staring well at him: for we were now at the iron rails of the Queen's Lodge.

I stopped; I could not ask him in; I saw he expected it, and was reduced to apologize, and tell him I must attend the Queen immediately.

He uttered again stronger and stronger exhortations for my retreat, accompanied by expressions which I was obliged to check in their bud. But finding he had no chance for entering, he stopped me again at the gate, and said he would read me a part of his work.

There was no refusing this: and he began, with a letter of Dr. Johnson's to himself. He read it in strong imitation of the Doctor's manner, very well, and not caricature. But Mrs. Schwellenberg was at her window, a crowd was gathering to stand round the rails, and the King and Queen and Royal Family now

[33]To *farm out* is to rent; a *farm* is an arrangement by which the right to collect revenue is sold to someone for a fixed payment; a *farmer-general* is one who farms the revenues of a district.

approached from the Terrace. I made a rather quick apology, and, with a step as quick as my now weakened limbs have left in my power, I hurried to my apartment.

You may suppose I had inquiries enough, from all around, of "Who was the gentleman I was talking to at the rails?" And an injunction rather frank not to admit him beyond those limits.

[D'Arblay made this perilous journey through the Rhineland in July 1815, just a month after the English and Prussian armies had defeated Napoleon Bonaparte (Buonaparte) at the Battle of Waterloo. She started her account at her husband's request, but did not actually write it until after his death in 1818 (September 1824–July 1825). Alexander was their only child. The account starts in Brussels, whither she had fled from Paris when Napoleon returned from exile on Elba, dethroned the restored Bourbon King Louis XVIII, and entered Paris on March 20, 1815 to rule France for the "Hundred Days." Frances d'Arblay's husband, a general in the service of Louis XVIII, was injured while on duty in Trèves (Trier), Germany; and she had to cross what was still a war zone in order to join him. The most direct route by stagecoach would be directly southeast, via Luxembourg. Because of wartime travel conditions, however, she had to make a wide circle, which took her far to the east and a little to the north—via Aix-la-Chapelle (Aachen), Juliers (Jülich), Cologne (Köln), Bonn, Coblenz, and finally southwest back to Trier.]

In this my deplorably widowed state to do aught that was suggested by Him—the lord and darling of my heart—is all for which I now retain any voluntary spirit of exertion, save in what regards OUR Alexander, who occupies all that is left me of life:—My adored Departed wished me to write this narration, with other anecdotes, first for his own perusal, and next to ensure their future communication to our son. The former motive is ended—forever!—the latter still remains, and that shall urge me to occupy, whenever I have the power, some portion of my poor remnant hours to the development of those events of my life of which He who rendered twenty-five years of it almost supremely happy desired me—enjoined me—to leave some written trace.

I begin with that He most wished, my hazardous journey to join him at Trèves.

On the nineteenth of July, 1815, during the ever memorable

Hundred Days, I was writing to my heart's best friend, at our apartments in the Marché aux Bois, at Brussels; whither I had fled on the arrival of Buonaparte in Paris, and where my honored husband had left me, on a mission from his king, Louis XVIII to Trèves; when I received a visit from la Princesse d'Hénin, and Colonel de Beaufort, who entered the room with a sort of precipitancy and confusion that immediately struck me as the effect of evil tidings which they came to communicate. My ideas instantly flew to the expectation of new public disaster; for what was private, or personal, occurred not to me. . . . I was just imagining that Louis XVIII was again dethroned, when Madame d'Hénin faintly pronounced the name of M. d'Arblay—Alarmed, I started—certain that the evil, whatsoever it might be, was His!—I turned from one to the other, in speechless trepidation, dreading to ask, while dying to know what awaited me. Madame d'Hénin then, in a husky voice, scarcely articulate, said that M. de Beaufort had received a letter from M. d'Arblay.

This a little recovered me; yet, certain, by their distress, that some cruel tidings were impending, I became eager to learn them, that no time might be lost should there be anything to do. I commanded myself, therefore, to assume sufficient composure to entreat for immediate and faithful intelligence.

Fearfully, then, one aiding the other, while I listened with subdued, yet increasing terror, they acquainted me that M. d'Arblay had received on the calf of his leg from a wild horse, a furious kick, which had occasioned so bad a wound as to confine him to his bed: and that he wished M. de Beaufort to procure me some traveling guide, that I might join him as soon as it would be possible with safety and convenience.

I now started up, and with clasped hands, besought them to let me see the letter at once. This they resisted, but their resistance only added torture to affright, and I became so urgent, so vehement, so overpowering, that they were forced to give way—But oh Heaven!—What was my agony when I saw that the letter was not in his own hand!—I conjured them to leave me, and let me read it alone—They offered, one to find me out a clever femme de chambre,[34] the other, to enquire a guide for me, to aid me to set out, if able, the next day; but I rather know this from recollection than from having understood them at the time: I only entreated their absence—and, having consented to their return in a few hours, I forced them away.

[34]Maid.

No sooner were they gone, than, calming my spirits by earnest and devout prayer, which alone supports my mind, and even preserves my senses, in deep calamity, I ran over the letter, and conceiving that the wound, from the entrance of the iron hoof into so tender a part, which caused pain too acute to permit the poor sufferer even the use of his hand, must menace a gangrene, I called forth my utmost courage, and resolved to fly to him immediately.

What time, indeed, was there to lose, when the letter, written by M. de Premorel, his aide-de-camp, was dated the fourth day after the wound, and acknowledged that three incisions had been made in the leg, unnecessarily, by an ignorant surgeon, which had so aggravated the danger, as well as the suffering, that he was now in bed, not only from the pain of the lacerated limb, but also from a nervous fever! and that no hope was held out to him of quitting it in less than a fortnight or three weeks.

I determined not to wait, though the poor sufferer himself had charged that I should, either for the femme de chambre of Mme. d'Hénin or the guide of M. de Beaufort, which they could not quite promise even for the next day—and to me the next hour seemed the delay of an age.

Never was I blessed with such personal courage as at this crisis—The one object I had in view divested me of every fear and every feeling of personal Danger, Prudence, Health, Strength, Expense, or Difficulty. To arrive in time to aid his recovery was my sole thought—to know it was his ardent wish was my constant consolation. . . .

[I] sent to order a chaise[35] at six, on the road to Luxembourg. The answer was that no horses were to be had!

Almost distracted, I flew myself to the inn that was recommended to me as the first for travelers—but the answer was repeated! The route to Luxembourg, the bookkeepers told me, was infested with straggling parties first from the wandering army of Grouchy,[36] now rendered pillagers from want of food; and next from the pursuing army of the Prussians, who made themselves pillagers also, through the rights of conquest—To travel in a chaise would be impracticable, they assured me, without a guard.

[35]A chaise (or chaise de poste, p. 324) was a private hired carriage. D'Arblay learned that, under the circumstances, the only safe way to travel was by the public diligence or stagecoach.
[36]One of Napoleon's generals.

I had already heard—though now in the perturbation of my haste I had set the intelligence aside, that all the roads from Brussels to Trèves were beset with desperate banditti, the refuse of all the armies: for my nephew, Charles Parr Burney, had called upon me two days previously, for letters to my poor General at Triers, where he, Charles Parr, meant to wait upon him; but he had called again the preceding evening, to tell me that he and his party had been forced to change their route, and content themselves with visiting Antwerp and Amsterdam, as they were warned that they might else become spoil to the wandering hordes who were, on the one hand, escaping from slaughter or captivity, and on the other, ferociously existing as banditti!

Constrained, thus, to give up going alone, or going immediately, I now resolved upon traveling in the diligence, and desired to secure a place in that for Triers (Trèves).

There was none to that city!—

"And what is the nearest town to Triers, whence I might go on in a chaise?" "Luxembourg."

I bespoke a place—but was told that the diligence had set off the very day before, and that none other would go for six days, as it only quitted Brussels once a week.

The misery of this intelligence, was almost equal to that which had been its origin. I quitted the bookkeeper's office in agony indescribable, [to] form some new plan, as staying another week was wholly out of the question. . . .

[A friend, Mme. de Spangen, suggests that d'Arblay travel with her brother-in-law, the Comte de Spangen, who will protect her as far as Liège and recommend her to the protection of others for the rest of her journey.]

Thence I proceeded to Messrs. de Noots, the banker's, for whom I had an unpresented letter of credit.—But what was my consternation to be told they had all dined abroad, and could not be followed, as they would not transact any further business that day!—

To write, or attempt any representation, would employ a time that would make me inevitably too late for my place; blessing, therefore, my benevolent Madame de Spangen, I resolved upon trusting to her kind recommendation, and borrowing money of the Comte her brother-in-law, whom, after my arrival at Trèves, I could pay by a draft.

I was hurrying home, to pack and prepare—but seeing from afar a figure upon the steps, I stopped, and looked with my glass: I then perceived Madame d'Hénin.—

I darted back like lightning—at fifteen I had not more agility than that with which I was endowed at this sight, from the fear of her persuasion, the grief of resisting her, and the dread lest the conflict should make me too late. I loitered about at a distance till I saw the coast clear, and that kind, anxious, really unhappy friend sent away.

I then entered my poor forlorn habitation, and set about my wretched packing. I had a very scanty wardrobe, the remnant of my flight from Paris; but abundance of small matters difficult to arrange. I had not even a trunk! nor power at such a moment to get one. I put all I had of value into a large flat hand basket, made of straw by a French prisoner, and which had been given to me by my dear Mrs. Locke, and all else I thrust into carpetbags. . . .

[D'Arblay barely managed to catch the coach for Liège, only to discover on her arrival there that the Comte de Spangen had come by an earlier coach and already left the city.]

What then was my affright!—I had but six Napoleons left when my passage to Liège was paid. I remained in a sort of stupor that made the bookkeeper regard me with wonder, though, as I had mentioned the Comte de Spangen, without any air of suspicion or ill opinion.

The stare of the man brought back to me some presence of mind. I then resolved to keep my own counsel with regard to my poverty, lest I should be stopped or affronted, and to go on as far as my six Napoleons would carry me, and when they were gone, to proceed by parting with my gold repeater and some trinkets which I carried in my basket.

As calmly as was in my power I then declared my purpose to go to Trèves, and begged to be put on my way.

I was come wrong, the bookkeeper answered: the road was by Luxembourg.

And how was I to get thither?

By Brussels, he said: and a week hence, the diligence having set off the day before.

Alas, I well knew that! and entreated some other means to forward me to Triers.

He replied that he knew of none from Liège; but that if I would go to Aix, I might there, perhaps, though it was out of the road, hear of some conveyance.

How desperate a resource! Yet I could hear of no other: and for Aix, he told me, a diligence would set off in about an hour.

I would now have secured a place; but he said I must first show my passport.

Passport? I repeated, I have none!

I could not, then, he dryly acquainted me, go on.

Astonished and affrighted, I pleaded my distress. I had not thought of a passport: none had been demanded for my quitting Brussels, and nothing of the kind had occurred to me: I had consulted no one; I had precipitated my flight to attend a sick friend, and I besought the bookkeeper to let me proceed. It was utterly, he asserted, impossible. I could not leave Liège without a passport from the Prussian Police Office, where I should only and surely be detained if I had not one to show from whence I came.

This, happily, reminded me of the one I had had from M. de Jaucourt in Paris, and which was, fortunately, though accidentally, in my hand basket. I begged, therefore, a guide to the Prussian office.

There arrived, I was shown to a room where two young officers received me very civilly; they were French, I believe; at least they spoke French well.

I told them my history, and gave them my passport, signed by M. de Jaucourt the fifteenth of March, and by Lieutenant Colonel Jones at Brussels the seventeenth of June.—

They seemed quite satisfied and carried the document to the next apartment—but what was my consternation—when I heard a voice of thunder vociferate rude reproaches to them, and saw them return with my unsigned passport, to tell me the Commandant refused his signature and ordered me to depart from the office!

Brutality so unauthorized, however it shocked, I would not suffer to intimidate me. Where, I asked, was I to go? I had a claim to a passport, and if refused it here must be directed elsewhere.

The Commandant, hearing me, burst into the room. He was a Prussian—but not like Prince Blücher, whom I had seen in England, and whose face, in private company, cast off all fiery hostility for pleased and pleasing benignity: this Mr. Kauffman had an air the most ferocious, and seemed rather to be pouncing upon some prey than coming forward to hear a reclamation of justice; and in a tone and manner of revolting roughness, he said I had brought a stale old useless passport, with which he would have nothing to do.

He spoke in bad and broken French, and was going to leave me: but I dropped my indignant sensations in my terror at this threatened failure, and eagerly represented that I had quitted Brussels too abruptly for seeking a new passport; but that this had been granted me at Paris in my flight from Buonaparte.

He cast his eyes momentarily on the passport, and then, in an inquisitorial voice, said "Vous êtes française?—"[37]

"Oui, Monsieur," I readily answered, being such in right of my dear husband, and conceiving that a recommendation, after having stated my escaping from Buonaparte. But he threw the passport instantly back to me, with marks of disdain, and said it would not do.

Earnestly then I required to know what step I must take, what course I must pursue?

Go back, he harshly answered, and get another.

And then he stalked away to the inner apartment.

Desperate from anguish, I followed him—I was traveling, I told him, to join a wounded General Officer, and should lose a whole week by returning, which might be fatal to me—he turned round, a little struck, yet as if amazed at my daring perseverance, and with undisguised contempt repeated "Vous êtes française?"

I then saw I had by no means made my court to him by my conjugal assumption, and that he was amongst that prejudiced mass that, confounding the good with the bad, made war against all the French. My affirmative, however, had been from a right I held too sacred to recall, and I again assented.

Taking up a newspaper, he turned away from me and walked towards a distant window.

I was then reduced to making use of the most earnest supplication, and the two young officers looked ready to join me, from understanding me more perfectly and evidently pitying my distress. But they had a tyrant to deal with whom it was clear they must implicitly obey.

At this deplorable moment, and when on the point of being

[37]"You are French?"

compelled back to Brussels, I had the exquisite good fortune to recollect the name of General Kleist, a Prussian Commander in Chief at Trèves, who had distinguished M. d'Arblay in a manner the most flattering and even cordial: and no sooner had I mentioned this, and with circumstances of detail that demonstrated the authenticity of what I uttered, than M. Kauffman gave the passport to the young officers, with leave to pass me on to Aix la Chapelle; There to present myself instantly to the commanding officer, to solicit permission *pour aller plus loin*.[38]

Ungracious as this was, I received it with the highest joy, and hastened to the bookkeeper to secure my place. This man, a German, whose compassion had now been awakened, saw my relief and delight with real satisfaction.

The diligence for Aix la Chapelle was not to set out till twelve: the bookkeeper offered me a boy to show me the town: and I gladly took a little stroll, happy to escape ordering any repast— for which my heart was too full, and my purse too empty!— . . .

From Thursday, 20 July

It was not till twelve at noon that the diligence set out by which I was to arrive at Aix la Chapelle. I was only going in search of a vehicle, and moving yet further from Trèves. All, however, seemed preferable to being sent back or kept stationary. A pleasing young female, with a baby and a gentle and respectful young man, were all my fellow travelers: They were Belgic, but as they concluded me to be French, they conversed together in English. This at some other time might have amused me; but I was not then amusable. I spared them, however, any indiscretion, by making known that I understood them. They looked simple, but were very courteous.

At Aix la Chapelle I lost them: for they arrived there to reside, not to travel further.

I now earnestly enquired for a conveyance to Trèves: none existed! nor could I hear of any at all, save a diligence to Juliers, which was to set out at four o'clock the next morning.

To lose thus a whole day, and even then to go only more north, instead of south, almost cast me into despair. But redress there was none! and I was forced to secure myself a place to Juliers, whence, I was told, I might get on.

At any more tranquil period I should have seized this interval

---

[38]To go further.

for visiting the famous old cathedral and the tomb of Char-
lemagne—but now, I thought not of them; I did not even recollect that Aix la Chapelle had been the capital of that emperor. I
merely saw the town through a misty, mizzling rain, and that
the road all around it was sandy and heavy—or that all was
discolored by my own disturbed view. . . .

[I left Aix on] the third day of my journey: and still, from the
time I left Liège, I was constantly but lengthening my distance
from the haven of my desires.

At about 10 miles from Aix la Chapelle some more passengers
entered the coach . . .

Of my new companions I now made earnest enquiry relative
to any route to Triers, expressing my unbounded eagerness to
pass over to it by the crossroad, if any carriage were obtainable.
An elderly, but stout and robust German, who had appeared
very ill disposed to everyone, sarcastic, severe, and sneering,
now suddenly cast off his malignancy and, as if surprised into
benevolence by my visible distress, offered to travel with and
protect and direct me himself, if I could procure a vehicle.

Transported, I accepted this offer; but when we stopped, at
someplace of which I have forgotten the name, to change horses
and take some refreshment, instead of demanding a chaise de
poste, I felt myself assailed by reflections that forced me to
relinquish my design. I knew nothing of this man; he might be
an adventurer, or something worse, who, conceiving my hand
basket, evidently heavy, to contain money or jewels, or papers
on some secret commission, might carry me what road he pleased,
to satisfy his curiosity or disburden me of my poor little trinkets.
I therefore thanked him, but I declined his offer; and I neither
spoke nor listened more till I arrived, at noon, at Juliers, on
Friday, 21st July.

We stopped at a rather large inn at the head of an immensely
long marketplace. It was nearly, at that moment, empty, except
where occupied by straggling soldiers, poor lame or infirm laborers, women and children. The universal war of the continent
left scarcely a man unmaimed to be seen, in civil life.

My fellow travelers, whoever they were, had ended their
journey and repaired to their homes; but while I was impatiently
asking for some conveyance to Trèves, a sergeant abruptly
accosted me, and desired I would forthwith accompany him to
the police office.

Perforce, I obeyed: and here I had precisely the same scene to

go through of gross authority and unfeeling harshness as that of
Liège: the same peremptory demands of who and what I was;
the same insolent contempt of my passport; the same irascible
menaces to send me back for one more recent and satisfactory.
The only difference I remember is that the Commandant here
seemed aware, by the words *laisser passer Madame d'Arblay,
née Burney,* of my Country, for he said "Vous êtes anglaise?"
Hoping to fare better than I had done as being *française,* I
readily answered "Oui, Monsieur;—Je suis du pays du brave
Wellington—"[39] but I instantly saw my mistake, by the deepened
scowl that darkened his brow and which was yet redoubled by
my saying I was going to a General Officer who was confined to
his bed merely in consequence of aiding *la cause commune.*
Pish!—he disdainfully uttered, in turning on his heel; and, en-
forcing all his arbitrary objections to letting me proceed, he was
pronouncing a positive refusal and making off from my remonstrances and petitions, when again I saved myself from so deadly
a blow by naming General Kleist and asserting his friendship for
my husband. To this he seemed afraid to be deaf, however
unwilling to listen; but my dauntless declaration that General
Kleist would be extremely hurt if my journey was impeded
forced a signature, of which I cannot read the handwriting, to
my passport. But he would forward me no further than to
Cologne, whither a carriage was going from Juliers almost immediately. I was fain to acquiesce, and returned to the inn. . . .

It was evening [when we arrived], but very light, and Cologne
had a striking appearance, from its general magnitude, and from
its profusion of steeples. . . .

I beheld the famed and venerable cathedral, but without any
means to visit or examine it, though the diligence stopped at a
part of its cloisters—stopped, or was stopped, I know not which—
but while I expected to be driven on to some *auberge,* a police
officer, in a Prussian uniform, came to the coach door and demanded
to look at our passports. My companion made herself known as a
native, and was let out directly. The officer, having cast his
eye over my passport, put his head through the window of the
carriage, and, in a low whisper, asked me whether I were French?

[39]Let pass Mme. d'Arblay, born Burney. . . . "You are English?" . . . "Yes, Sir, I am of
the country of the brave Wellington." D'Arblay hopes the Prussian will be more favorable
to an English than to a French national, and she reminds him of Wellington, the British
commander at Waterloo. She follows this up by referring to *la cause commune* (the common
cause), meaning the joint efforts of England and Prussia to defeat Napoleon.

French, by marriage, though English by birth, I hardly knew which to call myself: I said, however, "Oui."

He then, in a voice yet more subdued, gave me to understand that he could serve me. I eagerly caught at his offer, and told him I earnestly desired to go straight to Trèves, to a wounded Friend. I never, where I could escape its necessity, said *to my husband,* for the precipitance of my haste and my alarm had made me set out on my expedition in a mode so unbecoming his then high rank in actual service, that I knew he would never have consented to my scheme, though I was sure his best and tenderest feelings would gratulate its execution when it brought me the more quickly to his side—

He would do for me what he could, he answered, for he was French himself, though employed by the Prussians. He would carry my passport for me to the magistrate of the place, and get it signed without my having any further trouble; though only, he feared, to Bonn, or, at farthest, to Coblenz, whence I might probably proceed unmolested. He knew, also, and could recommend me to a most respectable lady and gentleman, both French and under the Prussian hard gripe, where I might spend the evening *en famille* and be spared entering any *auberge.*

This was delightful to me, after what I had suffered from the Prussian police officers—but, was there no imposition? no double dealing—I was disturbed—but my real and great distress seemed to interest this new voluntary friend, whose countenance, voice and manner were all accordant with pity and good will—and therefore I left the diligence and put myself into his hands.

He conducted me, in utter silence, to a house not far distant, passing through the cloisters, and very retired in its appearance. Arrived at a door, at which he knocked or rang, he still spoke not a word; but when an old man came to open it, in a shabby dress, but with a good and lively face, he gave him some directions in German, and in a whisper, and then—entrusted with my passport—he bowed to me very respectfully and hurried away.

There was something in this so singular, that I should have been extremely apprehensive of some latent mischief at any common period: but Now—I had no fear that opposed action: my fears were all occupied mentally! and my whole altered being was all courage for whatever, at any risk, could forward my journey to the sole object of my anxiety and my wishes. . . .

[D'Arblay is graciously received and put up for the night by an old French couple, impoverished refugee nobility, whose names she never learns. At 3:30 the next morning she sets out for the coach with their one old servant.]

The walk was immensely long; it was through the scraggy and hilly streets I have mentioned, and I really thought it endless. The good domestic carried my luggage. The height of the houses made the light merely not darkness; we met not a soul; and the painful pavement, and barred windows, and fear of being too late, made the walk still more dreary, lonely, and dread.

I was but just in time: the diligence was already drawn out of the inn yard, and some friends of some of the passengers were taking leave of one another. I eagerly secured my place—and never so much regretted the paucity of my purse as in my inability to recompense as I wished the excellent domestic whom I now quitted.

I found myself now in much better society than I had yet been, consisting of two gentlemen, evidently of good education, and a well-bred lady. They were all German, and spoke only that language to one another, though they occasionally addressed me in French; by occasionally, I mean as often as my own absorption in my own ruminations gave any opening for their civility.

And this was soon the case, by my hearing them speak of the Rhine; my thoughts were so little geographical that it had not occurred to me that Cologne was upon that river; I had not, therefore, looked for or perceived it the preceding evening: but upon my now starting at the sound of its name, and expressing my strong curiosity to behold it, they all began to watch for the first point upon which it became clearly visible, and all five with one voice called out, presently after, "Ah, la voilà!"[40]

I bent towards the coach window, and they all most obligingly facilitated my sight. But imagination had raised expectations that the Rhine, at this part of its stream, could by no means answer. It seemed neither so wide, nor so deep, nor so rapid, nor so grand as my mind had depicted it; nor yet were its waters so white or so bright as to suit my ideas of its fame. . . .

Arrived at Bonn, the guard or director, called, I think, le Conducteur, took all the charge of my passport, according to the

[40]"Ah, there it is!"

promise of my French-Prussian. Bonn is a fortress, and the residence of the *ci-devant*[41] Prince Bishop of Cologne. The palace is said to be a quarter of a mile in length. How modest and moderate are the palaces of England compared with those of even the minor potentates of the continent. I saw it not, however; I had not even any desire for the sight, nor for any other. We stopped at the Post Office. The house was quite magnificent. But I only entered the breakfast room, where I had the pain of hearing that we should remain at Bonn two hours. My fellow travelers, gay and social, ordered a festive repast: I was so fearful of wasting any of my small remaining cash that I only took a roll and a dish of coffee, at a table to which I stood, and then said I would while away the time by walking in the garden.

The garden was of a tolerable size and really pretty; but some company from this vast inn soon broke in upon my solitude, and I therefore stole off, resolving to take a view of the town—

I went out by a large iron gate, but could not venture to ask for a guide, in a poverty where every shilling became important. The street was entirely without mark or interest, and nearly without any inhabitants that were visible. The late absorbing war made that the case in every town I passed through. I walked straight on, till I came to a large marketplace. It seemed to me, after the narrow and dim and empty street, very gay, busy, populous and alive. I think it was a sort of fair. As I saw numerous avenues to it, I stopped at the corner to fix myself some mark for finding again my way back. And this was not difficult, for I soon observed an "unhappy divinity stuck in a niche"; and one as ludicrous as any mentioned in her passage through Germany by Lady Mary Wortley Montagu.[42] It was a short, thick, squabby little personage, whose wig, hose, sandals, coat, waistcoat, and trousers were of all the colors— save those of the rainbow—for, far from having the bright hues of that "radiant token," the gaudy, but most dingy, muddy and vulgar full blues, reds, and yellows of each part of the dress, and of the figure, seemed struggling with each other for which should be most obtrusively prominent—not graduating off into shades of evanescent softness. The wig, I think, was blue; the coat, red; the waistcoat, yellow; the sandals, green; the trousers, purple;

---

[41]Former, before his title was abolished under the French Revolutionary government.
[42]In her travel letters, Montagu had made fun of the gaudy statues she saw in Catholic Germany.

and the hose, pink. I am not certain, at this distance of time, that I give the right colors to their right places; I am only sure that the separate parts of the dress employed, separately, those colors, and that what rendered them almost as profane as they were risible, were some symbols—either of golden rays round the wig, or of a crucifix at the back, showed that this hideous little statue was meant for a young Jesus.[43]

I now strolled about the vast marketplace without fear of being lost. I observed, however, little besides cattle, toys, vegetables, crockery ware and cakes. There were forms innumerable, and almost all covered by seated women, very clean and tidy, with profusion of odd shaped white caps, but not one of them with a hat. At other parts, there might perhaps be other merchandise. The whole was eminently orderly. Nothing like a quarrel, a dispute, or even any grouping for gossiping. This is not, I imagine, a general picture of a German marketplace; for [nothing] now could be general, as nothing was natural. The issue of the war, still to all uncertain, while the army on the Loire, and the corps of Grouchy had not submitted, appeared to all the common inhabitants in the vicinity of France to await but some private project of Buonaparte for ending in his triumph. In all the few places I visited at this period I found this belief predominant, or, rather, universal; and that alike from the fears of his foes and the hopes of his adherents. Constraint, therefore, as well as consternation operated, as if by mute consent, in keeping all things, and all persons, tame, taciturn, and secretly expectant.

When I had taken a general survey of all that was within sight without venturing from the sides of the houses amongst the people, I looked for my guide in the niche and returned to the inn. There I heard that, from some cause I could not comprehend, the diligence was still to remain two hours longer. Unable to order any refreshment, I could not bring myself to enter any room for waiting so long a time. Again, therefore, I strolled out; and, having now seen all that led to the right, I turned to the left. I walked to the end of the street without finding anything to observe but common houses, without novelty, interest, or national peculiarity of any sort and differing only from ours by having fewer windows, less regularity, and less cheerfulness of

---

[43]Actually, it was not the infant Jesus, but "a crude allegorical representation of the rainbow" (as noted in the Clarendon edition of *Journals and Letters of Fanny Burney*).

aspect. In strolling leisurely back, I remarked, at the termination of a sort of lane, or outlet, something that looked like ruins. I eagerly advanced towards them and found myself on the skirts of a plain overlaid with the devastations of half consumed and still crumbling fortifications. I mounted some old broken steps, protuberating here and there through masses of dust, mortar, and heaped old half-burnt bricks; but the view that presented itself was only terrible, from showing the havoc of war, without including any remains that were noble, elegant, or curious in architecture, or that mixed any emotions of admiration with those of compassion that necessarily are awakened by the sight of dilapidations, whether owing to the hostility of time or of war.

When I had remained here till I was tired of my own meditations rather than investigation, for there was nothing to investigate, I descended my steps, to return to the inn. But I then perceived two narrow streets or lanes, so exactly resembling each other that I could not discern any difference that might lead me to ascertain by which I had arrived: and I had turned in so many directions while surveying the ruins, that, not having noticed a second street before I mounted them, I now knew not which way to turn.

Startled, I resolved to hasten down one of them at a venture, and then, if that should fail, to try the other.

This I did, and found myself in a long street that might well be that which I sought, but I could espy in it no jutting iron gate: I therefore hurried back, and made the same experiment down the other lane. This, however, led me on to some other street that I was sure I had not seen.

With yet greater speed I regained my ruins: but here a new difficulty arose. I saw a third straight passage, which had no more mark or likelihood than the two first. It might be, nevertheless, that this which had escaped me, was the right; and I essayed it directly. The same failure ensued, and I remounted it.

Vainly I looked around me for help—Dirty and ragged little children, of the lowest class, were playing about and chattering in German, but, though I attempted to speak to them repeatedly, they could not understand a word I uttered and ran, some laughing, others frightened, away.

Yet these poor little ones were all I met with in these lanes, which, as they lead only to a barren plain overrun with ruins, were unfrequented.

I was now dreadfully alarmed, lest I should miss the diligence: and I speeded again to the long street in search of anyone who could give me some succor.

I espied a good looking man, who was lame, at some distance.
I was with him in an instant and entreated him to direct me to
the Hotel de la Diligence.

He seemed good-naturedly sorry for the great perturbation in
which I spoke, but shook his head, and shrugged his shoulders,
in sign that he could not understand me.

I then saw a poor woman—and made the same request; but
with equal ill success.

Next I saw a boy—the same story!—Then a beggar—still the
same!

From side to side, straightforward and retrograding, I ran up
to every soul I saw—speaking first in French, next in English,
but meeting only with the lowest and most common Germans, who,
like all other common natives, know only their vernacular tongue.

I could now only resolve to return to my ruins, and in making
them my rallying point, to start from them, and back again, till I
had perambulated every street whatsoever that was in their
neighborhood.

But oh good Heaven! what now was my consternation! I had
started up and down in so desultory and precipitate a manner
that I could no longer find my way back to the ruins! I had
wandered, I have no knowledge how, from their immediate
vicinity, and could not discover any one of the three avenues by
which I had reached them. Turn which way I would, I met no
possible informant; all the men were in the various armies; the
higher sort of women were fled from Bonn, or remained in their
houses; and the lower sort were all, with the whole of the
general population, in the marketplace. At least so it was in the
streets I patrolled, for nothing did I behold but the maimed, or
beggars, or children. Most of those above probably would have
known a few words of French. And some of these poor souls,
when I addressed them, seemed very kindly concerned at my
evident distress; yet with a calm, a composure that was wide
from even striving to devise means for understanding or aiding
me: and their enquiries, in their own dialect, were so insupport-
ably slow and placid that the moment I found my French not
intelligible to them, I flew from their speech as I would have fled
from pestilence.

If I should be too late for the diligence, I too well knew not
another would pass for a week: and even if I could here meet
with a separate conveyance, the tales now hourly recounted of
marauders, straggling pillagers, and military banditti, with the

immense forests and unknown roads through which I must pass, made me tremble—as I now do, even now, nine years after—at looking back to my position at this fearful moment.

Oh! this was, indeed, nearly, the most tortured crisis of misery I ever experienced! one only has been yet more terrible! —nay, a thousand and ten thousand—ten million of times more terrible, because—alas! irretrievable![44] This, however, was a herald to my affrighted soul of what the other inflicted—To know my Heart's Partner wounded—ill—confined—attended only by strangers—to know, also, that if here detained, I could receive no news of him; for the diligence in which I traveled was the mail:—to know the dread anxiety, and astonishment that would consume his peace, and corrode all means of recovery, when day succeeding day neither brought me to his side, nor yet produced any tidings why I was absent—Oh gracious Heaven! in what a distracting state was my soul!—In a strange country— without money, without a servant—without a friend—and without language! Oh never—never shall I forget my almost frantic agony! Neither can I ever lose the remembrance of the sudden transport by which it was succeeded when, in pacing wildly to and fro, I was suddenly struck by the sight I have already described of the unhappy divinity stuck in a niche.

What rapture at that moment took place of anguish little short of despair—I now knew my way, and was at the hotel with a swiftness resembling flight. And there—what a confirmation I received of the timely blessing of my arrival, when I saw that the coach was just departing! The horses harnessed, every passenger entered, and the drivers with their whips in hand extended!—Oh my God! what an escape! and what thankful joy and gratitude I experienced!

Now then, at last, my heart became better tuned. A terror so dreadful averted, just when so near its consummation, opened me to feelings akin to happiness. I was now on my right road; no longer traveling zig zag and as I could procure any means to get on, but in the straight road, by Coblenz, to the city which contained the object of all my best hopes—solicitude—and impatience.

And now it was that my eyes opened to the beauties of Nature; now it was that the far famed Rhine found justice in these poor little eyes, which, hitherto, from mental preoccupation or from expectations too high raised, had refused a cordial

---

[44]The death of her husband.

tribute to its eminent merit; unless, indeed, its banks, till after
Bonn, are of inferior loveliness. Certain it is, that from this time
till my arrival at Coblenz, I thought myself in regions of
enchantment.

The Rhine from hence flows so continually through lofty mountains, and winds in such endless varieties, that it frequently
appears to be terminating in a lake; and those who sail upon it
must often believe themselves inevitably destined to land, as the
turnings are so rounded that no prolongation of the river is
apparent. And scarcely is there a reach that does not exhibit
some freshly charming view. Mountains, towers, castles, fortifications half demolished; interspersed with trees, hills, valleys,
plains, elevations covered with vineyards, thick woods of lime trees,
country seats, new plantations, and picturesque villages. The
houses were highly ornamental to the prospect, being mostly white,
covered with blue slate; looking brilliant, however diminutive,
because saved from all soil by the purity of the surrounding
air. . . .

[After two more days of excruciating delays—wakening the German authorities in Coblenz to persuade them to sign her passport, stopping for hours at grubby village inns—d'Arblay arrived
at Trèves on the evening of July 24. She sent for her husband's
valet, who assured her the danger was over.]

He was safe, I thanked God!—but danger, positive danger had
existed! Faint I felt, though in a tumult of grateful sensations; I
took his arm, for my tottering feet would hardly support me, and
made him a motion—for I was speechless—to lead me on. . . .

I recovered myself as we proceeded, and then demanded all
sort of details. François had delivered my note to his master—
who instantly divined that I was already arrived—Ah! could he
think me so little like himself as to know him ill, and suffer any
obstacle, that was surmountable, to keep me from him—Ah! how
different had then been our union from that which for so many
years made me the happiest of wives—and of women!— . . .

Oh Alexander! What a meeting of exquisite felicity!—to BOTH—

Yet, when he heard how I had traveled—with what risks, and
through what difficulties—which I poured forth to him in a
torrent of delighted exultation that I had conquered them—he
almost fainted!—though he learned them from myself, and saw
me not only in safety, but in gaiety of spirits unbounded!

Mary Hays
1760–1843

OVER a lifetime of writing, from her *Letters and Essays, Moral and Miscellaneous* (1793) to her *Memoirs of Queens* (1821), Mary Hays argued for women's rights and celebrated their achievements. Like her friend Mary Wollstonecraft, she was an ardent feminist whose assertion of the rights of women was reinforced by the ideals of the French Revolution. Hays was less theoretically acute than Wollstonecraft: though she attacked the abuses of sexual stereotyping, she failed to see what Wollstonecraft saw: that the sexual double standard had to be demolished. But her work complements Wollstonecraft's by filling in the homely domestic detail she overlooked; Hays shows us why sweet dependency cannot safeguard women's rights and how marriages might be made to work better. Her tone is neighborly, as if she hopes that men will have the sense and goodwill to agree with her once she makes the issues clear to them; she appeals to the men rather than vindicating the rights of women.

Hays, born to a family of middle-class Protestant Dissenters, was devoted to her exemplary father. Her sentimental romance with John Eccles terminated with his early death, and she never married, although she subsequently fell in love with a man who did not reciprocate her affection. This unhappy involvement provided the basis for her novel *Memoirs of Emma Courtney* (1796), in which she defended a woman's right to pursue the man she loves. Meanwhile, she had come to know many prominent liberal Dissenters and joined the intellectual circle of the radical publisher Joseph Johnson, which included Wollstonecraft, William Godwin, Tom Paine, and Anna Laetitia Barbauld. As the political climate turned reactionary, she was publicly attacked (most amusingly as Bridgetina Botherim in Elizabeth Hamilton's *Memoirs of Modern Philosophers*, 1800–1801); and she published *An Appeal to the Men of Great Britain in Behalf of Women* (1798) anonymously. Her large biographical dictionary, *Female Biography; or Memoirs of Illustrious and Celebrated Women of All Ages and Countries* (1803) kept her reputation alive in the nineteenth century.

from Letters IV and VI of Letters and Essays

I confess I am no advocate for cramping the minds and bodies of young girls, by keeping them forever poring over needlework (and when I see the tapestry and tent stitch of former times, I sigh at the waste of eyes, spirits, and time); nor do I think it so very important a part of female education as has generally been supposed. In well-regulated famililes, where nothing is left till tomorrow which can be done today, where every department is conducted with order and economy, where the business of the day is planned in the morning, and one thing concluded before another is begun; where the day is lengthened by early hours and short temperate meals, "eating to live, and not living only to eat," I am well assured there cannot be any occasion for this laborious and sempstress-like application: surely the covering of the body ought not to be the sole business of life. I doubt whether there will be any sewing in the next world, how then will those employ themselves who have done nothing else in this?

Sempronia had a large family of daughters, whom she early trained with unrelenting rigor to the duties of nonresistance and passive obedience. All attention to literature, she considered as mere waste of time, and valued herself upon being unacquainted with any other book than the Bible. The sole accomplishments which this notable lady deemed necessary to constitute a good wife and mother, were to scold and half starve her servants, to oblige her children to say their prayers and go stately to church, and to make clothes and household furniture[1] from morning till night; while to supply them with constant employment of this nature, more money was expended, and materials wasted, than would have paid for having the work done from home, and have purchased a handsome collection of books beside. The unfortunate girls submitted to this severe discipline from hard necessity, but not without murmuring; till at length, from close confinement, and the dull uniformity of one tedious pursuit, the bloom faded from their cheeks and the luster from their eyes, their tempers lost their sprightliness and their health

[1]Ornamental hangings, bed covers, etc.

its vigor. Their mother, who really loved them, and who thought that while she was blighting the tender blossom in its spring, she was performing the duties of a prudent and good parent, was alarmed at the change she perceived; and after vainly trying the efficacy of various quack medicines recommended as infallible restoratives, accompanied the young ladies to one of the fashionable watering places, in the hope of their receiving benefit from the salubrious effects of the sea air.

During their residence at Brighthelmstone, the languid charms of the elder daughter attracted the notice of the son of a wealthy citizen, who having received a liberal, though mercantile education, had been accustomed to amuse himself in the intervals of commercial business, with the study of the Belles-Lettres. His imagination had acquired by these pursuits a tincture of what is commonly called romance by the generality of the trading part of mankind; he had been disgusted with the venal daughters of fashion, and the really sweet, though fading countenance of our young lady (whom I shall call Serena), the bashfulness of her manners, and the meekness of her deportment, awakened his tenderness and flattered his vanity. The vulgar and confined notions of the mother he dignified with the name of simplicity; and as his Serena seldom ventured to converse freely in his presence, her silence he construed into the effect of a delicate timidity. He could not but perceive that her mind had been greatly neglected, but he consoled himself with the hope of giving it improvement and polish, and exclaimed with Rousseau, "Lovely ignorance! Happy will he be who is destined to instruct her."[2] Full of these ideas, he hastened their union, that he might remove his charming mistress out of a family where he conceived she was degraded, and transplant her into—

A richer soil, where vernal suns and showers,
Diffuse their warmest, largest influence.

Serena, by sea-bathing, recreation, and the attentions of her lover, which gave her thoughts a new turn, in some measure recovered her health and beauty, and in a few weeks became the wife of Melville, who now believed himself at the summit of

[2]From *Emile* (1762) by Jean-Jacques Rousseau, who argued that woman was created to please man and should accordingly be trained to make herself agreeable to him. The passage is quoted derisively by Mary Wollstonecraft in her *Vindication of the Rights of Woman* (1792), chapter 3.

human felicity. After the first congratulations and compliments were over, he conducted his bride to a pleasant villa, situated on the banks of the Thames, a few miles from the metropolis, intending before he introduced her to his connections (many of whom were among the polite and the literary) to devote his leisure hours to the cultivation and enlargement of her understanding.

For this purpose he furnished a commodious library with an elegant assortment of books, and when after the business of the day he returned from town, he would endeavor to entertain his Serena by reading select passages from the best English authors, particularly the works of the poets and moral essayists. But to his great mortification, when after repeating with enthusiasm some of the finest passages in Shakespeare, he glanced his eyes on his lady to perceive the effect it produced; the settled vacuity of her features announced the blank within. She seemed to listen and faintly smiled, but it was the forced smile of lassitude; she had no associations that could make her feel any interest in the glowing pictures of genius, and would interrupt the soul-harrowing scene between Hamlet and his guilty mother, to observe upon a phaeton that passed the window or return the caress of a favorite lap-dog. Poor Melville shuddered! the visionary scene of bliss began to fade from his imagination, he threw down his book, and to hide his chagrin, proposed to his wife a walk, as she had yet seen but little of the adjacent country. She readily agreed to accompany him, happy to be relieved from the irksome task, of giving a feigned attention to what she could not comprehend. Melville endeavored to direct her view as they passed to every sublime and beautiful feature in nature, the wood and the water, the hill and the valley, the wild health and the cultivated garden . . . But alas! the varied "shows and forms"[3] of nature were lost on the sterile fancy that had never received—"fair culture's kind enlivening aid." She entreated that they might return to the high road, for she was sure the path they had taken must be equally unsafe as dull and difficult, and she was every moment in terror, lest a robber should start out of the thicket. Her disgusted companion sighed as he silently acceded to her proposal, and began unwillingly to be convinced that true beauty must depend upon moral sentiment and that the mere varnish of a fair complexion could make no amends for a weak and empty mind.

[3]Hays supplied a note citing Robert Burns's poems. See "To William Simpson": "O Nature! a' thy shews an' forms / To feeling, pensive hearts hae charms!"

Vain was every subsequent attempt to give fire to this breathing clay, early habits had rendered the mental organs callous; the pretty insipid Serena would smile when he smiled, and weep when he frowned, but her tenderness flattered not; for there was no distinction in it. She had no will of her own (for the little energy she inherited from nature had been quenched by the despotic discipline of the good lady her mother) and Melville, wearied by the uniformity of her compliances, which gratified neither his judgment nor his heart, vainly exhorted her sometimes to have a taste of her own; for he would even have preferred opposition to the dead calm in which their days languished, and he dreaded to enliven them by society; for the gross inaccuracies and frivolity of his lady's conversation exposed him to the ridicule of his acquaintance and covered him with confusion.

Nor did the domestic management of his affairs afford him any consolation. His wife sought amusement in the company of her servants, she preserved no dignity of character, and acted not upon any plan; consequently her authority was despised, nothing was conducted with regularity, and while she sat whole days in loose dishabille to supernumerary needlework, which turned to little account, her house was filled with litter and disorder, her children ran wild, and her domestics quarreled among themselves and defrauded their master, as amid frequent changes, the certain consequence of mismanagement, it could not be expected that they would all be honest.

The unfortunate Melville, whose mind was formed for elegant and domestic tenderness, execrated his fate in the bitterness of his soul and desperately sought to forget his disappointment in scenes of dissipation and extravagance, and in a few years his expenses abroad and the want of order and economy at home involved them in the miseries of insolvency.

• • •

Martha, the second daughter, married a Mr. C., a reputable tradesman, who making no pretensions to refinement himself, was not disgusted with the narrow views and vulgar dialect of his lady; who, with a mind as uninformed as Serena's, was far from possessing the same gentle and placid disposition. On the contrary, her naturally strong passions and volatile temper seemed to have acquired additional force from the painful constraint she had been obliged reluctantly to submit to under the arbitrary jurisdiction of her mother. She married to gain her liberty, without feeling any particular tenderness or esteem for the man to whom she gave her hand. Coercive measures may have a restraining effect for a time, but can never subdue an untractable spirit: it is only by engaging the affections and enlarging the understanding, that the heart can be meliorated or principles be formed; for like a bow forcibly bent, the mind recoils from oppression with elastic power. The husband of Martha, a man of probity and plain common sense, wished to find in a wife a cheerful companion and an economical manager of his domestic affairs. Martha's lively manner and strict education afforded him the most flattering expectations, that he had made a suitable choice.

He gave way to her plan of dissipation for the first month after their marriage, without remonstrance, as he imagined that after the display of her bridal ornaments and the round of congratulatory visits usual on such occasions, that she would assume a matron-like behavior and engage in the employments of domestic life; but, to his great mortification, he soon began to find that he had deceived himself: one scheme of amusement prepared the way for another; the circle of their acquaintance became every day more extensive; and while he was engaged in his warehouse and counting house, Mrs. C. was all over the town, in the park, at the theaters, at card-parties, and assemblies; and returned at all hours fatigued and exhausted in the pursuit of those pleasures, which from their novelty and former prohibition were sought by her with additional ardor and spirit. In vain Mr. C. entreated, expostulated, and even threatened; when she could no longer prevail on him by artful flattery and caresses, she awed him into silence by the violence of her temper; he was fond of peace, and too frequently purchased it at an expensive rate.

Mrs. C. became a mother, and her husband now hoped the cares of her nursery would engage her attention, and have a more powerful influence over her mind than all his hitherto ineffectual remonstrances. For a few weeks, his hopes seemed realized; but Martha had none of that refinement which, by associating a thousand tender circumstances, gives additional poignancy to natural affections and binds them more closely to the heart. She soon became tired of performing the duties of a nurse to her offspring: when a girl, she had imagined herself fond of children, because she had considered them as a sort of live dolls and they supplied the place of baby-house amusements, which she had just been persuaded to resign. But the attention they now required appeared a very different affair; to sacrifice her rest by night, and her liberty in the day, to watch over them in sickness, and perform the numberless tender and delicate attentions necessary to their fragile age—was an insupportable fatigue, of which she fancied herself incapable; she persuaded Mr. C. that the delicacy of her constitution incapacitated her for performing the duty of a mother, and prevailed on him to suffer her to resign the child to the care of a hireling, where it soon after perished by the smallpox, which raged in the neighborhood, and which it caught in the natural way: for Mrs. C. had an invincible prejudice against inoculation, and all her prejudices were passions; for taking up her opinions without examination, she prided herself upon ever obstinately adhering to them.

Martha's manner of life began to affect the income of her husband; for she had contracted several debts, which he had been obliged to discharge. He now earnestly wished for a separation, for his wife was incapable of attending to reason and was seldom at home, but in the intervals of lassitude. Her temper, naturally acrimonious, was still more embittered by his sharp and repeated expostulations. They met only to quarrel, and parted with mutual contempt and aversion; till he at last came to a determination to give up trade, to collect his effects, and retire into a distant country, and should his wife refuse to accompany him, to allow her a stipulated separate maintenance, and to insist on her returning to reside with her mother. This proposal she absolutely rejected, and after much unavailing recrimination, agreed to accompany him into the country. He took care to reside in a remote house, in a village situated as far as possible from any market-town; when Martha, in despair at being torn from London and its amusements, took an unhappy resolution of drowning reflection by constant inebriation, which, in a short time, brought on a complication of disorders that terminated her useless and wretched existence—and relieved her husband from a ruinous and worthless companion.

The younger daughters, Ann and Charlotte, possessing fewer personal attractions than their elder sisters, remained unmarried. Ann, naturally of a gloomy and timid disposition, rendered still more splenetic by an infirm constitution, accidentally hearing a charity-sermon preached at their parish church by a popular Methodist teacher, was struck by the vehemence of his manner and alarmed by the severity of his doctrines. Her religious ideas (if ideas they could be called) had been taken upon trust, without ever once suspecting that religion is a personal concern, in which, as every individual would be accountable only for himself, neither the state or our forefathers could have any possible right of interference: she had no notion that belief must be founded upon evidence and consisted in a real assent to a clear proposition; and being no mathematician, took for granted that the dogmatist who erected his own judgment into an infallible tribunal, must be divinely inspired and could be liable to no mistake. Her pride was flattered by the fancy of spiritual superiority, and her spleen gratified by drawing a narrow circle and saying "Surely we are the people, and wisdom shall die with us."[4] The fact is, bigotry is ever the child of ignorance, and the cultivation of the understanding is the only radical cure for it. . . .

Ann, now become a proselyte to the rigid supralapsarian system, grew every day more narrow and morose; the most innocent cheerfulness she considered as unpardonable levity, her days were consumed in attending lectures and sermons, and her rest broken at night by superstitious terrors. Her former acquaintance she regarded with horror, as in a state of reprobation; or, if she vouchsafed to enter into conversation with them, representing the Deity after her own gloomy conceptions, she falsely described the paths of piety as strewed with thorns and briars, so that despairing of ideal perfection, they were ready to give up all virtue as unattainable. Incapable of generalizing ideas and comparing Scripture with itself, she understood nothing of the gentle spirit of the gospel, which teaches that without charity, all other sanctimonious pretensions are as a "sounding brass, and a tinkling cymbal."[5] The repeated precepts of love and confidence in God, kindness to our neighbor, purity, and benevolence of heart, were not sufficiently sublime and mystical to engage the notice of our devotee: particular figurative expressions, clothed in the symbolical language of the early periods of the world, engrossed her whole attention. She overlooked the description of the day of final retribution, represented with majestic simplicity by the Savior of the world: "I was hungry, and ye fed me; sick, and in prison, and ye visited me, etc."[6] And

[4]Adapted from Job 12:2
[5]I Corinthians 13:1
[6]Quoted, not quite accurately, from Matthew 25:35–36.

supposed that salvation would be the reward, not of right conduct, but of sound opinions.

These associations continually dwelt on, at length, from the constant pressure of the same ideas, had a physical effect on the brain, and produced that state of nervous irritability—that tends to hypochondriac melancholy; a shattered constitution became yet more impaired; and this unhappy victim to gross ignorance and abject superstition became a prey to that dreadful train of nervous affections, which admit of no cure, and by which the vital powers are consumed in cruel agitation and insupportable terrors.

Charlotte, the younger daughter, though not possessed of that superior genius, which notwithstanding all local disadvantages will educate itself, was not devoid either of capacity or tastes; but being kept from books and confined to the society of narrow minded and illiterate people, she made but little improvement. . . . Precluded from mental pursuits, her ingenuity could display itself only in drawing the pattern and shading the colors for a carpet or a fire screen, and her taste in fancying the ornaments to decorate her person. In such or similar occupations, she spent her early youth in innocence, and tolerable tranquility, and amused herself by forming many little plans (should she ever change her situation) for the disposition of the nuptial finery, the furnishing of her house, and the style of her equipage. In these dreams her youth passed away; every rising beauty became her rival; and every charm, as it faded, gave a pang to her heart, which was alternately harrowed by jealousy, by envy, by disappointed hope, and unavailing regret.

Fond of distinction, she knew not how to resign with a grace those obsequious attentions, so flattering, and too often so pernicious to the young female mind. She had no acquirements to substitute in the place of the allurements of youth and sprightliness, and she found herself, by degrees, neglected, and alone in a crowd. She had many acquaintances, but no friends; for intellect and virtue alone capacitate for friendship. By virtue, I do not mean the mere absence of gross vice: virtue is active—"It is sense, and spirit with humanity," and must be the result of reflection, and fixed principle. The weak and the ignorant can never be properly termed virtuous; they may have a happy temperament ("But mere good-nature is a fool"), and if they chance to fall into good hands, may be preserved from any glaring misconduct and pass decently through life; but like the chamelion, the color of their minds must depend entirely on the surrounding circumstances; and even in the most favorable situations, "the spaniel fool (as is observed by one of the periodical writers) will frequently turn mule fool." Every evil, both physical and moral, may be ultimately traced up to limited faculties and the want of knowledge.

Charlotte found no resource in the company of her sister, who entered not into the social spirit of Christianity, but passed her time in a monastic seclusion from the world. This unfortunate woman, who knew not how to throw a luster over her declining years by the dignity which intellectual attainments bestow, vainly endeavored to conceal the ravages of time by affecting the gaiety of youth; the very attempt, as it bespoke the vacant mind, pointed the "bitter scorn of grinning ridicule." Without resources in herself, solitude she found intolerable, and sought a relief from the weariness of *ennui* in visiting from house to house, in watching the conduct of her neighbors, and circulating the anecdotes she collected in her rambles; and, though this was done without malice, merely to enliven the insipidity of a commerce where neither the heart, nor the understanding had any share, it involved her in many inconvenient and disagreeable circumstances. At the card table, she tried to beguile the tedious hours by the vivid emotions, which gaming seldom fails to excite; but unskilled in the science, her temper became soured, and her fortune injured; till, at length, mere weariness for want of a sufficiently interesting pursuit and disgust with life, brought on a languor that terminated in a jaundice and slow fever and delivered her from the dreadful vacuity of having nothing to do, to hope, or to fear. The excellent Dr. Priestley,[7] in his treatise on education, justly says that "The mind suffers more in a state of suspense and uncertainty, how to get the time over, than in almost any exertion whatever"; and that this "is perhaps more frequently the cause of suicide, from life becoming absolutely insupportable, than all the other causes of it put together."

[7]Joseph Priestley, a distinguished Unitarian theologian, educator, and scientist, published several books on education between 1765 and 1778, as well as many other works.

from An Appeal to the Men of Great Britain

"Implicit faith, all hail! Imperial Man
Exacts submission."

[Ann] Yearsley

Of all the systems—if indeed a bundle of contradictions and absurdities may be called a system—which human nature in its moments of intoxication has produced, that which men have contrived with a view to forming the minds and regulating the conduct of women, is perhaps the most completely absurd. And, though the consequences are often very serious to both sexes, yet if one could for a moment forget these, and consider it only as a system, it would rather be found a subject of mirth and ridicule than serious anger.

What a chaos!—What a mixture of strength and weakness—of greatness and littleness—of sense and folly—of exquisite feeling and total insensibility—have they jumbled together in their imaginations—and then given to their pretty darling the name of woman! How unlike the father of gods and men, the gay, the gallant Jupiter, who on producing wisdom the fruit of his brains, presented it to admiring worlds under the character of a female!

But in the composition of Man's woman, wisdom must not be spoken of, nay nor even hinted at, yet strange to tell! there it must be in full force, and come forth upon all convenient occasions. This is a mystery which, as we are not allowed to be amongst the initiated, we may admire at an awful distance, but can never comprehend.

Again, how great in some parts of their conduct, and how insignificant upon the whole, would men have women to be! For one example—when their love, their pride, their delicacy; in short, when all the finest feelings of humanity are insulted and put to the rack, what is the line of conduct then expected from them?

I need not explain that the situation I here allude to is—when a woman finds that the husband of her choice, the object of her most sincere and constant love, abandons himself to other attachments; and not only this, but when—the natural consequences of these—estrangement of affection and estrangement of confidence follow, which are infinitely cutting to a woman of sensibility and soul; what I say is the line of conduct then expected from a creature declared to be—weak by nature, and who is rendered still weaker by education?

Now here is one of those absurdities of which I accuse men in their system of contradictions. They expect that this poor weak creature, setting aside in a moment love, jealousy, and pride, the most powerful and universal passions interwoven in the human heart, and which even men, clothed in wisdom and fortitude, find so difficult to conquer that they seldom attempt it—that she shall notwithstanding lay all these aside as easily as she would her gown and petticoat, and plunge at once into the cold bath of prudence, of which though the wife only is to receive the shock and make daily use of, yet if she does so, it has the virtue of keeping both husband and wife in a most agreeable temperament. Prudence being one of those rare medicines which affect by sympathy, and this being likewise one of those cases, where the husbands have no objections to the wives acting as principals, nor to their receiving all the honors and emoluments of office; even if death should crown their martyrdom, as has been sometimes known to happen. . . .

There are no vices to which a man addicts himself, no follies he can take it into his head to commit, but his wife and his nearest female relations are expected to connive at, are expected to look upon, if not with admiration, at least with respectful silence and at awful distance. Any other conduct is looked upon as a breach of that fanciful system of arbitrary authority, which men have so assiduously erected in their own favor; and any other conduct is accordingly resisted with the most acrimonious severity.

A man, for example, is addicted to the destructive vice of drinking. His wife sees with terror and anguish the approach of this pernicious habit, and by anticipation beholds the evils to be dreaded to his individual health, happiness, and consequence; and the probable misery to his family. Yet with this melancholy prospect before her eyes, it is reckoned an unpardonable degree of harshness and imprudence if she by any means whatever endeavor to check in the bud, this baleful practice; and she is in this case accused at all hands of driving him to pursue in worse places that which he cannot enjoy in peace at home. And, when this disease gains ground and ends in an established habit, she is treated as a fool for attempting a cure for what is incurable.

Thus there is no stage of this disorder, or any other to which man is morally liable, when it is accounted necessary or proper for women to interfere; or if they do so, men suppose themselves fully justified to plunge deeper and deeper into those vices which create most misery to their wives, in order to punish their presumption. And thus it is that the designs of Providence seem to be counteracted by the pride and obstinacy of man. For, the design of Providence seems evidently to be—that the sexes should restrain, discourage, and prevent vice in each other; as much as they should encourage, promote, and reward virtue.

Again, women are often connected with men whose shameful extravagance leave little for their families to hope for but poverty and the consequent neglect of a hard-hearted world. In this case perhaps, in the little sphere in which she is permitted to move, a wife may likewise be permitted to economize; but the fruits of her economy are still at the mercy of an imperious master, who thinks himself entitled to spend upon his unlawful pleasures what might have procured her innocent enjoyment and rational delight. And, I am sorry to add, that the men in general are but too apt in these cases, as well as upon most other occasions, to take the part of their own sex; and to consider nothing as blameable in them to such a degree as to justify opposition from the women connected with them. . . .

The highest pitch of virtue to which a woman can possibly aspire on the present system of things, is to please her husband, in whatever line of conduct pleasing him consists. And to this great end, this one thing needful, men are impolitic enough to advance, and to expect, that everything else should be sacrificed. Reason, religion—or at least many of the most important maxims of religion—private judgment, prejudices; all these, and much more than these must be swallowed up in the gulf of authority; which requiring everything as a right, disdains to return anything but as a concession.

I wish not however to be misunderstood, if even but for a moment; for though this is not the place to enlarge upon the subject, it must be acknowledged, that to please a reasonable and worthy husband—let me repeat my own words—in whatever pleasing him consists, is one of the most heartfelt and purest pleasures which a woman such as she ought to be, can possibly enjoy. But for women to be obliged to humor the follies, the caprice, the vices of men of a very different stamp, and to be obliged to consider this as their duty, is perhaps as unfortunate a system of politics in morals, as ever was introduced for degrading the human species.

I could here enumerate numberless instances of WHAT MEN WOULD HAVE WOMEN TO BE, under circumstances the most trying and the most humiliating; but as I neither wish to tire out the reader nor myself with what may be well imagined without repetition, I shall only say that, though they are allowed, and even expected, to assume upon proper occasions, and when it happens to indulge the passions or fall in with the humors of men, all that firmness of character and greatness of mind commonly esteemed masculine; yet this is in so direct opposition and so totally inconsistent with that universal weakness which men first endeavor to affix upon women for their own convenience, and then for their own defense affect to admire; that really it requires more than female imbecility and credulity to suppose that such extremes can unite with any degree of harmony in such imperfect beings as we all of us, men and women, must acknowledge ourselves to be. And therefore, except a woman has some schemes of her own to accomplish by this sort of management—which necessity is most galling to an ingenuous mind; or except she is herself a mere nothing—in which case her merit is next to nothing; these violent extremes—these violent exertions of the mind—are by no means natural or voluntary ones; but are on the contrary at variance with nature, with reason, and with common sense. . . .

Notwithstanding this declaration of their own superiority however, it is a compliment which men are by no means backward in paying to women, that they are better formed by nature than themselves for the perfection of virtue; and especially of those virtues which are of most difficult attainment, and which occur most commonly in life. Perhaps this may be true; but if so, it is granting all and more than I wish; for the moment that this is admitted, you either degrade virtue and all good morals, by supposing them capable of being best perfected by, and best suited for, beings of an inferior order—upon which terms no order of rational beings can be supposed very anxious about the attainment of them—Or, leaving these, I mean virtue and good morals, in their proper places, and supposing them inherent in the soul of man, because planted there by the hand of God; and yet still insisting on the necessary and propriety of women practicing them in a stricter degree than men, you from that moment, I say, tacitly grant to women that superiority of mind, which you have not generosity enough openly to avow.

But we relinquish willingly this kind of preference which you force upon us, and which we have no title to; and which indeed is an intolerable burden in the way you contrive to administer it; and instead of this, we only entreat of you to be fair, to be candid, and to admit that both sexes are upon a footing of equality when they are permitted to exert in their different spheres of action, the talents their Creator has been pleased to bestow upon them.

Do not therefore endeavor to degrade women on the one hand, and in every material point in life, and then suppose you make it up to them, by a few idle ceremonies and unmeaning words. . . .

Is it wonderful, since women cannot be in reality what men would have them to be, though they must often endeavor to appear so; since they dare not be what they really ought to be, because it clashes with the pretensions and prejudices of the stronger party; since they are compelled upon the one hand and restrained upon the other—is it wonderful I say if they pursue a trifling, a dissipated, and often a hypocritical and vicious conduct? Or in other words, is it wonderful if they are what they are? I believe I may readily answer the question. It is not wonderful. It is perfectly in the course of nature. It is an effect, resulting of necessity from a cause.

The seeds of pride and vanity are originally planted in the breast of every human being, man and woman; for in fact they differ but little. Or shall we say the seeds of ambition; for the same things are often called by different names; and men are ashamed of even acknowledging under one, that which they boast of under another. By whatever name we choose, however, to distinguish the passion to which we allude, it is a certain tendency, a certain inexplicable impulse in the mind to rise, which prompts us to excel by some means or other. The seeds of this, like those of all the other passions, are planted by a wise and unerring hand; and reason and experience prove to us that according to the management of these, the consequences are. They are evidently calculated to produce pleasure and utility on the whole, when kept within due bounds and directed to proper objects; but if these rules are neglected, they as evidently tend to destruction. Now this passion to distinguish themselves—this rage to excel—women are admitted to possess in as great perfection, if not perhaps in a stronger degree than men. With this difference only, that when applied to woman it commonly receives the denomination of vanity, or at best of pride; but I think seldom or never of ambition. No—that high sounding term is too sublime for woman, and is reserved to varnish over the passions and crimes of man; while those of the other sex, called by their proper names and seen in their natural colors, impose not on mankind.

The different objects however on which the vanity, or the pride, or the ambition of the sexes is employed, give a distinction and superiority to the men to which they are by no means entitled in reality; because it is not yet clearly proven that the choice of everything that is most consequential, decorous, pleasant, and profitable for their own sphere of action, is not a usurpation; and for other powerful reasons, which would lead into too large a field of controversy if here touched upon. I repeat, however, that men are by no means entitled to superior respect and consideration upon such grounds, when we reflect that women are compelled on the one hand to adopt a conduct they cannot approve of, nor feel easy and natural; and are restrained on the other, from the exercise of one more congenial to the rights of human nature; and therefore it is very difficult to say if they were not thus limited, how far it might not appear that they are equal to any sphere of action, however great or good.

But taking women on the footing they now are, and on which they will probably remain for some time at least, the tide of their passions must waste itself upon something; and thus being forced into wrong channels, there it flows; but for the honor of the sex I trust

> Still it murmurs as it flows,
> Panting for its native home.

Thus many a good head is stuffed with ribbons, gauze, fringes, flounces, and furbelows, that might have received and communicated far other and more noble impressions. And many a fine imagination has been exhausted upon these, which had they been turned to the study of nature, or initiated into the dignified embellishments of the fine arts, might have adorned, delighted, and improved society. For oh! what patience and industry, what time and trouble, what acute observation, what intense thought, what ceaseless anxiety, what hopes and fears, alternately elate and depress thy trembling spirit, thou busy priestess of vanity! The half of the talents, the perseverance, the resolution and attention, hadst thou been but a man, might have placed thee on the woolsack, or have put a miter on thy head, or a long robe on thy back, or a truncheon in thy hand. Or, being even what thou art, the fiftieth part of thy misemployed talents if turned into proper channels, might have made thee what is tantamount to a Chancellor, a Bishop, a Judge, or a General—A useful, an amiable, and an interesting woman. . . .

No reasonable woman, no woman with a spark of common sense, dreams that a husband is to continue a lover, in the romantic sense of the word; or if she does so she is soon undeceived, and very properly forced to submit to reason. But what is infinitely absurd and unfair, though undeniably true; men coming under the same description, men otherwise wise enough and reasonable enough to outward appearance, do seriously suppose that their wives are to turn out the angels their imaginations had painted. Or if they do not seriously suppose it, which after all is possible, they act precisely as if they did. They either expect, or affect to expect, that the same sweetness of temper, the same equality and flow of spirits, the same eagerness to please, shall uniformly prevail in the wife, when the amiable, the devoted lover, is metamorphosed into the sullen and tyrannical husband. Such expectations, however, are above the reach of almost any human being to fulfill; and from such unreasonable and unfair expectations may often therefore be traced the many disagreements and disappointments which but too frequently occur in that state, which is certainly, however, of all others in this sublunary world, that most capable of promoting and preserving—pure, lasting, and interesting attachments.

Alas! were men but half as anxious to fulfill their own share of the engagements entered into in the most important concern in life as they are to press home matrimonial duties upon women, all might be well; but unfortunately for themselves, as well as those connected with them, they place their happiness, and what they seem to value more—their consequence—in being indulged and humored beyond all reasonable bounds, in whatever mode their fancy or passions suggest.

• • •

In fine, it seems to be expected that women should in a manner cease to exist, in a rational and mental point of view, before they resign life; by giving up along with their name every title to judge or act for themselves, but when their masters choose to bestow such privileges upon them. Were it possible however for women to fulfill such implicit articles of slavery, it were, perhaps, wrong to oppose anything which, not being of itself absolutely immoral, might contribute to the peace of society. But women, being formed by the power of the Almighty so nearly to resemble man in their desire after happiness, they must be supposed equally selfish in their pursuit of it; and having upon the same principles with men, wills and opinions of their own, they will of course ever be promoting the attainments of their own ends, either directly or indirectly. That the latter system is the one that women find themselves under the necessity of adopting, is but too evident; but if men persist in thinking it the only one suitable to their characters and situation, they have no right to expect that beings so unfortunately circumstanced, and so unfairly treated, should under such disadvantages act up to the perfection of their nature, nor do I pretend to allege that they do so. If they did, all attempts at reformation were vain and unnecessary.

The substance of what the writer has already presumed to recommend to men—and that which follows will be to the same purpose—is shortly this: generously, and in conformity with sound politics, to allow women such privileges, such degrees of liberty and equality as they will otherwise, as they ever have done, take in a worse way and in a greater degree. And if indeed women do avail themselves of the only weapons they are permitted to wield, can they be blamed? Undoubtedly not; since they are compelled to it by the injustice and impolicy of men. Petty treacheries—mean subterfuge—whining and flattery—feigned submission—and all the dirty little attendants which compose the endless train of low cunning, if not commendable, cannot with justice be very severely censured, when practiced by women. Since alas!—THE WEAK HAVE NO OTHER ARMS AGAINST THE STRONG! Since alas!—NECESSITY ACKNOWLEDGES NO LAW, BUT HER OWN!

[Since men "are ashamed in this enlightened age, to hold forth passive obedience, and unlimited authority, in all their horrors, even to women," they define female amiability as compliance with men's bad conduct and overbearing tempers.]

They likewise represent, and a very powerful argument it is, that this is the only method by which they [women] may hope to arrive at any indulgence they aim at; for that they have nothing to expect when claimed as rights, to which claims they constantly give the name of masculine, and unsufferable from women; but that they have everything to hope for when entreated as favors. This is a way indeed of cutting short every proposal for bettering the situation of women, and of quashing every hope or desire of a general improvement. It is however but a barbarous kind of policy, unworthy of man to advance and of women to acknowledge; and which, however long it may have taken place or even succeeded with regard to one party, can never bear examination when considered as a mutual benefit; because viewed in that light it is founded upon no one principle of justice or common sense.

Notwithstanding then that men have planned everything their own way, I must repeat that the consequences are not equal to their hopes or expectations; for they complain bitterly both in public and private of the folly, the inconsistency, the extravagance, and the general relaxation of manners amongst women. And they would be extremely well satisfied, if, without changing an iota of their own system and self indulgence, they could transform women in general into domestic wives, tender mothers, and dutiful and affectionate daughters; characters upon which they expatiate with enthusiasm and delight, and no wonder. But when it is at any time argued and proved that to bring about reformation, the first step ought to be the reformation of the moral conduct of the men themselves; and the next that of educating women on a more liberal and unprejudiced plan, and putting them on a more respectable footing in society; then it is that the generality of men fly off, and are not ashamed to declare that they would rather a thousand times take women as they are—weak, frail, dependent creatures. In comparison of the frightful certainty of having women declared their equals, and as such their companions and friends instead of their amusement, their dependents, and in plain and unvarnished terms their slaves, folly, vice, impertinence of every kind is delightful.

Then it is that we hear of the heavenly softness of the sex, that with a glance can disarm authority and dispel rage. Then it is that we hear them tell, with as much earnestness and gravity as if it were true, or even possible, consistently with human nature; that in woman's weakness consists her strength, and in her dependence her power. That though for wise and political purposes, men are vested with authority over women, yet that is only for their mutual good that it is designed, or ever ought to be exercised—(And it is well known that men never do, but what they *ought* to do.) That it is indeed rather a nominal authority taken up for conveniency's sake; for that upon the whole, what women lose of power in an acknowledged way and in name, they make up for in the private scenes of life, etc. etc. etc.

Now every one of these unmeaning, imposing, romantic ravings might be easily confuted and overturned; for the truth is that they have not a leg to stand upon, when examined upon the principles of reason and common sense, backed by the woeful experience of women. But waiving all discussion of what is but too obvious, I shall content myself with asking two very simple questions; and I think I know exactly how every honest man will answer them.

Are not the ideas which men have indulged themselves in with regard to the other sex rather the work of imagination than the operations of reason and common sense, and are they not therefore more calculated to amuse a youthful fancy and encourage romantic expectations than for the purposes of common life? And to bring this "home to men's business and bosoms,"[1] let me ask them the second question. Whether when they expatiate upon the immense powers of the female sex over the hearts and conduct of men, they do not always attach the ideas of youth and beauty to the picture? I believe it will be pretty generally acknowledged that these two queries must be answered in the affirmative.

Now having these pleasing images before their mind's eye, which work them up to a temporary sentiment of love and tenderness for the whole sex, no wonder if men suppose that such objects have no need of law or right on their side and have only to be seen to be obeyed. No wonder if they suppose the only danger here to be, that every indulgence shall be granted even beyond what reason would approve. For they very justly represent the empire of beauty as requiring no formal or written law in its favor, its law being engraved on the heart of man, and more powerful than all others. But men and brethren, awake out of your illusive dreams! and in order to do justice to the sex in general, quit the fields of romance, where

> Love and life are always young,
> And truth on every shepherd's tongue.[2]

---

[1]From Francis Bacon's "Dedication" (1625) to his *Essays*.
[2]Sir Walter Raleigh's "The Nymph's Reply to the Passionate Shepherd," quoted not quite accurately.

And descending to real life and what is constantly before your eyes, recollect that all women are not handsome, that all women, alas! are young but for a very short period indeed, and that consequently you are not always in love. It is therefore equally absurd and cruel to establish rules and principles, and even fixed laws, which could only answer if the reverse of all this were true.

If indeed this were the case, if the women were always handsome, and always young, and the men perpetually in love, the laws and opinions adopted concerning women would fit exactly; and the whole business of life on both sides would be to please. But I shall and must tell you—though the very name of them will freeze the blood in your veins—that ugly women, and old women, and indeed every description of women, after the charm of novelty and the first frenzy of love are over with the other sex, find that those soft and heavenly graces, etc. upon which the men flourish so much—taking care however not to come to particulars—are not only quite insufficient "to disarm authority, and dispel rage," but are even quite insufficient to procure them common justice, upon the most common occasions.

No!—If emanations of the divinity itself—if all the virtues, graces, and charities were sent upon earth through the medium of ugly women, or old women, or I believe, God forgive me, in the shape of almost any man's own wife—they would rarely meet with anything but neglect, and often with contempt and derision. . . .

I apprehend that, independent of their maternal character—I mean as mothers of the human race, which cannot be taken from them, though it is reduced to as low a pitch in point of consequence as possible—that independent of this, women are considered in two ways only.—In the lower classes as necessary drudges—In the higher as the ornaments of society, the pleasing triflers, who flutter through life for the amusement of men, rather than for any settled purpose with regard to themselves; and are accordingly, as it suits the caprice of their masters, the objects of adoration, or of torment, or of a passion unworthy of a name or a place in civilized society. In plain language, women are in all situations rendered merely the humble companions of men—the tools of their necessities—or the sport of their authority, of their prejudices, and of their passions. Women, viewed in this degrading light, are perhaps as well off with the trifling and corruptive mode of education generally allowed them, as with one which would rouse those talents and increase that desire after knowledge with which God and nature has from the beginning so liberally endowed them.

But the question here is—Are men warranted in forming upon light grounds such opinions with regard to women, and in compelling them in every essential point in life to act according to these preconceived and, as we think, erroneous opinions? The answer from the men is but too ready, but too persuasive; for say they—Our judgment disclaims your pretensions—we hold our judgment as superior to yours—and we are invested with powers to compel, if we cannot persuade.

From such a tribunal, then, is there no appeal?—Alas! none.

When men however deign to argue more to the point, they allege that when women are educated too much upon an equality with them, it renders them—presuming and conceited—useless in their families—masculine, and consequently disgusting in their manners.

[Hays refutes these charges by arguing that knowledge in general does not favor presumption, though all things may be misapplied; that an educated woman is more apt to fulfill her obligations to her family than is an empty-headed pleasure-seeker; and that emulation of virtues which are common to human nature (though often appropriated by men) is natural and honorable.]

The misconduct of women, generally speaking, originates in improper education and in the mistaken and ungenerous opinions adopted wherever the sex is concerned; but most particularly in the matrimonial engagement, by which a degree of domestic tyranny is established by the men, totally incompatible with natural justice, not always even consistent with humanity, and consequently ill calculated to promote the happiness of either party. For where so decided and invariable authority and superiority are claimed, they will never be yielded to with satisfaction or complacency; except the subjected party is convinced that the title is well founded, or that the right, such as it is, is exercised with justice and moderation. Of the first, women never were, nor I fear never will be convinced. And the last, the daily and sad experience of many, will not permit them to believe.

In every case, the more distinctly limits are defined, the less confusion and doubts ensue . . . the clearer rights on each side are made out, the less room there is for dispute; and . . . when due bounds are set to authority, though upon the one hand it prevents the abuse of it, yet on the other it is the most likely method to ensure a ready obedience to its just commands.

These truths are simple and obvious enough, and are now very readily acknowledged in all matters except where women are concerned. It is astonishing, however, that principles of private and domestic justice do not at least keep pace in the minds of men with those of a public and political nature. The reason that they do not so with regard to women, I fear does not say much for the generosity of the men. With respect to each other they enforce justice, because they have power so to do—where the weaker sex is concerned the inference is obvious—what cannot be *enforced*, remains *undone*.

To finish what I have to say on this head at once, I confess that I think the power of the men in the married state, like that of kings in a well regulated and limited monarchy, ought to be confined solely to that of doing good. For, while the power of doing mischief is left open, the will can never be wanting in either case. With reverence be it spoken, I believe there never was a king in this world from *Solomon* downwards—*George* the third, king of *Great Britain, France,* and *Ireland,* always excepted—who might not be tempted at a time to stretch his prerogative a *little* too far.—Nor do I believe there is a husband on the face of the whole earth with the exception of only one—another convenient *salvo*—who may not frequently pull the reins of authority too tight, perhaps so very tight as to crack; to the utter confusion of the whole domestic machine, which it is supposed men are able to guide with such exquisite skill and dexterity.

A very intelligent traveler makes a remark highly worthy of observation, and which struck me indeed very forcibly as being much to the purpose of the present argument. He has just been giving an account of the inhabitants of an island, where he describes the men and women as living together on a footing of perfect equality, at least as much so as their different duties and occupations permit; like people in short of the same species, who feel that they are of equal consequence to each other's happiness and comforts—the difference of sex there only endearing and producing variety—not, as in other places, *degrading* the one half of the human race. The traveler, without any view to system building, and merely speaking of the natural consequences of such a friendly and equitable intercourse, says, with the utmost *naiveté*, that "the women from being happy, are always in good humor."[3]

I most firmly believe that *good humor* is *one* of the happy consequences to be reasonably expected, if women were everywhere put on a rational and equitable footing. And as consequences, like misfortunes, rarely come alone, how many good ones might not be expected to follow that engaging quality! Everyone is daily and hourly witness either of the effects which arise from *good humor*—which never fails to operate like a charm in all society public and private—or of the bad effects of its *opposite*. Oh! that men would therefore attend to the important lesson included in the little sentence which I have just quoted; for in few words, and without the pride of reasoning, it perhaps contains the *essence* of all that ever was or ever will be said to the purpose on the subject! Let them but endeavor to make women happy—not by flattering their follies and absurdities—but by every reasonable means; and above all by considering them as rational beings upon a footing with themselves—influenced by the same passions—and having the same claims to all the rights of humanity; which, indeed, are so simple, that justice well defined includes the whole. And then "women from being happy, will always be in good humor"; and from being happy, and always in good humor, it is but reasonable to hope that they will at last be, what all wise and good men wish them, and what in reality they may—and OUGHT TO BE.

[3]Major Alexander Jardine, in his *Letters from Barbary, France, Spain, Portugal, &c.* (1788), showed remarkably enlightened interest in the condition of women. See particularly his letters 15, 16, and 17 from France, where he comments on the relative emancipation of French women and the benefits produced by maximizing association between the sexes and reducing sexual distinctions in character and occupation as much as possible.

Maria Edgeworth
1768–1849

MARIA EDGEWORTH, a member of the Anglo-Irish gentry, was born in England, to the first of her father's four wives, who died when Maria was five. Though her remote ancestors had been colorfully disreputable (they were, in fact, the models for the Rackrents of her *Castle Rackrent*), Maria's father, Richard Lovell Edgeworth, was an energetic, conscientious, and progressive man. He formed Maria's mind—educating her carefully, encouraging her writing, and urging her to take an interest in public affairs; and she idolized him. When she was fourteen, the Edgeworths settled in Ireland, where her father became a model landlord. He involved Maria in running the estate, so that she acquired both wide knowledge of the Irish people and habits of business and accuracy not generally available to eighteenth-century ladies. Maria never married, living with her family all her life. As the eldest daughter among twenty-one children, she took a major role in educating younger siblings. This experience qualified her to collaborate with her father on *Practical Education* (1798), a pioneering work on educational psychology, and to write engaging and authentic stories for children.

Her first tale for adults was *Castle Rackrent* (1800), chronicles of the Rackrent family as told by their loyal retainer (modeled on the Edgeworths' own steward); it is an innovative masterpiece of local color fiction. *Belinda* (1801), which centers on a young lady's entrance into the fashionable world, is a more typical eighteenth-century woman's novel. *The Absentee* (1812) and *Ormond* (1817) dramatize the problems of Ireland and the responsibilities of the landholding class. Almost all of Edgeworth's novels were critically acclaimed and highly profitable. She depended on her father and other members of her intelligent, close-knit family for criticism and emotional support; but they do not seem to have exerted undue influence on her writing.

Entertaining, good-humored, and kindly, Maria Edgeworth was a great social success when she visited London in 1813. She knew many of the celebrities of the day, including Anna Laetitia Barbauld, to whom she proposed collaboration on a politically liberal women's journal.

(Barbauld declined on the grounds that the leading women writers were ideologically divided: "Mrs. Hannah More would not write along with you or me, and we should probably hesitate at joining Miss Hays, or if she were living Mrs. [Mary Wollstonecraft] Godwin.") Walter Scott, a warm friend and admirer of Edgeworth, said that in his novels he hoped to do for Scotland what she had done for Ireland.

Her "Essay on the Noble Science of Self-Justification" (written in 1787) was included in her first publication, *Letters for Literary Ladies* (1795). (The other parts were letters debating whether women should become authors and a story attacking emotional self-indulgence.) Though Edgeworth satirizes the emotional rhetoric women use to control men, her aim is not to make women subservient, but to make them rational: that is, to assert just claims and rely on reasonable arguments. This is evident in her later expansion of this essay into an amusing short novel, *The Modern Griselda* (1805).

An Essay

ON THE

Noble Science of Self-Justification

"For which an eloquence that aims *to vex*,
With native tropes of anger arms the *sex*."
—*Parnell*.

Endowed as the fair sex indisputably are, with a natural genius for the invaluable art of self-justification, it may not be displeasing to them to see its rising perfection evinced by an attempt to reduce it to a science. Possessed, as are all the fair daughters of Eve, of an hereditary propensity, transmitted to them undiminished through succeeding generations, to be "soon moved with slightest touch of blame"; very little precept and practice will confirm them in the habit, and instruct them in all the maxims of self-justification.

Candid pupil, you will readily accede to my first and fundamental axiom—that a lady can do no wrong.

But simple as this maxim may appear, and suited to the level of the meanest capacity, the talent of applying it on all the important, but more especially on all the most trivial, occurrences of domestic life, so as to secure private peace and public dominion, has hitherto been monopolized by the female adepts in the art of self-justification.

Excuse me for insinuating by this expression, that there may yet be amongst you some novices. To these, if any such, I principally address myself.

And now, lest fired by ambition you lose all by aiming at too much, let me explain and limit my first principle. "That you can do no wrong." You must be aware that real perfection is beyond the reach of mortals, nor would I have you aim at it; indeed it is not in any degree necessary to our purpose. You have heard of the established belief in the infallibility of the sovereign pontiff, which prevailed not many centuries ago—if man was allowed to be infallible, I see no reason why the same privilege should not be extended to woman—but times have changed; and since the happy age of credulity is past, leave the opinions of men to their natural perversity—their actions are the best test of their faith. Instead then of a belief in your infallibility, endeavor to enforce implicit submission to your authority. This will give you infinitely less trouble, and will answer your purpose as well.

Right and wrong, if we go to the foundation of things, are, as casuists tell us, really words of very dubious signification, perpetually varying with customs and fashion, and to be adjusted ultimately by no other standards but opinion and force. Obtain power, then, by all means: power is the law of man; make it yours.

But to return from a frivolous disquisition about right, let me teach you the art of defending the wrong. After having thus pointed out to you the glorious end of your labors, I must now instruct you in the equally glorious means.

For the advantage of my subject I address myself chiefly to married ladies; but those who have not as yet the good fortune to have that common enemy, a husband, to combat, may in the meantime practice my precepts upon their fathers, brothers, and female friends; with caution, however, lest by discovering their arms too soon, they preclude themselves from the power of using them to the fullest advantage hereafter. I therefore recommend it to them to prefer, with a philosophical moderation, the future to the present.

Timid brides, you have, probably, hitherto been addressed as angels. Prepare for the time when you shall again become mortal. Take the alarm at the first approach of blame; at the first hint of a discovery that you are anything less than infallible—contradict, debate, justify, recriminate, rage, weep, swoon, do anything but yield to conviction.

I take it for granted that you have already acquired sufficient command of voice; you need not study its compass; going beyond its pitch has a peculiarly happy effect upon some occasions. But are you voluble enough to drown all sense in a torrent of words? Can you be loud enough to overpower the voice of all who shall attempt to interrupt or contradict you? Are you mistress of the petulant, the peevish, and the sullen tone? Have you practiced the sharpness which provokes retort, and the continual monotony which by setting your adversary to sleep effectually precludes reply? an event which is always to be considered as decisive of the victory, or at least as reducing it to a drawn battle—you and Somnus[1] divide the prize.

Thus prepared for an engagement, you will next, if you have not already done it, study the weak part of the character of your enemy—your husband, I mean: if he be a man of high spirit, jealous of command and impatient of control, one who decides for himself, and who is little troubled with the insanity of minding what the world says of him, you must proceed with extreme circumspection; you must not dare to provoke the combined forces of the enemy to a regular engagement, but harass him with perpetual petty skirmishes: in these, though you gain little at a time, you will gradually weary the patience, and break the spirit of your opponent. If he be a man of spirit, he must also be generous; and what man of generosity will contend for trifles with a woman who submits to him in all affairs of consequence, who is in his power, who is weak, and who loves him?

"Can superior with inferior power contend?" No; the spirit of a lion is not to be roused by the teasing of an insect.

But such a man as I have described, besides being as generous as he is brave, will probably be of an active temper: then you have an inestimable advantage; for he will set a high value upon a thing for which you have none—time; he will acknowledge the force of your arguments merely from a dread of their length; he will yield to you in trifles, particularly in trifles which do not militate against his authority; not out of regard for you, but for his time; for what man can prevail upon himself to debate three hours about what could be as well decided in three minutes?

Lest amongst infinite variety the difficulty of immediate selection should at first perplex you, let me point out, that matters of *taste* will afford you, of all others, the most ample and incessant

[1]The Roman god of sleep.

subjects of debate. Here you have no criterion to appeal to. Upon the same principle, next to matters of taste, points of opinion will afford the most constant exercise to your talents. Here you will have an opportunity of citing the opinions of all the living and dead you have ever known, besides the dear privilege of repeating continually:— "Nay, you must allow *that*." Or, "You can't deny *this,* for it's the universal opinion— everybody says so! everybody thinks so! I wonder to hear you express such an opinion! Nobody but yourself is of that way of thinking!" with innumerable other phrases, with which a slight attention to polite conversation will furnish you. This mode of opposing authority to argument, and assertion to proof, is of such universal utility, that I pray you to practice it.

If the point in dispute be some opinion relative to your character or disposition, allow in general, that "you are sure you have a great many faults"; but to every specific charge reply, "Well, I am sure I don't know, but I did not think *that* was one of my faults! nobody ever accused me of that before! Nay, I was always remarkable for the contrary; at least before I was acquainted with you, sir: in my own family I was always remarkable for the contrary: ask any of my own friends; ask any of them; they must know me best."

But if, instead of attacking the material parts of your character, your husband should merely presume to advert to your manners, to some slight personal habit which might be made more agreeable to him; prove, in the first place, that it is his fault that it is not agreeable to him; ask which is most to blame, "she who ceases to please, or he who ceases to be pleased" —His eyes are changed, or opened. But it may perhaps have been a matter almost of indifference to him, till you undertook its defense: then make it of consequence by rising in eagerness, in proportion to the insignificance of your object; if he can draw consequences, this will be an excellent lesson: if you are so tender of blame in the veriest trifles, how impeachable must you be in matters of importance! As to personal habits, begin by denying that you have any; or in the paradoxical language of Rousseau declare that the only habit you have is the habit of having none; as all personal habits, if they have been of any long standing, must have become involuntary, the unconscious culprit may assert her innocence without hazarding her veracity.

However, if you happen to be detected in the very fact, and a person cries, "Now, now, you are doing it!" submit, but declare at the same moment—"That it is the very first time in your whole life that you were ever known to be guilty of it; and therefore it can be no habit, and of course nowise reprehensible."

Extend the rage for vindication to all the objects which the most remotely concern you; take even inanimate objects under your protection. Your dress, your furniture, your property, everything which is or has been yours, defend, and this upon the principles of the soundest philosophy: each of these things all compose a part of your personal merit; all that connected the most distantly with your idea gives pleasure or pain to others, becomes an object of blame or praise, and consequently claims your support or vindication.

In the course of the management of your house, children, family, and affairs, probably some few errors of omission or commission may strike your husband's pervading eye; but these errors, admitting them to be errors, you will never, if you please, allow to be charged to any deficiency in memory, judgment, or activity, on your part.

There are surely people enough around you to divide and share the blame; send it from one to another, till at last, by universal rejection, it is proved to belong to nobody. You will say, however, that facts remain unalterable; and that in some unlucky instance, in the changes and chances of human affairs, you may be proved to have been to blame. Some stubborn evidence may appear against you; still you may prove an alibi, or balance the evidence. There is nothing equal to balancing evidence; doubt is, you know, the most philosophic state of the human mind, and it will be kind of you to keep your husband perpetually in this skeptical state.

Indeed the short method of denying absolutely all blameable facts, I should recommend to pupils as the best; and if in the beginning of their career they may startle at this mode, let them depend upon it that in their future practice it must become perfectly familiar. The nice distinction of simulation and dissimulation depends but on the trick of a syllable; palliation and extenuation are universally allowable in self-defense; prevarication inevitably follows, and falsehood "is but in the next degree."

Yet I would not destroy this nicety of conscience too soon. It may be of use in your first setting out, because you must establish credit; in proportion to your credit will be the value of your future asseverations.

In the meantime, however, argument and debate are allowed

to the most rigid moralist. You can never perjure yourself by swearing to a false opinion.

I come now to the art of reasoning: don't be alarmed at the name of reasoning, fair pupils; I will explain to you my meaning.

If, instead of the fiery-tempered being I formerly described, you should fortunately be connected with a man, who, having formed a justly high opinion of your sex, should propose to treat you as his equal, and who in any little dispute which might arise between you, should desire no other arbiter than reason; triumph in his mistaken candor, regularly appeal to the decision of reason at the beginning of every contest, and deny its jurisdiction at the conclusion. I take it for granted that you will be on the wrong side of every question, and indeed, in general, I advise you to choose the wrong side of an argument to defend; whilst you are young in the science, it will afford the best exercise, and, as you improve, the best display of your talents.

If, then, reasonable pupils, you would succeed in argument, attend to the following instructions.

Begin by preventing, if possible, the specific statement of any position, or if reduced to it, use the most *general terms,* and take advantage of the ambiguity which all languages and which most philosophers allow. Above all things, shun definitions; they will prove fatal to you; for two persons of sense and candor, who define their terms, cannot argue long without either convincing, or being convinced, or parting in equal good-humor; to prevent which, go over and over the same ground, wander as wide as possible from the point, but always with a view to return at last precisely to the same spot from which you set out. I should remark to you, that the choice of your weapons is a circumstance much to be attended to: choose always those which your adversary cannot use. If your husband is a man of wit, you will of course undervalue a talent which is never connected with judgment: "for your part, you do not presume to contend with him in wit."

But if he be a sober-minded man, who will go link by link along the chain of an argument, follow him at first, till he grows so intent that he does not perceive whether you follow him or not; then slide back to your own station; and when with perverse patience he has at last reached the last link of the chain, with one electric shock of wit make him quit his hold, and strike him to the ground in an instant. Depend upon the sympathy of the spectators, for to one who can understand *reason*, you will find ten who admire *wit*.

But if you should not be blessed with "a ready wit," if demonstration should in the meantime stare you in the face, do not be in the least alarmed—anticipate the blow. Whilst you have it yet in your power, rise with becoming magnanimity, and cry, "I give it up! I give it up! La! let us say no more about it; I do so hate disputing about trifles. I give it up!" Before an explanation on the word trifle can take place, quit the room with flying colors.

If you are a woman of sentiment and eloquence, you have advantages of which I scarcely need apprise you. From the understanding of a man, you have always an appeal to his heart, or, if not, to his affection, to his weakness. If you have the good fortune to be married to a weak man, always choose the moment to argue with him when you have a full audience. Trust to the sublime power of numbers; it will be of use even to excite your own enthusiasm in debate; then as the scene advances, talk of his cruelty, and your sensibility, and sink with "becoming woe" into the pathos of injured innocence.

Besides the heart and the weakness of your opponent, you have still another chance, in ruffling his temper; which, in the course of a long conversation, you will have a fair opportunity of trying; and if—for philosophers will sometimes grow warm in the defense of truth—if he should grow absolutely angry, you will in the same proportion grow calm, and wonder at his rage, though you well know it has been created by your own provocation. The bystanders, seeing anger without any adequate cause, will all be of your side.

Nothing provokes an irascible man, interested in debate, and possessed of an opinion of his own eloquence, so much as to see the attention of his hearers go from him: you will then, when he flatters himself that he has just fixed your eye with his *very best* argument, suddenly grow absent—your house affairs must call you hence—or you have directions to give to your children—or the room is too hot, or too cold—the window must be opened—or door shut—or the candle wants snuffing. Nay, without these interruptions, the simple motion of your eye may provoke a speaker; a butterfly, or the figure in a carpet may engage your attention in preference to him; or if these objects be absent, the simply averting your eye, looking through the window in quest of outward objects, will show that your mind has not been abstracted, and will display to him at least your wish of not attending. He may, however, possibly have lost the habit of watching your eye for approbation; then you may assault his ear: if all other resources fail, beat with your foot that dead march of the spirits, that incessant tattoo, which so well deserves its name. Marvelous must be the patience of the much-enduring man whom some or other of these devices do not provoke: slight causes often produce great effects; the simple scratching of a pick-axe, properly applied to certain veins in a mine, will cause the most dreadful explosions.

Hitherto we have only professed to teach the defensive: let me now recommend to you the offensive part of the art of justification. As a supplement to reasoning comes recrimination: the pleasure of proving that you are right is surely incomplete till you have proved that your adversary is wrong; this might have been a secondary, let it now become a primary object with you; rest your own defense on it for further security: you are no longer to consider yourself as obliged either to deny, palliate, argue, or declaim, but simply to justify yourself by criminating another; all merit, you know, is judged of by comparison. In the art of recrimination, your memory will be of the highest service to you; for you are to open and keep an account-current of all the faults, mistakes, neglects, unkindnesses of those you live with; these you are to state against your own: I need not tell you that the balance will always be in your favor. In stating matters of opinion, produce the words of the very same person which passed days, months, years before, in contradiction to what he is then saying. By displacing, disjointing words and sentences, by misunderstanding the whole, or quoting only a part of what has been said, you may convict any man of inconsistency, particularly if he be a man of genius and feeling; for he speaks generally from the impulse of the moment, and of all others can the least bear to be charged with paradoxes. So far for a husband.

Recriminating is also of sovereign use in the quarrels of friends; no friend is so perfectly equable, so ardent in affection, so nice in punctilio, as never to offend: then "Note his faults, and con them all by rote." Say you can forgive, but you can never forget; and surely it is much more generous to forgive and remember, than to forgive and forget. On every new alarm, call the unburied ghosts from former fields of battle; range them in tremendous array, call them one by one to witness against the conscience of your enemy, and ere the battle is begun take from him all courage to engage.

There is one case I must observe to you in which recrimination has peculiar poignancy. If you have had it in your power to confer obligations on anyone, never cease reminding them of it: and let them feel that you have acquired an indefeasible right to reproach them without a possibility of their retorting. It is a maxim with some sentimental people, "To treat their servants as if they were their friends in distress."—I have observed that people of this cast make themselves amends, by treating their friends in distress as if they were their servants.

Apply this maxim—you may do it a thousand ways, especially in company. In general conversation, where everyone is supposed to be on a footing, if any of your humble companions should presume to hazard an opinion contrary to yours, and should modestly begin with, "I think," look as the man did when he said to his servant, "You think, sir—what business have you to think?"

Never fear to lose a friend by the habits which I recommend: reconciliations, as you have often heard it said—reconciliations are the cement of friendship; therefore friends should quarrel to strengthen their attachment, and offend each other for the pleasure of being reconciled.

I beg pardon for digressing: I was, I believe, talking of your husband, not of your friend—I have gone far out of the way.

If in your debates with your husband you should want "eloquence to vex him," the dull prolixity of narration, joined to the complaining monotony of voice which I formerly recommended, will supply its place, and have the desired effect: Somnus will prove propitious; then, ever and anon as the soporific charm begins to work, rouse him with interrogatories, such as, "Did not you say so? Don't you remember? Only answer me that!"

By-the-by, interrogatories artfully put may lead an unsuspicious reasoner, you know, always to your own conclusion.

In addition to the patience, philosophy, and other good things which Socrates learned from his wife,[2] perhaps she taught him this mode of reasoning.

But, after all, the precepts of art, and even the natural susceptibility of your tempers, will avail you little in the sublime of our

---

[2]According to tradition, the wife of the great Greek philosopher Socrates was a notorious shrew. He is said to have expressed gratitude for her because she taught him patience.

science, if you cannot command that ready enthusiasm which will make you enter into the part you are acting; that happy imagination which shall make you believe all you fear and all you invent.

Who is there amongst you who cannot or who will not justify when they are accused? Vulgar talent! the sublime of our science is to justify before we are accused. There is no reptile so vile but what will turn when it is trodden on; but of a nicer sense and nobler species are those whom nature has endowed with antennæ, which perceive and withdraw at the distant approach of danger. Allow me another allusion: similes cannot be crowded too close for a female taste; and analogy, I have heard, my fair pupils, is your favorite mode of reasoning.

The sensitive plant is too vulgar an allusion; but if the truth of modern naturalists may be depended upon, there is a plant which, instead of receding timidly from the intrusive touch, angrily protrudes its venomous juices upon all who presume to meddle with it—do not you think this plant would be your fittest emblem?

Let me, however, recommend it to you, nice souls, who, of the mimosa kind, "fear the dark cloud, and feel the coming storm," to take the utmost precaution lest the same susceptibility which you cherish as the dear means to torment others should insensibly become a torment to yourselves.

Distinguish then between sensibility and susceptibility; between the anxious solicitude not to give offense, and the captious eagerness of vanity to prove that it ought not to have been taken; distinguish between the desire of praise and the horror of blame: can any two things be more different than the wish to improve, and the wish to demonstrate that you have never been to blame?

Observe, I only wish you to distinguish these things in your own minds; I would by no means advise you to discontinue the laudable practice of confounding them perpetually in speaking to others.

When you have nearly exhausted human patience in explaining, justifying, vindicating; when in spite of all the pains you have taken, you have more than half betrayed your own vanity; you have a never-failing resource in paying tribute to that of your opponent, as thus:

"I am sure you must be sensible that I should never take so much pains to justify myself if I were indifferent to your opinion. I know that I ought not to disturb myself with such trifles; but nothing is a trifle to me which concerns you. I confess I am too anxious to please; I know it's a fault, but I cannot cure myself of it now. Too quick sensibility, I am conscious, is the defect of my disposition; it would be happier for me if I could be more indifferent, I know."

Who could be so brutal as to blame so amiable, so candid a creature? Who would not submit to be tormented with kindness?

When once your captive condescends to be flattered by such arguments as these, your power is fixed; your future triumphs can be bounded only by your own moderation; they are at once secured and justified.

Forbear not, then, happy pupils; but, arrived at the summit of power, give a full scope to your genius, nor trust to genius alone: to exercise in all its extent your privileged dominion, you must acquire, or rather you must pretend to have acquired, infallible skill in the noble art of physiognomy; immediately the thoughts as well as the words of your subjects are exposed to your inquisition.

Words may flatter you, but the countenance never can deceive you; the eyes are the windows of the soul, and through them you are to watch what passes in the inmost recesses of the heart. There, if you discern the slightest ideas of doubt, blame, or displeasure; if you discover the slightest symptoms of revolt, take the alarm instantly. Conquerors must maintain their conquests; and how easily can they do this, who hold a secret correspondence with the minds of the vanquished! Be your own spies then; from the looks, gestures, slightest motions of your enemies, you are to form an alphabet, a language intelligible only to yourselves, yet by which you shall condemn them; always remembering that in sound policy suspicion justifies punishment. In vain, when you accuse your friends of the high treason of blaming you, in vain let them plead their innocence, even of the intention. "They did not say a word which could be tortured into such a meaning." No, "but they looked daggers, though they used none."[3]

And of this you are to be the sole judge, though there were fifty witnesses to the contrary.

How should indifferent spectators pretend to know the countenance of your friend as well as you do—you, that have a

[3] Adapted from *Hamlet* 3:2, line 402.

nearer, a dearer interest in attending to it? So accurate have been your observations, that no thought of their souls escapes you; nay, you often can tell even what they are going to think of.

The science of divination certainly claims your attention; beyond the past and the present, it shall extend your dominion over the future; from slight words, half-finished sentences, from silence itself, you shall draw your omens and auguries.

"I know what you were going to say"; or, "I know such a thing was a sign you were inclined to be displeased with me."

In the ardor of innocence, the culprit, to clear himself from such imputations, incurs the imputation of a greater offense. Suppose, to prove that you were mistaken, to prove that he could not have meant to blame you, he should declare that at the moment you mention, "You were quite foreign to his thoughts, he was not thinking at all about you."

Then in truth you have a right to be angry. To one of your class of justificators, this is the highest offense. Possessed as you are of the firm opinion that all persons at all times, on all occasions, are intent upon you alone, is it not less mortifying to discover that you were thought ill of, than that you were not thought of at all? "Indifference, you know, sentimental pupils, is more fatal to love than even hatred."

Thus, my dear pupils, I have endeavored to provide precepts adapted to the display of your several talents; but if there should be any amongst you who have no talents, who can neither argue nor persuade, who have neither sentiment nor enthusiasm, I must indeed—congratulate them; they are peculiarly qualified for the science of Self-justification: indulgent nature, often even in the weakness, provides for the protection of her creatures: just Providence, as the guard of stupidity, has enveloped it with the impenetrable armor of obstinacy.

Fair idiots! let women of sense, wit, feeling, triumph in their various arts: yours are superior. Their empire, absolute as it sometimes may be, is perpetually subject to sudden revolutions. With them, a man has some chance of equal sway: with a fool he has none. Have they hearts and understandings? Then the one may be touched, or the other in some unlucky moment convinced; even in their very power lies their greatest dangers—not so with you. In vain let the most candid of his sex attempt to reason with you; let him begin with, "Now, my dear, only listen to reason"—you stop him at once with, "No, my dear, you know I do not pretend to reason; I only say, that's my opinion."

Let him go on to prove that yours is a mistaken opinion—you are ready to acknowledge it long before he desires it. "You acknowledge it may be a wrong opinion; but still it is your opinion." You do not maintain it in the least either because you believe it to be wrong or right, but merely because it is yours. Exposed as you might have been to the perpetual humiliation of being convinced, nature seems kindly to have denied you all perception of truth, or at least all sentiment of pleasure from the perception.

With an admirable humility, you are as well contented to be in the wrong as in the right; you answer all that can be said to you with a provoking humility of aspect.

"Yes; I do not doubt but what you say may be very true, but I cannot tell; I do not think myself capable of judging on these subjects; I am sure you must know much better than I do. I do not pretend to say but that your opinion is very just; but I own I am of a contrary way of thinking; I always thought so, and I always shall."

Should a man with persevering temper tell you that he is ready to adopt your sentiments if you will only explain them; should he beg only to have a reason for your opinion—no, you can give no reason. Let him urge you to say something in its defense—no; like Queen Anne, you will only repeat the same thing over again, or be silent. Silence is the ornament of your sex; and in silence, if there be not wisdom, there is safety. You will, then, if you please, according to your custom, sit listening to all entreaties to explain, and speak—with a fixed immutability of posture, and a predetermined deafness of eye, which shall put your opponent utterly out of patience; yet still by persevering with the same complacent importance of countenance, you shall half persuade people you could speak if you would; you shall keep them in doubt by that true want of meaning, "which puzzles more than wit";[4] even because they cannot conceive the excess of your stupidity, they shall actually begin to believe that they themselves are stupid. Ignorance and doubt are the great parents of the sublime.

Your adversary, finding you impenetrable to argument, perhaps would try wit:—but, "On the impassive ice the lightnings play." His eloquence or his kindness will avail less; when in

[4] Pope, *Moral Essays*, "Epistle II. To a Lady," line 114.

yielding to you after a long harangue, he expects to please you, you will answer undoubtedly with the utmost propriety, "That you should be very sorry he yielded his judgment to you; that he is very good; that you are much obliged to him; but that, as to the point in dispute, it is a matter of perfect indifference to you; for your part, you have no choice at all about it; you beg that he will do just what he pleases; you know that it is the duty of a wife to submit; but you hope, however, you may have an *opinion* of your own."

Remember, all such speeches as these will lose above half their effect, if you cannot accompany them with the vacant stare, the insipid smile, the passive aspect of the humbly perverse.

Whilst I write, new precepts rush upon my recollection; but the subject is inexhaustible. I quit it with regret, though fully sensible of my presumption in having attempted to instruct those who, whilst they read, will smile in the consciousness of superior powers. Adieu! then, my fair readers: long may you prosper in the practice of an art peculiar to your sex! Long may you maintain unrivaled dominion at home and abroad; and long may your husbands rue the hour when first they made you promise "*to obey!*"

Katherine Philips
(1631–1664)

DAUGHTER of a merchant, Philips lived a retired life. She either cultivated or, more likely, imagined a circle of women friends to whom, writing as "Orinda," she addressed many of her poems. Her work circulated widely in manuscript, but was published without her authorization. By the time of her death, from smallpox, she had won the admiration of Dryden, Abraham Cowley, and Sir John Denham, among others. She was long remembered as "The Matchless Orinda."

A Retired Friendship. To Ardelia

Come, my Ardelia, to this bower,
  Where kindly mingling souls awhile,
Let's innocently spend an hour
  And at all serious follies smile.

Here is no quarreling for crowns,
  Nor fear of changes in our fate;
No trembling at the great ones' frowns,
  Nor any slavery of state.

Here's no disguise nor treachery,
  Nor any deep concealed design;
From blood and plots this place is free,
  And calm as are those looks of thine.

10

Here let us sit and bless our stars,
    Who did such happy quiet give
As that removed from noise of wars,
    In one another's hearts we live.

Why should we entertain a fear?
    Love cares not how the world is turned;
If crowds of dangers should appear,
    Yet Friendship can be unconcerned.   *20*

We wear about us such a charm,
    No horror can be our offense;
For mischief's self can do no harm
    To Friendship or to Innocence.

Let's mark how soon Apollo's beams
    Command the flocks to quit their meat,
And not entreat the neighboring streams
    To quench their thirst, but cool their heat.

In such a scorching age as this,
    Who would not ever seek a shade   *30*
Deserve their happiness to miss,
    As having their own peace betrayed.

But we (of one another's mind
    Assured) the boisterous world disdain;
With quiet souls and unconfined
    Enjoy what princes wish in vain.

An Answer to Another Persuading a Lady to Marriage

Forbear, bold youth, all's Heaven here,
    And what you do aver,
To others courtship may appear,
    'Tis sacrilege to her.

She is a public deity,
    And were 't not very odd
She should depose herself to be
    A petty household god?

First make the sun in private shine,
  And bid the world adieu,   *10*
That so he may his beams confine
  In compliment to you.

But if of that you do despair,
  Think how you do amiss
To strive to fix her beams which are
  More bright and large than this.

"Ephelia"
(fl. 1679)

"EPHELIA" is the pseudonym of the author of *Female Poems on Several Occasions* (1679). We know nothing about her; the tradition that she was Joan Philips, daughter of Katherine, apparently originated in the nineteenth century and has no foundation. *Female Poems* contains sixty-five poems in a wide range of verse forms; many of them tell a story, in the manner of a sonnet sequence, of Ephelia's love for "J. G.," who abandons her to marry another.

To One that Asked Me
Why I Loved J. G.

Why do I love? Go, ask the glorious sun
Why every day it round the world doth run;
Ask Thames and Tiber, why they ebb and flow;
Ask damask roses, why in June they blow;
Ask ice and hail, the reason why they're cold;
Decaying beauties, why they will grow old:
They'll tell thee Fate, that everything doth move,
Enforces them to this, and me to love.
There is no reason for our love or hate,
'Tis irresistible, as death or fate.   *10*
'Tis not his face; I've sense enough to see
That is not good, though doted on by me;
Nor is 't his tongue that has this conquest won,
For that at least is equalled by my own;

His carriage can to none obliging be,
'Tis rude, affected, full of vanity;
Strangely ill-natured, peevish, and unkind,
Unconstant, false, to jealousy inclined;
His temper could not have so great a power,
'Tis mutable, and changes every hour;   20
Those vigorous years that women so adore
Are past in him; he's twice my age and more;
And yet I love this false, this worthless man
With all the passion that a woman can;
Dote on his imperfections, though I spy
Nothing to love; I love, and know not why.
Sure 'tis decreed in the dark book of fate
That I should love, and he should be ingrate.

To Coridon,
on Shutting his Door against some Ladies

Conceited coxcomb! though I was so kind
To wish to see you, think not I designed
To force myself to your unwilling arms,
Your conversation[1] has no such charms;
Think less, those lovely virgins were[2] with me
Would thrust themselves into your company;
They've crowds of gallants for their favors sue,
And to be caressed, need not come to you.
'Gainst handsome women rudely shut your door!
Had it been sergeants,[3] you could do no more: 10
Faith, we expected with a horrid yelp,
Out of the window you'd have cried "Help! help!"
What outrage have you offered to our sex,
That you should dread we came but to perplex?
Or since I saw you last, what have I done,
Might cause so strange an alteration?
Till now, your wishing eyes have at my sight

[1]Pronounced as five syllables, as is "alteration" in line 16.
[2]That is, "virgins who were."
[3]Officers of the law.

Spoke you all rapture, ecstasy, delight;
But at the change I have a critic[4] guess:
So much of friendship you to me profess, 20
More than your lazy tongue can e'er express,
And your performance hath been so much less,
That debtor-like, you dare not meet my eyes,
Which was the reason of your late surprise.
I'll tell you, Sir, your kindness to requite,
A loving secret, merely out of spite:
A secret four and twenty moons I've kept;
I've sighed in private, and in private wept,
And all for you; but yet so much my pride
Surmounts my passion, that now were I tried, 30
And th' heart so long I've wished for, prostrate lay
Before my feet, I'd spurn the toy away;
And though, perhaps, I wish as much as you,
I'll starve myself, so I may starve you too:
And for a curse, wish you may never find
An open door, nor woman when she's kind.

[4]Skillful.

Anne Killigrew
(1660–1685)

THE subject of Dryden's ode "To the Pious Memory of the Accomplished Mrs. Anne Killigrew, Excellent in the Two Sister Arts of Poesy and Painting" was a niece of the playwright Thomas Killigrew and served as maid of honor to Mary of Modena. Her poems circulated in manuscript and were published after her death from smallpox. Several of them were written to accompany paintings.

Herodias' Daughter Presenting to Her Mother St. John's Head in a Charger, also Painted by Herself.[1]

Behold, dear Mother, who was late our fear,
Disarmed and harmless I present you here;
The tongue tied up that made all Jewry quake,
And which so often did our greatness shake;
No terror sits upon his awful brow,
Where fierceness reigned, there calmness triumphs now;
As lovers use, he gazes on my face
With eyes that languish, as[2] they sued for grace;
Wholly subdued by my victorious charms,
See how his head reposes in my arms.   10
Come, join then with me in my just transport,
Who thus have brought the hermit to the court.

[1]The story illustrated by Killigrew's painting is told in Matthew 14:1–11. "Hermit" in line 12 is explained by Matthew 3:1–3.
[2]That is, "as if."

Upon the Saying that My Verses Were Made by Another

Next Heaven my vows to thee (O sacred Muse!)
I offered up, nor didst thou them refuse.
O Queen of Verse, said I, if thou'lt inspire,
And warm my soul with thy poetic fire,
No love of gold shall share with thee my heart,
Or yet ambition in my breast have part,
More rich, more noble I will ever hold
The Muses' laurel, than a crown of gold.
An undivided sacrifice I'll lay
Upon thine altar, soul and body pay;   *10*
Thou shalt my pleasure, my employment be,
My All I'll make a holocaust to thee.
   The deity that ever does attend
Prayers so sincere, to mine did condescend.
I writ, and the judicious praised my pen:
Could any doubt ensuing glory then?
What pleasing raptures filled my ravished sense?
How strong, how sweet, Fame, was thy influence?
And thine, false hope, that to my flattered sight
Didst glories represent so near and bright?   *20*
By thee deceived, methought each verdant tree
Apollo's transformed Daphne seemed to be;
And every fresher branch, and every bough
Appeared as garlands to empale my brow.
The learned in love say, thus the Wingèd Boy[1]
Does first approach, dressed up in welcome joy;
At first he to the cheated lover's sight
Nought represents but rapture and delight,
Alluring hopes, soft fears, which stronger bind
Their hearts, than when they more assurance find.   *30*

   Emboldened thus, to Fame I did commit
(By some few hands) my most unlucky wit.
But, ah, the sad effects that from it came!
What ought t'have brought me honor, brought me shame!

[1]Cupid.

Like Aesop's painted jay[2] I seemed to all,
Adorned in plumes I not my own could call:
Rifled like her, each one my feathers tore,
And, as they thought, unto the owner bore.
My laurels thus another's brow adorned,
My numbers they admired, but me they scorned: 40
Another's brow,[3] that had so rich a store
Of sacred wreaths, that circled it before;
Where mine quite lost (like a small stream that ran
Into a vast and boundless ocean),
Was swallowed up with what it joined, and drowned,
And that abyss yet no accession found.
    Orinda,[4] (Albion's and her sex's grace)
Owed not her glory to a beauteous face,
It was her radiant soul that shone within,
Which struck a luster through her outward skin;   50
That did her lips and cheeks with roses dye,
Advanced her height, and sparkled in her eye.
Nor did her sex at all obstruct her fame,
But higher 'mong the stars it fixed her name;
What she did write, not only all allowed,
But every laurel to her laurel bowed!
    Th'envious age only to me alone
Will not allow what I do write, my own;
But let 'em rage, and 'gainst a maid conspire,
So deathless numbers from my tuneful lyre   60
Do ever flow; so, Phoebus, I by thee
Divinely inspired and possessed may be;
I willingly accept Cassandra's fate,
To speak the truth, although believed too late.

[2]In the fable of the jay who borrows other birds' feathers in order to look grand. Provoked by his vanity, the birds strip him naked.
[3]We have not discovered to whom Killigrew's verses were attributed.
[4]See Philips headnote.

Mary Collier
(fl. 1739–1762)

O F Collier, a country laborer, little is known. By her own account she came of "poor but honest" parents who taught her to read. She worked as a washerwoman at Petersfield to age 63, then managed a farmhouse for seven years and retired, incapacitated, in 1762. A local patron helped her to publish *The Woman's Labor* (1739); in 1762 she brought out a volume of poems.

The Woman's Labor:
TO
Mr. Stephen Duck[1]

Immortal bard! thou fav'rite of the Nine!
Enriched by peers, advanced by Caroline!
Deign to look down on one that's poor and low,
Rememb'ring you yourself was lately so;
Accept these lines: alas! what can you have
From her who ever was, and's still a slave?
No learning ever was bestowed on me;
My life was always spent in drudgery:
And not alone; alas! with grief I find,
It is the portion of poor womankind.   *10*

[1]Stephen Duck (d. 1756), thresher and self-taught poet, gained the notice of Joseph Spence, Professor of Poetry at Oxford, and eventually the patronage of Queen Caroline. His poem *The Thresher's Labor* (1736) told the hard life of a rural working man but gratuitously belittled the labors of working women. Collier addresses him in retaliation.

Oft have I thought as on my bed I lay,
Eased from the tiresome labors of the day,
Our first extraction from a mass refined[2]
Could never be for slavery designed;
Till time and custom by degrees destroyed
That happy state our sex at first enjoyed.
When men had used their utmost care and toil,
Their recompense was but a female smile;
When they by arts or arms were rendered great,
They laid their trophies at a woman's feet;   20
They, in those days, unto our sex did bring
Their hearts, their all, a free-will offering;
And as from us their being they derive,
They back again should all due homage give.

    Jove once descending from the clouds, did drop
In show'rs of gold on lovely Danae's lap;
The sweet-tongued poets, in those generous days,
Unto our shrine still offered up their lays:
But now, alas! that Golden Age is past,
We are the objects of your scorn at last.   30
And you, great DUCK, upon whose happy brow
The Muses seem to fix the garland now,
In your late poem boldly did declare
Alcides' labors can't with yours compare;[3]
And of your annual task have much to say,
Of threshing, reaping, mowing corn and hay;
Boasting your daily toil, and nightly dream,
But can't conclude your never-dying theme
And let our hapless sex in silence lie
Forgotten, and in dark oblivion die;   40
But on our abject state you throw your scorn,
And women wrong, your verses to adorn.
You of hay-making speak a word or two,
As if our sex but little work could do:[4]
This makes the honest farmer smiling say,
He'll seek for women still to make his hay;

[2]Probably Eve, who was "extracted" from Adam.
[3]Alcides is Hercules, who was required to perform twelve immense labors. Duck wrote, "Scarce Hercules e'er felt such toils as these!"
[4]"Our master comes, and at his heels a throng / Of prattling females, armed with rake and prong; / Prepared, whilst he is here, to make his hay; / Or, if he turns his back, prepared to play" (Duck).

For if his back be turned, their work they mind
As well as men, as far as he can find.
For my own part, I many a summer's day
Have spent in throwing, turning, making hay;   50
But ne'er could see, what you have lately found,
Our wages paid for sitting on the ground.[5]
'Tis true, that when our morning's work is done,
And all our grass exposed unto the sun,
While that his scorching beams do on it shine,
As well as you, we have a time to dine:
I hope, that since we freely toil and sweat
To earn our bread, you'll give us time to eat.
That over, soon we must get up again,
And nimbly turn our hay upon the plain;   60
Nay, rake and prow[6] it in, the case is clear;
Or how should cocks in equal rows appear?
But if you'd have what you have wrote believed,
I find that you to hear us talk are grieved:[7]
In this, I hope, you do not speak your mind,
For none but Turks, that ever I could find,
Have mutes to serve them, or did e'er deny
Their slaves, at work, to chat it merrily.
Since you have liberty to speak your mind,
And are to talk, as well as we, inclined.   70
Why should you thus repine, because that we,
Like you, enjoy that pleasing liberty?
What! would you lord it quite, and take away
The only privilege our sex enjoy?

    When ev'ning does approach, we homeward hie,
And our domestic toils incessant ply:
Against your coming home prepare to get
Our work all done, our house in order set,
Bacon and dumpling in the pot we boil,
Our beds we make, our swine we feed the while;   80
Then wait at door to see you coming home,
And set the table out against you come:

---

[5]"The hay-makers have time allowed to dine. / That soon dispatched, they still sit on the ground" (Duck).

[6]Pull? Not found in the *Oxford English Dictionary*.

[7]"Here's company, so they may chat their fill. . . . So loud's their speech, and so confused their noise, / Scarce puzzled Echo can return the voice" (Duck).

Early next morning we on you attend;
Our children dress and feed, their clothes we mend;
And in the field our daily task renew,
Soon as the rising sun has dried the dew.

   When harvest comes, into the field we go,
And help to reap the wheat as well as you;
Or else we go the ears of corn to glean;
No labor scorning, be it e'er so mean;   *90*
But in the work we freely bear a part,
And what we can, perform with all our heart.
To get a living we so willing are,
Our tender babes into the field we bear,
And wrap them in our clothes to keep them warm,
While round about we gather up the corn;
And often unto them our course do bend,
To keep them safe, that nothing them offend:
Our children that are able, bear a share
In gleaning corn, such is our frugal care.   *100*
When night comes on, unto our home we go,
Our corn we carry, and our infant too;
Weary, alas! but 'tis not worth our while
Once to complain, or *rest at ev'ry stile*;[8]
We must make haste, for when we home are come,
Alas! we find our work but just begun;
So many things for our attendance call,
Had we ten hands, we could employ them all.
Our children put to bed, with greatest care
We all things for your coming home prepare: *110*
You sup, and go to bed without delay,
And rest yourselves till the ensuing day;
While we, alas! but little sleep can have,
Because our froward children cry and rave;
Yet, without fail, soon as daylight doth spring,
We in the field again our work begin,
And there, with all our strength, our toil renew,
Till Titan's[9] golden rays have dried the dew;
Then home we go unto our children dear,
Dress, feed, and bring them to the field with care.   *120*

---

  [8]"Homewards we move, but spent so much with toil, / We slowly walk, and rest at ev'ry stile" (Duck).
  [9]The sun's.

Were this your case, you justly might complain
That day nor night you are secure from pain;
Those mighty troubles which perplex your mind
(*Thistles* before, and *females* come behind)[10]
Would vanish soon, and quickly disappear,
Were you, like us, encumbered thus with care.
What you would have of us we do not know:
We oft take up the corn that you do mow;
We cut the peas, and always ready are
In ev'ry work to take our proper share;   130
And from the time that harvest doth begin,
Until the corn be cut and carried in,
Our toil and labor's daily so extreme
That we have hardly ever *time to dream.*[11]

The harvest ended, respite none we find;
The hardest of our toil is still behind:
Hard labor we most cheerfully pursue,
And out, abroad, a-charring often go:
Of which I now will briefly tell in part,
What fully to declare is past my art;   140
So many hardships daily we go through,
I boldly say, the like *you* never knew.

When bright Orion glitters in the skies
In winter nights, then early we must rise;
The weather ne'er so bad, wind, rain, or snow,
Our work appointed, we must rise and go;
While you on easy beds may lie and sleep,
Till light does through your chamber windows peep.
When to the house we come where we should go,
How to get in, alas! we do not know: 150
The maid quite tired with work the day before,
O'ercome with sleep; we standing at the door
Oppressed with cold, and often call in vain,
Ere to our work we can admittance gain:
But when from wind and weather we get in,
Briskly with courage we our work begin;
Heaps of fine linen we before us view,

[10]"Before us we perplexing thistles find . . . Behind our master waits" (Duck). See also
n. 4.
[11]"Nor, when asleep, are we secure from pain . . . Our mimic Fancy ever restless seems;
/ And what we act awake, she acts in dreams" (Duck).

Whereon to lay our strength and patience too;
Cambrics and muslins, which our ladies wear,
Laces and edgings, costly, fine, and rare,   *160*
Which must be washed with utmost skill and care;
With holland shirts, ruffles and fringes too,
Fashions which our forefathers never knew.
For several hours here we work and slave,
Before we can one glimpse of daylight have;
We labor hard before the morning's past,
Because we fear the time runs on too fast.

At length bright Sol illuminates the skies,
And summons drowsy mortals to arise;
Then comes our mistress to us without fail,   *170*
And in her hand, *perhaps,* a mug of ale
To cheer our hearts, and also to inform
Herself, what work is done that very morn;
Lays her commands upon us, that we mind
Her linen well, nor *leave the dirt behind*;
Not this alone, but also to take care
We don't her cambrics nor her ruffles tear;
And *these* most strictly does of us require,
To save her soap, and sparing be of fire;
Tells us her charge is great, nay furthermore,   *180*
Her clothes are fewer than the time before.
Now we drive on, resolved our strength to try,
And what we can, we do most willingly;
Until with heat and work, 'tis often known,
Not only sweat, but blood runs trickling down
Our wrists and fingers; still our work demands
The constant action of our lab'ring hands.

Now night comes on, from whence you have relief,
But that, alas! does but increase our grief;
With heavy hearts we often view the sun,   *190*
Fearing he'll set before our work is done;
For either in the morning, or at night,
We piece the *summer*'s day with candlelight.
Though we all day with care our work attend,
Such is our fate, we know not when 'twill end:
When ev'ning's come, you homeward take your way,
We, till our work is done, are forced to stay;
And after all our toil and labor past,

Six-pence or eight-pence pays us off at last;
For all our pains, no prospect can we see   *200*
Attend us, but *old age* and *poverty*.

   The washing is not all we have to do:
We oft change work for work as well as you.
Our mistress of her pewter doth complain,
And 'tis our part to make it clean again.
This work, though very hard and tiresome too,
Is not the worst we hapless females do:
When night comes on, and we quite weary are,
We scarce can count what falls unto our share;
Pots, kettles, saucepans, skillets, we may see,   *210*
Skimmers and ladles, and such trumpery,
Brought in to make complete our slavery.
Though early in the morning 'tis begun,
'Tis often very late before we've done;
Alas! our labors never know an end;
On brass and iron we our strength must spend;
Our tender hands and fingers scratch and tear:
All this, and more, with patience we must bear.
Colored with dirt and filth we now appear;
Your threshing *sooty peas* will not come near.[12]   *220*
All the perfections woman once could boast
Are quite obscured, and altogether lost.

   Once more our mistress sends to let us know
She wants our help, because the beer runs low:
Then in much haste for brewing we prepare,
The vessels clean, and scald with greatest care;
Often at midnight from our bed we rise,
At other times even *that* will not suffice;
Our work at evening oft we do begin,
And ere we've done, the night comes on again.   *230*
Water we pump, the copper we must fill,
Or tend the fire; for if we e'er stand still,
Like you, when threshing, we a watch must keep,
Our wort boils over if we dare to sleep.

   But to rehearse all labor is in vain,
Of which we very justly might complain:

[12]"When sooty peas we thresh, you scarce can know / Our native color, as from work we
go" (Duck).

For us, you see, but little rest is found;
Our toil increases as the year runs round.
While you to Sisyphus yourselves compare,
With Danaus' daughters we may claim a share;[13]   *240*
For while *he* labors hard against the hill,
Bottomless tubs of water *they* must fill.

So the industrious bees do hourly strive
To bring their loads of honey to the hive;
Their sordid owners always reap the gains,
And poorly recompense their toil and pains.

[13]In Greek legend Sisyphus was condemned eternally to push up a hill a stone that constantly rolled down again, and the daughters of Danaus to try forever to fill, with broken pitchers, a water jar that had no bottom.

Elizabeth Carter
(1717–1806)

T H E Bluestocking Carter was renowned for erudition: she knew nine languages, including Arabic, and had studied music, astronomy, history, and geography. Her most famous work was a translation of Epictetus (1758), but she also published two volumes of poems. She never married, and lived for many years as her father's housekeeper. She suffered from chronic headache and periods of depression.

Written Extempore on the Sea-Shore.
1741.—By Moon Light

Thou restless fluctuating deep,
  Expressive of the human mind,
In thy for ever varying form,
  My own inconstant self I find.

How soft now flow thy peaceful waves.
  In just gradations to the shore:
While on thy brow, unclouded shines
  The regent of the midnight hour.

Blest emblem of that equal state,
  Which I this moment feel within: *10*
Where thought to thought succeeding rolls,
  And all is placid and serene.

As o'er thy smoothly flowing tide,
  Their light the trembling moon-beams dart,

My lov'd Eudocia's image smiles,
  And gaily brightens all my heart.

But ah! this flatt'ring scene of peace,
  By neither can be long possessed,
When Eurus[1] breaks thy transient calm,
  And rising sorrows shake my breast.   *20*

Obscur'd thy Cynthia's silver ray
  When clouds opposing intervene:
And ev'ry joy that Friendship gives
  Shall fade beneath the gloom of spleen.[2]

[1]The east wind.
[2]See Finch, "The Spleen," n. 1.

Mary Leapor
(1722–1746)

LEAPOR, daughter of a country gardener, was taught to read and write but discouraged from attempting verse. She spent her short life working as a housekeeper and cook, but managed to produce a substantial body of poems which circulated in her neighborhood. Although, when published, her poems were taken as examples of untutored talent, Leapor had studied Pope and Dryden.

The Sacrifice:
An Epistle to Celia

If you, dear Celia, cannot bear
The low delights that others share;
If nothing will your palate fit
But learning, eloquence and wit,
Why, you may sit alone (I ween)
Till you're devoured with the spleen.
But if variety can please
With humble scenes and careless ease;
If smiles can banish melancholy,
Or whimsy with its parent folly;   10
If any joy in these there be,
I dare invite you down to me.
   You know these little roofs of mine
Are always sacred to the Nine;
This day we make a sacrifice
To the Parnassian deities,

Which I am ordered by Apollo
To show you in the words that follow.
  As first we purge the hallowed room
With soft utensil called a broom;   *20*
And next for you a throne prepare,
Which vulgar mortals call a chair,
While zephyrs from an engine blow,
And bid the sparkling cinders glow;
Then gather round the mounting flames
The priestess and assembled dames,
While some inferior maid shall bring
Clear water from the bubbling spring.
Shut up in vase of sable dye,
Secure from each unhallowed eye,   *30*
Fine wheaten bread you next behold,
Like that which Homer sings of old,[1]
And by some unpolluted fair
It must be scorched with wond'rous care.
So far 'tis done. And now behold
The sacred vessels—not of gold:
Of polished earth must they be formed,
With painting curiously adorned.
These rites are past: And now must follow
The grand libation to Apollo,   *40*
Of juices drawn from magic weeds,
And pith of certain Indian reeds.[2]
For flow'r of milk the priestess calls,
Her voice re-echoes from the walls;
With hers the sister voices blend,
And with the od'rous steam ascend.
Each fair one now a sibyl grows,
And ev'ry cheek with ardor glows,
And (though not quite beside their wits)
Are seized with deep prophetic fits.   *50*
Some by mysterious figures show
That Celia loves a shallow beau;

[1] As in the *Iliad* (Pope's translation), XI.770: "Honey new-pressed, the sacred flow'r of wheat." Line 43 below ("flow'r of milk"—i.e., cream) echoes this and similar phrases throughout Pope's Homer translations; the description as a whole should be compared with passages such as *Iliad* XI. 768–778 (Nestor's entertainment of guests) and *Odyssey* XV. 147ff (ritual baths and feasts).

[2] Presumably tea with sugar, but suggestive of Homeric potions (e.g., *Odyssey*, IV.302–306 and X.265ff).

And some by signs and hints declare
That Damon will not wed Ziphair:[3]
Their neighbors' fortunes each can tell,
So potent is the mighty spell.
   This is the feast and this, my friend,
Are you commanded to attend.
Yes at your peril. But adieu,
I've tired both myself and you.   *60*

Upon Her Play Being Returned to Her, Stained with Claret[1]

Welcome, dear wanderer, once more!
  Thrice welcome to thy native cell!
Within this peaceful humble door
  Let thou and I contented dwell!

But say, O whither hast thou ranged?
  Why dost thou blush a crimson hue?
Thy fair complexion's greatly changed:
  Why, I can scarce believe 'tis you.

Then tell, my son, O tell me, where
  Didst thou contract this sottish dye?   *10*
You kept ill company, I fear,
  When distant from your parent's eye.

Was it for this, O graceless child!
  Was it for this, you learned to spell?
Thy face and credit both are spoiled:
  Go drown thyself in yonder well.

I wonder how thy time was spent:
  No news (alas!) hadst thou to bring.
Hast thou not climbed the Monument?
  Nor seen the lions, nor the king?[2]   *20*

[3]Classical names for rural people.
[1]Leapor left an unproduced play, "The Unhappy Father"; it is said to have been her favorite among her works.
[2]Standard "sights" for a visitor to London.

But now I'll keep you here secure,
  No more you view the smoky sky:
The Court was never made (I'm sure)
  For idiots,[3] like thee and I.

---

[3]Besides the usual meaning of *idiot*, other relevant senses are: an ignorant person, such as a rustic; and a person who has no professional standing.

Hannah More
(1745–1833)

FEW writers have been as influential as Hannah More. A fashionable playwright and poet turned evangelical Christian, she devoted her copious pen to the abolition of slavery and reformation of public manners. To combat the spread of radical ideas among the working class, she organized (and largely wrote) the "Cheap Repository Tracts," a series of ballads and broadsides similar to the most popular reading matter. At least two million circulated, an unprecedented number. More's importance rests on something more basic than contributions to literature—the propagation of literacy itself.

The Riot:
Or, Half a Loaf Is Better Than No Bread.
In a Dialogue Between Jack Anvil and Tom Hod

To the tune of "A Cobbler there was"
Written in ninety-five, a year of scarcity and alarm.[1]

---

[1]In the mid-1790s bad harvests resulted in high prices and social unrest. Hester Piozzi noted with alarm "the distress upon the poorer sort in every town and county . . . Handbills too . . . posted on our church doors . . . *demanding*, not *requesting* relief for the lower orders" (*Thraliana*, January 1795). It is said that a reading of "The Riot" pacified a violent mob in one town.

TOM

"Come, neighbors, no longer be patient and quiet,
Come, let us kick up a bit of a riot;
I'm hungry, my lads, but I've little to eat,
So we'll pull down the mills, and we'll seize all the meat;
I'll give you good sport, boys, as ever you saw,
So a fig for the justice, a fig for the law."

                                        Derry down.[2]

Then his pitchfork Tom seized.—"Hold a moment," says Jack,
"I'll show thee thy blunder, brave boy, in a crack,
And if I don't prove we had better be still
I'll assist thee straightway to pull down every mill;   10
I'll show thee how passion thy reason does cheat,
Or I'll join thee in plunder for bread and for meat!

"What a whimsey to think thus our bellies to fill,
For we stop all the grinding by breaking the mill!
What a whimsey to think we shall get more to eat
By abusing the butchers who get us the meat!
What a whimsey to think we shall mend our spare diet
By breeding disturbance, by murder and riot!

"Because I am dry, 'twould be foolish, I think,
To pull out my tap and to spill all my drink;   20
Because I am hungry and want to be fed,
That is sure no wise reason for wasting my bread:
And just such wise reasons for minding their diet
Are used by those blockheads who rush into riot.

"I would not take comfort from others' distresses,
But still I would mark how God our land blesses;
For though in old England the times are but sad,
Abroad, I am told, they are ten times as bad;
In the land of the Pope there is scarce any grain,
And 'tis worse still, they say, both in Holland and Spain.   30

"Let us look to the harvest our wants to beguile,
See the lands with rich crops how they ev'rywhere smile!
Meantime to assist us, by each western breeze,
Some corn is brought daily across the salt seas!

---

[2]A conventional ballad refrain. In the original it occurs after each stanza.

Of tea we'll drink little, of gin none at all,
And we'll patiently wait, and the prices will fall.

"But if we're not quiet, then let us not wonder
If things grow much worse by our riot and plunder;
And let us remember whenever we meet,
The more ale we drink, boys, the less we shall eat.   40
On those days spent in riot, no bread you brought home,
Had you spent them in labor, you must have had some.

"A dinner of herbs, says the wise man, with quiet,
Is better than beef amid discord and riot.[3]
If the thing could be helped I'm a foe to all strife,
And I pray for a peace ev'ry night of my life;
But in matters of state not an inch will I budge,
Because I conceive I'm no very good judge.

"But though poor, I can work, my brave boy, with the best;
Let the king and the parliament manage the rest;   50
I lament both the war and the taxes together,
Though I verily think they don't alter the weather.
The king, as I take it, with very good reason,
May prevent a bad law, but can't help a bad season.

"The parliament men, although great is their power,
Yet they cannot contrive us a bit of a shower;
And I never yet heard, though our rulers are wise,
That they know very well how to manage the skies;
For the best of them all, as they found to their cost,
Were not able to hinder last winter's hard frost.   60

"Besides, I must share in the wants of the times,
Because I have had my full share in its crimes;
And I'm apt to believe the distress which is sent,
Is to punish and cure us of all discontent.
But the harvest is coming—potatoes are come![4]
Our prospect clears up; ye complainers be dumb!

"And though I've no money, and though I've no lands,
I've a head on my shoulders, and a pair of good hands;
So I'll work the whole day, and on Sundays I'll seek

---

[3]Proverbs 15:17. Jack goes on to refer to the ongoing war with France, one reason for the distress in England.
[4]Potatoes, imported from Ireland, replaced wheat as the staple food of the working class. Actually, they were bitterly resented.

At church how to bear all the wants of the week.   70
The gentlefolks too will afford us supplies;
They'll subscribe[5]—and they'll give up their
     puddings and pies.

"Then before I'm induced to take part in a riot,
I'll ask this short question—what shall I get by it?
So I'll e'en wait a little, till cheaper the bread,
For a mittimus hangs o'er each rioter's head:
And when of two evils I'm asked which is best,
I'd rather be hungry than hanged, I protest."

Quoth Tom, "Thou art right; if I rise, I'm a Turk."
So he threw down his pitchfork, and went to his work.   80

___

[5]To relief funds for the poor.

Charlotte Smith
(1749–1806)

SMITH began writing in her teens but only took it up professionally when her husband was imprisoned for debt. She preferred poetry, and her first book, *Elegiac Sonnets* (1784), was well received; but the need to support a large family impelled her to write novels. Her best known work is *The Old Manor House* (1793). Despite success, her life was filled with disappointment, grief and, in her later years, illness.

Sonnet I

The partial Muse has from my earliest hours
   Smiled on the rugged path I'm doomed to tread,
And still with sportive hand has snatched wild flowers,
   To weave fantastic garlands for my head:
But far, far happier is the lot of those
   Who never learned her dear delusive art;
Which, while it decks the head with many a rose,
   Reserves the thorn to fester in the heart.
For still she bids soft Pity's melting eye
   Stream o'er the ills she knows not to[1] remove,   *10*
Points every pang, and deepens every sigh
   Of mourning friendship, or unhappy love.
Ah! then, how dear the Muse's favors cost,
   If those paint sorrow best—who feel it most![2]

[1]That is, "knows not how to."
[2]In a note, Smith cites Pope's *Eloisa to Abelard*, line 366: "He best can paint them, who shall feel them most."

Sonnet XLIV
Written in the Churchyard at Middleton in Sussex.

Pressed by the Moon, mute arbitress of tides,
  While the loud equinox its power combines,
  The sea no more its swelling surge confines,
But o'er the shrinking land sublimely rides.
The wild blast, rising from the western cave,
  Drives the huge billows from their heaving bed,
  Tears from their grassy tombs the village dead,[3]
And breaks the silent sabbath of the grave!
With shells and sea-weed mingled, on the shore
  Lo! their bones whiten in the frequent wave;   *10*
  But vain to them the winds and waters rave;
They hear the warring elements no more:
While I am doomed—by life's long storm opprest,
To gaze with envy on their gloomy rest.

[3]"Middleton is a village on the margin of the sea in Sussex. . . . There were formerly several acres of ground between its small church and the sea; which now, by its continual encroachments, approaches within a few feet of this half ruined . . . edifice. The wall which once surrounded the churchyard is entirely swept away, many of the graves broken up, and the remains of bodies interred washed into the sea: whence human bones are found among the sand and shingles on the shore" (Smith).

Ann Yearsley
(1752 or 1756–1806)

BORN near Bristol, Yearsley was brought up to be a milkwoman like her mother. She was rescued from desperate poverty by Hannah More, who edited and published her first book of poems (1784). But Yearsley's pride was insulted when More put her literary income into trust, and they quarreled. Afterwards Yearsley operated a circulating library, and published two more books of verse, a novel, and a play. Of independent temper, she attacked both slavery and class snobbery.

Addressed to Ignorance,

Occasioned by a Gentleman's Desiring the Author Never to Assume a Knowledge of the Ancients.

Lend me thy dark veil.—Science darts her strong ray;
    In the orb of bright learning she sits.
Haste! haste! Clothed by thee, I can yet keep my way,
    Still secure from her critics, or wits.

All slight thee; no beauty e'er boasts of thy pow'r,
    No beau on thy influence depends;
No statesman shall own[1] thee, no poet implore,
    But Lactilla[2] and thou must be friends.

Then come, gentle goddess, sit full in my looks,[3]
    Let my accents be sounded by thee;   *10*

---

[1]Acknowledge as an acquaintance or possession.
[2]"Milkmaid," Yearsley's poetical name for herself.
[3]Alluding to Pope's *Dunciad*—i.e., "gentle Dulness" (II.34) and "In each she marks her image full exprest" (I.107).

While Crito in pomp bears his burden of books,
  On the plains of wild Nature I'm free.

When Ign'rance forbids me in ambush to move,
  Or to feed on the scraps of the sage,
I am blind to the ancients—yet Fancy would prove
  That Pythagoras lives through each age.[4]

She shows me blind Homer, who ne'er must be still,
  To motion perpetual decreed;[5]
Forgetful of Ilium, he now turns a mill,
  While old Nestor, quite dumb, roves the mead.   20

In a tiger Achilles bounds o'er the wide plain;
  As a fox sly Ulysses is seen;
Doubly horned, Menelaus now scorns to complain,
  But more blest, in a buck skips the green.[6]

Fond Paris three changes with sighs has gone through,
  First a goat, then a monkey complete;
Enraged, to the river Salmacis he flew,
  Washed his face—and forgot his fair mate.[7]

But Zeno, Tibullus, and Socrates grave,
  In the bodies of wan garreteers,[8]   30
All tattered, cold, hungry, by turns sigh and rave
  At their publisher's bill of arrears.

Diogenes lives in an ambling old beau,[9]
  Plato's spirit is damped in yon fool;

[4]Pythagoras (6th cent. B.C.) preached the transmigration of the soul from one body to another, even of different species—and also, often, from one condition to its opposite. Most of the poem is based on this idea.

[5]Legend says that Homer wandered, a beggar, through all the cities of Greece. Below: Ilium is Troy; Nestor is a wise, articulate, senior warrior in the *Iliad*.

[6]In the *Iliad* Achilles is noted for fierce courage (like a tiger's), Ulysses for foxlike cunning. Menelaus is "doubly horned" (1) because cuckolded (by Paris, who seduced his wife Helen), and (2) as a buck. Also, in one legend Menelaus angered Artemis by killing a sacred deer.

[7]Paris, son of Priam, King of Troy, is a *goat* in two ways: (1) he is sexually promiscuous, and (2) in Pope's *Iliad* (III.38) he is a "goat," whereas Menelaus is a "lion." He is also a *monkey* (one who plays antics) in that he dresses "outlandishly" (Euripides, *Iphigenia at Aulis*, line 75) and seems more like a "gay dancer" than a warrior (*Iliad*, III.486). The river Salmacis is appropriate for him to wash in, for its waters make men effeminate (Ovid, *Metamorphoses*, IV.285ff). Here they also work like those of Lethe, causing forgetfulness: Paris had wedded Oenone, but he forgot her when offered a more beautiful woman.

[8]One who lives in a garret, the usual residence of penniless authors and literary hacks. Zeno (5th cent.B.C.) was a philosopher who pioneered the Socratic method, Tibullus (d.c. 19 B.C.) a Roman poet noted for his artistry. In one of his elegies he calls himself poor.

[9]Diogenes (4th cent.B.C.) was a wandering philosopher who lived austerely.

While the soul of Lycurgus to Tyburn must go,
  In yon thief that's hanged by his rule.[10]

Longinus now breathes in a huntsman, and swears
  "That each critic rides over his brother;
That Muses are jilts, and that poor garreteers
  Should in Helicon drown one another."[11]   40

There's Virgil, the courtier, with hose out at heel,
  And Hesiod, quite shoeless his foot;
Poor Ovid walks shivering behind a cart-wheel,
  While Horace cries, "Sweep for your soot."[12]

Fair Julia sees Ovid, but passes him near,
  An old broom o'er her shoulder is thrown;
Penelope lends to five lovers an ear,
  Walking on with one sleeve to her gown.[13]

But Helen, the Spartan, stands near Charing Cross,
  Long laces and pins doomed to cry;[14]   50
Democritus, Solon, bear baskets of moss,
  While Pliny sells woodcocks hard by.[15]

In Billingsgate Nell Clytemnestra moves slow,
  All her fishes die quick in the air;

---

[10]Lycurgus (4th cent.B.C.), Spartan lawgiver. In his code thieves were punished severely. Tyburn: the gallows in London.

[11]These are thoughts that Longinus, in *On the Sublime* (1st cent. A.D.), would call "ignoble," and are thus the opposite of what he urges (Chap. 9). They are more appropriate to fox-hunting country squires. Helicon was a mountain sacred to the Muses, where arose two springs thought to inspire poetry.

[12]Virgil (70–19 B.C.), the greatest Roman poet, was patronized by the emperor Augustus; his family had lost their property. Hesiod (8th cent. B.C.) in his *Works and Days* warns against going shoeless in winter. Ovid, Roman poet, was banished (A.D. 8) to Tomi, on the Black Sea; in his *Tristia* he complains of the heavy labor and hard winters there. Horace (65–8 B.C.) in *Odes* I.9 urges defending against cold weather by "heaping the hearth with new / Supplies of firewood"; he also describes himself as round-bellied—not the physique for a chimney sweep.

[13]Julia was the granddaughter of the emperor Augustus; it was for his part in her adultery that Ovid was banished. Penelope, "severely chaste" (Pope's *Odyssey*, XVI.36), resisted her twenty suitors for ten years.

[14]Helen, queen of Sparta; see n. 6. In Homer she weaves tapestries, gives a veil as a gift, and owns a large wardrobe.

[15]Democritus (5th–4th cent. B.C.), atomic theorist, also wrote *The Causes of Seeds, Plants and Fruits*. Solon (early 6th cent. B.C.), Athenian lawgiver: according to Plutarch he regulated the size of the baskets carried by women. Pliny the Elder (A.D. 23–79) in his *Natural History* tells anecdotes of exotic birds. The woodcock, a bird esteemed in Europe as a delicacy, is of interest also to naturalists.

Agamemnon peeps stern, through the eye of old Joe,
　　At Aegisthus, who, grinning, stands there.[16]

Stout Ajax the form of a butcher now takes,
　　But the last he passed through was a calf;
Yet no revolution his spirit awakes,
　　For no Troy is remembered by Ralph.[17]　　　　　　　　*60*

More modern Voltaire joyless sits on yon bench,
　　Thin and meager, bewailing the day
When he gave up his Maker to humor a wench,[18]
　　And then left her in doubt and dismay.

Wat Tyler, in Nicholson, dares a King's life,
　　At St. James's the blow was designed;[19]
But Jove leaned from heaven and wrested the knife,
　　Then in haste lashed the wings of the wind.

Here's Trojan, Athenian, Greek, Frenchman and I,
　　Heaven knows what I was long ago;　　　　　　　　*70*
No matter, thus shielded, this age I defy,
　　And the next cannot wound me, I know.

[16]Billingsgate was the London fishmarket, famed for the foul speech of the women who worked there. In Aeschylus's *Agamemnon* Clytemnestra, Agamemnon's wife, is brutally outspoken; she also likens herself to a fisherman in describing (line 1382) how she caught Agamemnon in her "net." Aegisthus is the lover for whom she murders him.

[17]When Achilles' armor was given to Ulysses Ajax, mad with disappointment, slaughtered a herd of sheep (Ovid, *Metamorphoses*, XIII). A *calf* is a stupid person; Ajax was known for stupidity. Ralph is his present embodiment.

[18]Voltaire (1694–1778), French author and philosopher, though never an atheist, was notorious for his aggressive deism. The "wench" is perhaps Mme. du Châtelet, with whom Voltaire lived for some years and who encouraged his studies.

[19]Margaret Nicholson, a housemaid, attempted to stab George III at St. James's Palace in August 1786. Wat Tyler (d. 1381) was the leader of an English peasant revolt.

Bibliography

GENERAL WORKS: The standard reference work on the writers is *A Dictionary of British and American Women Writers 1660–1800,* ed. Janet Todd (Totowa, N.J.: Rowman and Allanheld, 1985). A good critical introduction to the period is Katharine M. Rogers, *Feminism in Eighteenth-Century England* (Urbana: University of Illinois Press, 1982). For further information, see *Annotated Bibliography of Twentieth-Century Critical Studies of Women and Literature 1660–1800,* ed. Paula Backscheider et al. (New York: Garland, 1977) and the annual volumes of *The Eighteenth Century: A Current Bibliography* and of the *MLA Bibliography. First Feminists: British Women Writers 1578–1799,* ed. Moira Ferguson (Bloomington: Indiana University Press, 1985) presents selections from twenty-eight writers, with an emphasis on political significance. Pieces by twenty-four women appear in *The New Oxford Book of Eighteenth Century Verse,* ed. Roger Lonsdale (Oxford: Oxford University Press, 1984).

D'ARBLAY, FRANCES BURNEY: No complete edition of the journals exists. Our extracts are drawn from three partial editions: *Early Diary,* ed. Annie R. Ellis (London: George Bell, 1907), vols. 1 and 2 (for 1768–1775); *Diary and Letters,* ed. Charlotte Barrett and Austin Dobson (London: Macmillan, 1904–1905), vols. 1, 2, and 4 (for 1778–1790); and *Journals and Letters,* ed. Joyce Hemlow et al. (Oxford: Clarendon Press, 1972–1984), vol. 8 (for 1815), reprinted by permission of Oxford University Press. See Joyce Hemlow's biography, *The History of Fanny Burney* (Oxford: Clarendon Press, 1958) and Michael Adelstein's critical study, *Fanny Burney* (New York: Twayne, 1968).

ASTELL, MARY: Our selections come from *A Serious Proposal*

to the Ladies for the Advancement of Their True and Greatest Interest, Part I (4th ed., London: R. Wilkins, 1701) and Part II (London: R. Wilkins, 1697), and from *Some Reflections upon Marriage* (4th ed., 1730), reprinted by Source Book Press (New York, 1970). See Ruth Perry, *The Celebrated Mary Astell* (Chicago: University of Chicago Press, 1986).

BARBAULD, ANNA LAETITIA: Our selections come from *Works*, ed. Lucy Aikin (London: Longman, 1825), vols. 1 and 2. On Barbauld's life and work see Betsy Rodgers, *Georgian Chronicle: Mrs. Barbauld and Her Family* (London: Methuen, 1958).

BEHN, APHRA: All texts are reprinted from *Works*, ed. Montague Summers (London: Heinemann, 1915), vols. 1, 5, and 6. Popular biography by Angeline Goreau, *Reconstructing Aphra* (New York: Dial Press, 1980); bibliography by Mary Ann O'Donnell (New York: Garland, 1984); critical study by Frederick M. Link, *Aphra Behn* (New York: Twayne, 1968).

CARTER, ELIZABETH: Our text comes from *Poems on Several Occasions* (London: J. Rivington, 1762).

COLLIER, MARY: We print from the first edition, *The Woman's Labor: An Epistle to Mr. Stephen Duck* (London: J. Roberts, 1739). See Moira Ferguson, "Introduction" to a facsimile reprint of that edition (Los Angeles: Augustan Reprint Society, 1985).

EDGEWORTH, MARIA: "An Essay on the Noble Science of Self-Justification" is reprinted from *Tales and Novels* (1893, rptd. New York: AMS Press, 1967), vol. 4. See Marilyn Butler, *Maria Edgeworth: A Literary Biography* (Oxford: Clarendon Press, 1972).

"EPHELIA": Our texts are from *Female Poems on Several Occasions* (London: W. Downing, 1679).

FINCH, ANNE, COUNTESS OF WINCHILSEA: Most of our poems come from *The Poems of Anne Countess of Winchilsea*, ed. Myra Reynolds (Chicago: University of Chicago Press, 1903). The last two, "An Apology . . ." and "A Supplication . . . ," are printed by courtesy of the Wellesley College Library, from a manuscript in their English Poetry Collection.

HAYS, MARY: Our selections are from *Letters and Essays* (1793) and *An Appeal to the Men of Great Britain in Behalf of*

Women (1798), in facsimile reprint by Garland (New York, 1974). See Gina M. Luria, "Mary Hays, A Critical Biography" (New York University dissertation, 1972).

KILLIGREW, ANNE: Our texts are taken from *Poems* (1686), in facsimile reprint by Scholars' Facsimiles (Gainesville, Fla., 1967).

LEAPOR, MARY: We print from *Poems upon Several Occasions* (London: J. Roberts): "The Sacrifice" from vol. 1 (1748) and "Upon Her Play Being Returned" from vol. 2 (1751).

MANLEY, DELARIVIÈRE: "The Wife's Resentment" is taken from *The Power of Love* (London: J. Barber, 1720). See Paul B. Anderson, "Delarivière Manley's Prose Fiction," *Philological Quarterly* 13 (1934): 168–88, and "Mistress Delarivière Manley's Biography," *Modern Philology* 33 (1936) :261–278.

MONTAGU, LADY MARY WORTLEY: Our texts of "The Lover" and all but one of the letters come from *Letters and Works*, ed. W. Moy Thomas (1861; rpt. New York: AMS Press, 1970), vols. 1 and 2; the letter of 10 Jan. 1713, from the authoritative *Complete Letters*, ed. Robert Halsband (Oxford: Clarendon, 1965–1967), vol. 1; No. 6 of *The Nonsense of Common Sense*, from Halsband's edition (Evanston: Northwestern University, 1947); and "The Reasons that Induced Dr. S[wif]t . . . ," from Halsband's reprint of its first (1734) edition in *The Augustan Milieu*, ed. H. K. Miller et al. (Oxford: Clarendon Press, 1970). We have corrected these texts from Montagu's *Complete Letters* and *Essays and Poems*, ed. Halsband and Isobel Grundy (Oxford: Clarendon Press, 1977). See Halsband's biography, *The Life of Lady Mary Wortley Montagu* (Oxford: Oxford University Press, 1956). The letter of 10 Jan. and "The Reasons that Induced Dr. S[wif]t" are reprinted by permission of Oxford University Press.

MORE, HANNAH: "The Riot" is reprinted from *Works* (New York: Harper, 1855), vol. 1. For life and work, see M. G. Jones, *Hannah More* (Cambridge: Cambridge University Press, 1952).

PHILIPS, KATHERINE: Our texts come from *Minor Poets of the Caroline Period*, ed. George Saintsbury (Oxford: Clarendon Press, 1905), vol. 1. See biography by Philip W. Souers, *The Matchless Orinda* (Cambridge: Harvard University Press, 1931).

PIOZZI, HESTER THRALE: Our extracts come from *Thraliana*, ed. Katharine C. Balderston (Oxford: Clarendon Press, 1942).

Reprinted by permission of Oxford University Press. "The Three Warnings" is reprinted from its first edition, *Miscellanies in Prose and Verse* by Anna Williams (London: Davies, 1766); the elegy on Carter from the *St. James's Chronicle* (4 March 1806), corrected by the text in *Thraliana*. See James L. Clifford, *Hester Lynch Piozzi*, 2d ed. (Oxford: Clarendon Press, 1952) and William McCarthy, *Hester Thrale Piozzi* (Chapel Hill: University of North Carolina Press, 1985).

SMITH, CHARLOTTE: We print from *Elegiac Sonnets*, 5th ed. (London: Cadell, 1789).

YEARSLEY, ANN: Our text comes from *Poems on Various Subjects* (London: Robinson, 1787). See J.M.S. Tompkins, "The Bristol Milkwoman," in *The Polite Marriage . . . Eighteenth Century Essays* (Cambridge: Cambridge University Press, 1938).

PL59

Ⓟ **PLUME**   **MERIDIAN**

EXCEPTIONAL PLAYS

(0452)

☐ **A RAISIN IN THE SUN by Lorrain Hansberry.** From one of the most potent voices in the American theater comes A RAISIN IN THE SUN, which touched the taproots of black American life as never before and won the New York Critics Circle Award. This Twenty-Fifth Anniversary edition also includes Hansberry's last play, THE SIGN IN SIDNEY BRUSTEIN'S WINDOW, which became a theater legend. "Changed American theater forever!"—*New York Times*   (259428—$8.95)

☐ **BLACK DRAMA ANTHOLOGY Edited by Woodie King and Ron Milner.** Here are twenty-three extraordinary and powerful plays by writers who brought a dazzling new dimension to the American theater. Includes works by Imamu Amiri Baraka (LeRoi Jones), Archie Shepp, Douglas Turner Ward, Langston Hughes, Ed Bullins, Ron Zuber, and many others who gave voice to the anger, passion and pride that shaped a movement, and continue to energize the American theater today.

(009022—$6.95)

☐ **THE NORMAL HEART by Larry Kramer.** An explosive drama about our most terrifying and troubling medical crises today: the AIDS epidemic. It tells the story of very private lives caught up in the heartrending ordeal of suffering and doom—an ordeal that was largely ignored for reasons of politics and majority morality. "The most outspoken play around."—Frank Rich, *The New York Times*   (257980—$6.95)

☐ **FENCES: A play by August Wilson.** The author of the 1984-85 Broadway season's best play, *Ma Rainey's Black Bottom*, returns with another powerful, stunning dramatic work. "Always absorbing . . . The work's protagonist—and great creation—is a Vesuvius of rage . . . the play's finest moments perfectly capture that inky almost emperceptibly agitated darkness just before the fences of racism, for a time, can crash down."—Frank Rich, *The New York Times*.   (264014—$7.95)

☐ **IBSEN: The Complete Major Prose Plays, Translated and with an Introduction by Rolf Fjelde.** Here are the masterpieces of a writer and thinker who blended detailed realism with a startlingly bold imagination, infusing prose with poetic power, and drama with undying relevance and meaning. This collection includes *Pillars of Society, A Doll House, Ghosts, An Enemy of the People, Hedda Gabler, When We Dead Awaken,* and Ibsen's six other prose plays in chronological order.

(262054—$16.95)

☐ **A WALK IN THE WOODS by Lee Blessing.** "Best new American play of the season" —Clive Barnes, *The New York Post.* A stunningly powerful and provocative drama, based on an event that actually took place . . . probes the most important issue of our time—the very survival of civilization.   (264529—$7.95)

Prices slightly higher in Canada

Buy them at your local bookstore or use this convenient coupon for ordering.

NEW AMERICAN LIBRARY
P.O. Box 999, Bergenfield, New Jersey 07621

Please send me the books I have checked above. I am enclosing $_____ (please add $1.50 to this order to cover postage and handling). Send check or money order—no cash or C.O.D.'s. Prices and numbers are subject to change without notice.

Name_____

Address_____

City_____ State_____ Zip Code_____

Allow 4-6 weeks for delivery.
This offer, prices and numbers are subject to change without notice.